Acclaim for Orhan Pamuk's

Snow

"Powerful.... Astonishingly timely.... A deft melding of political intrigue and philosophy, romance and noir.... [*Snow*] is forever confounding our expectations."
— *Vogue*

"A novel of profound relevance to the present moment. [The] debate between the forces of secularism and those of religious fanaticism ... is conducted with subtle, painful insight into the human weakness that can underlie both impulses."
— *The Times* (London)

"A work of art.... Alternating between the snowstorm's hush and philosophical conversations reminiscent of Dostoevsky's great novels, *Snow* proves a ... timely and gripping read."
— *Minneapolis Star Tribune*

"Marvelous ... as quiet and transformative as a blizzard and as coldly beautiful."
— *St. Petersburg Times*

"In *Snow*, Pamuk uses his powers to show us the critical dilemmas of modern Turkey. How European a country is it? How can it respond to fundamentalist Islam? And how can an artist deal with these issues? ... The author's high artistry and fierce politics take our minds further into the age's crisis than any commentator could. Orhan Pamuk is the sort of writer for whom the Nobel Prize was invented."
— *The Daily Telegraph* (London)

"Part political thriller, part farce, *Snow* is [Pamuk's] most dazzling fiction yet. One of the top books of the year."
— *The Village Voice*

"It comes as no surprise that political prescience should be yet another of the many gifts of Turkish novelist Orhan Pamuk. With *Snow*, Pamuk gives convincing proof that the solitary artist is a better bellwether than any televised think-tanker. . . . The work is a melancholy farce full of rabbit-out-of-a-hat plot twists that, despite the locale, looks uncannily like the magic lantern show of misfire, denial and pratfall that appears daily in our newspapers."
                                        —*Independent on Sunday*

"Pure magic. . . . *Snow* is excellent."   —*San Francisco Chronicle*

"'How much can we ever know about love and pain in another's heart? How much can we hope to understand those who have suffered deeper anguish, greater deprivation and more crushing disappointments than we ourselves have known?' Such questions haunt the poet Ka . . . [in] this novel [that is] as much about love as it is about politics."
                                        —*The Observer* (London)

"*Snow* has already been a bestseller in Turkey—given Pamuk's stature as a novelist and the novel's content it could hardly fail to be. But what makes it a brilliant novel is its artistry. Pamuk keeps so many balls in the air that you cannot separate the inquiry into the nature of religious belief from the examination of modern Turkey, the investigation of East-West relations, and the nature of art itself. . . . All this rolled into a gripping political thriller."
                                        —*The Spectator*

"Brilliant. . . . Pamuk writes with such grace and deep respect for his conflicted characters that this rich novel passes like a dream, encompassing every aspect of love and belief."
                                        —*People*

Orhan Pamuk
Snow

Orhan Pamuk's novel *My Name Is Red*
won the 2003 IMPAC Dublin Literary
Award. His work has been translated into
more than thirty languages. He lives in
Istanbul.

INTERNATIONAL

Snow

He draws a schematic of
a snowflake & writes the
titles of his poems on the
axes ....

Every life is like a snowflake
whose forms appear
identical from afar but
are determined by any
number of mysterious
forces, making each one
singular ......

www.orhanpamuk.net/articles/
sara hemily miano.htm

Snow

—◆◆◆◆◆—

Orhan Pamuk

Translated from the Turkish by Maureen Freely

VINTAGE INTERNATIONAL
Vintage Books
A Division of Random House, Inc.
New York

FIRST VINTAGE INTERNATIONAL EDITION, AUGUST 2005

The Library of Congress has cataloged the Knopf edition as follows:
Pamuk, Orhan [date]
[Kar, English]
Snow / Orhan Pamuk ; translated from the Turkish by Maureen Freely—1st American ed.
p. cm.
I. Freely, Maureen, [date] II. Title.
PL248.P34K36513 2004
894'.3533—dc22
2003065935

Vintage ISBN: 0-375-70686-0

Book design by Robert C. Olsson

www.vintagebooks.com

Printed in the United States of America
10 9 8 7 6 5 4 3 2 1

To Rüya

Our interest's on the dangerous edge of things.
The honest thief, the tender murderer,
The superstitious atheist.
    —Robert Browning, "Bishop Blougram's Apology"

Politics in a literary work are a pistol-shot in the middle of a concert, a crude affair though one impossible to ignore. We are about to speak of very ugly matters.
    —Stendhal, *The Charterhouse of Parma*
    Richard Howard's translation

Well, then, eliminate the people, curtail them, force them to be silent. Because the European enlightenment is more important than people.
    —Dostoevsky, notebooks for *The Brothers Karamazov*

The Westerner in me was discomposed.
    —Joseph Conrad, *Under Western Eyes*

CONTENTS

Contents

Snow

———— ◆◆◆ ————

CHAPTER ONE

The Silence of Snow

THE JOURNEY TO KARS

The silence of snow, thought the man sitting just behind the bus driver. If this were the beginning of a poem, he would have called the thing he felt inside him the silence of snow.

He'd boarded the bus from Erzurum to Kars with only seconds to spare. He'd just come into the station on a bus from Istanbul—a snowy, stormy, two-day journey—and was rushing up and down the dirty wet corridors with his bag in tow, looking for his connection, when someone told him the bus for Kars was leaving immediately.

He'd managed to find it, an ancient Magirus, but the conductor had just shut the luggage compartment and, being "in a hurry," refused to open it again. That's why our traveler had taken his bag on board with him; the big dark-red Bally valise was now wedged between his legs. He was sitting next to the window and wearing a thick charcoal coat he'd bought at a Frankfurt *Kaufhof* five years earlier. We should note straight-away that this soft, downy beauty of a coat would cause him shame and disquiet during the days he was to spend in Kars, while also furnishing a sense of security.

As soon as the bus set off, our traveler glued his eyes to the window next to him; perhaps hoping to see something new, he peered into the wretched little shops and bakeries and broken-down coffeehouses that lined the streets of Erzurum's outlying suburbs, and as he did it began to snow. It was heavier and thicker than the snow he'd seen between Istanbul and Erzurum. If he hadn't been so tired, if he'd paid a bit more attention to the snowflakes swirling out of the sky like feathers, he might have realized that he was traveling straight into a blizzard; he might have seen at the start that he was setting out on a journey that would change his life forever and chosen to turn back.

But the thought didn't even cross his mind. As evening fell, he lost himself in the light still lingering in the sky above; in the snowflakes whirling ever more wildly in the wind he saw nothing of the impending blizzard but rather a promise, a sign pointing the way back to the happiness and purity he had known, once, as a child. Our traveler had spent his years of happiness and childhood in Istanbul; he'd returned a week ago, for the first time in twelve years, to attend his mother's funeral, and having stayed there four days he decided to take this trip to Kars. Years later, he would still recall the extraordinary beauty of the snow that night; the happiness it brought him was far greater than any he'd known in Istanbul. He was a poet and, as he himself had written—in an early poem still largely unknown to Turkish readers—it snows only once in our dreams.

As he watched the snow fall outside his window, as slowly and silently as the snow in a dream, the traveler fell into a long-desired, long-awaited reverie; cleansed by memories of innocence and childhood, he succumbed to optimism and dared to believe himself at home in this world. Soon afterward, he felt something else that he had not known for quite a long time and fell asleep in his seat.

Let us take advantage of this lull to whisper a few biographical details. Although he had spent the last twelve years in political exile in Germany, our traveler had never been very much involved in politics. His real passion, his only thought, was for poetry. He was forty-two years old and single, never married. Although it might be hard to tell as he curled up in his seat, he was tall for a Turk, with brown hair and a pale complexion that had become even paler during this journey. He was shy and enjoyed being alone. Had he known what would happen soon after he fell asleep—with the swaying of the bus his head would come to lean first on his neighbor's shoulder and then on the man's chest—he would have been very much ashamed. For the traveler we see leaning on his neighbor is an honest and well-meaning man and full of melancholy, like those Chekhov characters so laden with virtues that they never know success in life. We'll have a lot to say about melancholy later on. But as he is not likely to remain asleep for very long in that awkward position, suffice it for now to say that the traveler's name is Kerim Alakuşoğlu, that he doesn't like this name but prefers to be called Ka (from his initials), and that I'll be doing the same in this book. Even as a schoolboy, our hero stubbornly insisted on writing *Ka* on his homework and exam papers; he signed *Ka* on university registration forms; and he took every opportunity to defend his right to continue to do so, even if it meant conflict with teachers and government officials. His mother, his family, and his friends all called him Ka, and, having also published some poetry collections under this name, he enjoyed a small enigmatic fame as Ka, both in Turkey and in Turkish circles in Germany.

That's all we have time for at present. As the bus driver wished his passengers a safe journey as we departed Erzurum station, let me just add these words: "May your road be open, dear Ka." But I don't wish to deceive you. I'm an old friend of Ka's, and I begin this story knowing everything that will happen to him during his time in Kars.

After leaving Horasan, the bus turned north, heading directly for Kars. As it climbed the winding road, the driver had to slam on the brakes to avoid a horse and carriage that had sprung up out of nowhere on one of the hairpin bends, and Ka woke up. Fear had already fostered a strong fellow feeling among the passengers; before long, Ka too felt at one with them. Even though he was sitting just behind the bus driver, Ka was soon behaving like the passengers behind him: Whenever the bus slowed to negotiate a bend in the road or avoid going over the edge of a cliff, he stood up to get a better view; when the zealous passenger who'd committed himself to helping the driver by wiping the condensation from the windshield missed a corner, Ka would point it out with his forefinger (which contribution went unnoticed); and when the blizzard got so bad that the wipers could no longer keep the snow from piling up on the windshield, Ka joined the driver in trying to guess where the road was.

Once caked with snow, the road signs were impossible to read. When the snowstorm began to rage in earnest, the driver turned off his brights and dimmed the lights inside the bus, hoping to conjure up the road out of the semidarkness. The passengers fell into a fearful silence with their eyes on the scene outside: the snow-covered streets of destitute villages, the dimly lit, ramshackle one-story houses, the roads to farther villages that were already closed, and the ravines barely visible beyond the streetlamps. If they spoke, it was in whispers.

So it was in the gentlest of whispers that Ka's neighbor, the man onto whose shoulder Ka had fallen asleep earlier, asked him why he was traveling to Kars. It was easy to see that Ka was not a local.

"I'm a journalist," Ka whispered in reply. This was a lie. "I'm interested in the municipal elections—and also the young women who've been committing suicide." This was true.

"When the mayor of Kars was murdered, every newspaper in Istanbul ran the story," Ka's neighbor replied. "And it's the same for the women who've been committing suicide." It was hard for Ka to know whether it was pride or shame he heard in the man's voice. Three days later, standing in the snow on Halitpaşa Avenue with tears streaming from his eyes, Ka was to see this slim handsome villager again.

During the desultory conversation that continued on and off for the rest of the bus journey, Ka found out that the man had just taken his mother to Erzurum because the hospital in Kars wasn't good enough, that he was a livestock dealer who served the villages in the Kars vicinity, that he'd been through hard times but hadn't become a rebel, and that—for mysterious reasons he did not disclose to Ka—he was sorry not for himself but for his country and was happy to see that a well-read, educated gentleman like Ka had taken the trouble to travel all the way from Istanbul to find out more about his city's problems. There was something so noble in the plainness of his speech and the pride of his bearing that Ka felt respect for him.

His very presence was calming. Not once during twelve years in Germany had Ka known such inner peace; it had been a long time since he had had the fleeting pleasure of empathizing with someone weaker than himself. He remembered trying to see the world through the eyes of a man who could feel love and compassion. As he did the same now, he no longer felt so fearful of the relentless blizzard. He knew they were not destined to roll off a cliff. The bus would be late, but it would reach its destination.

When, at ten o'clock at night, three hours behind schedule, the bus began its crawl through the snow-covered streets of Kars, Ka couldn't recognize the city at all. He couldn't even see the railroad station, where he'd arrived twenty years earlier by steam engine, nor could he see any sign of the hotel to which his driver had taken him that day (following a full tour of the city): the Hotel Republic, "a telephone in every room." It was as if everything had been erased, lost beneath the snow. He saw a hint of the old days in the horse-drawn carriages here and there, waiting in garages, but the city itself looked much poorer and sadder than he remembered. Through the frozen windows of the bus, Ka saw the same concrete apartments that had sprung up all over Turkey during the past ten years, and the same Plexiglas panels; he also saw banners emblazoned with campaign slogans strung above every street.

He stepped off the bus. As his foot sank into the soft blanket of snow, a sharp blast of cold air shot up past the cuffs of his trousers. He'd booked a room at the Snow Palace Hotel. When he went to ask the conductor where it was, he thought two of the faces among the travelers waiting for their luggage looked familiar, but with the snow falling so thick and fast he couldn't work out who they were.

He saw them again in the Green Pastures Café, where he went after setting into his hotel: a tired and careworn but still handsome and eye-catching man with a fat but animated woman who seemed to be his life-long companion. Ka had seen them perform in Istanbul in the seventies, when they were leading lights of the revolutionary theater world. The man's name was Sunay Zaim. As he watched the couple, he let his mind wander and was eventually able to work out that the woman reminded him of a classmate from primary school. There were a number of other men at their table, and they all had the deathly pallor that speaks of a life on the stage; what, he wondered, was a small theater company doing in this forgotten city on a snowy night in February? Before leaving the restaurant, which twenty years ago had been full of government officials in coats and ties, Ka thought he saw one of the heroes of the seventies' militant left sitting at another table. But it was as if a blanket of snow had settled over his memories of this man, just as it had settled over the restaurant and the failing, gasping city itself.

Were the streets empty because of the snow, or were these frozen pavements always so desolate? As he walked he took careful notice of the writing on the walls—the election posters, the advertisements for schools and restaurants, and the new posters that the city officials hoped would end the suicide epidemic: HUMAN BEINGS ARE GOD'S MASTERPIECES, AND SUICIDE IS BLASPHEMY. Through the frozen windows of a half-empty tea-house, Ka saw a group of men huddled around a television set. It cheered him just a little to see, still standing, these old stone Russian houses that in his memory had made Kars such a special place.

The Snow Palace Hotel was one of those elegant Baltic buildings. It was two stories high, with long narrow windows that looked out onto a courtyard and an arch that led out to the street. The arch was 110 years old and high enough for horse-drawn carriages to pass through with ease; Ka felt a shiver of excitement as he walked under it, but he was too tired to ask himself why. Let's just say it had something to do with one of Ka's reasons for coming to Kars.

Three days earlier, Ka had paid a visit to the Istanbul offices of the *Republican* to see a friend from his youth. It was this friend, Taner, who had told him about the municipal elections coming up and how—just as in the city of Batman—an extraordinary number of girls in Kars had succumbed to a suicide epidemic. Taner went on to say that if Ka wanted to write about this subject and see what Turkey was really like after his twelve-year absence, he should think of going to Kars; with no one else available for this assignment, he could provide Ka with a current press card; what's more, he said, Ka might be interested to know that their old classmate İpek was now living in Kars. Although separated from her husband, Muhtar, she'd stayed on in the city and was living with her father and sister in the Snow Palace Hotel. As Ka listened to Taner, who wrote political commentaries for the *Republican,* he remembered how beautiful İpek was.

Cavit, the hotel clerk, sat in the high-ceilinged lobby watching television. He handed Ka the key, and Ka went up to the second floor to Room 203; having shut the door behind him, he felt calmer. After careful self-examination, he concluded that, notwithstanding the fears that had plagued him throughout his journey, neither his heart nor his mind were troubled by the possibility that İpek might be here in the hotel. After a lifetime in which every experience of love was touched by shame and suffering, the prospect of falling in love filled Ka with an intense, almost instinctive dread.

In the middle of the night, before getting into bed, Ka padded across the room in his pajamas, parted the curtains, and watched the thick, heavy snowflakes falling without end.

———◆———

CHAPTER TWO

Our City Is a Peaceful Place

THE OUTLYING DISTRICTS

Veiling as it did the dirt, the mud, and the darkness, the snow would continue to speak to Ka of purity, but after his first day in Kars it no longer promised innocence. The snow here was tiring, irritating, terrorizing. It had snowed all night. It continued snowing all morning, while Ka walked the streets playing the intrepid reporter—visiting coffeehouses packed with unemployed Kurds, interviewing voters, taking notes—and it was still snowing later, when he climbed the steep and frozen streets to interview the former mayor and the governor's assistant and the families of the girls who had committed suicide. But it no longer took him back to the white-covered streets of his childhood; no longer did he think, as he had done as a child standing at the windows of the sturdy houses of Nişantaş, that he was peering into a fairy tale; no longer was he returned to a place where he could enjoy the middle-class life he missed too much even to visit in his dreams. Instead, the snow spoke to him of hopelessness and misery.

Early that morning, before the city woke up and before he had let the snow get the better of him, he took a brisk walk through the shantytown below Atatürk Boulevard to the poorest part of Kars, to the district known as Kalealtı. The scenes he saw as he hurried under the ice-covered branches of the plane trees and the oleanders—the old decrepit Russian buildings with stovepipes sticking out of every window, the thousand-year-old Armenian church towering over the wood depots and the electric generators, the pack of dogs barking at every passerby from a five-hundred-year-old stone bridge as snow fell into the half-frozen black waters of the river below, the thin ribbons of smoke rising out of the tiny shanty houses of Kalealtı sitting lifeless under their blanket of snow—made him feel so melancholy that tears welled in his eyes. On the opposite bank were two children, a girl and a boy who'd been sent out early to buy bread, and as they danced along, tossing the warm loaves back and forth or clutching them to their chests, they looked so happy that Ka could not help smiling. It wasn't the poverty or the helplessness that disturbed him; it was the thing he would see again and again during the days to come—in the empty windows of photography shops, in the frozen windows of the crowded teahouses where the city's unemployed passed the time playing cards, and in the city's empty snow-covered squares. These sights spoke of a strange and powerful loneliness. It was as if he were in a place that the whole world had forgotten, as if it were snowing at the end of the world.

Ka's luck stayed with him all morning, and when people asked him who he was they wanted to shake his hand; they treated him like a famous journalist from Istanbul; all of them, from the governor's assistant to the poorest man, opened their doors and spoke to him. He was introduced to the city by Serdar Bey, the publisher of *Border City News* (circulation three hundred and twenty), who sometimes sent local news items to the *Republican* in Istanbul (mostly they didn't print them). Ka had been told to visit "our local correspondent" first thing in the morning, as soon as he left the hotel, and no sooner had he found this old journalist ensconced in his office than he realized this man knew everything there was to know in Kars. It was Serdar Bey who was the first to ask him the question he would hear again hundreds of times during his three-day stay.

"Welcome to our border city, sir. But what are you here for?"

Ka explained that he had come to cover the municipal elections and also perhaps to write about the suicide girls.

"As in Batman, the stories about the suicide girls have been exaggerated," the journalist replied. "Let's go over to meet Kasım Bey, the assistant chief of police. They should know you've arrived—just in case."

That all newcomers, even journalists, should pay a visit to the police was a provincial custom dating back to the forties. Because he was a political exile who had just returned to the country after an absence of many years, and because, even though no one had mentioned it, he sensed the presence of Kurdish separatist guerillas (PKK) in the city, Ka made no objection.

They set off into the blizzard, cutting through a fruit market and continuing past the stores of spare parts and hardware on Kâzım Karabekir

Avenue, past teahouses where gloomy unemployed men sat watching television and the falling snow, past dairy shops displaying huge wheels of yellow cheese; it took them fifteen minutes to cut a diagonal across the city.

Along the way, Serdar Bey stopped to show Ka the place where the old mayor had been assassinated. According to one rumor, he'd been shot over a simple municipal dispute: the demolition of an illegal balcony. They'd caught the assailant after three days in the village to which he'd escaped; when they found him hiding in a barn, he was still carrying the weapon. But there had been so much gossip during those three days before his capture, no one wanted to believe that this was indeed the culprit: the simplicity of the motivation was disappointing.

The Kars police headquarters was in a long three-story building on Faikbey Avenue, where the old stone buildings that had once belonged to wealthy Russians and Armenians now housed mostly government offices. As they sat waiting for the assistant chief of police, Serdar Bey pointed out the high ornate ceilings and explained that between 1877 and 1918, during the Russian occupation of the city, this forty-room mansion was first home to a rich Armenian and later a Russian hospital.

Kasım Bey, the beer-bellied assistant chief of police, came into the corridor and ushered them into his room. Ka could see at once that they were in the company of a man who did not read national newspapers like the *Republican,* considering them left-wing, that he was not particularly impressed to see Serdar Bey praising anyone simply for being a poet, but that he feared and respected him as the owner of the leading local paper. After Serdar Bey had finished speaking, the police chief turned to Ka. "Do you want protection?"

"Pardon?"

"I'm only suggesting one plainclothes policeman. To set your mind at ease."

"Do I really need it?" asked Ka, in the agitated voice of a man whose doctor has just told him he should start walking with a cane.

"Our city is a peaceful place. We've caught all the terrorists who were driving us apart. But I'd still recommend it, just in case."

"If Kars is a peaceful place, then I don't need protection," said Ka. He was secretly hoping that the assistant chief of police would take this opportunity to reassure him once again that Kars was a peaceful place, but Kasım Bey did not repeat his statement.

They headed north to Kalealtı and Bayrampaşa, the poorest neighborhoods. The houses here were shanties made of stone, brick, and corrugated aluminum siding. With the snow continuing to fall, they made their way from house to house: Serdar Bey would knock on a door, and if a woman answered he would ask to see the man of the house, and if Serdar Bey recognized him he would say in a voice inspiring confidence that his friend, a famous journalist, had come to Kars all the way from Istanbul to report on the elections and also to find out more about the city—to write, for example, about why so many women were committing suicide—and if these citizens could share their concerns, they would be doing a good thing for Kars. A few were very friendly, perhaps because they thought Ka and Serdar Bey might be candidates bearing tins of sunflower oil, boxes of soaps, or parcels full of cookies and pasta. If they decided to invite the two men in out of curiosity or simple hospitality, the next thing they did was to tell Ka not to be afraid of the dogs. Some opened their doors fearfully, assuming, after so many years of police intimidation, that this was yet another search, and even once they had realized that these men were not from the state, they would remain shrouded in silence. As for the families of the girls who had committed suicide (in a short time, Ka had heard about six incidents), they each insisted that their daughters had given them no cause for alarm, leaving them all shocked and grieved by what had happened.

They sat on old divans and crooked chairs in tiny icy rooms with earthen floors covered by machine-made carpets, and every time they moved from one house to the next, the number of dwellings seemed to have multiplied. Each time they went outside they had to make their way past children kicking broken plastic cars, one-armed dolls, or empty bottles and boxes of tea and medicine back and forth across the way. As they sat next to stoves that gave out no heat unless stirred continuously, and electric heaters that ran off illegal power lines, and silent television sets that no one ever turned off, they heard about the never-ending woes of Kars.

They listened to mothers who were in tears because their sons were out of work or in jail, and to bathhouse attendants who worked twelve-hour shifts in the *hamam* without earning enough to support a family of eight, and to unemployed men who were no longer sure they could afford to go to the teahouse because of the high price of a glass of tea. These people complained and complained about the unemployment rate, their bad luck, the city council, and the government, tracing their every problem to the nation and the state. As they traveled from house to house, listening to these tales of hardship, a moment arrived when, in spite of the white light coming in through the windows, Ka came to feel as if they had entered a shadow world. The rooms were so dark he could barely make out the shape of the furniture, so when he was compelled to look at the snow outside, it blinded him—it was as if a curtain of tulle had fallen before his eyes, as if he had retreated into the silence of snow to escape from these stories of misery and poverty.

The suicide stories he heard that day were the worst; they would haunt him for the rest of his life. It wasn't the elements of poverty or helplessness that Ka found so shocking. Neither was it the constant beatings to which these girls were subjected, or the insensitivity of fathers who wouldn't even let them go outside, or the constant surveillance of jealous husbands. The thing that shocked and frightened Ka was the way these girls had killed themselves: abruptly, without ritual or warning, in the midst of their everyday routines.

There was one sixteen-year-old girl, for example, who had been forced into an engagement with an elderly teahouse owner; she had eaten her evening meal with her mother, father, three siblings, and paternal grandmother, just as she had done every evening; after she and her sisters had cleared the table with the usual amount of giggling and tussling, she went from the kitchen into the garden to fetch the dessert, and from there she climbed through the window into her parents' bedroom, where she shot herself with a hunting rifle. The grandmother, who heard the gunshot, ran upstairs to find the girl supposed to be in the kitchen lying dead on the floor in her parents' bedroom in a pool of blood; this old woman could not understand how her girl had managed to get from the kitchen to the bedroom, let alone why she would have committed suicide. There was another sixteen-year-old who, following the usual evening scuffle with her two siblings over what to watch on television and who would hold the remote control, and after her father came in to settle the matter by giving her two hard whacks, went straight to her room and, finding a big bottle of a veterinary medicine, Mortalin, knocked it back like a bottle of soda. Another girl, who had married happily at the age of fifteen, had given birth six months ago; now, terrorized by the beatings given her by her depressed and unemployed husband, she locked herself in the kitchen after the daily quarrel. Her husband guessed what she was up to, but she had already prepared the rope and the hook in the ceiling, so before he could break down the door she had hanged herself.

It fascinated Ka, the desperate speed with which these girls had plunged from life into death. The care they had taken—the hooks put into the ceiling, the loaded rifles, the medicine bottles transferred from pantry to bedroom—suggested suicidal thoughts they'd carried around with them for a long time.

The first such suicide had come from the city of Batman, a hundred kilometers from Kars. All over the world, men are three or four times more likely to kill themselves than women; it was a young civil servant in the National Office of Statistics in Ankara who had first noticed that in Batman the number of female cases was three times greater than the number for males and four times greater than the world average for females. But when a friend of his at the *Republican* published this analysis in "News in Brief," no one in Turkey took any notice. A number of correspondents for French and German newspapers, however, did pick up on the item, and only after they had gone to Batman and published stories in the European press did the Turkish press begin to take an interest: at this point, quite a few Turkish reporters paid visits to the city.

According to officials, the press interest had served only to push more girls over the edge. The deputy governor of Kars, a squirrel-faced man with a brush mustache, told Ka that the local suicides had not reached the same statistical level as those in Batman, and he had no objection "at present" to Ka's speaking to the families, but he asked Ka to refrain from using the word *suicide* too often when speaking to these people and to take care not to exaggerate the story when he wrote it up in the *Republican*. A committee of suicide experts—including psychologists, police officers, judges, and officials from the Department of Religious Affairs—was already preparing to decamp from Batman to Kars; as a preliminary measure the Department of Religious Affairs had plastered the city with its SUICIDE IS BLASPHEMY posters, and the governor's office was to distribute a pamphlet with the slogan as its title. Still, the deputy governor worried that these measures might produce the result opposite from the one intended—not just because girls hearing of others committing suicide might be inspired to do the same, but also because quite a few might do it out of exasperation with the constant lecturing from husbands, fathers, preachers, and the state.

"What is certain is that these girls were driven to suicide because they were extremely unhappy. We're not in any doubt about that," the deputy governor told Ka. "But if unhappiness were a genuine reason for suicide, half the women in Turkey would be killing themselves." He suggested that these women might be offended if they had to listen to a chorus of male voices remonstrating "Don't commit suicide!" This, he told Ka proudly, was why he had written to Ankara asking that the antisuicide propaganda committee include at least one woman.

The idea that suicide might spread contagiously like the plague had first been suggested after a girl traveled all the way from Batman to Kars just to kill herself. Her family now refused to let Ka and Serdar Bey into the house, but the girl's maternal uncle agreed to speak with them outside. Smoking a cigarette, seated under the oleander trees of a snow-covered garden in the Atatürk district, he told her story. His niece had married two years earlier; forced to do housework from morning till night, she had also endured the incessant scolding of her mother-in-law for failing to conceive a child. But this alone would not have been enough to drive the girl to suicide; it was clear that she had got the idea from the other women killing themselves in Batman. Certainly the dear departed girl had seemed perfectly happy on visiting with her family here in Kars, so it was all the more shocking when—on the very morning she was due to return to Batman—they found a letter in her bed saying that she had taken two boxes of sleeping pills.

One month after the suicide idea had, as it were, infected Kars, this girl's sixteen-year-old cousin committed the first copycat suicide. With the uncle's coaxing, and having got Ka to promise that he would include the full story in his report, her tearful parents explained that the girl had been driven to suicide after her teacher accused her of not being a virgin. Once the rumor had spread all over Kars, the girl's fiancé called off the engagement, and the other young suitors—still coming to the house to ask for this beautiful girl's hand despite the betrothal—stopped coming too. At that point, the girl's maternal grandmother had started to say, "Oh, well, looks like you're never going to find a husband." Then one evening, as the whole family was watching a wedding scene on television and her father, drunk at the time, started crying, the girl stole her grandmother's sleeping pills and, having swallowed them all, went to sleep (not only the idea of suicide but also the method having proved contagious). When the autopsy revealed that the girl had actually been a virgin, her father blamed not just the teacher for spreading the lie but also his relative's daughter for coming from Batman to kill herself. And so, out of a wish to dispel the baseless rumors about their child's chastity and to expose the teacher who had started the malicious lie, the family decided to tell Ka the full story.

Ka thought it strangely depressing that the suicide girls had had to struggle to find a private moment to kill themselves. Even after swallow-ing their pills, even as they lay quietly dying, they'd had to share their rooms with others. Ka had grown up in Nişantaş reading Western litera-ture, and in his own fantasies of suicide he had always thought it impor-tant to have a great deal of time and space; at the very least you needed a room you could stay in for days without any knocking on the door. In his fantasies, suicide was a solemn ceremony with sleeping pills and whiskey, a final act performed alone and of one's own free will; in fact, every time he had ever imagined doing away with himself, it was the indispensable loneliness of it that scared him off. For that reason, he had to admit, he had never been seriously suicidal.

The only suicide who had delivered him back to that loneliness was the covered girl who had killed herself almost six weeks ago. This suicide was one of the famous "head-scarf girls." When the authorities had out-lawed the wearing of head scarves in educational institutions across the country, many women refused to comply; the noncompliant young women at the Institute of Education in Kars had been barred first from the classrooms and then, following an edict from Ankara, from the entire campus. Among the families Ka met, that of the head-scarf girl was the most well off; the distraught father owned a little grocery store. Offering Ka a Coca-Cola from the store refrigerator, he explained that his daugh-ter had discussed her plans with both family and friends. As for the ques-tion of the head scarf, clearly her mother, who wore one, had set the example—with the blessing of the whole family—but the real pressure had come from those of her school friends running the campaign against the banishment of covered women from the Institute. Certainly it was they who taught her to think of the head scarf as a symbol of "political Islam." And so despite her parents' express wish that she remove her head scarf, the girl refused, thus ensuring that she herself would be removed, by the police and on many occasions, from the halls of the Institute of Education. When she saw some of her friends giving up and uncovering their heads, and others forgoing their head scarves to wear wigs instead, the girl began to tell her father and her friends that life had no meaning and she no longer wanted to live. But as the state-run Department of Religious Affairs and the Islamists had joined forces by now to condemn suicide as one of the greatest sins, and there were posters and pamphlets all over Kars proclaiming the same truth, no one expected a girl of such piety to take her own life. It seems that the girl, Teslime, had spent her last evening silently watching the television show called *Marianna*. After making tea and serving it to her parents, she went to her room and readied herself for her prayers, washing her mouth, her feet, and her hands. When she had finished her ablutions, she knelt down on her prayer rug and lost herself for some time in thought, and then in prayer, before tying her head scarf to the lamp hook from which she hanged herself.

CHAPTER THREE

Give Your Vote to God's Party

POVERTY AND HISTORY

R aised in Istanbul amid the middle-class comforts of Nişantaş—a
lawyer for a father, a housewife for a mother, a beloved sister, a
devoted maid, rooms full of furniture, a radio, curtains—Ka knew nothing of poverty; it was something beyond the house, in another world.
Shrouded in a dangerous and impenetrable darkness, this other world took
on a metaphysical charge in Ka's childhood imagination. And so it may
be hard to understand that Ka's sudden decision to travel to Kars was at
least partly motivated by a desire to return to his childhood.

Returning to Istanbul after twelve years in Frankfurt, looking up old
friends and revisiting the streets and shops and cinemas they'd shared as
children, he found almost nothing he recognized; if they hadn't been torn
down, they'd lost their souls. As for Kars, though he'd been living abroad
for some time, Ka was still aware of it as the poorest, most overlooked
corner of Turkey. For this reason, he may have been taken by a desire to
look farther afield for childhood and purity: If the world he knew in
Istanbul was no longer to be found, his journey to Kars can be seen as an
attempt to step outside the boundaries of his middle-class childhood, to
venture at long last into the other world beyond. In fact, when he found
the shop windows in Kars displaying things that he remembered from his
childhood, things you never saw in Istanbul anymore—Gislaved gym
shoes, Vesuv stoves, and (the first thing any child learned about Kars)
those round boxes of the city's famous processed cheese divided into six
wedges, he felt happy enough even to forget the suicide girls: Kars
brought him that peace of mind he once knew.

Around noon, after Serdar Bey and he had parted, he met with spokesmen for the People's Equality Party and for the Azeris, and after these interviews were over he stepped out again into the flurry of snowflakes—how large they were!—to take a solitary stroll through the city. Passing the barking dogs of Atatürk Avenue, he moved with sad determination toward the city's poorest neighborhoods, through a silence broken only by more barking dogs. As the snow covered the steep mountains no longer visible in the distance, covered the Seljuk castle and the shanties that sprawled among the ruins, it seemed to have swept everything off to another world, a world beyond time; when it occurred to him that he might be the only person to have noticed, his eyes filled with tears. He passed a park in Yusuf Paşa that was full of dismantled swings and broken slides; next to it was an open lot where a group of teenage boys were playing football. The high lampposts of the coal depot gave them just enough light, and Ka stopped for a while to watch them. As he listened to them, shouting and cursing and skidding in the snow, and gazed at the white sky and the pale yellow glow of the streetlights, the desolation and remoteness of the place hit him with such force that he felt God inside him.

It was less a certainty than a faint image at this point, like struggling to remember a particular picture after taking a swift tour through the galleries of a museum. You try to conjure up the painting only to lose it again. It wasn't the first time Ka had had this sensation.

Ka had grown up in a secular republican family and had had no religious teaching outside school. Although he'd had similar visions on occasion over the past few years, they had caused him no anxiety, nor had they inspired any poetic impulse. At most he would feel happy that the world was such a beautiful thing to behold.

When he returned to his hotel room for a bit of warmth and rest, he spent some time leafing happily through the histories of Kars he had brought with him from Istanbul, confusing what he read with the stories he had been hearing all day and with the tales from childhood that these books brought to mind.

Once upon a time in Kars, there had been a large and prosperous middle class, and although it had been far removed from Ka's own world it had engaged in all the rituals Ka remembered from childhood; there had been great balls in those mansions, festivities that went on for days. Kars was an important station on the trade route to Georgia, Tabriz, and the Caucasus; being on the border between two empires now defunct, the

Ottoman and the Russian, the mountain city also benefited from the protection of the standing armies each power had in turn placed in Kars for that purpose. During the Ottoman period, many different peoples had made Kars their home. There had been a large Armenian community; it no longer existed, but its thousand-year-old churches still stood in all their splendor. Many Persians fleeing first the Moghul and later the Iranian armies had settled in Kars over the years; there were Greeks with roots going back to the Byzantine and Pontus periods; there were also Georgians and Kurds and Circassians from various tribes. Some of the Muslims were driven out when the Russian army took possession of the city's five-hundred-year-old castle in 1878, and thereafter the pasha's mansions and *hamams* and the Ottoman buildings on the slopes below the castle fell into decay. Kars was still prosperous and diverse when the czar's architects went to work along the southern bank of the Kars River, and soon they had built a thriving new city defined by five perfectly straight parallel avenues and by streets that intersected these avenues at right angles, something never before seen in the East. Czar Alexander came here for the hunting—and to meet secretly with his mistress. To the Russians, Kars was a gateway to the south and to the Mediterranean, and with an eye to controlling the trade routes running through it they invested a great deal in civic projects. These were the things that had so impressed Ka during his stay twenty years earlier. The streets and the large cobblestone pavements, the plane trees and the oleanders that had been planted after the founding of the Turkish Republic—these gave the city a melancholy air unknown in Ottoman cities, whose wooden houses burned down during the years of nationalist struggle and tribal warfare.

After endless wars, rebellions, massacres, and atrocity, the city was occupied by Armenian and Russian armies at different times and even, briefly, by the British. For a short time, when the Russian and Ottoman forces had left the city following the First World War, Kars was an independent state; in October 1920, the Turkish army entered under the command of Kâzım Karabekir, the general whose statue now stood in Station Square. This new generation of Turks made the most of the grand plan initiated by the czar's architects forty-three years earlier: The culture that the Russians brought to Kars now fit perfectly with the Republic's westernizing project. But when it came to renaming the five great Russian avenues, they couldn't think of enough great men from the city's history who weren't soldiers, so they ended up memorializing five great pashas.

These were the city's westernizing years, as Muzaffer Bey, the ex-mayor from the People's Party, related with both pride and anger. He talked about the great balls in the civic centers, and the skating competitions held under the now rusty and ruined wrought-iron bridges Ka had crossed during his morning walk. When a theater company from Ankara came to perform *Oedipus Rex,* the Kars bourgeoisie received them with great enthusiasm, even though less than twenty years had passed since the war with Greece. The elderly rich in coats with fur collars would go out for rides on sleighs pulled by hearty Hungarian horses adorned with roses and silver tassels. At the National Gardens, balls were held under the acacia trees to support the football team, and the people of Kars would dance the latest dances as pianos, accordions, and clarinets were played in the open air. In summertime, girls could wear short-sleeved dresses and ride bicycles through the city without being bothered. Many lycée students who glided to school on ice skates expressed their patriotic fervor by sporting bow ties. In his youth, Muzaffer Bey had been one of them, and when as a lawyer he eagerly returned to the city to run for office, he took to wearing them again; his party associates warned him that this fashion was a vote-loser, likely to inspire people to dismiss him as the worst sort of poseur, but Muzaffer Bey paid no mind.

Now they were lost, those endless cold winters, and to listen to Muzaffer Bey it was as if this explained the city's plunge into destitution, depression, and decay. Having described the beauty of those winters— dwelling in particular on the powdered faces of the half-naked actors who had come all the way from Ankara to perform Greek plays—the old mayor went on to tell how in the late forties he himself had invited a youth group to perform a revolutionary play in the civic center. "This work tells of the awakening of a young girl who has spent her life enveloped in a black scarf," he said. "In the end she pulls it off and burns it." In the late forties they'd had to search the entire city for a black scarf to use in the play; in the end they had had to phone Erzurum to ask for one to be sent. "Now the streets of Kars are filled with young women in head scarves of every kind," Muzaffer Bey added. "And because they've been barred from their classes for flaunting this symbol of political Islam, they've begun committing suicide."

Ka refrained from asking questions, as he would for the rest of his stay in Kars whenever anyone mentioned the rise of political Islam or the head-scarf question. He also refrained from asking why it was, if indeed not a single head scarf could be had in Kars in the late forties, that a group of fiery youths had felt compelled to stage a revolutionary play urging women not to cover their heads. During his long walks through the city that day, Ka had paid little attention to the head scarves he saw and didn't attempt to distinguish the political kind from any other; having been back in the country for only a week, he had not yet acquired the secular intellectual's knack of detecting political motive when seeing a covered woman in the street. But it is also true that, since childhood, he had scarcely been in the habit of noticing covered women. In the westernized upper-middle-class circles of the young Ka's Istanbul, a covered woman would have been someone who had come in from the suburbs—from the Kartal vineyards, say—to sell grapes. Or she might be the milkman's wife or someone else from the lower classes.

In time, I was also to hear many stories about former owners of the Snow Palace Hotel, where Ka was staying. One was a West-leaning professor whom the czar had exiled to Kars (a gentler option than Siberia); another was an Armenian in the cattle trade; subsequently the building housed a Greek orphanage. The first owner had equipped the 110-year-old structure with the sort of heating system typical of so many houses built in Kars at that time: a stove set behind the walls to radiate heat to four surrounding rooms. It was not until Kars had become part of the Turkish Republic and the building had its first Turkish owner that it was converted to a hotel, but, being unable to figure out how to operate the Russian heating system, that owner installed a big brass stove beside the door opening onto the courtyard. Only much later was he converted to the merits of central heating.

Ka was lying on his bed with his coat on, lost in daydreams, when there was a knock on the door; he jumped up to answer it. It was Cavit, the desk clerk who spent his days beside the stove watching television; he had come to tell Ka something he had forgotten when Ka came in.

"I forgot to tell you. Serdar Bey, owner of the *Border City Gazette*, wants to see you immediately."

Downstairs, Ka was about to walk out of the lobby when he was stopped dead in his tracks; just at that moment, coming through the door behind the reception desk, was İpek. He'd forgotten how beautiful she was during their university days, and now, suddenly reminded, he felt slightly nervous in her presence. Yes, exactly—that's how beautiful she was. First they shook hands in the manner of the westernized Istanbul bourgeoisie, but after a moment's hesitation they moved their heads forward, embracing without quite letting their bodies touch, and kissed on the cheeks.

"I knew you were coming," İpek said, as she stepped back. Ka was surprised to hear her speaking so openly. "Taner called to tell me." She looked straight into Ka's eyes when she said this.

"I came to report on the municipal elections and the suicide girls."

"How long are you staying?" asked İpek. "I'm busy with my father right now, but there's a place called the New Life Pastry Shop, right next door to the Hotel Asia. Let's meet there at half past one. We can catch up then."

If they'd run into each other in Istanbul—somewhere in Beyoğlu, say—this would have been a normal conversation: it was because it was happening in Kars that Ka felt so strange. He was unsure how much of his agitation had to do with İpek's beauty. After walking through the snow for some time, Ka found himself thinking, I'm so glad I bought this coat!

On the way to the newspaper office, his heart revealed a thing or two that his mind refused to accept: First, in returning to Istanbul from Frankfurt for the first time in twelve years, Ka's purpose was not simply to attend his mother's funeral but also to find a Turkish girl to make his wife; second, it was because he secretly hoped that this girl might be İpek that he had traveled all the way from Istanbul to Kars.

If a close friend had suggested this second possibility, Ka would never have forgiven him; its truth would cause Ka guilt and shame for the rest of his life. Ka, you see, was one of those moralists who believe that the greatest happiness comes from never doing anything for the sake of personal happiness. On top of that, he did not think it appropriate for an educated, westernized, literary man like himself to go in search of marriage to someone he hardly knew. In spite of this, he felt quite content when he arrived at the *Border City Gazette*. This was because his first meeting with İpek—the thing he had been dreaming of from the moment he stepped on the bus in Istanbul—had gone much better than he could have predicted.

The *Border City Gazette* was on Faikbey Avenue, one street down from Ka's hotel, and its offices and printing facilities took up only slightly more space than Ka's small hotel room. It was a two-room affair with a wooden partition on which were displayed portraits of Atatürk, calendars, sample business cards and wedding invitations (a printing sideline), and photographs of the owner with important government officials and other famous Turks who had paid visits to Kars. There was also a framed copy of the newspaper's first issue, published forty years before. In the background was the reassuring sound of the press's swinging treadle; 110 years old, it was manufactured in Leipzig by the Baumann Company for its first owners in Hamburg. After working it for a quarter century, they sold it to a newspaper in Istanbul (this was in 1910, during the free press period following the establishment of the second constitutional monarchy). In 1955—just as it was about to be sold off as scrap—Serdar Bey's dear departed father bought the press and shipped it to Kars.

Ka found Serdar Bey's twenty-two-year-old son moistening his finger with spit, about to feed a clean sheet into the machine with his right hand while skillfully removing the printed paper with his left; the collection basket had been broken during an argument with his younger brother eleven years earlier. But even performing the complex maneuver, he was able to wave hello to Ka. Serdar Bey's second son was seated before a jet-black table, its top divided into countless small compartments and surrounded by rows of lead letters, molds, and plates. The elder son resembled his father, but when Ka looked at the younger he saw the slant-eyed, moon-faced, short, fat mother. Hand-setting advertisements for the issue due out in three days, this boy showed the painstaking patience of a calligrapher who has renounced the world for his art.

"So now you see what difficult conditions we in the Eastern Anatolian press have to work under," said Serdar Bey.

At that very moment, the electricity went off. As the printing press whirred to a halt and the shop fell into an enchanted darkness, Ka was struck by the beautiful whiteness of the snow falling outside.

"How many copies did you print?" Serdar Bey asked. Lighting a candle, he sat Ka down on a chair in the front office.

"I've done a hundred and sixty, baba."

"When the electricity comes back on, bring it up to three hundred and forty. Our sales are bound to increase, what with the visiting theater company."

The *Border City Gazette* was sold at only one outlet, just across from the National Theater, and this outlet sold on average twenty copies of each edition; including subscriptions, the paper's circulation was 320, a fact that inspired not a little pride in Serdar Bey. Of these, 240 went to government offices and places of business; Serdar Bey was often obliged to report on their achievements. The other 80 went to "honest and important people of influence" who had moved to Istanbul but still maintained their links with the city.

When the electricity came back on, Ka noticed an angry vein popping out of Serdar Bey's forehead.

"After you left us, you had meetings with the wrong people, and these people told you the wrong things about our border city," said Serdar Bey.

"How could you know where I've been?" asked Ka.

"Naturally, the police were following you," said the newspaperman. "And for professional reasons, we listen in on police communication with this transistor radio. Ninety percent of the news we print comes from the office of the governor and the Kars police headquarters. The entire police force knows you have been asking everyone why Kars is so backward and poor and why so many of its young women are committing suicide."

Ka had heard quite a few explanations as to why Kars had fallen into such destitution. Business with the Soviet Union had fallen off during the Cold War, some said. The customs stations on the border had shut down. Communist guerillas who had plagued the city during the 1970s had chased the money away. The rich had pulled out what capital they could and moved to Istanbul and Ankara. The nation had turned its back on Kars, and so had God. And one must not forget Turkey's never-ending disputes with bordering Armenia. . . .

"I've decided to tell you the real story," said Serdar Bey.

With a clarity of mind and an optimism he hadn't felt in years, Ka saw at once that the heart of the matter was shame. It had been for him too, during his years in Germany, but he'd hidden the shame from himself. It was only now, having found hope for happiness, that he felt strong enough to admit the truth.

"In the old days we were all brothers," said Serdar Bey. He spoke as if betraying a secret. "But in the last few years, everyone started saying, I'm an Azeri, I'm a Kurd, I'm a Terekemian. Of course we have people here from all nations. The Terekemians, whom we also call the Karakalpaks, are the Azeris' brothers. As for the Kurds, whom we prefer to think of as a tribe: In the old days, they didn't even know they *were* Kurds. And it was that way through the Ottoman period: None of the people who chose to stay went around beating their chests and crying, 'We are the Ottomans!' The Turkmens, the Posof Laz, the Germans who had been exiled here by the czar—we had them all, but none took any pride in proclaiming themselves different. It was the Communists and their Tiflis Radio who spread tribal pride, and they did it because they wanted to divide and destroy Turkey. Now everyone is prouder—and poorer."

When he was confident that his point was not lost on Ka, Serdar Bey moved on to another subject.

"As for these Islamists, they go from door to door in groups, paying house visits; they give women pots and pans, and those machines that squeeze oranges, and boxes of soap, cracked wheat, and detergent. They concentrate on the poor neighborhoods; they ingratiate themselves with the women; they bring out hooked needles and sew gold thread onto the children's shoulders to protect them against evil. They say, 'Give your vote to the Prosperity Party, the party of God; we've fallen into this destitution because we've wandered off the path of God.' The men talk to the men, the women talk to the women. They win the trust of the angry and humiliated unemployed; they sit with their wives, who don't know where the next meal is coming from, and they give them hope; promising more gifts, they get them to promise their votes in return. We're not just talking about the lowest of the low. Even people with jobs—even tradesmen— respect them, because these Islamists are more hardworking, more honest, more modest than anyone else."

The owner of the *Border City Gazette* went on to say that the recently assassinated mayor had been universally despised. It was not because this man, having decided the city's horses and carriages were too old-fashioned, had tried to ban them. (To no avail, as it turned out; once he was dead, the plan was abandoned.) No, Serdar Bey insisted, the people of Kars had hated this mayor because he took bribes and lacked direction. But the republican parties on both the right and the left had failed to capitalize on this hatred; divided as they were by blood feuds, ethnic issues, and other destructive rivalries, they had failed to come up with a single viable candidate of their own. "The only candidate the people trust is the one who is running for God's party," said Serdar Bey. "And that candidate is Muhtar Bey, the ex-husband of İpek Hanım, whose father Turgut Bey owns your hotel. Muhtar's not very bright, but he's a Kurd, and the Kurds make up forty percent of our population. The new mayor will belong to God's party."

Outside, the snow was falling thicker and faster than ever; just the sight of it made Ka feel lonely. He was also worried that the westernized world he had known as a child might be coming to an end. When he was in Istanbul, he had returned to the streets of his childhood, looking for the elegant old buildings where his friends had lived, buildings dating back to the beginning of the twentieth century, but he found that many of them had been destroyed. The trees of his childhood had withered or been chopped down; the cinemas, shuttered for ten years, still stood there, surrounded by rows of dark, narrow clothing stores. It was not just the world of his childhood that was dying; it was his dream of returning to Turkey one day to live. If Turkey were taken over by a fundamentalist Islamist government, he now thought, his own sister would be unable to go outside without covering her head.

The neon sign of the *Border City Gazette* had created a small pocket of light in the darkness outside; the giant snowflakes wafting slowly through the glow were the stuff of fairy tales, and as Ka watched them continue to fall, he had a vision of himself with İpek in Frankfurt: They were in the same *Kaufhof* where he had bought the charcoal-gray coat he now wrapped so tightly around him; they were shopping together on the second floor, in the women's shoe section. . . .

"This is the work of the international Islamist movement that wants to turn Turkey into another Iran," Serdar Bey said.

"Is it the same with the suicide girls?" Ka asked, turning from the window.

"We're now gathering denunciations from people who say what a shame it was that these girls were so badly deceived, but because we don't want to put more pressure on other young women, thus perhaps driving more of them to suicide, we haven't yet printed any of the statements. They say that Blue, the infamous Islamist terrorist, is in our city, to advise the covered girls—and the suicidal ones, too."

"Aren't Islamists against suicide?"

Serdar Bey did not answer this question. The printing press stopped and a silence fell over the room. Ka returned his gaze to the miraculous snow. The knowledge that he was soon to see İpek was making him nervous. The problems of Kars were a welcome distraction, but all he wanted now was to think about İpek and prepare for their meeting at the pastry shop; it was twenty past one.

With a pomp and ceremony befitting some precious handmade gift, Serdar Bey presented Ka with a copy of the front page that his huge older son had just printed. Ka's eyes, accustomed to scanning for his name in literary journals, were quick to spot the item in the corner:

KA, OUR CELEBRATED POET, COMES TO KARS

KA, the celebrated poet whose fame now spreads throughout Turkey, has come to pay a visit to our border city. He first won the appreciation of the entire country with two collections entitled *Ashes and Tangerines* and *The Evening Papers*. Our young poet, who is also the winner of the Behcet Necatigil Prize, has come to Kars to cover the municipal elections for the *Republican*. For many years, KA has been studying Western poetry in Frankfurt.

"My name is printed wrong," said Ka. "The A should be lowercase." He regretted saying this. "But it looks good," he added, as if to make up for his bad manners.

"My dear sir, it was because we weren't sure of your name that we tried to get in touch with you," said Serdar Bey. "Son, look here, you printed our poet's name wrong." But as he scolded the boy there was no surprise in his voice. Ka guessed that he was not the first to have noticed that his name had been misprinted. "Fix it right now."

"There's no need," said Ka. At the same moment, he saw his name printed correctly in the last paragraph of the new lead item.

NIGHT OF TRIUMPH FOR THE SUNAY ZAIM PLAYERS AT THE NATIONAL THEATER

The Sunay Zaim Theatrical Company, which is known throughout Turkey for its theatrical tributes to Atatürk, the Republic, and the Enlightenment, performed to a rapt and enthusiastic audience at the National Theater yesterday evening. The performance, which went on until the middle of the night and was attended by the deputy governor, the mayoral candidate, and the leading citizens of Kars, was punctuated by thunderous clapping and applause. The people of Kars, who have long been thirsting for an artistic feast of this caliber, were able to watch not just from the packed auditorium but also from the surrounding houses. Kars Border Television worked tirelessly to organize this first live broadcast in its two-year history so that all of Kars would be able to watch the splendid performance. Although it still does not own a live-transmission vehicle, Kars Border Television was able to stretch a cable from its headquarters in Halitpaşa Avenue the length of two streets to the camera at the National Theater. Such was the feeling of goodwill among the citizens of Kars that some residents were kind enough to take the cable into their houses to avoid snow damage. (For example, our very own dentist, Fadıl Bey, and his family let them take the cable in through the window overlooking his front balcony and pass it into the gardens in the back.) The people of Kars now wish to have other opportunities to enjoy highly successful broadcasts of this order.

The management of Kars Border Television also announced that in the course of the city's first live broadcast, all Kars workplaces had been so kind as to broadcast advertisements.

The show, which was watched by the entire population of our city, included republican vignettes, the most beautiful scenes from the most important artistic works of the Western Enlightenment, theatrical sketches criticizing advertisements that aim to corrode our culture, the adventures of Vural, the celebrated goalkeeper, and poems in praise of Atatürk and the nation. Ka, the celebrated poet, who is now visiting our city, recited his latest poem, entitled "Snow." The crowning event of the evening was a performance of *My Fatherland or My Scarf,* the enlightenment masterwork from the early years of the republic, in a new interpretation entitled *My Fatherland or My Head Scarf.*

"I don't have a poem called 'Snow,' and I'm not going to the theater this evening. Your newspaper will look like it's made a mistake."

"Don't be so sure. There are those who despise us for writing the news before it happens. They fear us not because we are journalists but because we can predict the future; you should see how amazed they are when things turn out exactly as we've written them. And quite a few things do happen only because we've written them up first. This is what modern journalism is all about. I know you won't want to stand in the way of our being modern—you don't want to break our hearts—so that is why I am sure you will write a poem called 'Snow' and then come to the theater to read it."

Scanning the rest of the paper—announcements of various campaign rallies, news of a vaccine from Erzurum that was now being administered in the city's lycées, an upbeat article describing how all city residents were to be granted an additional two months to pay their water bills—Ka now noticed a news item he had missed earlier.

ALL ROADS TO KARS CLOSED

The snow that has been falling for two days has now cut all our city's links to the outside world. The Ardahan Road closed yesterday morning, and the road to Sarıkamış was impassable by afternoon. Due to excess snow and ice in the affected area, road closures forced a bus owned by the Yılmaz Company to return to Kars.

The weather office has announced that cold air coming straight from Siberia and the accompanying heavy snowfall will continue for three more days. And so for three days, the city of Kars will have to do as it used to do during the winters of old—stew in its own juices. This will offer us an opportunity to put our house in order.

Just as Ka was standing up to leave, Serdar Bey jumped from his seat and held the door so as to be sure his last words were heard.

"As for Turgut Bey and his daughters, who knows what they'll tell you?" he said. "They are educated people who entertain many friends like me in the evening, but don't forget: İpek Hanım's ex-husband, Muhtar Bey, is the mayoral candidate for Party of God. Her father, Turgut Bey, is an old Communist. Her sister, who came here to complete her studies, is rumored to be the leader of the head-scarf girls. Imagine that! There is not a single person in Kars who has the slightest idea why they chose to come here during the worst days of the city four years ago."

Ka's heart sank as he took in this disturbing news, but he showed no emotion.

CHAPTER FOUR

Did You Really Come Here to Report on the Election and the Suicides?

KA MEETS İPEK IN THE NEW LIFE PASTRY SHOP

Why, despite the bad news he'd just received, was there a faint smile on Ka's face as he walked through the snow from Faik-bey Avenue to the New Life Pastry Shop? Someone was playing Peppino di Capri's "Roberta," a melodramatic pop song from the sixties, and it made him feel like the sad romantic hero of a Turgenev novel, setting off to meet the woman who has been haunting his dreams for years. Let's tell the truth: Ka loved Turgenev and his elegant novels, and like the Russian writer Ka too had tired of his own country's never-ending troubles and come to despise its backwardness, only to find himself gazing back with love and longing after a move to Europe. Ka was not haunted by the image of İpek, but in his mind was the vision of a woman very much like her. Perhaps İpek had entered his thoughts from time to time, but it was only when he'd heard of her divorce that he began to think about her; indeed, it was precisely because he had *not* dreamed of her enough that he was now so keen to stoke his feelings with music and Turgenevist romanticism.

But as soon as he had entered the pastry shop and joined her at her table, all thoughts of such romanticism vanished, for İpek seemed even more beautiful now than at the hotel, lovelier even than she had been at university. The true extent of her beauty—her lightly colored lips, her pale complexion, her shining eyes, her open, intimate gaze—unsettled Ka. There was a moment when she seemed so sincere that he feared his studied composure would fail him. (This was his worst fear, after that of writing bad poems.)

"On the way here, I saw workmen drawing a live-transmission cable all the way from Border City Television to the National Theater. They were stretching it like a clothesline," he said, hoping to break the awkward silence. But not wanting to seem critical of the shortcomings of provincial life, he was careful not to smile.

It took some effort to keep up the conversation, but they both applied themselves to the task with admirable determination. The snow was one thing they could discuss with ease. When they had exhausted this subject, they moved on to the poverty of Kars. After that it was Ka's coat. Then a mutual confession that each found the other quite unchanged, and that neither had been able to give up smoking. The next subject was distant friends: Ka had just seen many of them in Istanbul. But it was the discovery that both their mothers were now dead and buried in Istanbul's Feriköy Cemetery that induced the greater intimacy both were seeking. And so by the time they had discovered a common astrological sign, the revelation—illusory or not—produced a frisson that brought them even closer.

Relaxed now, they were able to chat (briefly) about their mothers and (at greater length) about the demolition of the old Kars train station. They soon turned to the pastry shop in which they were sitting; it had been an Orthodox church until 1967, when the door had been removed and taken away to the museum. A section of the same museum commemorated the Armenian Massacre (naturally, she said, some tourists came expecting to see remnants of the Turks' massacre of the Armenians, and it was always a jolt to discover that in this museum the story was the other way around). The next topic was the pastry shop's sole waiter, half deaf, half a ghost. Then the price of coffee, which, apparently, was no longer sold in the city's teahouses because it was too expensive for the unemployed clientele. They went on to discuss the political views of the newspaperman who had given Ka his tour of the city, those of the various local papers (all supporters of the military and the present government), and tomorrow's issue of the *Border City Gazette,* which Ka now fished out of his pocket.

As he watched İpek scan the front page, Ka was overcome by the fear that, like his old friends in Istanbul, she was so much consumed by Turkey's internal problems and miserable political intrigues that she would never even consider living in Germany. He looked for a long time at İpek's small hands and her elegant face; her beauty still shocked him.

"For which article did they sentence you, and how long was your sentence?"

Ka told her. In the small political newspapers of the late seventies, considerable freedom of expression had been exercised, much more than the penal code allowed. Anyone tried and found guilty of insulting the state tended to feel rather proud of it. But no one ended up in prison, as the police made no serious effort to pursue the editors, the writers, or the translators in their ever-shifting whereabouts. But after the military coup of 1980, the authorities slowly got around to tracking down everyone who'd earlier evaded prison simply by changing address, and it was at this moment that Ka, having been tried for a hastily printed political article he had not even written, fled to Germany.

"Was it hard for you in Germany?" asked İpek.

"The thing that saved me was not learning German," said Ka. "My body rejected the language, so I was able to preserve my purity and my soul."

He was suddenly afraid he was making a fool of himself, but in his delight to have İpek as his audience, he went on to tell a story he'd never told anyone—about the silence buried inside him, the silence that had kept him from writing a single poem for the past four years.

"I rented a small place next to the train station; it had a window looking out over the rooftops of Frankfurt. In the evening, when I thought back on the day, I found that my memories were shrouded in a sort of silence. At first, out of this silence would come a poem. Over time, I had gained some recognition in Turkey as a poet, and now I began to get invitations to give readings. The approaches came from Turkish immigrants, city councils, libraries, and third-class schools hoping to draw in Turkish audiences, and also from Turks hoping to acquaint their children with a poet writing in Turkish."

So, when invited, Ka would board one of those orderly, punctual German trains he so admired; through the smoky mirror of the window, he'd watch the delicate church towers rising above remote villages. He'd peer into the beech forests, searching for the darkness at their heart. He'd see the sturdy children returning home with their rucksacks, and that same silence would descend on him; because he could not understand the language, he felt as safe, as comfortable, as if he were sitting in his own house, and this was when he wrote his poems.

On days when he wasn't traveling, he'd leave home at eight in the morning, walk the length of Kaiserstrasse, and go to the city library on the Zeil and read books. "There were enough English books there to last me twenty lifetimes." Here he read magnificent nineteenth-century novels, English romantic poetry, histories of engineering and related topics, museum catalogs—he read whatever he wanted, and he read it all with the pleasure of a child who knows death is too far off to imagine. As he sat in the library turning pages, stopping now and again to study the illustrations in old encyclopedias, rereading Turgenev's novels from cover to cover, he was able to block out the buzz of the city; he was surrounded by silence, just as he was on trains. Even after dark, when he would go by another route, walking in front of the Jewish Museum and the length of the River Main; even on weekends, when he walked from one end of the city to the other, this silence still enveloped him.

"Four years ago these silences took over my entire life. I needed noise—it was only by shutting out noise that I was able to write poetry," said Ka. "But now I lived in utter silence. I wasn't speaking with any Germans, and my relations with the Turks weren't good either—they dismissed me as a half-crazed, effete intellectual. I wasn't seeing anyone, I wasn't talking to anyone, and I wasn't writing poems."

"But it says in the paper that you're going to be reading your latest poem tonight."

"I don't have a latest poem, so how can I read it?"

There were only two other customers in the pastry shop. They were seated at a table on the other side of the room, in a corner next to the window. One was a tiny young man; his companion, old, thin, and tired, was patiently trying to explain something to him. Behind them, on the other side of the plate-glass window, great snowflakes were falling into the darkness; the pastry shop's neon sign tinged the flakes with pink. Set against this backdrop, the two men locked in intense conversation in the far corner of the pastry shop looked like characters in a grainy black-and-white film.

"My sister Kadife was at university in Istanbul, but she failed her finals in the first year," İpek said. "She managed to transfer to the Institute of Education here in Kars. The thin man sitting just behind me, way in the back, is Dr. Yılmaz, the director of the Institute. When my mother died in a car accident, my father, who adores my sister and didn't want to be alone, decided to move here and bring her along to live with my husband and me. But no sooner had my father moved here—this was three years ago—than Muhtar and I split up. So now the three of us live together. We own the hotel with some relatives; it's full of ghosts and tormented dead souls. We take up three rooms."

During their years in the student left, Ka and İpek had had nothing to do with each other. When, at seventeen, he first entered the high-ceilinged corridors of the literature department, Ka did not immediately single out İpek—there were plenty of other beautiful girls—and when they met the following year, she was already Muhtar's wife. Muhtar was a poet friend of Ka's who belonged to the same political group; like İpek, he came from Kars.

"Muhtar took over his father's Arçelik and Aygaz appliance distributorship," said İpek, "and once we were settled here, I tried to get pregnant. When nothing happened, he starting taking me to doctors in Erzurum and Istanbul; when I still couldn't conceive, we separated. But instead of remarrying, Muhtar gave himself to religion."

"Why are so many people giving themselves to religion all of a sudden?" Ka asked.

İpek didn't answer, and for a while they just watched the black-and-white television bracketed to the wall.

"Why is everyone in this city committing suicide?" asked Ka.

"It's not everyone who's committing suicide, it's just girls and women," said İpek. "The men give themselves to religion, and the women kill themselves."

"Why?"

İpek gave him a look that told him he would get nowhere by pressing her for quick answers; he was left feeling that he had overstepped. For a time, they were both silent.

"I have to speak to Muhtar as part of my election coverage," Ka said.

İpek rose at once, walked over to the cash register, and made a phone call. "He's at the branch headquarters of the party until five," she said, when she returned. "He'll expect you then."

Another silence fell between them, and Ka began to panic. If the roads had not been closed, he would have jumped on the next bus leaving Kars. He felt a pang of despair for this failing city and its forgotten people. Without intending it, he turned his head to look out the window. For a long time, he and İpek watched the snow listlessly, as if they had all the time in the universe and not a care in the world. Ka felt helpless.

"Did you really come here for the election and the suicide girls?" İpek asked finally.

"No," said Ka. "I found out in Istanbul that you and Muhtar had separated. I came here to marry you."

İpek laughed as if Ka had just told a very good joke, but before long her face turned deep red. During the long silence that followed, he looked into İpek's eyes and realized that she saw right through him. So you couldn't even take the time to get to know me, her eyes told him. You couldn't even spend a few minutes flirting with me. You're so impatient that you couldn't hide your intentions at all. Don't try to pretend you came here because you always loved me and couldn't get me out of your mind. You came here because you found out I was divorced and remembered how beautiful I was and thought I might be easier to approach now that I was stranded in Kars.

By now Ka was so ashamed of his wish for happiness, and so determined to punish himself for his insolence, that he imagined İpek uttering the cruelest truth of all: The thing that binds us together is that we have both lowered our expectations of life. But when she spoke, İpek said something very different from what he had imagined.

"I always knew you had it in you to be a good poet," she said. "I'd like to congratulate you on your work."

The walls of the pastry shop were, like the walls of every teahouse, restaurant, and hotel lobby in the city, decorated with photographs of mountain vistas—not the beautiful mountains of Kars but the mountains of Switzerland. Stacked on the display counters were trays of chocolates and braided cakes; their oiled surfaces and wrappings glittered in the pale light. The old waiter who had just served them tea was now sitting next to the till, facing Ka and İpek's table but with his back to the other customers and happily watching a film on the wall TV, having turned up the sound so he could hear. Ka, who was eager to avoid İpek's eyes, gave the television his full attention. A blond bikini-clad Turkish actress was running across the sand, while a man with a thick mustache chased her. At that moment, the tiny man who had been sitting at the dark table at the far end of the pastry shop rose to his feet and, pointing a gun at the director of the Institute of Education, muttered a few things Ka could not hear. When the director spoke back, the gun fired—but Ka worked this out only later. The gun made hardly any noise at all; it was only when he saw the director shudder violently and fall from his chair that Ka realized the man had been shot in the chest.

Seeing Ka's horror, İpek turned around to find out what had happened.

Ka looked over to where the old waiter had been only a moment ago, but he was gone. The tiny man, still standing in the same spot, continued to point the gun straight at the director, who lay still on the ground. The director was trying to tell him something, but with the TV now turned up so high, it was impossible to make out what he was saying. The tiny man pumped three more bullets into his victim, made for the door behind him, and disappeared. Ka had not seen his face.

"Let's go," said İpek. "We shouldn't stay here."

"Help!" said Ka, in a thin voice. Then he added, "Let's call the police." But he couldn't move a muscle. Moments later, he was running behind İpek. As they rushed through the double doors of the pastry shop and down the stairs into the street, they did not see a soul.

Once they'd reached the snowy pavement, they began to walk very fast. No one saw us leave, Ka said to himself, and this brought him some comfort, because now he felt as if it were he who had committed the murder. This was what he got—what he deserved—for proposing so abruptly to İpek. The mere memory made him cringe with shame. He couldn't bear to look anyone in the eye.

Ka's fears had not abated by the time they reached the corner of Kâzım Karabekir Avenue, although the shooting had given them a secret to share and he was glad to have even this silent intimacy with her. But in the light shining on the crates of oranges and apples outside the Halıl Paşa Arcade and from the naked bulb reflected in the mirror in the neighboring barbershop, Ka was alarmed to see tears in İpek's eyes.

"The director of the Institute of Education wasn't letting covered girls into the classroom," İpek explained. "That's why that poor dear man was killed."

"Let's tell the police," said Ka, even as he remembered that once upon a time, when he was a left-wing student, such an idea would have been unthinkable.

"There's no need; they'll find out anyway. They probably know about it already. The branch headquarters of the Prosperity Party is on the second floor there." İpek pointed at the entrance to the market. "Tell Muhtar what you've seen, so he won't be surprised when MİT pulls him in. And there's something else I have to tell you: Muhtar wants to marry me again, so watch what you say."

———— •=••=• ————

CHAPTER FIVE

I Hope I'm Not Taking Too Much of Your Time?

THE FIRST AND LAST CONVERSATION BETWEEN
THE MURDERER AND HIS VICTIM

When, in full view of Ka and İpek, the tiny man in the New Life Pastry Shop shot him in the head and the chest, the director of the Institute of Education was wearing a concealed tape recorder. The device—an imported Grundig—had been secured to his chest with duct tape by the diligent agents of the Kars branch of MİT, the national intelligence agency. The director had received a number of threats after barring covered girls from the classroom. When the civil security agents who keep track of fundamentalist activities confirmed that these threats were serious, the Kars branch decided it was time to offer the potential victim some protection. But the director did not wish to have an agent lumbering like a bear after him. Although he identified himself with the secular political camp, he believed in fate as much as any other religious man. He preferred to record the death threats, with a view to having the guilty parties arrested later. He had stepped into the New Life Pastry Shop on a whim, to have one of those walnut-filled crescent pastries he loved so much. When he saw a stranger approach, he switched on the tape recorder, as was now his practice in all such situations. The device took two bullets—not enough to save his life—but the tapes survived intact. Years later, I was able to acquire a transcript from the director's widow, her eyes still not dry, and his daughter, who by then had become a famous model.

—Hello, sir. Do you recognize me?
—No, I'm afraid I don't.
—That's what I thought you'd say, sir. Because we haven't ever met. I did try to come and see you last night and then again this morning.

Yesterday the police turned me away from the school doors. This morning I managed to get inside, but your secretary wouldn't let me see you. I wanted to catch you before you went into class. That's when you saw me. Do you remember me now, sir?

—No, I don't.

—Are you saying you don't remember me, or are you saying you don't remember seeing me?

—What did you want to see me about?

—To tell you the truth, I'd like to talk to you for hours, even days, about everything under the sun. You're an eminent, enlightened, educated man. Sadly, I myself was not able to pursue my studies. But there's one subject I know backward and forward, and that's the subject I was hoping to discuss with you. I'm sorry, sir. I hope I'm not taking too much of your time?

—Not at all.

—Excuse me, sir, do you mind if I sit down? We have a great deal of ground to cover.

—Please. Be my guest.

(The sound of someone pulling out a chair.)

—I see you're eating a pastry with walnuts. We have lots of walnut trees in Tokat. Have you ever been to Tokat?

—I'm sorry to say I haven't.

—I'm so sorry to hear that, sir. If you ever do come to visit, you must stay with me. I've spent my whole life in Tokat, all thirty-six years. Tokat is very beautiful. Turkey is very beautiful too. But it's such a shame that we know so little about our own country, that we can't find it in our hearts to love our own kind. Instead we admire those who show our country disrespect and betray its people. I hope you don't mind if I ask you a question, sir. You're not an atheist, are you?

—No, I'm not.

—People say you are, but I myself would find it hard to believe that a man of your education would—God forbid—deny God's existence. But you're not a Jew either, are you?

—No, I'm not.

—You're a Muslim?

—Yes. Glory be to God, I am.

—You're smiling, sir. I'd like to ask you to take my question seriously and answer it properly. Because I've traveled all the way from Tokat in the dead of winter just to hear you answer it.

—How did you come to hear of me in Tokat?

—There has been nothing in the Istanbul papers, sir, about your decision to deny schooling to girls who cover their heads as dictated by their religion and the Holy Koran. All those papers care about are scandals involving fashion models. But in beautiful Tokat we have a Muslim radio station called Flag that keeps us informed about the injustices perpetrated on the faithful in every corner of the country.

—I could never do an injustice to a believer. I too fear God.

—It took me two days to get here, sir, two days on snowy, stormy roads. While I was sitting on that bus I thought of no one but you, and believe me, I knew all along that you were going to tell me you feared God. And here's the question I imagined asking you next, sir. With all due respect, Professor Nuri Yılmaz, if you fear God, if you believe that the Holy Koran is the word of God, let's hear your views on the beautiful thirty-first verse of the chapter entitled Heavenly Light.

—Yes, it's true. This verse states very clearly that women should cover their heads and even their faces.

—Congratulations, sir! That's a good straight answer. And now, with your permission, sir, I'd like to ask you something else. How can you reconcile God's command with this decision to ban covered girls from the classroom?

—We live in a secular state. It's the secular state that has banned covered girls, from schools as well as classrooms.

—Excuse me, sir. May I ask you a question? Can a law imposed by the state cancel out God's law?

—That's a very good question. But in a secular state these matters are separate.

—That's another good straight answer, sir. May I kiss your hand? Please, sir, don't be afraid. Give me your hand. Give me your hand and watch how lovingly I kiss it. Oh, God be praised. Thank you. Now you know how much respect I have for you. May I ask you another question, sir?

—Please. Go right ahead.

—My question is this, sir. Does the word *secular* mean *godless*?

—No.

—In that case, how can you explain why the state is banning so many girls from the classroom in the name of secularism, when all they are doing is obeying the laws of their religion?

—Honestly, my son. Arguing about such things will get you nowhere.

They argue about it day and night on Istanbul television, and where does it get us? The girls are still refusing to take off their head scarves and the state is still barring them from the classroom.

—In that case, sir, may I ask you another question? I beg your pardon, but when I think about these poor hardworking girls of ours—who have been denied an education, who are so polite and so hardworking and who have bowed their heads to God-only-knows how many decrees already—the question I cannot help asking is, How does all this fit in with what our constitution says about educational and religious freedom? Please, sir, tell me. Isn't your conscience bothering you?

—If those girls were as obedient as you say they are, they'd have taken off their head scarves. What's your name, my son? Where do you live? What sort of work do you do?

—I work at the Happy Friends Teahouse, which is just next door to Tokat's famous Mothlight Hamam. I'm in charge of the stoves and the teapots. My name's not important. I listen to Flag radio all day long. Every once in a while I'll get really upset about something I've heard, about an injustice done to a believer. And because I live in a democracy, because I happen to be a free man who can do as he pleases, I sometimes end up getting on a bus and traveling to the other end of Turkey to track down the perpetrator, wherever he is, and have it out with him face-to-face. So please, sir, answer my question. What's more important, a decree from Ankara or a decree from God?

—This discussion is going nowhere, son. What hotel are you staying at?

—What, are you thinking of turning me in to the police? Don't be afraid of me, sir. I don't belong to any religious organizations. I despise terrorism. I believe in the love of God and the free exchange of ideas. That's why I never end a free exchange of ideas by hitting anyone, even though I have a quick temper. All I want is for you to answer this question. So please excuse me, sir, but when you think about the cruel way you treated those poor girls in front of your institute—when you remember that these girls were only obeying the word of God as set out so clearly in the Confederate Tribe and Heavenly Light chapters of the Holy Koran— doesn't your conscience trouble you at all?

—My son, the Koran also says that thieves should have their hands chopped off, but the state doesn't do that. Why aren't you opposing this?

—That's an excellent answer, sir. Allow me to kiss your hand. But how can you equate the hand of a thief with the honor of our women?

According to statistics released by the American Black Muslim professor Marvin King, the incidence of rape in Islamic countries where women cover themselves is so low as to be nonexistent and harassment is virtually unheard of. This is because a woman who has covered herself is making a statement. Through her choice of clothing, she is saying, Don't harass me. So please, sir, may I ask you a question? Do we really want to push our covered women to the margins of society by denying them the right to an education? If we continue to worship women who take off their head scarves (and just about everything else too), don't we run the risk of degrading them as we have seen so many women in Europe degraded in the wake of the sexual revolution? And if we succeed in degrading our women, aren't we also running the risk of—pardon my language—turning ourselves into pimps?

—I've finished my pastry, son. I'm afraid I have to leave.

—Stay in your seat, sir. Stay in your seat and I won't have to use this. Do you see what this is, sir?

—Yes. It's a gun.

—That's right, sir. I hope you don't mind. I came a long way to see you. I'm not stupid. It crossed my mind that you might refuse to hear me out. That's why I took precautions.

—What's your name, son?

—Vahit Süzme. Salim Feşmekân. Really, sir, what difference does it make? I'm the nameless defender of nameless heroes who have suffered untold wrongs while seeking to uphold their religious beliefs in a society that is in thrall to secular materialism. I'm not a member of any organization. I respect human rights and I oppose the use of violence. That's why I'm putting my gun in my pocket. That's why all I want from you is an answer to my question.

—Fine.

—Then let us go back to the beginning, sir. Let's remember what you did to these girls whose upbringing took so many years of loving care. Who were the apples of their parents' eyes. Who were so very, very intelligent. Who worked so hard at their studies. Who were all at the top of the class. When the order came from Ankara, you set about denying their existence. If one of them wrote her name down on the attendance sheet, you erased it—just because she was wearing a head scarf. If seven girls sat down with their teacher, you pretended that the one wearing the head scarf wasn't there, and you'd order six teas. Do you know what you did to these girls? You made them cry. But it didn't stop there. Soon there was another directive from Ankara, and after that you barred them from their classrooms. You threw them out into the corridors, and then you banned them from the corridors and threw them out into the street. And then, when a handful of these heroines gathered trembling at the doors of the school to make their concerns known, you picked up the phone and called the police.

—We're not the ones who called the police.

—I know you're afraid of the gun in my pocket. But please, sir, don't lie. The night after you had those girls dragged off and arrested, did your conscience let you sleep? That's my question.

—Of course, the real question is how much suffering we've caused our womenfolk by turning head scarves into symbols and using women as pawns in a political game.

—How can you call it a game, sir? When that girl who had to choose between her honor and her education—what a pity—sank into a depression and killed herself, was that a game?

—You're very upset, my boy. But has it never occurred to you that foreign powers might be behind all this? Don't you see how they might have politicized the head-scarf issue so that they can turn Turkey into a weak and divided nation?

—If you'd let those girls back into your school, sir, there would be no head-scarf issue.

—Is it really my decision? These orders come from Ankara. My own wife wears a head scarf.

—Stop sucking up to me. Answer the question I just asked you.

—Which question was that?

—Is your conscience bothering you?

—My child, I'm a father too. Of course I feel sorry for those girls.

—Look. I'm very good at holding myself back. But once I blow my fuse, it's all over. When I was in prison, I once beat up a man just because he forgot to cover his mouth when he yawned. Oh, yes, I made men of all of them in there. I cured every man in that prison wing of all his bad habits. I even got them praying. So stop trying to squirm out of this. Let's hear an answer to my question. What did I just say?

—What *did* you say, son? Lower that gun.

—I didn't ask you if you have a daughter but if you're sorry.

—Pardon me, son. What did you ask?

—Don't think you have to butter me up, just because you're afraid of the gun. Just remember what I asked you. *(Silence.)*

—What did you ask me?

—I asked you if your conscience was troubling you, infidel!

—Of course it's troubling me.

—Then why do you persist? Is it because you have no shame?

—My son, I'm a teacher. I'm old enough to be your father. Is it written in the Koran that you should point guns at your elders and insult them?

—Don't you dare let the word *Koran* pass your lips. Do you hear? And stop looking over your shoulder like you're asking for help. If you shout for help I won't hesitate. I'll shoot. Is that clear?

—Yes, it's clear.

—Then answer this question: What good can come to this country if women uncover their heads? Give me one good reason. Say something you believe with all your heart. Say, for example, that by uncovering themselves they'll get Europeans to start treating them like human beings. At least then I'll understand what your motives are and I won't shoot you. I'll let you go.

—My dear child. I have a daughter myself. She doesn't wear a head scarf. I don't interfere with her decision, just as I don't interfere with my wife's decision to wear one.

—Why did your daughter decide to uncover herself—does she want to become a film star?

—She's never said anything of the sort. She's in Ankara studying public relations. But she's been a tremendous support to me since I've come under attack over this head-scarf issue. Whenever I get upset about the things people say, whenever I am slandered or threatened, whenever I have to face the wrath of my enemies—or people like you, who have every right to be angry—she calls me from Ankara and—

—And she says, Grit your teeth, Dad. I'm going to be a film star.

—No, son, she doesn't say that. She says, Father dear, if I had to go into a classroom full of covered girls, I wouldn't dare go in uncovered. I'd wear a head scarf even if I didn't want to.

—So what if she didn't want to cover herself, what harm could come of it?

—Honestly, I couldn't tell you. You asked me to give you a reason.

—So tell me, you shameless brute. Do you mean to tell me that this was your thinking when you allowed the police to club these devout girls who have covered their heads at God's command? Are you trying to tell me that you drove them to suicide just to please your daughter?

—There are plenty of women in Turkey who think the way my daughter does.

—When ninety percent of women in this country wear head scarves, it's hard to see who these film stars think they're speaking for. You might be proud to see your daughter exposing herself, you shameless tyrant, but get this into your head. I might not be a professor, but I know a lot more about this subject than you do.

—My good man, please don't point your gun at me. You're very upset. If the gun goes off, you'll live to regret it.

—Why would I regret it? Why would I have spent two days traveling through this miserable snow if not to wipe out an infidel? As the Holy Koran states, it is my duty to kill any tyrant who visits cruelty on believers. But because I feel sorry for you I'm going to give you one last chance. Give me just one reason why your conscience doesn't bother you when you order covered women to uncover themselves, and I swear I won't shoot you.

—When a woman takes off her head scarf, she occupies a more comfortable place in society and gets more respect.

—That might be what that film-star daughter of yours thinks, but the opposite is true. Head scarves protect women from harassment, rape, and degradation. It's the head scarf that gives women respect and a comfortable place in society. We've heard this from many women who've chosen later in life to cover themselves. Women like the old belly dancer Melahat Şandra. The veil saves women from the animal instincts of men in the street. It saves them the ordeal of entering beauty contests to compete with other women. They don't have to live like sex objects, they don't have to wear makeup all day. As the American Black Muslim professor Marvin King has already noted, if the celebrated film star Elizabeth Taylor had spent the last twenty years covered, she would not have had to worry so much about being fat. She would not have ended up in a mental hospital. She might have known some happiness. Pardon me, sir. May I ask you a question? Why are you laughing, sir? Do you think I'm trying to be funny? *(Silence.)* Go ahead and tell me, you shameless atheist. Why are you laughing?

—My dear child, please believe me! I'm not laughing! Or if I did laugh, I was laughing out of nerves.

—No, you weren't. You were laughing with conviction!

—Please believe me, I feel nothing but compassion for all the people in this country—like you, like those covered girls—who are suffering for this cause.

—Sucking up to me will get you nowhere. I'm not suffering one bit. But you're going to suffer now for laughing about those girls who committed suicide. And now that you've laughed at them, there's no chance you'll show remorse. So let me tell you where things stand now. It's quite some time now since the Freedom Fighters for Islamic Justice condemned you to death. They reached their verdict in Tokat five days ago and sent me here to execute the sentence. If you hadn't laughed, I might have relented and forgiven you. Take this piece of paper. Let's hear you read out your death sentence. *(Silence.)* Stop crying like a woman. Read it out in a good strong voice. Hurry up, you shameless idiot. If you don't hurry up, I'm going to shoot.

—"I, Professor Nuri Yılmaz, am an atheist"—my dear child, I'm not an atheist!

—Keep reading.

—My child, you're not going to shoot me while I'm reading this, are you?

—If you don't keep reading it, I'm going to shoot you.

—"I confess to being a pawn in a secret plan to strip the Muslims of the secular Turkish Republic of their religion and their honor and thereby to turn them into slaves of the West. As for the girls who would not take off their head scarves, because they were devout and mindful of what is written in the Koran, I visited such cruelty on them that one girl could bear it no more and committed suicide. . . ." My dear child, with your permission, I'd like to make an objection here. I'd be grateful if you could pass this on to the committee that sent you. This girl didn't hang herself because she was barred from the classroom. And it wasn't because of the pressure her father put on her either. MİT has already told us she was suffering from a broken heart.

—That's not what she said in her suicide note.

—Please forgive me, but my child, I think you should know—please lower that gun—that even before she got married, this uneducated girl was naïve enough to give herself to a policeman twenty-five years her senior. And—it's an awful pity—but it was after he'd told her he was married and had no intention of marrying her—

—Shut up, you disgrace. That's something your prostitute of a daughter would do.

—Don't do this, my son, don't do this. If you shoot me, you're only darkening your own future.

—Say you're sorry.

—I'm sorry, son. Don't shoot.

—Open your mouth. I want to shove the gun inside. Now put your finger on top of mine and pull the trigger. You'll still be an infidel but at least you'll die with honor. *(Silence.)*

—My child, look what I've come to. At my age, I'm crying. I'm begging you. Take pity on me. Take pity on yourself. You're still so young. And you're going to become a murderer.

—Then pull the trigger yourself. See for yourself how much suicide hurts.

—My child, I'm a Muslim. I'm opposed to suicide.

—Open your mouth. *(Silence.)* Don't cry like that. Didn't it ever cross your mind that one day you'd have to pay for what you've done? Stop crying or I'll shoot.

(The voice of the old waiter in the distance.)

—Should I bring your tea to this table, sir?

—No, thank you. I'm about to leave.

—Don't look at the waiter. Keep reading your death sentence.

—My son, please forgive me.

—I said read.

—"I am ashamed of all the things I have done. I know I deserve to die and in the hope that God Almighty will forgive me . . ."

—Keep reading.

—My dear child. Let this old man cry for a few moments. Let me think about my wife and my daughter one last time.

—Think about the girls whose lives you destroyed. One had a nervous breakdown, four were kicked out of school in their third year. One committed suicide. The ones who stood trembling outside the doors of your school all came down with fevers and ended up in bed. Their lives were ruined.

—I am so very sorry, my dear, dear child. But what good will it do if you shoot me and turn yourself into a murderer? Think of that.

—All right. I will. *(Silence.)* I've given it some thought, sir. And here's what I've worked out.

—What?

—I'd been wandering around the miserable streets of Kars for two days and getting nowhere. Then I decided it must be fate, so I bought my return ticket to Tokat. I was drinking my last glass of tea when—

—My child, if you thought you could kill me and then escape on the last bus out of Kars, let me warn you. The roads are closed due to the snow. The six o'clock bus has been canceled. Don't live to regret this.

—Just as I was turning around, God sent you into the New Life Pastry Shop. And if God's not going to forgive you, why should I? Say your last words. Say, "God is great."

—Sit down, son. I'm warning you—this state of ours will catch you all—and hang you.

—Say, "God is great."

—Calm down, my child. Stop. Sit down. Think it over one more time. Don't pull that trigger. Stop. *(The sound of a gunshot. The sound of a chair pushed out.)* Don't, my son! *(Two more gunshots. Silence. A groan. The sound of a television. One more gunshot. Silence.)*

———•◆•———

CHAPTER SIX

He Kissed My Hand

LOVE, RELIGION, AND POETRY:
MUHTAR'S SAD STORY

After İpek left him at the entrance to Halıl Paşa Arcade and returned to the hotel, Ka waited before climbing the stairs to the second-floor branch headquarters of the Prosperity Party; he spent some time mingling with the apprentices, the unemployed, and the idle poor who were loitering in the corridors on the ground floor. In his mind's eye he kept seeing the director of the Institute of Education lying on the floor in his death agony; racked by remorse and guilt, he told himself that he should be phoning some of the contacts he'd made that morning: the assistant chief of police, perhaps, or someone in Istanbul, or the news office of the *Republican,* or someone else he knew. But even though the building was teeming with teahouses and barbershops, he couldn't find a single place with a telephone.

Still searching, he went into an establishment whose door read THE SOCIETY OF ANIMAL ENTHUSIASTS. There was a telephone here but someone was using it. And by now he was no longer sure he wanted to make a call after all. Going through the half-open door on the other side of the front office, he found a hall whose walls were decorated with pictures of roosters; in the middle of the hall was a small fighting ring. Suddenly Ka realized he was in love with İpek. And realizing that this love would determine the rest of his life, he was filled with dread.

Among the rich animal enthusiasts who enjoyed cockfights, there was one man who would remember very well how Ka came into the hall that day, sat down on one of the empty benches in the viewing area, and appeared to lose himself in thought. He drank a glass of tea as he read the list of sporting rules posted in big letters on the wall:

No rooster touched without permission of its owner.

A rooster that goes down 3 times in a row and doesn't peck its beak will be declared a loser.

Owners may take 3 minutes to treat a wounded spur and 1 minute to dress a broken claw.

In the event a rooster falls down and his rival steps on his neck, the fallen rooster will be brought back to his feet and the fight will continue.

In the event of electricity outage there will be a 15-minute time-out, by which time—if power is not restored—the match will be canceled.

When he left the Society of Animal Enthusiasts at a quarter past two, Ka was trying to figure out how he might induce İpek to escape with him from Kars. The lights were out now in the old lawyer Muzaffer Bey's People's Party office, which Ka now noticed was only three doors down from Muhtar's Prosperity Party—separated by the Friends' Teahouse and the Green Tailor. So much had happened to Ka since his visit to the lawyer that morning that, even as he entered the branch headquarters of the Prosperity Party, Ka could scarcely believe he was back on the same floor.

Ka had not seen Muhtar for twelve years. After embracing him and kissing him on both cheeks, Ka noticed that he now had a large belly and his hair was thinning and turning gray, but this was more or less what Ka had expected. Even in university days, there had been nothing special about Muhtar. Now, as then, one of those cigarettes he chain-smoked was hanging from the corner of his mouth.

"They've killed the director of the Institute of Education," Ka said.

"He didn't die; they just said so on the radio," said Muhtar. "How do you know this?"

"He was sitting at the other end of the place İpek called you from," said Ka. "The New Life Pastry Shop." He told Muhtar what they'd seen.

"Have you called the police?" asked Muhtar. "What did you do next?"

Ka told him that İpek had gone back to the hotel and he had come straight here.

"There are only five days until the election, and everyone knows we're going to win, so the state is knitting a sock to pull over our heads. It's prepared to say anything to bring us down," said Muhtar. "All across

Turkey, our support of the covered girls is the key expression of our political vision. Now someone's tried to assassinate the wretch who refused to let those girls past the entrance of the Institute of Education, and a man who was at the scene of the crime comes straight to our party headquarters without even stopping to call the police." Muhtar paused to compose himself and then added, with some delicacy, "I'd appreciate it if you called the police right now. Please tell them everything." He passed him the receiver as a proud host might offer a refreshment. Once Ka had taken it, Muhtar looked up and dialed the number.

"I've already met the assistant chief of police. His name's Kasım Bey," Ka said.

"Where do you know him from?" Muhtar asked, in a suspicious voice that irritated Ka.

"He was the first person Serdar Bey, the newspaper publisher, took me to meet this morning," Ka said, but before he could continue, the girl at the switchboard had connected him to the assistant chief of police. Ka told him exactly what he had seen at the New Life Pastry Shop. Muhtar lurched toward him and, with a clumsy gesture that was faintly flirtatious, pressed his ear up next to Ka's and tried to listen in. To help him hear better, Ka lifted the receiver and held it closer to Muhtar's ear. Now they were so close they could feel each other's breath on their faces. Although Ka had no idea why Muhtar would want to be part of his conversation with the assistant chief of police, instinct told him to go along. He explained that he had not seen the assailant's face but described his build as tiny, and then he took care to repeat these facts.

"We'd like you to come right over so we can take your statement," the police chief said, in a friendly voice.

"I'm at the headquarters of the Prosperity Party," Ka said. "It won't take me long to reach you."

There was a silence at the other end of the line.

"Just a moment," said the police chief.

Ka and Muhtar could hear him covering the phone and whispering to his colleagues.

"I hope you don't mind, but I've ordered a patrol car for you," the police chief said. "This snow just isn't letting up. We will send a car in a few minutes to pick you up from the party headquarters."

"It's good you told them you were here," Muhtar said, when Ka had hung up. "In any case, they already knew. They have surveillance everywhere. And I don't want them to get the wrong idea about the possibly suspicious things I just said to you."

A wave of anger swept over Ka; this dated back to his first political encounters during his bourgeois days in Nişantaş. When he was a lycée student, men like this used to turn people against each other by pinching their butts and trying to push them into the passive position. Later on this turned into a game; the object was to get people to denounce one another, particularly their political enemies, as police informers. It was the fear of police cars and the fear of being caught in a situation in which he'd be obliged to inform—forced to tell the police which houses to raid—that had put Ka off politics for good. Now here was Muhtar, running on the Islamist fundamentalist ticket, something he would have found despicable ten years earlier, and here was Ka, still making excuses for this and so much else.

The phone rang. Muhtar resumed a respectable pose and set about bargaining with someone from Kars Border Television over the price for a commercial for Muhtar's family's appliance dealership that was to run during that evening's live transmission.

After he had hung up the phone, the two men were silent, like two peeved children with nothing to say to each other, and as they sat there Ka imagined their discussing all the things that had happened to them during the twelve years since they'd last met.

First he imagined each describing what was on his mind: Now that we've both been forced into exile, without having managed to achieve much or succeed at anything, or even find happiness, we can at least agree that life's been hard! It isn't enough even to be a poet . . . that's why politics still casts such a shadow over our lives. But even having said this, neither would find it in him to add what he could not admit even to himself: It's because we failed to find happiness in poetry that we find ourselves longing for the shadow of politics.

Ka despised Muhtar more than ever. But then he reminded himself that Muhtar might have found a bit of happiness in having brought himself to the brink of an election victory, just as he, Ka, had found a little in having gained a middling reputation as a poet—better than no reputation at all. But as neither man was ever going to admit to happiness at these things, they could not broach the big subject, the bitter truth that stood between them: They had both inured themselves to defeat and to the pitiless unfairness of life. Ka feared that both of them longed for İpek as a symbol of escape from this defeatist state of mind.

"I hear you're going to be reading your latest poem at the performance this evening," said Muhtar, with a barely perceptible smile.

For a few moments Ka stared fiercely into the beautiful hazel eyes of this man who had once been married to İpek. He could not detect even the trace of a smile in them.

"Did you see Fahir while you were in Istanbul?" asked Muhtar, this time with something closer to a grin.

Now Ka was able to smile with him, and not disingenuously: the man Muhtar named was someone for whom he had some respect. Fahir was a contemporary of theirs, for twenty years a staunch defender of Western modernist poetry. He'd studied at St. Joseph, the French lycée; once a year he would dip into the inheritance from his crazy but rich grandmother—who was said to have come from the palace—and off he would go to Paris, where he would fill his suitcase with poetry collections from the booksellers of Saint-Germain. Back in Istanbul, he would translate them into Turkish, for publication either in the magazines he'd founded or as volumes for the poetry lists of foundering publishing houses; he secured the same accommodations for his own poems and those of several other Turkish poets in the modernist camp. But while everyone respected him for these efforts, Fahir's own poetry—written as it was under the influence of the poems he'd translated into affected "pure Turkish"—was generally found to be, at best, devoid of inspiration and, at worst, incomprehensible.

Ka told Muhtar that he had been unable to see Fahir in Istanbul.

"There was a time when I really wanted Fahir to like my poetry," said Muhtar. "Sadly, he despised poets like me, who were interested not in pure poetry but in folklore and the beauties of our country. Years went by, the military took over and we all went to prison, and like everyone else, when I was released I drifted like an idiot. The people I had once tried to imitate had changed, those whose approval I once wanted had disappeared, and none of my dreams had come true, not in poetry or in life. Rather than continue my abject, penniless frenzy in Istanbul, I came back to Kars and took over my father's shop, which had once caused me such shame, but even with all these changes I was not happy. I couldn't take the people here seriously, and when I saw them I did just as Fahir had done when he saw my poems: I turned up my nose. The city of Kars and the people in it—it was as if they weren't real. Everyone wanted to die or to leave. But I had nowhere left to go. It was as if I'd been erased from history, banished from civilization. The civilized world seemed far away and I couldn't imitate it. God wouldn't even give me a child who might do all the things I had not done, who might release me from my misery by becoming the westernized, modern, self-possessed individual I had always dreamed of becoming."

Ka was impressed by the way Muhtar could occasionally mock himself; his faint smile seemed to radiate from within.

"In the evenings I would drink, and to avoid arguing with my beautiful İpek, I would come home late. Once, very late, on one of those Kars nights when everything, even the birds in the sky, seems to have frozen, I was the last patron to leave the Green Pastures Café. I was walking toward Army Avenue, where İpek and I were living, not more than a ten-minute walk away but a long distance by Kars standards. The raki had gone to my head, and I hadn't gone more than two blocks before I lost my way. There wasn't a soul on the streets. Kars looked like an abandoned city, as it always does on such cold nights; even when I knocked on a door there was no answer, either because it was one of those Armenian houses no one's lived in for eighty years, or else because the people inside were buried under many quilts and, like hibernating animals, unwilling to leave the warmth of their holes.

"It pleased me, in a way, to see the whole city looking abandoned and unpopulated. Soon a sweet drowsiness was spreading through my body, thanks to the drink and the cold. I decided to leave this life, so I took three or maybe five more steps before stretching out on the frozen pavement under a tree to wait for sleep and death to take me. In a drunken stupor, you can withstand that sort of cold for four or five minutes before freezing to death. As the soft drowsiness spread through my veins, I saw before me the child I never had. What a joy it was to see this child, a boy, already grown, and wearing a tie, his manner nothing like that of our tie-wearing bureaucrats—no, this son of mine was a true European. Just as he was about to tell me something, he stopped and kissed the hand of an old man. Light radiated from this good-hearted old man in all directions. At the same moment, a shaft of light pierced the place where I lay; shining right into my eyes, it went straight through me and woke me up.

"Feeling shame and hope in equal measure, I rose to my feet. I looked and there, just across from me, I saw light pouring through an open door as people came and went. The voice inside me told me to follow them in. The new arrivals accepted me into their group and took me into the bright and warm little house. They were nothing like the hopeless and downtrodden folk who populate the city of Kars; these were happy people and, even more amazing, they were all from Kars; I even knew some of them. I realized now that this was the secret lodge of His Excellency Saadettin Efendi, the Kurdish sheikh I had heard so many rumors about. I'd been told he had many disciples in the civil service and also among the rich, that their number was growing daily, and that, at their invitation, he had come down from his village in the mountains to perform his rites for the city's poor, unemployed, and disconsolate, but knowing the police would never permit such an antirepublican display I had paid little attention to the rumors.

"Now here I was, climbing the sheikh's staircase step by step, tears streaming from my eyes. Something was happening that I had secretly dreaded for a long time and that in my atheist years I would have denounced as weakness and backwardness: I was returning to Islam. Those caricatures you see of sheikhs with their long robes and their round-trimmed beards—the truth is, I found them frightening, and so even as I climbed those stairs of my own free will I began to cry. The sheikh was kind. He asked me why I was crying. Of course, I was not about to say, I'm crying because I've fallen among reactionary sheikhs and their disciples. Anyway, I was also deeply ashamed of the raki fumes pouring from my mouth like smoke from a chimney. So I said I'd lost my key. This must have occurred to me because I had in fact let my key ring drop in the place where I'd stretched out to die. My declaration launched his sycophant followers into a discussion of the possible metaphorical meanings of *the key,* but the sheikh soon sent them all out to look for the real one. Once we were alone, he smiled sweetly. I realized that he was the good-hearted old man in my dream, so I relaxed.

"I felt such awe before this august man with his saintly expression that I kissed his hand. Then he did something that shocked me greatly: He kissed my hand too. A feeling of peace spread through me; I had not felt this way for years. I immediately understood that I could talk to him about anything, tell him all about my life, and he would bring me back to the path I had always believed in, deep down inside, even as an atheist: the road to God Almighty. I was joyous at the mere expectation of this salvation. Meanwhile, they had found my key.

"I went home and slept, and in the morning I remembered what had happened and felt ashamed. My memories were vague, not least because I didn't want to remember any of it. I promised myself I would never return to the sheikh's lodge. But I was worried about what might happen if I were to run into one of the disciples who'd seen me there. Then one night, again on my way home from the Green Pastures Café, my feet took me back there. Despite my nightly crises of shame, this kept happening, evening after evening. The sheikh would seat me right beside him; as he listened to my sorrows, he filled my heart with God's love. I kept crying, and this made me feel at peace. By day, I would keep the secrets of the lodge by carrying around the *Republican,* the most secular newspaper in Turkey, and railing against the religious revivalists who were taking over the country as enemies of the Republic; I'd ask why the Atatürk Thought Association didn't have meetings here anymore.

"My double life went on until the night İpek asked me if there was another woman. I burst into tears and told her everything. She cried too. 'Now that you've gone religious, are you going to wrap a scarf around my head?' I promised her I would make no such demand. And as I was worried that she might think my change might be due to economic reasons, I was quick to assure her that everything was going well at the store and that in spite of all the electricity outages the new Arçelik stoves were selling well—I said all this to calm her down. To tell the truth, I was happy that I would now be able to pray at home and bought myself a how-to-pray manual at the bookseller's. My new life stretched out before me.

"After I had pulled myself together, a bolt of inspiration came to me one night and I wrote an important poem. In this poem I described the entire crisis: my shame, the love of God growing inside me, the peace, the first time I climbed the sheikh's staircase, even the real and metaphorical meanings of my key. As a poem it was flawless. I swear to you, it was as good as those fashionable Western poems Fahir translated into Turkish. I posted it to him with a letter at once. I waited six months, but the poem never appeared in *Achilles Ink,* his magazine at the time. By now I had written three more poems. Every two months, I would send them to him. For a year I waited impatiently, but he didn't publish a single one.

"My unhappiness at this time had nothing to do with our remaining childless, or with İpek's continuing resistance to the teachings of Islam, or even the taunts of my old secular and leftist friends who knew of my turn to religion. So many were turning to religion with equal ardor that they scarcely had time to pay much attention to me. No, the most upsetting thing was the fact that the poems I'd sent to Istanbul weren't being published. At the beginning of every month, with the appearance of the new issue of *Achilles Ink,* time stood still. I would take comfort every time by telling myself that this month, at last, they would publish a poem. The truths in these poems deserved to stand alongside the truths in Western poetry. In my view, the only person in Turkey who could make this happen was Fahir.

"The injustice of his continuing indifference began to anger me and to poison the happiness I had found through Islam. It got so that I was thinking about Fahir even when I was praying in the mosque; once again, I was miserable. One night I decided to disclose my sorrow to the sheikh but he knew nothing of modernist poetry, René Char, the broken sentence, Mallarmé, Joubert, the silence of an empty line.

"This undermined my confidence in my sheikh. After all, he hadn't been offering me anything new for some time, just *Keep your heart clean, and God's love will deliver you from oppression* and eight or ten other lines like that. I don't want to be unfair, he is not a simple man; it's just that he had a simple education. It was at this point that some devil within—half utilitarian, half rationalist, a remnant of my atheist days—began to goad me. People like me find peace only when fighting for a cause in a political party with like-minded people. This is why I joined the Prosperity Party; I knew it would give me a deeper and more meaningful spiritual life than I had found with the men in the lodge. This is, after all, a religious party, a party that values the spiritual side. My experience as a party member during my Marxist years prepared me well."

"In what ways?" Ka asked.

The lights went out. There was a long silence.

"The electricity's gone off," Muhtar said finally, in a mysterious voice. Ka did not answer him; he sat in the darkness, perfectly still.

——————◆◆◆◆——————

CHAPTER SEVEN

Political Islamist Is Only a Name That Westerners and Seculars Give Us

AT PARTY HEADQUARTERS, POLICE HEADQUARTERS, AND ONCE AGAIN IN THE STREETS

It was spooky sitting in darkness and total silence, but Ka preferred this to sitting in a well-lit room and chatting with Muhtar like old friends. Now all they had in common was İpek, and while part of Ka was very eager to discuss her, another part was just as keen to conceal his feelings. He also feared that Muhtar might tell more stories, revealing himself to be even more stupid, and in that case Ka would be compelled to wonder why İpek had stayed married to this man for so many years. He had no wish to discover her unworthy of his devotion.

So he relaxed when Muhtar, losing patience with his own story, changed the subject to left-wing friends and political exiles who had fled to Germany. Ka smiled and told him what he'd heard about Tufan, their curly-haired friend from Malatya, who had once written about third-world issues for various periodicals: It seems he'd lost his mind. Ka last saw him in the central station in Stuttgart; he had a great long pole in his hands with a wet cloth tied to the end, and he was racing back and forth mopping the floor, whistling as he worked. Then Muhtar asked about Mahmut, the man who, never one to mince words, had once caused so much upset. Ka explained how Mahmut had joined the fundamentalist group of Hayrullah Efendi; he now devoted himself to its internal wranglings with the same argumentative fury he had shown as a leftist, except that now his issue was who got to control which mosque. As for the lovable Süleyman, Ka smiled when he told how he had been living off the dole of a church charity that had given refuge to many political exiles from the third world, but having grown so bored with life in the small town of Traunstein, he'd returned to Turkey, even knowing full well he'd be thrown into prison the moment he got there.

Ka spoke about Hikmet, who had died under mysterious circumstances while working as a chauffeur in Berlin; Fadıl, who had married the elderly widow of a Nazi officer and now ran a small hotel with her; and Tarık the theoretician, who had made a fortune working with the Turkish mafia in Hamburg. As for Sadık, who alongside Muhtar, Ka, Taner, and İpek had once folded periodicals fresh off the press, he was now running a gang that smuggled illegal immigrants over the Alps and into Germany. Muharrem, the famous sulker, was now living a happy underground life with his family in the Berlin metro, in one of those ghost stations abandoned at the time of the Cold War and the wall. As the train sped between the Kreuzberg and Alexanderplatz stations, the retired Turkish socialists on board would stand to attention just as the old bandits of Istanbul would salute whenever passing through Arnavutköy, gazing into the swirling waters where a legendary gangster had driven over the edge and perished. Even if they didn't recognize one another, the political exiles standing to attention in the car would cast furtive looks about them to see whether any fellow passengers might also be honoring the legendary hero of their secret cause. It was in such a metro car that Ka met up with Ruhi, who had once been so critical of his leftist friends for their refusal to engage with psychology; Ka found out that Ruhi was now working as a test subject in a study measuring the effectiveness of an advertising campaign for a new type of lamb pastrami pizza marketed to Turkish workers in the lowest income bracket.

Of all the political exiles Ka had met in Germany, the happiest was Ferhat, who had joined the PKK and was now attacking various offices of Turkish Airlines with revolutionary fervor; he'd also been seen on CNN, throwing Molotov cocktails at Turkish consulates; apparently he was now learning Kurdish and dreaming of a second career as a Kurdish poet. As for the few others Muhtar asked about with a strange note of concern in his voice, Ka had long forgotten them; he could only guess that they had followed in the paths of so many others, who joined small gangs, worked for the secret services or some segment of the black market, or otherwise vanished or went underground. Some, no doubt, had ended up by some violent means at the bottom of a canal.

His old friend had lit a match by now, so Ka was able to see the ghostly furniture of the branch party headquarters, and once he had located the old coffee table and the gas stove, he stood up and moved to the window, where he fixed his attention on the falling snow.

The flakes wafting past him were huge and ripe. Ka found a soothing elegance in their slow, white fullness, which was all the more luminous when a bluish light from an unknown part of the city shone through them. His mind returned to the snowy evenings of his childhood, when storms caused power outages and all through the house Ka would hear fearful whispers—"God save the poor!"—and his childish heart beat faster and he was so glad to have a family. He watched sadly as a horse and carriage struggled through the snow: in the darkness he could see only the head of the burdened creature, swinging from side to side.

"Muhtar, do you still pay visits to your sheikh?"

"Do you mean His Excellency Saadettin Efendi?" asked Muhtar. "Yes, I do, every once in a while. Why do you ask?"

"What does this man have to offer you?"

"A little companionship and, even if it doesn't last very long, a little compassion. He's well-informed."

In his voice Ka heard not serenity but disillusionment. "I live a very solitary life in Germany," Ka said, obstinately continuing the conversation. "When I look over the rooftops of Frankfurt in the middle of the night, I sense that the world and my life are not without purpose. I hear sounds inside me."

"What sorts of sounds?"

"It may just have to do with fear of getting old and dying," Ka said, with embarrassment. "If I were an author and Ka were a character in a book, I'd say, 'Snow reminds Ka of God!' But I'm not sure it would be accurate. What brings me close to God is the silence of snow."

"The religious right, this country's Muslim conservatives"—Muhtar was speaking rapidly, as though willing himself to be carried away by a false hope—"after my years as a leftist atheist, these people came as such a great relief. You should meet them. I'm sure you'd warm to them too."

"Do you really think so?"

"Well, for one thing, all these religious men are modest, gentle, understanding. Unlike westernized Turks, they don't instinctively despise the common people; they're compassionate and wounded themselves. If they got to know you, they'd like you. There would be no harsh words."

As Ka knew from the beginning, in this part of the world faith in God was not something achieved by thinking sublime thoughts and stretching one's creative powers to their outer limits; nor was it something one could do alone; above all it meant joining a mosque, becoming part of a community. Nevertheless, Ka was still disappointed that Muhtar could talk so much about his group without once mentioning God or his own private faith. He despised Muhtar for it. But as he pressed his fore-head against the window, he said something altogether different.

"Muhtar, if I started to believe in God, you would be disappointed, and I think you'd despise me."

"Why?"

"The idea of a solitary westernized individual whose faith in God is private is very threatening to you. An atheist who belongs to a community is far easier for you to trust than a solitary man who believes in God. For you, a solitary man is far more wretched and sinful than a nonbeliever."

"I am a solitary man," said Muhtar.

The fact that he could say these words with such sincerity and convic-tion filled Ka with rancor and pity. It seemed to him that darkness had given them both a certain drunken confidence. "I know I'm not going to be one, but say I did become the sort of believer who prays five times a day. Why would that disturb you? Perhaps because you can embrace your religion and your community only if godless secularists like me are over-seeing business and government affairs. A man can't pray to his heart's content in this country unless he can depend on the efficiency of the atheist who's an expert at managing the West and the other aspects of worldly business."

"But you're not one of those godless businessmen. I can take you to see His Excellency the Sheikh whenever you like."

"I think our friendly policemen have arrived!" said Ka.

Through the icy window they saw two plainclothes cops struggling to get out of a patrol car parked just below, at the entrance to the arcade.

"I'm going to ask a favor now," said Muhtar. "In a moment these men are going to come upstairs and take us off to the station. They won't arrest you, they'll just take your statement and let you go. You can go back to your hotel, and in the evening Turgut Bey will invite you to dinner and you'll join him at his table. Of course his devoted daughters will be there too. So what I'd like is for you to say the following to İpek. Are you listen-ing to me? Tell İpek that I want to marry her again! It was a mistake for me to ask her to cover herself in accordance with Islamic law. Tell her I'm through acting like a jealous provincial husband and that I'm shamed and sorry for the pressures I put on her during our marriage!"

"Haven't you already said these things to her?"

"I have, but I got nowhere. It's possible that she didn't believe me, seeing as I'm the district head of the Prosperity Party. But you're a different sort of man; you've come all the way from Istanbul, all the way from Germany even. If you tell her, she'll believe it."

"Seeing as you're the district head of the Prosperity Party, isn't it going to cause you political difficulties if your wife isn't covering herself?"

"With God's permission I'm going to win the election in four days' time and become the mayor," said Muhtar. "But it's far more important to me that you tell İpek how sorry I am; I'll probably still be behind bars. Brother, could you do this for me?"

Ka had a moment of indecision. Then he said, "Yes, I will."

Muhtar embraced Ka and kissed him on both cheeks. Ka felt a mixture of pity and revulsion; he despised himself for not being pure and openhearted like Muhtar.

"And I'd be very grateful if you would take this poem to Istanbul and deliver it by hand to Fahir," said Muhtar. "It's the one I just mentioned to you, its title is 'The Staircase.' "

Ka was just putting the poem into his pocket when three plain-clothes policemen entered the darkened room; two were carrying huge flashlights. They were capable and efficient and it was clear from their demeanor that they knew exactly what Ka was doing there with Muhtar; it was clear to Ka that they were from MİT. They insisted all the same on seeing Ka's identity card and asking him his business. Ka said once again that he had come to cover the municipal elections and the suicide girls for the *Republican*.

"It's because people like you are writing about them in the Istanbul papers that these girls are committing suicide in the first place," said one of the policemen.

"No, it's not," Ka said stubbornly.

"What's your explanation then?"

"They're committing suicide because they're unhappy."

"We're unhappy too, but we don't commit suicide."

While this conversation was going on, they were combing the branch headquarters with their flashlights, opening cabinets, taking out drawers, dumping their contents onto tabletops, and leafing through files. They turned Muhtar's table upside down to look for weapons, and they pulled out one of the heavy filing cabinets to look behind that. They treated Ka much better than they treated Muhtar.

"After you saw the director of the Institute being shot, why did you come here instead of going straight to the police?"

"I had an appointment here."

"Why?"

"We're old friends from university," said Muhtar, in an apologetic voice. "And the daughter of the owner of the Snow Palace Hotel, where he's staying, is my wife. Just before the incident, they called me and made an appointment. Our phones here at party headquarters are tapped, so you'll have no trouble verifying this."

"What do you know about our tapping your phones?"

"I beg your pardon," said Muhtar, without the slightest annoyance. "I don't know for sure—I was only guessing. Maybe I am wrong."

Ka felt a tinge of respect for Muhtar, who had ingratiated himself with the policemen treating him roughly, who was taking their pushing and shoving with equanimity, who, like the rest of Kars, shrugged off the power outages and the dreary muddiness of the roads.

Having searched every corner of the branch headquarters, overturned every drawer, and emptied every file folder, the policemen bound a few discoveries together with string, noting them for the official record, and threw the bundle into a sack. Then they took Ka and Muhtar down to the patrol car. As they sat in the back side by side like two mum and guilty children, Ka saw subordination return to the huge white hands resting like two fat old dogs on Muhtar's knees.

As the patrol car inched its way through the dark snow-covered streets, the two stared miserably at the weak orangey lights shining out through the half-drawn curtains of the old Armenian mansions, at the elderly clutching plastic bags and struggling down the icy pavements, at the dark old empty houses, lonely as ghosts. On the billboard in front of the National Theater a poster announced that evening's performance. The workmen were still out on the streets installing the cable for the live transmission. The crowds milling around the bus station looked ever more impatient with the roads still closed.

The snowflakes now seemed large as the ones in those *boules de neige* Ka had played with as a child; as the police car trundled slowly through the snow he felt as if he were inside a fairy tale. Because the driver was taking great care, even this short trip took seven or eight minutes, but all the while he exchanged only one look with Muhtar; he could tell from his friend's miserable look of resignation that when they reached police headquarters Muhtar would get a beating while he himself would be spared.

He read something else into the look his friend gave him, and it would stay with him many years: Muhtar thought he deserved the beating he was about to get. Even with the certainty of his winning the election in four days' time, there was something so unsettling about his composure as to make him seem contrite for what had not yet happened; it was almost as if he were thinking, I deserve this beating not just for having insisted on settling in this godforsaken city but for having succumbed once again to the desire for power; I won't let them break my spirit, but I still hate myself for knowing all this and so I feel inferior to you. Please, when you look me straight in the eye, don't throw my shame back at me.

While the plainclothesmen didn't separate Ka from Muhtar after parking the patrol car in the inner courtyard of police headquarters, there was nevertheless a marked difference in the treatment of the two men. Ka was a famous journalist from Istanbul who could, if he wrote something critical, get them into a lot of trouble, so they treated him like a witness who was there to help the authorities with their investigation. But with Muhtar it was as if to say, Not you again! and so even when they returned to Ka it was as if to say, What is a man like you doing with a man like him? Innocently Ka assumed it was Muhtar's ingratiating replies that made them think him, on the one hand, stupid (do you really think we're going to let you take over the country?) and, on the other, confused (if only you could get your own life in order). Only much later would Ka make the painful discovery that the police were pursuing a different line altogether.

Hoping he might be able to identify the tiny man who had shot the director of the Institute of Education, they took Ka into a side room to peruse an archive of about a hundred black-and-white photographs. Here was every political Islamist from Kars and the surrounding areas who had ever been detained even once by the police. Most of them were young Kurds, from the villages or else unemployed, but there were also mug shots of street vendors, students attending religious high schools or universities, teachers, and Sunni Turks. As Ka looked at photograph after photograph of doleful youths staring miserably into the police camera, he thought he recognized two teenagers from his walk around the city earlier in the day, but he saw no one who resembled the tiny and, it seemed to him, older man who'd committed the murder.

Ka returned to find Muhtar hunched on the same stool, but his nose was bleeding and one eye was shot with red. Muhtar made one or two shameful gestures and then hid his face behind a handkerchief. In the silence Ka imagined that Muhtar had found redemption in this beating; it might have released him from the guilt and spiritual agony he felt at the misery and stupidity of his country. Two days later, just before receiving the unhappiest news of his life—and having by then fallen into the same state as Muhtar—Ka would have reason to recall his foolish fantasy.

Moments later, they returned Ka to the side room to give his statement. Sitting across from a young policeman using the same old Remington typewriter he remembered his lawyer father using on nights when he brought work home, Ka described the slaying of the director of the Institute of Education, and as he spoke it occurred to him that they had shown him Muhtar in order to frighten him.

He was released soon afterward, but Muhtar's face remained before his eyes for some time. In the old days, the provincial police weren't quite so ready to beat up religious conservatives. But Muhtar was not from one of the center-right parties; he was a proponent of radical Islam. Once again Ka wondered if this stance had something to do with Muhtar's personality. He walked through the snow for a long, long time. At the end of Army Avenue, he sat down on a wall and smoked a cigarette, while he watched a group of children slipping and sliding on a side street in the lamplight. The poverty and the violence he had seen that day had tired him, but he was propped up by the hope that with İpek's love he would be able to begin a new life.

Later on, walking through the snow again, he found himself on the pavement across the street from the New Life Pastry Shop. The window was broken and the navy-blue light atop the police patrol car parked out front was flashing; it cast an almost spiritual glow over the shop employees and the pack of children gathered around the car, and it imbued the falling snow with a divine patience. When Ka joined the crowd, the police were still interrogating the old waiter.

Someone tapped timidly on Ka's shoulder. "You're Ka the poet, aren't you?" It was a teenage boy with large green eyes and a good-natured childish face. "My name is Necip. I know you've come to Kars to report on the elections and the suicide girls for the *Republican,* and you've already met with quite a few groups. But there's one more important person in Kars whom you should see."

"Who?"

"Could we move a little to the side?"

Ka liked the teenager's air of mystery. They moved in front of the Modern Buffet, "world-famous for its sharbats and saleps."

"My instructions are such that I cannot give you the name of the person you need to meet unless you first agree to meet him."

"How can I agree to see someone without first knowing who he is?"

"You're right," said Necip. "But this person is in hiding. I can't tell you who he's hiding from or why unless you agree to see him."

"All right, I agree to see him," said Ka. Striking a pose that came straight out of an adventure comic, he added, "I hope this isn't a trap."

"If you can't put your trust in people, you'll never get anywhere in life," said Necip, also striking a pose straight out of an adventure comic.

"I trust you," said Ka. "Who is this person I need to see?"

"After you find out his name, you'll meet him. But you must also keep his hiding place a secret. Now think about it one more time. Shall I tell you who he is?"

"Yes," said Ka. "You have to trust me too."

"This person's name is Blue," said Necip in a voice full of awe. He looked disappointed when Ka offered no reaction. "Did you never hear about him when you were in Germany? In Turkey he's famous."

"I know," said Ka, in a soothing voice. "I'm ready to meet him."

"But I don't know where he is," said Necip. "What's more, I myself have never seen him even once in my whole life."

For a moment they smiled doubtfully at each other.

"Someone else is going to take you to see Blue. My job is to help you make contact with that person."

They walked together down Little Kâzımbey Avenue, amid the posters and small campaign banners. There was something about Necip's wiry body and his nervous, childish manner that reminded Ka of himself at that age, so he warmed to the boy. For a moment he found himself trying to imagine what the world looked like through those green eyes.

"What did you hear about Blue in Germany?" asked Necip.

"I read in the Turkish papers that he was a militant political Islamist," said Ka. "I read other nasty things about him, too."

Necip quickly interrupted him. "Political Islamist is only a name that Westerners and seculars give us Muslims who are ready to fight for our religion," he said. "You're a secularist, but please don't let yourself fall for the lies about Blue in the secular press. He hasn't killed anyone, not even in Bosnia, where he went to defend his Muslim brothers, or in Grozny, where a Russian bomb left him crippled."

They came to a corner, where he made Ka stop.

"You see that store across the street, the Communication Bookstore? It belongs to the Followers, but all Islamists in Kars use it as a gathering place. The police know this and so does everyone else; some of the sales-clerks spy for them. I'm a pupil at the religious high school. It's against the rules for me to go in there. If I do I'll be disciplined, but I have to let the people inside know you're here. In three minutes you'll see a tall bearded young man wearing a red skullcap come out the door. Follow him. When you've gone two streets, if there aren't any plainclothes police around, he'll approach you and take you to the place you need to go. Do you understand? May God be your helper."

With that, Necip vanished into a cloud of snowflakes. Ka's heart went out to him.

CHAPTER EIGHT

Suicide Is a Terrible Sin

BLUE AND RÜSTEM

K a stood across the street from the Communication Bookstore. The snow was falling faster, and by now he was tired of waiting and of dusting snow off his head, his coat, his shoes. He was about to go back to the hotel when he looked across the street and in the dim light of the streetlamp saw a tall bearded youth walking along the pavement opposite. When he realized that the snow had turned the boy's skullcap from red to white, Ka's heart began to race and he set off after him.

After walking all the way down Kâzım Karabekir Avenue—which the mayoral candidate of the Motherland Party, following the new fashion set by Istanbul, had promised to turn into a pedestrian precinct—they turned into Faikbey Avenue and then took the second right into Station Square. The statue of General Kâzım Karabekir that Ka remembered seeing earlier in the middle of the square was now buried and looked like a giant ice-cream cone. In the darkness Ka could still see that the bearded youth had entered the train station; he hurried after him. Finding no one in the waiting hall, he imagined that his guide must have gone out to the platform, so Ka went also; at the end of the platform he was just able to see someone moving into the darkness beyond, so Ka followed onto the tracks. Just as Ka was considering that were he to be shot dead here, his body would probably lie undiscovered till spring, he came face-to-face with the bearded young man.

"No one's following us," he said, "though you can still change your mind. But if you decide to continue you must keep your mouth shut from here on. You can never tell anyone how you got here. The penalty for treachery is death."

This threat didn't scare Ka, if only because, pronounced in a high-pitched voice, it sounded almost funny. They continued along the tracks, passing the silo and then turning into Stew Street, right next to the military barracks, where the bearded youth pointed to an apartment building and told him which bell to ring.

"Don't be insolent to the Master," he said. "Don't interrupt him, and when you're through don't hang around, just get up and leave."

This was how Ka discovered that among his admirers Blue was also known as the Master. But it was just about the only thing Ka knew about Blue—aside from his being a political Islamist of some notoriety. He remembered reading in the Turkish newspapers he saw from time to time in Germany that Blue had been implicated in a murder years ago. Still, many political Islamists killed, and none of them was famous. What had made Blue notorious was the claim that he was responsible for the murder of an effeminate exhibitionist and TV personality named Güner Bener, on whose quiz show, broadcast on a minor channel, contestants vied for cash prizes. Bener wore gaudy suits and had a penchant for indecent remarks, favoring jokes about "the uneducated." One day, during a live broadcast, this freckled master of sarcasm was making fun of one of his poorer and clumsier contestants when by some slip of the tongue he uttered an inappropriate remark about the Prophet Muhammad.

Most likely it was noticed only by a few devout men dozing in front of their TV sets, who probably forgot the quip as soon as they had heard it, but Blue sent a letter to all the Istanbul papers threatening to kill the host unless he made a formal apology on the next show and promised never to make such a joke again. The Istanbul press gets threats like this all the time and might well have paid no attention to this one. But the television station had such a commitment to its provocative secularist line, and to showing just how rabid these political Islamists could be, that the managers invited Blue to appear on the show. He took this opportunity to make even fiercer threats, and he was such a hit as the "wild-eyed scimitar-wielding Islamist" that he was invited to repeat the performance on other channels.

Around this time, the public prosecutor issued a warrant for Blue's arrest on the charge of making a public death threat, so Blue marked his first burst of celebrity by going into hiding. Meanwhile Güner Bener, who had also captured much attention by now for his role, appeared on his daily live TV show to defy his would-be assassins, proclaiming with unexpected vehemence that he was "not afraid of Atatürk-hating antirepublican perverts"; the next day, in his luxury hotel room in Izmir where he stayed for the show, they found him strangled with the same loud tie festooned with beach balls he'd been wearing during the broadcast.

Blue had an alibi—he'd been attending a conference in Manisa in support of the head-scarf girls—but he stayed in hiding to avoid the press, which had by now made sure the whole country knew about the incident and Blue's part in it. Some of the Islamist press were as critical as the secularists; they accused Blue of "bloodying the hands" of political Islam, of allowing himself to become the plaything of the secularist press, of enjoying his media fame in a manner unbefitting a Muslim, of being in the pay of the CIA. This may explain why Blue went underground and stayed there for a good long time. It was while he was in hiding that stories spread in Islamist circles of his having gone to Bosnia to fight the Serbs and his having been heroically wounded fighting the Russians in Grozny, but there were those who claimed that these rumors were false.

(Those who would know Blue's own version of these matters might consult his short autobiography entitled "My Execution," which can be found on the fifth page of this book's thirty-fifth chapter, "Ka with Blue in His Cell" subtitled "I'M NOT AN AGENT FOR ANYONE," though I am not sure everything Blue tells us there is entirely correct.)

True, many lies were told about Blue. The fact is that some of them fed his legend, and certainly it could be said that Blue was nourished by his own mysterious reputation. It was also suggested that, by his later silence, Blue had tacitly agreed with all the barbs he attracted in some Islamist circles for his earlier proclamations; many would even suggest that a Muslim appearing so much in the secularist, Zionist, bourgeois media had only got what he deserved. In fact, as our story will show, Blue did indeed enjoy talking to the media.

As for his reasons for being in Kars, as is so often the case with rumors in small places, the stories spread fast but just didn't add up. Some said he had come to shore up the local operations of a Kurdish Islamist organization, the government having crushed the Diyarbakır-based national operations center; Blue, it was said, had been dispatched to Kars to "secure the organization's secrets." Others discounted this story, as the organization in question had no members in Kars, apart from one or two raving lunatics. Some said Blue had come to repair relations between the Marxist-revolutionary Kurds and the Islamist Kurds—there was increasing conflict between them in the cities of the East—and according to this story he had come to urge that they all try to act like peaceful well-behaved militants. The tension between the Marxist-revolutionary Kurds and the Islamist Kurds had begun in violent arguments, exchanges of insults, beatings, and street fights, and in many cities matters escalated to knifings and attacks with meat cleavers; in recent months partisans had been shooting and killing one another, taking captives and interrogating them under torture (with both sides using familiar methods like pouring melted plastic onto a prisoner's skin or squeezing his testicles), and there were also reports of strangulations. It was said that a secret group of mediators had formed who believed this war was "playing right into the hands of the state" and so wanted to end it, and that this group had dispatched Blue to reconnoiter in the towns of the affected area, but according to his enemies Blue's black past and relative youth disqualified him from such an important mission. There were other rumors, spread by the young Islamists, that he had come to Kars to "straighten out" Hakan Özge, Kars Border Television's effeminate young shiny-suit-wearing host and disc jockey, who had been making mischievous jokes and sly insinuations about our glorious Islam and now constantly referred to God and prayer time on his program. Others still imagined that Blue was a go-between for an international Islamist terrorist ring. It was said that even the Kars intelligence and security units had heard about this Saudi-backed network with plans to terrorize thousands of women—pouring into Turkey from the old Soviet Union to work as prostitutes—by killing some of them. Blue had done nothing to deny these rumors, just as he had done nothing to deny the rumors about the suicide girls, the head-scarf girls, or the rumor that he had come to observe the municipal election. His failure to respond to what was said about him, coupled with his refusal to come out of hiding, gave him an air of mystery that appealed to the students at the religious high school and the young in general. He wasn't just hiding from the police; he stayed off the streets as a way of maintaining his legend, and toward this end it suited him to keep people guessing as to whether or not he was in their city.

Ka rang the doorbell that the youth with the skullcap had indicated and immediately decided that the short man who welcomed him inside the apartment was the one who had shot the director of the Institute of Education at the New Life Pastry Shop an hour and a half earlier. Ka's heart began to beat faster.

"I hope you won't take offense," this man said, raising his arms in the air as a prompt for his guest to do likewise. "Over the past two years they've made three attempts to assassinate the Boss, so I'm going to have to frisk you."

Ka held out his arms to be searched—it took him back to his university days. As the man's little hands passed carefully over his shirt, Ka was afraid he would notice how fast his heart was beating. But once the search was over, Ka felt calmer and his heartbeat returned to normal. No, in fact this was not the director's assassin. This pleasant middle-aged man, who rather resembled Edward G. Robinson, seemed neither decisive nor strong enough to shoot anyone.

Ka heard the sobs of a baby and the sweet sounds of a mother tenderly trying to comfort it.

"Shall I take off my shoes?" he asked, and removed them without waiting for an answer.

"We're guests here," said a second voice. "We don't want to be a burden to our hosts."

Ka suddenly realized there was someone else in the little entry hall. Although he knew at once that it was Blue, a part of him was doubtful; perhaps he had been expecting the meeting to be far more carefully staged. He followed Blue into a sparsely furnished room, where a black-and-white television set was playing. Here a tiny infant with his fist in his mouth was staring with happy and deeply serious eyes at his mother, who was changing him and whispering to him sweetly in Kurdish. His eyes fixed first on Blue and then on Ka as they entered the room. As in all the old Russian houses, there was no hallway. The two men continued into a second room.

Ka's mind was on Blue. He saw a bed made so perfectly that it would have passed military inspection, and a pair of striped pajamas neatly folded beside the pillow; sitting on the bed was an ashtray inscribed ERSIN ELECTRIC and on the wall a calendar showing scenes of Venice; there was a large window, its shutters open, looking out over the melancholy lights of the snow-covered city. Blue closed the window and turned to face Ka.

His eyes were deep blue—almost midnight blue—a color you never saw in a Turk. He was brown-haired and beardless, much younger than Ka had expected; he had an aquiline nose and breathtakingly pale skin. He was extraordinarily handsome, but his gracefulness was born of self-confidence. In his manner, expression, and appearance there was nothing of the truculent, bearded, provincial fundamentalist whom the secularist press had depicted with a gun in one hand and a string of prayer beads in the other.

"Please don't take off your coat until the room has warmed up. . . . It's a beautiful coat. Where did you buy it?"

"In Frankfurt."

"Frankfurt . . . Frankfurt," Blue murmured, and he lifted his eyes to the ceiling and lost himself in thought. Then he explained that "some time ago" he had been found guilty under Article 163 of promoting the establishment of a state based on religious principles and had for this reason escaped to Germany.

There was a silence. Ka knew he should take this opportunity to establish cordial terms between them, so when his mind went blank, he began to panic. He sensed that Blue was talking to calm himself.

"When I was in Germany, at whatever Muslim association I happened to be visiting, in whatever city—it could be Frankfurt or Cologne, somewhere between the cathedral and the station, or one of the wealthy neighborhoods of Hamburg—wherever I happened to be walking, there was always one German who stood out of the crowd as an object of fascination for me. The important thing was not what I thought of him but what I thought he might be thinking about me; I'd try to see myself through his eyes and imagine what he might be thinking about my appearance, my clothes, the way I moved, my history, where I had just been and where I was going, who I was. It made me feel terrible but it became a habit; I became used to feeling degraded, and I came to understand how my brothers felt. . . . Most of the time it's not the Europeans who belittle us. What happens when we look at them is that we belittle ourselves. When we undertake the pilgrimage, it's not just to escape the tyranny at home but also to reach to the depths of our souls. The day arrives when the guilty must return to save those who could not find the courage to leave. Why did you come back?"

Ka remained silent. The threadbare room, with its unpainted walls and its flaking plaster, did not invite confidences, nor did the naked bulb that hung from the ceiling, piercing his eyes.

"I don't want to bore you with questions," said Blue. "When the dear departed Mullah Kasım Ensari received visitors at his tribal encampment on the banks of the Tigris River, this was always the first thing he'd say: 'I'm very glad to meet you, sir, and now would you tell me who you're spying for?'"

"I'm spying for the *Republican*," said Ka.

"That much I know. But I still have to ask why they're so interested in Kars as to have taken the trouble to send someone all the way out here."

"I volunteered. I'd also heard that my old friend Muhtar and his wife were living here."

"But they've separated—hadn't you heard?" Blue corrected him, looking straight into Ka's eyes.

"I had heard," said Ka. He blushed. Thinking of everything that Blue had to be noticing right then, Ka hated him.

"Did they beat Muhtar at the police station?"

"Yes, they did."

"Did he deserve to be beaten?" Blue asked, in a strange, almost insinuating voice.

"No, of course he didn't," Ka replied angrily.

"And why didn't they beat you? Are you pleased with yourself?"

"I have no idea why they didn't beat me."

"Of course you know why: You belong to the Istanbul bourgeoisie. Anyone can tell, just by looking at your skin and the way you hold yourself. He must have friends in high places—that's what they said to one another, there's no doubt about it. As for Muhtar, one look and you know he has no connections, no importance whatsoever. In fact, the reason Muhtar went into politics in the first place was to be able to stand up to those people the way you can. But even if he wins the election, to take office he still has to prove that he's the sort of person who can take a beating from the state. That's why he was probably glad to be getting one."

Blue was not smiling at all; his expression was even sad.

"No one can be happy about a beating," Ka said, feeling himself to be ordinary and superficial next to Blue.

Blue's face said, Let's move on to the subject we're really here to talk about. "You've been meeting with the families of the girls who committed suicide," he said. "Why did you want to talk to them?"

"To research an article."

"For newspapers in the West?"

"Yes, for newspapers in the West," said Ka, with a certain pride, despite his having no contacts in the German press. "And also in Turkey, for the *Republican*," he added with embarrassment.

"The Turkish press is interested in its country's troubles only if the Western press takes an interest first," said Blue. "Otherwise it's offensive to discuss poverty and suicide; they talk about these things as if they happen in a land beyond the civilized world. Which means that you too will be forced to publish your article in Europe. This is why I wanted to meet you: You are not to write about the suicide girls, either for a Turkish paper or a European one! Suicide is a terrible sin. It's an illness that grows the more attention you pay it, particularly this most recent case. If you write that she was a Muslim girl making a political statement about head scarves, it will be more lethal for you than poison."

"But it's true," said Ka. "Before she committed suicide, this girl did her ritual ablutions and then said her prayers. I understand the head-scarf girls have a lot of respect for her because she did that."

"Girls who commit suicide are not even Muslims!" said Blue. "And it's wrong to say they're taking a stand over head scarves. If you publish lies like this, you'll only spread more rumors—about quarrels among the head-scarf girls, about the poor souls who have resorted to wearing wigs, about how they've been destroyed by the pressure put on them by the police and their mothers and fathers. Is this what you came here for, to encourage more poor girls to commit suicide? These girls who for the love of God find themselves caught between their schools and their families are so miserable and so alone that they see no course but to imitate the suicidal martyr."

"The deputy governor said that the Kars suicides have been exaggerated."

"Why did you meet with the deputy governor?"

"For the same reason I went to see the police: so that they wouldn't feel obliged to follow me around all day."

"When they heard the news that the covered girls thrown out of school were committing suicide, they were very pleased!" said Blue.

"I will write things as I see them," said Ka.

"Your insinuation is directed not just against the state and the deputy governor, it's directed at me too. When you imply that neither the secular governor nor the political Islamists want anything written about the suicide girls, I know you're trying to provoke me."

"Yes, I am."

"That girl didn't kill herself because they threw her out of school, she killed herself over a love affair. But if you write that a covered girl killed herself—sinned against God—on account of a broken heart, the boys at the religious high school will be furious. Kars is a small place."

"I was hoping to discuss all this with the girls themselves."

"Fine," said Blue. "Why don't you ask these girls whether they'd like you to write in the German press about their sisters who, having stood up for the right to cover their heads, were so devastated by the repercussions that they departed this world in a state of sin."

"I'd be more than happy to ask them!" Ka said stubbornly, even as he was beginning to feel afraid.

"I had another reason for having you come here," said Blue. "You just witnessed the assassination of the director of the Institute of Education. This was a direct result of the anger of our believers over the cruelty that the state has visited on our covered girls. But of course the whole thing is a state plot. First they used this poor director to enforce their cruel measures, and then they incited some madman to kill him so as to pin the blame on the Muslims."

"Are you claiming responsibility or are you condemning the incident?" Ka asked sharply, as if he really were a journalist.

"I haven't come to Kars for political reasons," said Blue. "I came, perhaps, to stop this suicide epidemic." Suddenly he put his hands on Ka's shoulders, pulled him close, and kissed him on both cheeks. "You are a modern-day dervish. You've withdrawn from the world to devote yourself to poetry. You would never want to be the pawn of those who would denigrate innocent Muslims. Just as I've decided to trust you, you've decided to trust me—and you came through all this snow that we might meet. Now, to show my thanks, I would like to tell you a story with a moral." Again he looked Ka straight in the eye. "Shall I tell you the story?"

"Tell me the story."

"Long, long ago, there was a tireless warrior of unequaled bravery who lived in Iran. Everyone who knew him loved him. They called him Rüstem, and so shall we. One day, while hunting, he lost his way, and then, as he slept encamped that same night, he lost his horse. While he was looking for Raksh, his horse, Rüstem wandered into Turan, which was an enemy land. But because his reputation preceded him, they treated him well. The shah of Turan welcomed him as a guest and arranged a feast in his honor. And after the feast, the shah's daughter paid Rüstem a visit in his room to proclaim her love for him. She told him that she wished to have his child. She seduced him with her beauty and her fine words, and before long they were making love.

"The following morning, Rüstem returned to his own country, but he left a token—a wristband—for his future child. When the child was born, they called him Suhrab, so let's call him that too. Years later, his mother told him that his father was none other than the legendary Rüstem. 'I'm going to Iran,' the boy said, 'to depose the wicked Shah Keykavus and install my father as his successor . . . and then I'll return to Turan and do exactly the same thing to the wicked Shah Efrasiyab, and when I've done that, I'll install myself as his successor. And then my father Rüstem and I will bring just rule to Iran and Turan—in other words, to the entire universe!'

"So said the pure and good-hearted Suhrab, little knowing that his enemies were far more cunning and sly than he. For while Efrasiyab, the shah of Turan, lent his support to the war with Iran, he also placed spies in the army to make sure Suhrab wouldn't recognize his father.

"After many tricks and ruses, and cruel twists of fate and coincidence, engineered for all he knew by the Sublime Almighty, the day arrived when Suhrab and his father Rüstem came face-to-face on the battlefield, each with his army behind him. Neither could have known the other's face, but no matter: Both were in armor, and needless to say they did not recognize each other. Rüstem would of course have wanted to remain anonymous inside his armor: otherwise this hero facing him might unleash the full fury of his force against Rüstem in particular. As for Suhrab, his childish heart allowed him only one vision, that of his father on the throne of Iran, so he never stopped even to wonder who his adversary might be. And so it came to pass that these two great and good-hearted warriors who were father and son, standing before their respective watchful armies, jumped forward and drew their swords."

Blue paused. Before looking into Ka's eyes, he added in a childish voice, "Although I've read this story hundreds of times, I always shudder when I get to this part, and my heart starts pounding. I don't know why, but for some reason I identify with Suhrab as he prepares to kill his father. Who would want to kill his father? What soul could bear the pain of that crime, the weight of that sin? Especially my own Suhrab with his innocent heart! The only hope at this point is that Suhrab will kill his foe without discerning his identity.

"As these thoughts pass through my mind, the two warriors begin to fight, and in a struggle that goes on for hours neither is able to defeat the other. Soaked and exhausted, they scabbard their swords. When we come to the evening of the first day, I'm as troubled for the father as I am for Suhrab, and when I continue the story, it's as if I'm reading it for the first time; I dare to dream that father and son will be unable to kill each other and find some way out of their predicament.

"On the second day, the two armies line up once more, and once again father and son face each other in their armor and engage each other in merciless combat. After a long struggle, luck smiles on Suhrab—but can we even call this luck?—and he throws Rüstem off his horse and pins him to the ground. He takes out his dagger and as he prepares to bring it down on his father's neck, they say this to him: 'In Iran it is not the tradition for enemy heroes to take away a head on the first occasion. Don't kill him; that would be too crude.' So Suhrab does not kill his father.

"When I read this part I get very confused. I'm full of love for Suhrab. What is the meaning of this fate God has arranged for this father and his son? As for the third day of the fight, a day I have awaited with such trepidation—against all my expectations, it's over in a moment. Rüstem knocks Suhrab off his horse and, leaping forward, plunges his sword into him and kills him. The speed of the event is horrifying, shocking. When he sees the wristband and realizes that he has killed his son, Rüstem kneels down, takes his son's bloody corpse onto his lap, and cries.

"At this point in the story I always cry too, not just because I share Rüstem's grief but because I now understand the meaning of Suhrab's death. It is Suhrab's love for his father that kills him. But now I move beyond the childish and good-hearted love Suhrab felt for his beloved father; what I feel most acutely now is the deeper and far more dignified anguish of the father as he struggles to honor both his son and the codes that bind him. My sympathies, which have been throughout with the rebellious and individualistic Suhrab, pass over to Rüstem, the strong responsible father who is his own man."

Blue paused for a moment. Ka felt very jealous of his ability to tell this story—or, indeed, any story—with such conviction.

"But I didn't tell you this beautiful story to show you what it means to me or how I relate it to my life; I told it to point out that it's forgotten," said Blue. "This thousand-year-old story comes from Firdevsi's *Shehname*. Once upon a time, millions of people knew it by heart—from Tabriz to Istanbul, from Bosnia to Trabzon—and when they recalled it they found the meaning in their lives. The story spoke to them in just the same way that Oedipus' murder of his father and Macbeth's obsession with power and death speak to people throughout the Western world. But now, because we've fallen under the spell of the West, we've forgotten our own stories. They've removed all the old stories from our children's textbooks. These days, you can't find a single bookseller who stocks the *Shehname* in all of Istanbul! How do you explain this?"

Both men fell silent.

"Let me guess what you're thinking," said Blue. "Is this story so beautiful that a man could kill for it? That's what you're thinking, isn't it?"

"I don't know," said Ka.

"Then think about it," said Blue, and he left the room.

CHAPTER NINE

Are You an Atheist?

A NONBELIEVER WHO DOES
NOT WANT TO KILL HIMSELF

When Blue left the room, Ka was not sure what to do. At first he thought Blue was coming back to quiz him on his "thoughts." But it soon dawned on him that he had misread this man. In his posturing, insinuating way, Blue was giving him a message. Or was it a threat?

In either case, it wasn't danger Ka sensed but rather the fact of not belonging here. The room in which he had seen the mother and the baby was now empty; so, too, was the entryway. As he closed the front door behind him, it was all he could do not to run down the stairs.

When he looked up at the sky, Ka's first thought was that the snowflakes had stopped moving; as he watched them hover in midair, it seemed as if time itself had stopped. It also seemed that a great deal had changed and a great deal of time had passed while he'd been inside. But Ka's meeting with Blue had lasted only twenty minutes.

He made his way along the train track, past the snow-covered silo that loomed overhead like a great white cloud, and was soon back inside the station. As he passed through the empty, dirty building, he saw a dog approaching, wagging its curly tail in a friendly way. It was a black dog with a round white patch on its forehead. As he looked across the filthy waiting hall, Ka saw three teenage boys, who were beckoning the dog with sesame rolls. One of them was Necip; he broke away from his friends and ran toward Ka.

"On no account are you to let my classmates know how I knew you'd be coming through here," he said. "My best friend, Fazıl, has a very important question to ask you. If you can give him a moment of your time, he'll be very happy."

"All right," said Ka, and he walked over to the bench where the other teenagers were sitting.

One poster on the wall behind them urgently reminded travelers how important the railroads were to Atatürk; another sought to strike fear in the heart of any girl contemplating suicide. The boys rose to their feet to shake Ka's hand, but then shyness overtook them.

"Before Fazıl asks his question, Mesut would like to tell you a story he's heard," said Necip.

"No, I can't tell it myself," said Mesut, hardly containing his excitement. "Please—could you tell the story for me?"

While Necip told the story, Ka watched the black dog frolicking about the dirty half-lit station.

"The story takes place in a religious high school in Istanbul, or that's what I heard," Necip began. "A typical slapdash place in a suburb on the edge of the city. The director of this school had an appointment with a city official in one of those new Istanbul skyscrapers we've seen on television. He got into this enormous elevator and began to go up. There was another man in the elevator, a tall man younger than he; this man showed the director the book in his hand, and as some of its pages were still uncut he took out a knife with a mother-of-pearl handle while he recited a few lines. When the elevator stopped on the nineteenth floor, the director got out.

"During the days that followed, he began to feel very strange. He became obsessed with death, he couldn't find the will to do anything, and he couldn't stop thinking about the man in the elevator. The school director was a devout man, so he went to see some Cerrahi dervishes, hoping to find solace and guidance. He sat there until morning, pouring out all his woes, and after he had done this, the celebrated sheikh made the following diagnosis:

" 'It seems you've lost your faith in God,' he said. 'What's worse, you don't even know it, and as if that weren't bad enough, you're even proud of not knowing it! You contracted this disease from the man in the elevator. He's turned you into an atheist.' The director rose to his feet in tears to deny what the illustrious sheikh had said, but there was still one part of his heart that was pure and honest, and this part assured him that the sheikh was telling the truth.

"Infected by the disease of atheism, the director began to put unreasonable pressure on his lovely little pupils; he tried to spend time alone with their mothers; he stole money from another teacher whom he envied. And the worst of it was, he felt proud for having committed these sins. He would assemble the whole school to accuse them of blind faith; he told them their traditions made no sense and asked why they couldn't be free as he was; he couldn't utter a sentence without stuffing it with French words; he spent the money he had stolen on the latest European fashions. And wherever he went, he made sure to let people know how much he despised them for being 'backward.'

"Before long, the school had descended into anarchy. One group of pupils raped a beautiful classmate, another group beat up an elderly Koran teacher, and the whole place was on the brink of revolt. The director would go home in tears, contemplating suicide, but because he lacked the courage to follow through, he kept hoping that someone else would kill him. To make this happen, he—God forbid—cursed His Excellency the Prophet Muhammad in front of one of his most God-fearing pupils. But knowing by now that he had lost his mind, his pupils didn't lay a finger on him. He took to the streets, to proclaim—God forbid—that God did not exist, that mosques should be turned into discotheques, and that we'd only become as rich as people in the West if we all converted to Christianity. But now that the young Islamists wanted to kill him, he lost his resolve and hid from them.

"Hopeless and unable to find any way to satisfy his death wish, the director returned to the same fateful skyscraper in Istanbul and, stepping into the same elevator car, found himself face-to-face once again with the tall man who had first exposed him to atheism. The man smiled in a way to indicate that he knew the director's whole story, and then he presented the book as he had the time before—the cure for atheism was to be found in it too. As the director stretched out a trembling hand, the man took out the knife with the mother-of-pearl handle, as if preparing to cut the pages of the book, but with the elevator still moving, he plunged it into the director's heart."

When Necip finished the story, Ka realized that he'd heard it before, from Islamist Turks in Germany. In Necip's version, the mysterious book at the end of the story remained unnamed, but Mesut now named one or two Jewish writers known to be agents of atheism, as well as a number of columnists who had led the media campaign against political Islam—one of these would be assassinated three years later.

"The director is not alone in his anguish—there are many atheists in our midst. They've been seduced by the devil and now roam among us, desperate for peace and happiness," said Mesut. "Do you share this view?"

"I don't know."

"What do you mean, you don't know?" Mesut asked, with some annoyance. "Aren't you an atheist too?"

"I don't know," said Ka.

"Then tell me this: Do you or don't you believe that God Almighty created the universe and everything in it, even the snow that is swirling down from the sky?"

"The snow reminds me of God," said Ka.

"Yes, but do you believe that God created snow?" Mesut insisted.

There was a silence. Ka watched the black dog run through the door to the platform to frolic in the snow under the dim halo of neon light.

"You're not giving me an answer," said Mesut. "If a person knows and loves God, he never doubts God's existence. It seems to me that you're not giving me an answer because you're too timid to admit that you're an atheist. But we knew this already. That's why I wanted to ask you a question on my friend Fazıl's behalf. Do you suffer the same terrible pangs as the poor atheist in the story? Do you want to kill yourself?"

"No matter how unhappy I was, I'd still find suicide terrifying," said Ka.

"But why?" asked Fazıl. "Is it because it's against the law? But when the state talks about the sanctity of human life, they get it all wrong. Why are you afraid of committing suicide? Explain this."

"Please don't take offense at my friend's insistence," said Necip. "Fazıl's asking you this question for a reason—a very special reason."

"What I wanted to ask," said Fazıl, "is this: Aren't you so troubled and unhappy that you want to commit suicide?"

"No," said Ka. He was beginning to get annoyed.

"Please, don't try to hide anything from us," said Mesut. "We won't do anything bad to you just because you're an atheist."

There was a tense silence. Ka rose to his feet. He had no desire to let them see how he felt. He started walking.

"Where are you going? Please don't go," said Fazıl. Ka stopped in his tracks but said nothing.

"Maybe I should speak instead," said Necip. "The three of us are in love with girls who have put everything at risk for the sake of their faith.

The secular press calls them *covered girls*. For us they are simply Muslim girls, and what they do to defend their faith is what all Muslim girls must do."

"And men too," said Fazıl.

"Of course," said Necip. "I'm in love with Hicran. Mesut is in love with Hande. Fazıl was in love with Teslime, but now she's dead. Or she committed suicide. But we can't bring ourselves to believe that a Muslim girl ready to sacrifice everything for her faith would be capable of suicide."

"Perhaps she could no longer bear her suffering," Ka suggested. "After all, she'd been thrown out of school, and her family was putting pressure on her to take off her head scarf."

"No amount of suffering can justify a believer's committing this sin," Necip said excitedly. "If we even forget or miss our morning prayers, we're so worried about our sinful state that we can hardly sleep at night. The more it happens, the earlier we run back to the mosque. When someone's faith is this strong, he'll do anything to keep from committing such a sin—even submit to a life of torture."

"We know that you went to see Teslime's family," Fazıl said. "Do they think she committed suicide?"

"They do. She watched *Marianna* on TV with her parents, washed herself, and said her prayers."

"Teslime never watched soap operas," Fazıl said, in a soft voice.

"How well did you know her?" Ka asked.

"I didn't know her personally; we never actually spoke," said Fazıl, with some embarrassment. "I saw her once from far away, and she was pretty well covered. But as a soulmate, of course I knew her very well; when you love someone above all others, you know everything there is to know about her. The Teslime I knew would never have committed suicide."

"Maybe you didn't know her well enough."

"And maybe the Westerners sent you here to cover up Teslime's murder," said Mesut, with a swagger.

"No, no, we trust you," said Necip. "Our leaders say you're a recluse, a poet. It's because we trust you that we wanted to talk to you about something that's making us very unhappy. Fazıl would like to apologize for what Mesut has just said."

"I apologize," said Fazıl. His face was beet red. Tears were forming in his eyes.

Mesut remained silent as peace was restored.

"Fazıl and I are blood brothers," said Necip. "Most of the time, we think the same things; we can read each other's thoughts. Unlike me, Fazıl has no interest in politics. Now we'd like to know if you could do us both a favor. The thing is, we can both accept that Teslime might have been driven to the sin of suicide by the pressures from her parents and the state. It's very painful; Fazıl can't stop thinking that the girl he loved committed the sin of suicide. But if Teslime was a secret atheist like the one in the story, if she was one of those unlucky souls who don't even know they are atheists, or if she committed suicide because she was an atheist, for Fazıl this is a catastrophe: It means he was in love with an atheist.

"You're the only one who can answer this terrible suspicion that's plaguing us. You're the only one who can offer Fazıl comfort. Do you understand what we're thinking?"

"Are you an atheist?" asked Fazıl, with imploring eyes. "And if you are an atheist, do you want to kill yourself?"

"Even on days when I am most certain that I'm an atheist, I feel no urge to commit suicide," said Ka.

"Thank you for giving us a straight answer to our question," said Fazıl. He looked calmer now. "Your heart is full of goodness, but you're afraid of believing in God."

Seeing that Mesut was still glaring at him, Ka was eager to put some distance between them. His mind was already far, far away. He felt a desire stirring inside him, and a dream connected to that desire, but at the same time he was unable to give himself over to this dream on account of the activity around him. Later, when he could think carefully, he would understand that this dream rose from his yearning for İpek as well as from his fear of dying and his failure to believe in God. And at the last moment, Mesut added something else.

"Please don't misunderstand us," said Necip. "We have no objection to someone's becoming an atheist. There's always room for atheists in Muslim societies."

"Except that the cemeteries have to be kept separate," said Mesut. "It would bring disquiet to the souls of believers to lie in the same cemeteries as the godless. When people go through life concealing their lack of faith, they bring turbulence not only to the land of the living but also to cemeteries. It's not just the torment of having to lie beside the godless till Judgment Day; the worst horror would be to rise up on Judgment Day only to find oneself face-to-face with a luckless atheist. . . . Mr. Poet, Ka Bey, you've made no secret of the fact that you were once an atheist. Maybe you still are one. So tell us, Who makes the snow fall from the sky? What is the snow's secret?"

For a moment they all looked outside to watch the snow falling onto the empty tracks.

What am I doing in this world? Ka asked himself. How miserable these snowflakes look from this perspective, how miserable my life is. A man lives his life, and then he falls apart and soon there is nothing left. Ka felt as if half his soul had just abandoned him but still the other half remained; he still had love in him. Like a snowflake, he would fall as he was meant to fall; he would devote himself heart and soul to the melancholy course on which his life was set. His father had a certain smell after shaving, and now this smell came back to him. He thought of his mother making breakfast, her feet aching inside her slippers on the cold kitchen floor; he had a vision of a hairbrush; he remembered his mother giving him sugary pink syrup when he woke up coughing in the night, he felt the spoon in his mouth, and as he gave his mind over to all the other little things that make up a life and realized how they all added up to a unified whole, he saw a snowflake. . . .

So it was that Ka heard the call from deep inside him: the call he heard only at moments of inspiration, the only sound that could ever make him happy, the sound of his muse. For the first time in four years, a poem was coming to him; although he had yet to hear the words, he knew it was already written; even as it waited in its hiding place, it radiated the power and beauty of destiny. Ka's heart rejoiced. He told the three youths he had to leave them and hurried away through the snow, thinking all the while of the poem he would write when he was back at the hotel.

—————◦•◦—————

CHAPTER TEN

What Makes This Poem Beautiful?

SNOW AND HAPPINESS

K a threw off his coat the moment he got into his room, opened the green notebook he'd brought with him from Frankfurt, and wrote out the poem as it came to him, word by word. It was like copying down a poem someone was whispering into his ear, but he gave the words on the page his full attention nevertheless. Because he'd never before written a poem like this, in one flash of inspiration, without stopping, there was a corner of his mind where he doubted its worth. But as line followed line, it seemed to him that the poem was perfect in every way, which made his joyful heart beat faster. And so he carried on writing, hardly pausing at all, leaving spaces only here and there for the words he had not quite heard, until he had written thirty-four lines.

The poem was made up of many of the thoughts that had come to him all at once a short while earlier: the falling snow, cemeteries, the black dog running happily around the station building, an assortment of childhood memories, and the image that had lured him back to the hotel: İpek. How happy it made him just to imagine her face—and also how terrified! He called the poem "Snow."

Much later, when he thought about how he'd written this poem, he had a vision of a snowflake; this snowflake, he decided, was his life writ small; the poem that had unlocked the meaning of his life, he now saw sitting at its center. But—just as the poem itself defies easy explanation—it is difficult to say how much he decided at that moment and how much of his life was determined by the hidden symmetries this book is seeking to unveil.

Before finishing the poem, Ka went silently to the window and watched the scene outside: the large snowflakes floating so elegantly through the air. He had the feeling that simply by watching the snow fall he would be able to bring the poem to its predetermined end.

There was a knock on the door. Just as he opened it, the last two lines came to him, but then he lost them—and they would remain lost for the duration of his stay in Kars.

It was İpek. "I have a letter for you," she said, handing it to him.

Ka took the letter and threw it aside without even looking at it. "I'm so happy," he said.

He'd always thought that only vulgar people said things like "I'm so happy," but when he said it now, he felt no shame at all.

"Come inside," he said to İpek. "You're looking very beautiful."

İpek entered nonchalantly, as if she knew the rooms of the hotel as well as her own home. The time they had spent apart seemed to Ka only to have intensified their intimacy.

"I can't say how it happened," said Ka, "but it's possible that this poem came to me thanks to you."

"The condition of the director of the Institute of Education has worsened," İpek said.

"That's good news, considering we thought he was already dead."

"The police are widening their net. They've raided the university dormitories, and now they're doing the hotels. They came here and looked at our books and asked about each and every one of our guests."

"What did you say about me? Did you tell them we're getting married?"

"You're very sweet, but my mind's on other things right now. We've just heard that they picked up Muhtar and beat him. But apparently they let him go afterward."

"He asked me to pass on a message: He's ready to do anything to get you to marry him again. He apologizes a thousand times over for trying to force you to wear a head scarf."

"Muhtar's already said this to me; he says it every day," said İpek. "After the police let you go, what did you do?"

"I wandered around the city," Ka said. He had a moment of indecision.

"Go on, tell me."

"They took me to see Blue. I was told not to tell anyone."

"So you shouldn't," said İpek. "And you shouldn't say anything to Blue about us, or about my father either."

"Have you ever met him?"

"For a while Muhtar was very much taken with him, so he paid a few visits to our house. But when Muhtar decided he wanted a more moderate and democratic form of Islamism, he distanced himself."

"He says he came here for the suicide girls."

"Be afraid that you heard that and don't discuss it with anyone," said İpek. "There's a high probability that his hiding place is bugged by the police."

"Then why can't they catch him?"

"They will when it suits them."

"Why don't you and I just get out of this city right now?" Ka said.

Rising up inside him was that feeling he had always known as a child and as a young man at moments of extraordinary happiness: a prospect of future misery and hopelessness.

In a panic, he tried to bring this happy moment to a close: this, he hoped, would lessen the unhappiness he was ultimately sure to suffer. The safest way to calm himself, he thought, would be simply to accept the inevitable: that the love he felt for İpek—the source of his anxiety—would be his undoing; that any intimacy he might chance to enjoy with her would dissolve him as salt dissolves ice; that he didn't deserve this happiness, but rather the disgrace and denigration that would surely result. He braced himself for it.

But it didn't happen. Instead, İpek wrapped her arms around him. First they just held each other, and then their friendly embrace turned to passion; they began to kiss, and soon they were lying side by side on the bed. His pessimism was no match for his sexual excitement. Soon he had given himself over to a boundless desire; soon, he dreamed, they would be taking off each other's clothes and making love for hours and hours.

But İpek stood up. "I find you very attractive, and I too want to make love, but I haven't been with anyone for three years and I'm just not ready," she said.

I haven't made love with anyone for four years, Ka said to himself. He was sure İpek could see these words on his face.

"And even if I were ready," said İpek, "I could never make love with my father so near, in the same house."

"Does your father have to be out of the hotel for you to be in bed with me naked?" Ka asked.

"Yes. And he hardly ever leaves the hotel. He doesn't much like the icy streets of Kars."

"All right, then, let's not make love now, but let's kiss a bit longer," said Ka.

"All right."

İpek leaned over Ka, who was sitting on the edge of the bed, for a long and serious kiss before permitting him to approach her.

"Let me read you my poem," he said, when he felt sure the kiss was over. "Don't you want to know how it goes?"

"Read this letter first. A young man delivered it to the door."

Ka opened the letter and read it out in a loud voice.

"Ka, my dear son:

"If you'd prefer me not to call you my son, I offer my sincere apologies. Last night I saw you in my dreams. It was snowing in my dream, and every snowflake that fell to the earth shone with divine radiance. I asked myself if it was a sign, and then this afternoon I saw outside the same snow I'd seen in my dream falling right in front of my window. You walked past our humble home, number 18 Baytarhane Street. Our esteemed friend Muhtar, whom God Almighty has just subjected to a severe test, has explained to me the meaning you take from this snow. We are travelers on the same road. I am waiting for you, sir.

"Signed:
Saadettin Cevher"

"Sheikh Saadettin," said İpek. "Go to him at once. Then you can come back and have dinner with my father this evening."

"Am I supposed to pay my respects to every lunatic in Kars?"

"I told you to be afraid of Blue; don't be so quick to dismiss him as a lunatic. The sheikh is cunning too, and he isn't stupid."

"I want to forget about all of them. Shall I read you my poem now?"

"Go ahead."

Ka sat down at the little table and began to read in an excited but confident voice, but then he stopped. "Go over there," he said to İpek. "I want to see your face while I'm reading." When he was sure he could see her from the corner of his eyes, he began his poem again. "Is it beautiful?" he asked her a few moments later.

"Yes, it's beautiful!" said İpek.

Ka read a few more lines aloud and then asked her again, "Is it beautiful?"

"It's beautiful," İpek replied.

When he finished reading the poem, he asked, "So what was it that made it beautiful?"

"I don't know," İpek replied, "but I did find it beautiful."

"Did Muhtar ever read you a poem like this?"

"Never," she said.

Ka began to read the poem aloud again, this time with growing force, but he still stopped at all the same places to ask, "Is it beautiful?" He also stopped at a few new places to say, "It really is very beautiful, isn't it?"

"Yes, it's very beautiful!" İpek replied.

Ka was so happy that he felt (as he had felt only once before, early in his career, when he wrote a poem for a child) as if a strange and beautiful light were enveloping him, and seeing in a shaft of this light the reflection of İpek, he was even happier. Taking it as a sign that the rules were suspended, he began to embrace İpek again, but now she gently pulled away.

"Listen. Go to our esteemed sheikh at once. He counts as a very important person here, much more important than you think; many people in this city go to see him, even people who regard themselves as seculars, lots of army officers. It's even said the governor's wife goes there, and lots of rich people, lots of soldiers. He's on the side of the state. When he said that the covered girls in the university should take off their head scarves, the Prosperity Party didn't make a peep. In a place like Kars, when a man this powerful invites you over, you don't turn him down."

"Was it you who sent poor Muhtar to see him?"

"Are you worried that the sheikh will discover a God-fearing part of you and send you scurrying back into the fold?"

"I'm very happy right now, I have no need for religion," said Ka. "And anyway, that's not what brought me back to Turkey. Only one thing could have brought me back: your love. . . . Are we going to get married?"

İpek sat down on the edge of the bed. "Come on, go," she said. She gave Ka a warm and bewitching smile. "But be careful, too. There's no one better at finding the weak point in your soul, and like a genie he'll work his way inside you."

"What will he do to me?"

"He'll speak to you, and then all of a sudden he'll throw himself on the floor. He'll take some ordinary thing you said and say how wise it is; he'll insist you're a real man. Some people even think he's making fun of them at this point! But that's His Excellency's special gift. He does it so convincingly you end up believing that he really thinks what you've said is wise and that he believes as you do with all his heart. He acts as if there is something great inside you. After a while, you begin to see this inner beauty too, and because you have never before sensed the beauty within you, you think it must be the presence of God, and this makes you happy. In other words, the world becomes a beautiful place when you're near this man. And you'll love our esteemed sheikh because he's brought you to this happiness. All the while, another voice is whispering inside you that this is all a game the sheikh is playing and you are a miserable idiot. But as far as I could figure out from what Muhtar told me, it seems you no longer have the strength to be that miserable idiot. You're so wretchedly unhappy that all you want is for God to save you. Now, your mind—which knows nothing of your soul's desires—objects a little but not enough; you embark on the road the sheikh has shown you because it is the only road in the world that will let you stand on your own two feet. Sheikh Efendi's greatest gift is to make the wretch sitting before him feel special, even more as one with the universe than His Excellency himself. To most men in Kars this feels like a miracle, for they know only too well that no one else in Turkey could be as wretched, poor, and unsuccessful as they. So you come to believe, first in the sheikh and then in the long-forgotten teachings of your Islamic faith. Contrary to what they think in Germany and to the pronouncements of secularist intellectuals, this is not a bad thing. You can become like everyone else, you can become one with the people, and, even if it's only for a little while, you can escape from unhappiness."

"I'm not unhappy," said Ka.

"In fact, someone that unhappy is not unhappy at all. Even the most miserable people have hidden consolations and hopes they secretly embrace. It's not like Istanbul; there are no mocking nonbelievers. Things are simpler here."

"I'm going now, but only because you want me to. Where is Baytarhane Street? How long should I stay there?"

"Stay there till your soul finds some solace!" said İpek. "And don't be afraid of believing." She helped Ka put on his coat. "Is your knowledge of Islam fresh in your mind?" she asked. "Do you remember the prayers you learned at primary school? You might embarrass yourself."

"When I was a child, our maid used to take me to Teşvikiye Mosque," said Ka. "It was more an occasion to get together with the other women who worked as maids than it was to worship. They would have a good long gossip waiting for the prayers to begin, and I would roll around on the carpets with the other children. At school, I memorized all the prayers to ingratiate myself with the teacher—he helped us memorize the *fatiha* by hitting us, picking us up by the hair, squeezing our heads under the lids of our desks where the 'religious book' stood open. I learned everything they taught us about Islam, but then I forgot it. Now it's as if everything I know about Islam is from *The Message*—you know, that film starring Anthony Quinn." Ka smiled. "It was showing not long ago on the Turkish channel in Germany—but, for some strange reason, in German. You're here this evening, aren't you?"

"Yes."

"Because I want to read you my poem again," said Ka, as he put his notebook into his pocket. "Do you think it's beautiful?"

"Yes, really, it's beautiful."

"What's beautiful about it?"

"I don't know, it's just beautiful," said İpek. She opened the door to leave.

Ka threw his arms around her and kissed her on the mouth.

CHAPTER ELEVEN

Do They Have a Different God in Europe?

KA WITH SHEIKH EFENDI

K a left the hotel at a gallop; a number of people told me later that they remember seeing him race through the snow under the long line of propaganda banners in the direction of Baytarhane Street. He was so happy that, just as in his most joyful moments of childhood, two films were running simultaneously in the cinema of his imagination. In the first, he was somewhere in Germany—though not his Frankfurt house—making love to İpek. This film ran in a loop, and sometimes the place where they were making love was his hotel room. On the second imaginary screen, he could see words and visions relating to the last two lines of his poem "Snow."

He stopped first at the Green Pastures Café to ask for directions. There, inspired by the row of bottles on the shelf beside the picture of Atatürk and the Swiss vistas, he took a table and—with the decisiveness of a man in a great hurry—ordered a double raki and a plate of white cheese and roasted chickpeas. According to the announcer on television, preparations for Kars's first ever live broadcast were almost complete despite the heavy snowfall; there followed a summary of local and national news. It seemed that in the interests of peace and avoiding any further trouble for the deputy governor, the authorities had phoned the station to bar them from mentioning the shooting of the director of the Institute of Education. While he was taking all this in, Ka downed his double raki like a glass of water.

After polishing off a third raki, he set off for the sheikh's lodge; four minutes later, they were buzzing him in from upstairs. As he climbed the steep steps, he remembered that he was still carrying Muhtar's poem,

"Staircase," in his jacket pocket. He was sure everything would go well here, but he still felt that spine-tingling chill that a child feels on his way to the doctor's office, even when he's sure he won't be getting a shot. Having reached the top of the stairs, he was sorry he had come.

Ka could tell that the sheikh felt the fear in his heart the moment he appeared. But there was something about the sheikh that kept Ka from feeling ashamed. On the wall of the landing there was a mirror with a carved walnut frame. His first glimpse of Sheikh Efendi was in this mirror. The house itself was so crowded that the room was warm with breath and body heat. Scarcely a moment later, Ka found himself kissing the sheikh's hand, before he'd had even time to take in his surroundings or look to see who else was in the room.

There were about twenty others, come to attend the simple ceremony held every Tuesday, to listen to the sheikh in conversation and to unburden their hearts. Five or six were tradesmen or teahouse or dairy owners who took every opportunity to spend time with the sheikh for the happiness it gave them; there was also a young paraplegic, a cross-eyed bus company manager, an elderly man who was the bus manager's friend, a night watchman from the electricity board, a man who had been the janitor of the Kars hospital for forty years, and a few others.

Reading the confusion in Ka's face, the sheikh bowed down to kiss Ka's hand. There was something almost childish in the gesture; it was as if he were paying his respects. And although it was exactly what Ka had expected the sheikh to do, he was still astonished. Fully aware that everyone else in the room was watching them, the two men began to converse.

"May God bless you for accepting my invitation," said the sheikh. "I saw you in my dream. It was snowing."

"I saw you in my dream, Your Excellency," said Ka. "I came here to find happiness."

"It makes us happy to know that it was here in Kars that your happiness was born," said the sheikh.

"This place, this city, this house . . . they make me afraid," said Ka, "because you all seem so strange to me. Because I've always shied away from these things. I have never wanted to kiss anyone's hand—or let anyone kiss mine."

"It seems that you spoke most openly of the beauty within you to our brother Muhtar," said the sheikh. "So tell us, what does this blessed snowfall remind you of?"

At the far end of the divan on which the sheikh sat, right next to the window's edge, Ka now noticed Muhtar. There were a few bandages on his forehead and his nose. To hide the purple bruises around his eyes, he wore big dark glasses like those of old people who have been blinded by smallpox. He was smiling at Ka, but his expression was far from friendly.

"The snow reminded me of God," said Ka. "The snow reminded me of the beauty and mystery of creation, of the essential joy that is life."

He fell silent for a moment; all eyes in the crowded room were still on him. Seeing the sheikh looking as serene as ever, Ka was annoyed.

"Why did you summon me here?" he asked.

"Please don't say such a thing!" cried the sheikh. "After Muhtar Bey told us what you had said to him, it seemed you might want to open your heart to us, talk to us, find a friend."

"All right, let's talk then," said Ka. "Before I came here, I had three glasses of raki."

"But why are you so afraid of us?" asked the sheikh, his eyes opening up very wide, as if he were surprised; he was just a sweet fat man. Everyone around him was wearing the same sincere smile. "Aren't you going to tell us why you're so afraid of us?"

"I'll tell you, but I don't want you to take offense."

"We won't take offense," said the sheikh. "Please, come over here, sit next to me. It's very important to understand why you're afraid of us."

The sheikh's expression was half serious and half joking, ready to make his disciples laugh at a moment's notice. Ka liked his demeanor, and as soon as he had taken his place next to the sheikh he was tempted to imitate it.

"I've always wanted this country to prosper, to modernize. . . . I've wanted freedom for its people," Ka said. "But it seemed to me that our religion was always against all this. Maybe I'm mistaken. I beg your pardon. Maybe I'm just admitting this because I've had too much to drink."

"Please don't say such a thing!"

"I grew up in Istanbul, in Nişantaş, among society people. I wanted to be like the Europeans. I couldn't see how I could reconcile my becoming a European with a God who required women to wrap themselves in scarves, so I kept religion out of my life. But when I went to Europe, I realized there could be an Allah who was different from the Allah of the bearded provincial reactionaries."

"Do they have a different God in Europe?" asked the sheikh jokingly. He patted Ka's back.

"I want a God who doesn't ask me to take off my shoes in his presence and who doesn't make me fall to my knees to kiss people's hands. I want a God who understands my need for solitude."

"There is only one God," said the sheikh. "He sees everything and understands everyone—even your need for solitude. If you believed in him, if you knew he understood your need for solitude, you wouldn't feel so alone."

"That's very true, Your Excellency," said Ka, feeling as if he were really speaking to everyone in the room. "It's because I'm solitary that I can't believe in God. And because I can't believe in God, I can't escape from solitude. What should I do?"

Although he was drunk and unexpectedly pleased to be speaking with such courage to a real sheikh, a part of him still knew that he was entering dangerous territory, so when the sheikh fell silent he was afraid.

"Do you really want guidance from me?" asked the sheikh. "We're those people you just mentioned: bearded provincial reactionaries. Even if we shaved off our beards, there is no cure for provincialism."

"I'm provincial too, and I want to become even more provincial. I want to be forgotten in the most unknown corner of the world under a blanket of snow," said Ka.

He kissed the sheikh's hand again. When he saw how easily he could do this, he felt pleased with himself. But one part of his mind still operated differently, in a Western manner, so he also despised himself.

"I hope you will forgive me, but before I came here I had something to drink," he said again. "I felt guilty about having refused all my life to believe in the same God as the uneducated—the aunties with their heads wrapped in scarves, the uncles with the prayer beads in their hands. There's a lot of pride involved in my refusal to believe in God. But now I want to believe in that God who is making this beautiful snow fall from the sky. There's a God who pays careful attention to the world's hidden symmetry, a God who will make us all more civilized and refined."

"Of course there is, my son," said the sheikh.

"But that God is not among you. He's outside, in the empty night, in the darkness, in the snow that falls inside the hearts of outcasts."

"If you want to find God by yourself, go ahead—walk out into the darkness, revel in the snow, use it to fill yourself with God's love. We have no desire to turn you from this path. But don't forget that arrogant men who think too much of themselves always end up alone. God doesn't have any time for pride. Pride was what got Satan expelled from heaven."

Once again, Ka found himself overcome with the fear that he would find so shaming afterward. He also dreaded the things he knew they would say about him if he left. "So what shall I do, Your Excellency?" he asked. He was just about to kiss the sheikh's hand again when he changed his mind. He could tell that everyone around him knew how confused he was, and how drunk, and looked down on him for this. "I want to believe in the God you believe in and be like you, but because there's a Westerner inside me, my mind is confused."

"If your intentions are this sincere, this is a good beginning," said the sheikh. "The first thing you need to learn is humility."

"How can I do that?" Ka asked. Once again, he could feel the mocking devil inside him.

"After the evening meal, anyone who wants to talk comes to join me in this corner, on the divan where you're sitting right now," said the sheikh. "Everyone here is a brother."

It now dawned on Ka that the great crowd of men sitting on the chairs and the cushions around him were in fact queuing up to sit on the corner of this divan. He guessed that what the sheikh wanted most from him now was his respect for this imagined queue, so the best course was to make his way to the end of it and wait patiently like a European; with this in mind, he rose to his feet. He kissed the sheikh's hand one more time and went to sit on a cushion in the far corner.

Sitting next to him was a short, kindly man with gold-capped molars who worked at one of the teahouses on İnönü Avenue. The man was so small, and Ka so addled, that Ka found himself wondering whether the man had come to see the sheikh about a remedy for dwarfism. When he was a child in Nişantaş, there had been a very elegant dwarf who would go to the Gypsies in the square every evening to buy a bouquet of violets and a single carnation. The little man told Ka he had seen him passing in front of his teahouse earlier that day; he was sorry Ka hadn't come in, and he would be very happy if Ka dropped by tomorrow. At this point the cross-eyed bus company manager with the elderly friend chimed in; in a whisper, he told Ka of having gone through a very bad spell on account of a girl—he had given himself to drink and become rebellious to the point of losing all sight of God—but in the end he had been able to put everything behind him. Before Ka could ask, Did you marry the girl?

the bus company manager added, "We came to see that this girl was not right for us."

The sheikh then said a few words against suicide. The men nearby listened in silence, some nodding at the wisdom of his words, while the three in the corner continued their whispering.

"There have been a few more suicides," the short man said, "but the state has decided not to tell us, for the same reason as when it decides not to tell us that the temperature is dropping—they don't want to upset us. But here's the real reason for this epidemic: It's because they're selling these girls to elderly clerks, men they don't love."

The bus company manager objected. "When my wife first met me," he said, "she didn't love me either." He went on to declare that the epidemic had many causes: for example, unemployment, high prices, immorality, and lack of faith. Because he agreed with everything both men said, Ka began to feel rather two-faced. When the elderly companion began to nod off, the cross-eyed manager woke him up.

There was a long silence. A feeling of peace rose up inside Ka. They were so far from the center of the world, one couldn't even imagine going there, and as he fell under the spell of the snowflakes that seemed to hang in the sky outside, he began to wonder if he had entered a world without gravity.

When everyone had ceased to pay any attention to him, another poem came to Ka. He had his notebook with him, and, as with his first poem, he gave himself fully to the voice now rising up inside him, but this time he wrote down all thirty-six lines of the poem in one fell swoop. Because his mind was still foggy with drink, he was not sure the poem was any good. But when a new rush of inspiration overtook him, he rose to his feet and, begging the sheikh's pardon, rushed out of the room; when he sat himself down on the stairs to read what he had written, he could see that this poem, like the first, was flawless.

The poem draws upon the events Ka had just lived and witnessed. Four lines allude to a conversation with a sheikh about the existence of God; there are also references to Ka's shameful look following his mention of the uneducated man's God, some proposals concerning solitude, the world's secret symmetry and the creation of life; there is a man with gold teeth and one who is cross-eyed and a gentle dwarf holding a carnation, all standing with him, telling their life stories.

Shocked at the beauty of his own words, Ka could not help but ask himself, What does it all mean? It seemed to be a poem someone else had written—this, he thought, was why he was able to see its beauty. But also, finding it beautiful was a shock considering its contents, considering his own life. How to understand the beauty in this poem?

The light timer in the stairwell clicked off and he was plunged into darkness. When he had found the button and turned the light back on, he took one last look at the notebook and the title came to him: "Hidden Symmetry." Later he would point to the speed with which this happened as proof that this and all the poems that followed it were—like the world itself—not of his own creation. With this in mind, he would move it to the position of the first poem on the Reason axis.

CHAPTER TWELVE

If God Does Not Exist, How Do You Explain All the Suffering of the Poor?

THE SAD STORY OF NECIP AND HICRAN

On leaving His Excellency's lodge, Ka headed back to the hotel, and as he trudged through the snow his mind turned to İpek. It wouldn't be long, he realized, before he'd see her again. On his way down Halitpaşa Avenue, he passed first a group of People's Party campaigners and then a crowd of students on their way out of a university-entrance-exam course. The students were talking about what they were going to watch on television that night and about how easy it was to fool their chemistry teacher; they were needling each other just as mercilessly as Ka and I used to do when we were their age.

Ka saw a mother and father leading their tearful child by the hand from an apartment building where they'd just visited the dentist upstairs. It was clear from their clothes that this couple were barely making ends meet, but they had decided to take their beloved child not to the state dispensary but rather to a private dentist, whose treatment they hoped would be less painful. Through the open door of a shop that sold women's stockings, bolts of cotton cloth, colored pencils, batteries, and cassettes, he heard once again the strains of Peppino di Capri's "Roberta" and remembered hearing it on the radio when he was a child and his uncle had taken him out for a drive on the Bosphorus.

As his heart began to soar, it occurred to Ka that there might be a new poem coming to him, so he stepped into the first teahouse he could find and, sitting down at the first empty table, took out his pencil and his notebook.

After gazing through moist eyes at the empty page for some time, he revised his forecast: Actually, there was no poem coming to him, but this didn't dampen his spirits in the slightest. The teahouse was packed with unemployed men and students, and all around him the walls were plastered not just with scenes of Switzerland but also with theatrical posters, newspaper cartoons, assorted clippings, an announcement of the terms and conditions of the civil service exam, and a schedule of the soccer matches to be played by Karsspor that year. The results of past matches—most of them losses—were penciled in by various hands; next to the 6–1 loss to Erzurumspor, someone had written the lines that Ka would incorporate into "All Humanity and the Stars," the poem he would write tomorrow while sitting in the Lucky Brothers Teahouse:

> *Even if your mother came down from heaven to take you into her arms,*
> *Even if your wicked father let her go without a beating for just one night,*
> *You'd still be penniless, your shit would still freeze, your soul would*
>   *still wither, there is no hope!*
> *If you're unlucky enough to live in Kars, you might as well flush yourself*
>   *down the toilet.*

Smiling happily as he copied these lines into his notebook, he was soon joined by Necip, who was sitting at a table in the back; it was clear from his expression that he was stunned to see Ka in this place and also very pleased.

"I'm so happy you're here," said Necip. "Are you writing a poem? I would like to apologize for my friends, especially the one who called you an atheist. It's the first time in their lives they've come face-to-face with a nonbeliever. But it seems to me that you couldn't really be an atheist, because you're such a good person." He went on to say a few other things that he'd felt unable to say earlier: He and his friends had sneaked out of school to attend the show at the theater that evening, but they were going to sit way in the back, because of course they didn't want the school directors to spot them on live TV. Necip was elated to have escaped from school and to be meeting his friends at the National Theater. They all knew that Ka was going to read a poem there. Everyone in Kars wrote poems, but Ka was the first person Necip had ever met to have his poems published. Could he offer Ka a glass of tea?

Ka explained that he was short of time.

"In that case, I'll just ask you one question, one last question," said Necip. "I'm not like my friends, I'm not trying to show you disrespect. I'm just very curious."

"Yes."

Necip lit a cigarette with shaky hands. "If God does not exist, that means heaven does not exist either. And that means the world's poor, those millions who live in poverty and oppression, will never go to heaven. And if that is so, then how do you explain all the suffering of the poor? What are we here for, and why do we put up with so much unhappiness, if it's all for nothing?"

"God exists. So does heaven."

"No, you're just saying that to console me, because you feel sorry for us. As soon as you're back in Germany, you'll start thinking God doesn't exist, just like you did before."

"For the first time in years, I'm very happy," said Ka. "Why shouldn't I believe the same things as you?"

"Because you belong to the intelligentsia," said Necip. "People in the intelligentsia never believe in God. They believe in what Europeans do, and they think they're better than ordinary people."

"I may belong to the intelligentsia in Turkey," said Ka. "But in Germany I'm a worthless nobody. I was falling apart there."

Necip's beautiful eyes turned inward, and Ka could see that the teenager was considering his case, trying to put himself in Ka's shoes. "Then why did you get angry at your country and flee to Germany?" he asked. Seeing Ka's face fall, he said, "Never mind! Anyway, if I were rich, I'd be so ashamed of my situation that I'd believe in God even more."

"One day, God willing, we'll all be rich," said Ka.

"Nothing is as simple as you say—that's what I think. I'm not that simple either, and I don't want to be rich. What I want is to be a writer. I'm writing a science-fiction novel. It might get published—in one of the Kars papers, the one called the *Lance*—but I don't want to be published in a paper that sells seventy-five copies; I want to be published in an Istanbul paper that sells thousands. I have a synopsis of the novel with me. If I read it to you, could you tell me whether you think an Istanbul paper might publish it?"

Ka looked at his watch.

"It's very short!" said Necip.

The electricity went out and all of Kars was plunged into darkness. The only light in the teahouse was coming from the stove. Necip ran over to the counter and grabbed a candle; he lit it and dripped a few drops of wax onto a plate, a seal by which to affix the burning candle to the plate, which he set on the table. Retrieving a few sheets of crumpled paper from his pocket, he began to read in a hesitant voice, stopping from time to time to gulp with excitement.

"In the year 3579, there was a red planet we haven't even discovered yet. Its name was Gazzali and its people were rich, and their lives were much easier than our lives are today, but contrary to what materialists would have predicted, their rich and easy lives did not bring the inhabitants of this planet any spiritual satisfaction. To the contrary, everyone was deeply anxious about being and nothingness, man and the universe, God and his people.

"And so it came to pass that a number of Gazzalians traveled to the most remote corner of their planet to set up the Islamic Lycée for the Study of Science and Oration. It took only the cleverest and most hardworking students.

"Two close friends attended this lycée. Inspired by books written 1600 years earlier, books that illuminated this East–West problem so beautifully they could have been written yesterday, they called each other Necip and Fazıl. Together they read *The Great East,* their revered master's finest book, over and over, and in the evenings they would meet secretly in Fazıl's bed, the higher bunk, where under the covers they would lie side by side watching the blue snowflakes fall onto the glass roof above them and disappear just like planets. Here they would whisper into each other's ears about the meaning of life and the things they hoped to do when they were older.

"The evil-hearted tried in vain to tarnish this pure friendship with snide and jealous jokes. But then one day the two came under a cloud. It so happened that they had simultaneously fallen in love with the same girl, a virgin named Hicran. Even when they discovered that Hicran's father was an atheist, they couldn't cure themselves of their hopeless longing; on the contrary, their love grew all the more intense.

"In this way they came to realize that there was no longer enough room on Gazzali for both of them; they knew in their hearts that one of them would have to die. But they made the following promise. After spending some time in the next world, no matter how many light-years away it was, the one who died would come back to this world to visit his surviving friend and answer his most urgent questions—about life after death.

"As for the question of who would kill whom and how it would be done, they just couldn't make up their minds—mainly because they both knew that true happiness could only come for the one who sacrificed his own life for the other. So, for example, if one of them—let's say it was Fazıl—said, 'Let's both stick our naked hands into the sockets at the same time and electrocute ourselves together,' Necip would see it at once for what it was: a clever trick Fazıl had invented to sacrifice himself for his friend (clearly, Fazıl would have arranged for Necip's socket to be harmless). After many months of hemming and hawing, months that caused both boys great pain, the question was decided in a matter of seconds: Necip returned from his evening lessons one night to discover his dear friend lying dead in his bed, riddled with bullets.

"The following year, Necip married Hicran, and on their wedding night he told her what had passed between him and his friend and how one day Fazıl would return from the spirit world. Hicran told him she had really loved Fazıl; after his death she had cried for days, cried so much that blood had run from her eyes, and she had married Necip only because he was Fazıl's friend and bore him some resemblance. They decided not to consummate their marriage and agreed that the ban on love should continue until Fazıl returned from the other world.

"But as the years passed, they began to long for each other. First their longing was spiritual, and then it became physical. One night, during an interplanetary inspection, while shining their beams on a city on Earth that went by the name of Kars, they were no longer able to control themselves; they fell upon each other like crazy people and made passionate love. You might think this meant they had forgotten Fazıl, whose memory had for so long plagued them like a toothache. But they had not forgotten him, and the shame in their hearts scared them as it grew with every day.

"A night arrived when they awoke suddenly, having both decided at the same time that this strange cocktail of fear and other emotions was going to destroy them. At the same moment, the television across the room turned on by itself, and there, shining brightly, the ghostly form of Fazıl took shape. The deadly shots to the forehead were still fresh, and his lower lip and other wounds were still dripping with blood.

" 'I am racked with pain,' said Fazıl. 'There is not a single corner of the other world I have not seen.' [I will write about these travels in full detail using Gazzali's *Victories of Mecca* and Ibn Arabi as my inspi-rations, said Necip.] 'I have earned the highest compliments of God's angels, and I have traveled to what is thought to be the summit of the highest plain of heaven; I have seen the terrible punishments meted out in hell to tie-wearing atheists and arrogant colonialist posi-tivists who make fun of the common people and their faith—but everywhere happiness eluded me, because my mind was here with you.'

"Husband and wife were overwhelmed with fearful admiration as they listened to the sad ghost.

" 'The thing that made me so unhappy all those years was not the thought that I might one day see you two sitting so happily together, as I am seeing you tonight. On the contrary, I longed for Necip's happiness more than I longed for my own. Because of the profound feeling between us, we had been unable to find any way to kill either ourselves or each other. Because each valued the other's life more than his own, it was as if we were both wearing protec-tive armor that made us immortal. How happy that made me feel! But my death proved to me that I had been wrong to believe in this feeling.'

" 'No!' Necip cried. 'Not once did I give my own life more value than I gave to yours!'

" 'If this had been true, I never would have died,' said Fazıl's ghost, 'and you would never have married the beautiful Hicran. I died because you harbored a secret wish—a wish so secret you even hid it from yourself—to see me dead.'

"Necip objected violently to this accusation, but the ghost refused to listen.

" 'It was not just the suspicion that you wished me dead that deprived me of peace in the other world,' said the ghost. 'It was also that you had a hand in my murder, for it was you who so treacher-ously shot me in the head, and here, and here, as I lay in my bed sleeping. And there was another fear, too—the fear that you acted as an agent for the enemies of the Holy Koran.' By now Necip had given up objecting and fallen silent.

" 'There is only one way for you to deliver me from my suffering and restore me to heaven, and only by following this same path can you deliver yourself from suspicion in this heinous crime,' said the ghost. 'Find my killer, whoever he might be. In seven years and seven months, they haven't found a single suspect. And when you've found whoever killed me or wanted me dead, I want to see the crime avenged. An eye for an eye. So long as that villain remains unpunished, there is no peace for me in this life, nor will there be any peace for you in the transitory realm that you still insist on calling the "real world."'

"Neither Necip nor Hicran could think what to say; they watched in tearful amazement as the ghost vanished from the screen."

"And then what? What happened next?" Ka asked.

"I haven't decided yet," said Necip, "but if I wrote the whole story, do you think I could sell it?" When he saw Ka hesitating, he added, "Listen, every line I write comes from the bottom of my heart. They all express my deepest convictions. What does this story mean to you? What did you feel when I was reading it to you?"

"It shook me to the core, because it showed me that you believe with all your heart that this world is nothing more than a preparation for the next."

"Yes, I do believe that," said Necip with excitement. "It's not enough, though. God wants us to be happy in this world too. But that's the hardest thing."

They fell silent as they pondered the hardest thing.

After a moment the lights came back on, but the people in the teahouse remained as silent as they had been in the darkness. And the television screen was still dark; the owner began to hit it with his fist.

"We've been sitting here together for twenty minutes now," said Necip. "My friends must be dying of curiosity."

"Who are your friends?" asked Ka. "Is one of them Fazıl? And are those your real names?"

"No, of course not. I'm using an assumed name, just like the Necip in the story. You're not a policeman; stop interrogating me! As for Fazıl, he refuses to come to places like this," Necip told him, turning quite mysterious. "Fazıl is the most religious person in our group, and he's the person I trust more than anyone else in the world. But he's worried that if he gets involved in politics, he'll get a police file and be kicked out of school. He has an uncle in Germany who's going to send for him, and we love each other just as much as the two boys in the story, so if someone killed me, I am certain that he would take revenge. In fact, it's just as in the story—we're so close that no matter how far apart we are, we can always tell what the other is doing."

"So what's Fazıl doing right now?"

"Hmmm," said Necip, assuming a strange pose. "He's in the dormitory, reading."

"Who is Hicran?"

"That's not a real name either. But it's not a name she took herself, it's a name we've given her. Some of us write her love letters and poems nonstop, but we're too afraid to send them. If I had a daughter, I'd want her to be as beautiful, as intelligent, and as courageous as she is. She's the leader of the head-scarf girls, and she's afraid of nothing. Her mind is her own.

"To tell you the truth, in the beginning she was an infidel—this was because she was under the influence of her atheist father. She was a model in Istanbul; she'd go on television and bare her bottom and flaunt her legs. She came here to do a shampoo commercial for television. In it she was going to be walking along Ahmet Muhtar the Conqueror Avenue—the meanest, dirtiest street in Kars but also the most beautiful. Then when she stopped in front of the camera, she was to swing her magnificent waist-length brown hair like a flag and say, 'Even in the filth of the beautiful city of Kars, my hair is still sparkling clean—thanks to Blendax.' The commercial was going to be shown everywhere; the whole world would laugh at us.

"At that time, the head-scarf business at the Institute of Education was just getting started, and two of the girls had seen Hicran on television and also recognized her from photographs in gossip magazines that had reported on her behavior with rich kids in Istanbul. Secretly, the girls admired her, so they invited her for tea. Hicran accepted, though for her it was a big joke. She got bored with the girls almost immediately, and do you know what she said? 'If our religion'—no, she didn't say *our* religion, she said *your* religion—'if your religion requires you to hide your hair, and the state forbids you to wear a head scarf, why don't you be like so-and-so'—here she gave the name of a foreign rock star—'and just shave your hair off and wear a nose ring? Then the whole world would stand up and take notice!'

"Our poor girls were so taken aback to hear these affronts that they couldn't even keep from laughing with her! This made Hicran even bolder, so she said, 'These scarves are sending you back to the Middle Ages. Why don't you take them off and flaunt your beautiful hair?'

"And as Hicran was about to remove the scarf from the silliest girl among them, her hand froze. Suddenly, Hicran threw herself at the silly girl's feet—this girl's brother is one of our classmates, and he's so stupid even the morons call him a moron—and begged the girl's pardon. Hicran returned the next day, and the day after that, and in the end she joined them instead of going back to Istanbul. She's one of the saints who'll help turn the head scarf into the flag of Anatolia's oppressed Muslim women—mark my words!"

"Then why did you say nothing about her in your story except that she was a virgin?" asked Ka. "Why didn't Necip and Fazıl ask for her opinion before deciding to kill themselves for her sake?"

There was a tense silence, during which Necip raised his beautiful eyes, one of which, in two hours and three minutes, would be shattered by a bullet; he looked up at the dark street to watch the snow fall slowly, like a poem. Then he whispered, "There she is. It's her!"

"Who?"

"Hicran! She's out there in the street!"

CHAPTER THIRTEEN

———◦◦◦◦———

I'm Not Going to Discuss
My Faith with an Atheist

A WALK THROUGH THE SNOW WITH KADIFE

S he was wearing a purple raincoat, her eyes were hidden behind futuristic dark glasses, and on her head was one of those nondescript head scarves Ka had seen thousands of women wearing since childhood and which were now the symbol of political Islam. When he saw that this young woman entering the teahouse was walking directly toward him, Ka jumped to his feet as though the teacher had just entered the classroom.

"I'm İpek's sister, Kadife," said the woman, smiling faintly. "Everyone's expecting you for dinner. My father sent me to tell you."

"How did you know I was here?" Ka asked.

"In Kars everyone always knows about everything that's going on," said Kadife. She wasn't smiling at all now. "If it's happening in Kars, of course."

Ka could detect some pain in her expression, but he had no idea where it came from. Necip made the introductions: "Meet my poet-novelist friend!" he said. They looked each other over but did not shake hands. Ka took it for a sign of tension. Much later, looking back on these events, he would work out that the omission was out of deference to Islamic convention. Necip turned ghostly white, looking at Kadife as if looking at a Hicran just arrived from outer space, but Kadife's manner was so matter-of-fact that not a single man in the crowded teahouse even turned around to look at her. She wasn't as beautiful as her sister, either.

But as he walked with her through the snow and down Atatürk Avenue, Ka felt very happy. She was wrapped up in a scarf, and though plainer than her sister's her face was pleasant and clean. When he looked right into her eyes, hazel like İpek's, he found he was able to talk to her with great ease; this made her attractive to him, so much so that he felt as if he were betraying her older sister.

First, to Ka's surprise, they discussed meteorology. Kadife knew everything there was to know about the subject; she rattled off the details like one of those old people who do nothing all day but listen to the radio. She told him that the low-pressure front coming down from Siberia was going to last two more days, that if this snow continued the roads would also be closed for another two days, that 160 centimeters had fallen in Sarıkamış, and that the inhabitants of Kars no longer believed the weather reports. In fact, she said, everyone was talking about how the state, not wishing to upset the populace, routinely announced air temperatures five or six degrees higher than they actually were (no one had mentioned this to Ka). She talked about how, as children in Istanbul, she and İpek always wanted the snow to continue. The sight of snow made her think how beautiful and short life is and how, in spite of all their enmities, people have so very much in common; measured against eternity and the greatness of creation, the world in which they lived was narrow. That's why snow drew people together. It was as if snow cast a veil over hatreds, greed, and wrath and made everyone feel close to one another.

They fell silent for a while. All the shops along Şehit Cengiz Topel Street were closed, and they didn't see a soul. This walk with Kadife through the snow brought Ka as much anxiety as happiness. He locked his eyes on the lights in the window of a shop at the very end of the street, as if he was afraid that if he kept turning to look into Kadife's face he would fall in love with her. Was he really in love with her older sister? His desire to fall madly in love had a logic to it, that much he knew. When they reached the end of the street, he stopped to look at the sign in the window of the Joyous Beer Hall, written on a piece of notepaper:

Due to tonight's theatrical event, the honorable Zihni Sevük, candidate for the Free People's Party, has postponed this evening's meeting.

Through the window of the small and narrow Joyous Beer Hall, he could see Sunay Zaim, sitting at the head of a table with his entire troupe; with only twenty minutes to go before the show began, they were all drinking thirstily.

As he perused the campaign posters in the window of the beer hall, his eye fell on the yellow one announcing "HUMAN BEINGS ARE GOD'S MASTERPIECES AND SUICIDE IS BLASPHEMY," and this prompted Ka to ask Kadife what she thought about Teslime's suicide.

"I'm sure you know enough already to turn Teslime into a very interesting story for your friends in Germany—not to mention the Istanbul press," she said, sounding faintly annoyed.

"I'm new to Kars," said Ka. "Even as I come to understand how things work here, I'm beginning to think I'll never be able to make it clear to anyone on the outside. My heart breaks to see these people's fragile livelihoods and their needless suffering."

"The only people who worry about needless suffering are atheists who've never suffered a thing," said Kadife. "Because, after all, it takes only the tiniest discomfort for atheists to decide that they can't bear life without faith anymore, and the next thing you know they've returned to the fold."

"But Teslime's suffering was so great that she left the fold and committed suicide," Ka said. The drink had made him stubborn.

"Well, if Teslime did indeed kill herself, it's possible to say she committed a terrible sin. If you turn to the twenty-ninth line of the Nisa verse of the glorious Koran, you'll see that suicide is clearly prohibited. But the thought that she might have sinned and killed herself is nothing next to the love we feel for her; there is still a corner of our hearts where we remember her with deep love and affection."

"So you mean to say that even if this luckless girl has committed an insult against our faith, we still love her," Ka said, trying to lead Kadife. "We don't believe in God with our whole hearts anymore; we no longer need to, because now, as in the West, we confirm our beliefs by reason and logic. Is this what you're saying?"

"The Holy Koran is the word of God, and when God makes a clear and definite command, it's not a matter for ordinary mortals to question," Kadife said. She sounded very sure of herself. "But do not assume from this that our religion leaves no room for discussion. I will say only that I'm not going to discuss my faith with an atheist, or even a secularist. I beg your pardon."

"You're right."

"And I'm not one of those Islamist toadies who go around trying to convince secularists that Islam can be a secular religion," Kadife added.

"Right again," said Ka.

"That's the second time you've said I'm right," Kadife said, with a smile, "but I don't think you really mean it."

"No, you are right again," said Ka, but he wasn't smiling.

For a time they walked in silence. Could it be that he would fall in love with Kadife and not her sister? Ka knew only too well that he would never feel sexually attracted to a woman in a head scarf, but still he couldn't stop flirting with this secret thought.

As they joined the crowds on Karadağ Avenue, he brought the conversation around to his poetry, and then, in an awkward aside, he mentioned that Necip was also a poet and asked whether she was aware of having quite a few admirers in the religious high school who worshiped her by the name of Hicran.

"By what name?"

Ka told her a few of the other stories he'd heard about Hicran.

"None of those stories are true," said Kadife. "I haven't heard any of the religious high school boys of my acquaintance telling them." She walked a few more steps and then she said, "But I've heard that shampoo story before." She smiled. In fact it wasn't she but rather a rich and much-hated Istanbul journalist who had first suggested to the head-scarf girls that they shave their heads—and this had been said only to attract media attention in the West and make the girls look important. "There's only one thing that's true in these stories. The first time I went to see the head-scarf girls, I did go to make fun of them, but I was also curious. Put it like this: I went out of devilish curiosity."

"And then what happened?"

"I came to Kars because the Institute of Education would take me, and also because my sister was here already. So in the end these girls were my classmates, and if you still don't believe me, go visit them in their homes when they invite you. Their mothers and fathers brought them up to be as they are. So did the religious instruction they received during their state education. Then suddenly, after having been told all their lives to keep their heads covered, these girls were told, 'The state wants you to take your scarves off.'

"As for me, I put on a head scarf one day to make a political statement. I just did it for a laugh, but it also felt frightening. Maybe it was because I remembered I was the daughter of a man who had been an enemy of the state since the beginning of time. I'm very sure I intended to wear it for only one day; it was one of those revolutionary gestures that you laugh about years later, when you're remembering the good old days when you were political. But the state, the police, and the local press came down on me so hard I could scarcely think of it as a joke anymore—I had painted myself into a corner and couldn't get out. They arrested us on the charge of staging a demonstration without a permit. But when they released us the next day, if I had said, 'Forget the scarf; I never really meant it anyway,' the whole of Kars would have spat in my face. Now I've come to see that God put me through all this suffering to help me find the path of truth. Once I was an atheist like you. Don't look at me like that; you look as if you pity me."

"I'm not looking at you like that."

"Yes, you are. I don't think my situation is any funnier than yours. I don't feel superior to you, either—I want you to know that, too."

"What does your father say to all this?"

"So far we're managing. But the way things are going, I'm not sure how much longer we can—and this scares us, because we love each other very much. In the beginning, my father was proud of me; the day I went to school with my head covered, he acted as if I had found a special new form of rebellion. He stood with me in front of my mother's old mirror with the brass frame as I tried the scarf on, and while we were still in front of the mirror, he gave me a kiss. Although we never talked about it much, this much was clear: What I was doing was worthwhile not as a defense of Islam but as a defiance of the state. He made as if to say, My daughter looks just fine like this, but deep down inside he was as scared as I was.

"I knew he was scared when they threw us in jail, and I knew he felt guilty. He insisted that the political police didn't care about me but were still interested in him. In the old days, MİT kept files on leftists and democrats, but now they're most interested in the Islamists; still, you can imagine why he saw it as the same old gun being turned now on his daughter.

"It was even more difficult when I began to take my stance seriously. My father went out of his way to support me at every step, but it was still difficult for him. You know how it is sometimes with old people—no matter how much noise there is in the house, no matter how much the stove clatters, no matter how loudly the wife complains about who knows what, no matter how much the door hinges creak, whatever reaches their ears it's as if they've heard nothing—well, that's my father when it comes to the head-scarf issue. If one of those girls comes to the house, he'll sometimes play the atheist bastard, but before long he's encouraging them to stand up to the state. And because I've seen to it that these girls are mature enough to stand up to him, I have meetings at home. One of them is joining us tonight; her name is Hande.

"After Teslime committed suicide, Hande's parents pressured her to take off her head scarf and she did, but she's not comfortable with the decision. My father says it all reminds him of his old days as a Communist. There are two kinds of Communists: the arrogant ones, who enter the fray hoping to make men out of the people and bring progress to the nation; and the innocent ones, who get involved because they believe in equality and justice. The arrogant ones are obsessed with power; they presume to think for everyone; only bad can come of them. But the innocents? The only harm they do is to themselves. But that's all they ever wanted in the first place. They feel so guilty about the suffering of the poor, and are so keen to share it, that they make their lives miserable on purpose.

"My father was a teacher, but then they took his job away. During one torture session they pulled out one of his fingernails; following another session they threw him into prison. Still, he did what he could. For years he and my mother ran a stationery store; they did photocopying; they even translated a few novels from French into Turkish. At times they would go door-to-door selling encyclopedias on the installment plan. When the poverty was just too much to bear, he'd put his arms around us and cry. He was always so afraid something bad would happen to us. And so when the police came to see us after the director of the Institute of Education was shot, he got very frightened—even though he grumbled at them too. I've heard that you went to see Blue. Please don't tell my father."

"I won't tell him," Ka said. He stopped to brush the snow off his coat. "Aren't we going this way—straight to the hotel?"

"You can go this way too. The snow doesn't end, and neither will the list of things we have to discuss. Besides, I'd like to show you Butcher Street. . . . What did Blue want from you?"

"Nothing."

"Did he say anything about us—my father or my sister?"

Ka saw an anxious expression on Kadife's face. "I can't remember," he said.

"Everyone's afraid of him. We are too. . . . These are the most famous butcher shops in the city."

"How does your father spend his days?" Ka asked. "Does he ever leave the house—the hotel?"

"He's the one who manages the hotel. He gives the orders to the housekeeper, the cleaner, the laundrywoman, and the busboys. My sister and I help out. But my father almost never goes out. What's your sign?"

"Gemini," said Ka. "Geminis are supposed to tell lots of lies, but I'm not so sure."

"Are you saying that you're not sure whether Geminis tell lies, or you're not sure whether *you* do?"

"If you believe in astrology, you must be able to figure out why today is such a special day for me."

"Yes, my sister told me; today you wrote a poem."

"Does your sister tell you everything?"

"We have two diversions here. We talk about everything that happens to us, and we watch television. We even talk while watching television. And while we're talking, we watch television too. My sister is very beautiful, don't you think?"

"Yes, she's very beautiful," said Ka, with reverence. "But you're also beautiful," he added politely. "And now are you going to tell her that too?"

"No, I'm not going to tell her. Let's have one secret we can share. It's the best way to begin a friendship." And she brushed off the snow that had piled up on her long purple raincoat.

CHAPTER FOURTEEN

How Do You Write Poems?

THE DINNER CONVERSATION TURNS TO
LOVE, HEAD SCARVES, AND SUICIDE

They saw a crowd milling in front of the National Theater; in just a few minutes, the show would begin. The relentless snowfall seemed to have deterred no one, or perhaps the snow itself had made people decide that, with so much going wrong, they might as well seize this one chance for an enjoyable evening out. Many of those gathered on the pavement in front of the 110-year-old building came from the ranks of the unemployed; there were youths who had left their homes and dormitories in shirt and tie, and youngsters who had sneaked out of the house. Many had brought their children. For the first time since arriving in Kars, Ka saw an open black umbrella. Kadife knew Ka was on the program and scheduled to recite a poem, but when Ka said he had no intention of taking part and had no time for it anyway, she made no attempt to persuade him.

He could feel another poem coming. He stopped talking and rushed back to the hotel as fast as he could. He excused himself, saying that he needed to nip back to his room to collect himself; no sooner had he opened the door than he threw off his coat, sat down at the small table, and began scribbling furiously. The poem's main themes were friendship and secrecy. Snowflakes and stars were also featured, as were a number of motifs that suggested special happy days.

A number of Kadife's remarks went straight into the poem without alteration; as one line followed another, Ka surveyed the page with the pleasure and excitement of a painter watching a picture appear on his easel. He could see now that his conversation with Kadife had a hidden logic; in this poem, entitled "Stars and Their Friends," he elaborated on the theory that every person has a star, every star has a friend, and for every person carrying a star there is someone else who reflects it, and everyone carries this reflection like a secret confidante in the heart. Although he could hear the poem's music in his head and exalted in its perfection, he had to skip a word that eluded him here and there; there were a few lines missing too. He would later say that this was because of his preoccupation with İpek, his not having had his dinner yet, and his being happier than ever before.

As soon as he finished the poem, he rushed down to the lobby and into the owners' private quarters. Sitting at a bountifully set table in the middle of a spacious room with high ceilings, flanked on either side by his daughters, Kadife and İpek, was Turgut Bey. There was a third girl as well, sitting to one side; she wore a stylish purple head scarf, and Ka knew at once she must be Kadife's friend Hande. Across from her was Serdar Bey, the newspaperman; he seemed at home in this group. As Ka surveyed all the dishes on the table—what a strange and beautiful disorder— and watched the Kurdish maid, Zahide, gracefully darting in and out of the back kitchen, he imagined that Turgut Bey and his daughters were accustomed to spending long evenings at this table.

"I've been thinking about you all day, and all day I've been worrying about you," said Turgut Bey. "Why are you so late?" He rose to his feet and leaned over to wrap his arms around Ka in such a way that Ka thought the man was about to cry. "Terrible things can happen at any time," he said, with a tragic air.

He sat down in the place Turgut Bey indicated, right across from him, at the other end of the table; the maid served Ka a bowl of lentil soup, which he devoured hungrily. The two other men returned to their raki, their eyes drifting toward the television right behind him; when Ka saw that everyone else had done the same, he did something he'd been dreaming of for a long time: He stared at İpek's beautiful face.

Because he would later describe his boundless ecstasy quite vividly in his notes, I know exactly how he felt at that moment—like a happy child, he couldn't keep his arms or legs still. He could not have been more jittery and impatient if he and İpek were rushing to catch the train that would take them back to Frankfurt. He looked at Turgut Bey's worktable—piled high with books, newspapers, receipts, hotel record books—and as he gazed at the circle cast by the lamp below its shade, he conjured up the vision of another circle of light, one on his own worktable, in the little office he would share with İpek when they returned to live happily ever after in Frankfurt.

Just then he saw that Kadife's eyes were on him. Meeting her gaze, Ka thought he saw a flash of jealousy cross her face, which was not as beautiful as her sister's, but she managed to conceal it with a conspiratorial smile.

His dinner companions remained mesmerized by the television set; even in the thick of conversation, they kept glancing at it out of the corners of their eyes. The live telecast from the National Theater had begun; the tall thin emcee swaying this way and that on the stage was one of the actors Ka had seen while getting off the bus the previous evening. They had not been watching him long when Turgut Bey picked up the remote control and changed the channel. For a long time they sat staring at a fuzzy picture flecked with white dots; they had no idea what they were watching, but it seemed to be in black-and-white.

"Father," said İpek, "what are you watching?"

"It's snow," said her father. "If nothing else, it is an accurate description of our weather here. This counts as real news. Anyway, you know that if I watch one channel for too long, I feel robbed of my dignity."

"Then, Father, why don't you just turn the television off? Something else is going on here that's robbing us all of our dignity."

"Well, tell our guest what's happened," said her father, looking rather shamefaced. "It makes me uneasy that he doesn't know."

"That's how I feel too," said Hande. There was anger in her beautiful black eyes. For a moment everyone fell silent.

"Why don't you tell the story, Hande?" said Kadife. "There's nothing to be ashamed of."

"No, that's not true. There's a great deal to be ashamed of, and that's why I want to talk about it," Hande said. Her large eyes flashed with a strange joy. She smiled as if recalling a happy memory and said, "It's forty days exactly since our friend Teslime's suicide. Of all the girls in our group, Teslime was the one most dedicated to the struggle for her religion and the word of God. For her, the head scarf did not just stand for God's love, it also proclaimed her faith and preserved her honor. None of us could have ever imagined she would kill herself. Despite pressure both at school and at home to take off her scarf—her father and her teachers were relentless—Teslime held her ground. She was about to be expelled from school in her third year of study, just on the verge on graduating. Then one day her father had some visitors from police headquarters; they told him that if he didn't send his daughter to school scarfless, they would close down his grocery store and run him out of Kars.

"The father threatened to throw Teslime out of the house, and when this tactic failed he entered into negotiations to marry her off to a forty-five-year-old policeman who had lost his wife. Things had gone so far that the policeman was coming to the store with flowers. So revolted was Teslime by this gray-eyed widower, she told us, she was thinking of taking off her head scarf if it would save her from this marriage, but she just couldn't bring herself to do it.

"Some of us agreed that she should uncover her head to avoid marrying the gray-eyed widower, and some of us said, 'Why don't you threaten your father with suicide?' I was the one who urged this most strongly. I really didn't want Teslime to give up her head scarf. I don't know how many times I said, 'Teslime, it's far better to kill yourself than to uncover your head.' But I was just saying it for the sake of conversation. We believed what the papers said—that the suicide girls had killed themselves because they had no faith, because they were slaves to materialism, because they had been unlucky in love; all I was trying to do was give Teslime's father a fright. Teslime was a devout girl, so I assumed she would never seriously consider suicide. But when we heard she had hanged herself, I was the first to believe it. And what's more, I knew that, had I been in her shoes, I would have done the same thing."

Hande began to cry. İpek went to her side, gave her a kiss, and began to caress her; Kadife joined them. With the girls wrapped in each other's arms, Turgut Bey was waving the remote control and soon also trying to comfort Hande. Before long they were all telling jokes to keep her from crying. As though trying to distract a weeping child, Turgut Bey pointed out the giraffes on the screen; then, like a child not yet certain she's ready to relent, Hande gazed at the screen with tearful eyes. For a long while, the girls forgot their own lives as they watched two giraffes in slow motion, in a faraway land, perhaps in the middle of Africa, in a field shaded by a heavy growth of trees.

"After Teslime's suicide, Hande decided to take off her head scarf and go back to school; she didn't want to cause her parents any more distress," Kadife explained. "They'd made so many sacrifices, gone without so much, to give her the right sort of upbringing; the things most parents do for an only son, they did for her. Her parents have always assumed that Hande would be able to support them one day, because Hande is very clever."

She was speaking in a soft voice, almost whispering, but still loud enough for Hande to hear her, and like everyone else in the room, Hande was listening, even with her tear-filled eyes still fixed to the television screen.

"At first the rest of us tried to talk her out of removing her scarf, but when we realized that her going uncovered was better than her committing suicide, we supported her decision. When a girl has accepted the head scarf as the word of God and the symbol of faith, it's very difficult for her to take it off. Hande spent days locked up inside her house trying to concentrate."

Like everyone else in the room, Ka was cowering with embarrassment by now, but when his arm brushed against İpek's arm a wave of happiness spread through him. As Turgut Bey jumped from channel to channel, Ka tried to find more happiness by brushing his arm against İpek's arm. When İpek did the same, he forgot all about the sad story he'd just heard.

Once again, the television was tuned to the National Theater. The tall thin man was saying how proud he was to be taking part in Kars's first live telecast and announced the program for the evening, promising miraculous renditions of the world's greatest legends; secret confessions of a national goalkeeper; shocking revelations that would bring shame to our political history; unforgettable scenes from Shakespeare and Victor Hugo; amorous disasters; the greatest, most glittering stars of Turkish film and theater; as well as jokes, songs, and earth-shaking surprises. Ka heard himself described as "our greatest poet, who has returned to our country in silence after many years." Reaching under the table, İpek took Ka's hand.

"I understand that you don't want to take part in the performance," said Turgut Bey.

"I'm very happy where I am, sir, very happy indeed," said Ka, pressing his arm against İpek's even harder.

"I really wouldn't want to do anything to disrupt your happiness," said Hande, setting everyone in the room on edge, "but I came here tonight to meet you. I haven't read any of your books, but it's enough for me that you're a poet and have been to places like Germany. Do you mind if I ask whether you've written any poems lately?"

"Quite a few poems have come to me since I arrived in Kars," said Ka.

"I wanted to meet you because I thought you could tell me how I might go about concentrating. Do you mind if I ask a question? How do you write poems? Isn't it by concentrating?"

Whenever he gave readings for Turks in Germany, this was the most common question from women in the audience, but every time they asked, Ka recoiled as if he'd been asked something personal. "I have no idea how poems get written," he said now. "A good poem always seems to come from outside, from far away." He saw Hande's eyes filling with suspicion, and added, "Why don't you explain to me what you mean when you use the word *concentrate*?"

"I try all day, but I can't conjure up the vision I want to see, the vision of myself without a head scarf. Instead, I keep seeing all the things I want to forget."

"For example?"

"When they first noticed how many of us were wearing head scarves, they sent a woman from Ankara to try to talk us out of it. This 'agent of persuasion' sat in the same room for hours on end, talking to each of us alone. She asked things like, 'Did your parents beat you? How many children are there in your family? How much does your father earn in a month? What sort of clothes did you wear before you adopted religious dress? Do you love Atatürk? What sort of pictures do you have hanging on the walls at home? How many times a week do you go to the movies? In your view, are men and women equals? Is God greater than the state, or is the state greater than God? How many children do you want to have? Have you ever suffered from abuse in the home?' She asked us hundreds of questions like this, and she wrote down all our answers, filling out a long form for each of us.

"She was a very stylish woman—painted nails, dyed hair, no head scarf, of course—and she wore the sort of clothes you see in magazines, but at the same time she was—how should I put this?—plain. Even though some of her questions made us cry, we liked her. We even hoped that the muddy streets of Kars weren't causing her too much trouble. Afterward I began to see her in my dreams. At first I didn't read too much into it, but now, whenever I try to imagine myself walking through crowds with my hair flying all around me, I see myself as the 'agent of persuasion.' In my mind's eye I'm as stylish as she is, wearing stiletto heels and dresses even shorter than hers, and men are looking at me with interest. I find this pleasing—and at the same time very shaming."

"Hande, you don't have to describe your shame unless you want to," said Kadife.

"No, I'm going to talk about it. Even though I feel shame in my dreams, that doesn't mean I'm ashamed *of* my dreams. Even if I did take off my head scarf, I don't think I'd become the kind of woman who flirts with men or who can't think of anything but sex. After all, when I do take off my head scarf, I won't be doing it of my own free will. Still, I know people can be overcome by sexual feelings even when they do something like this without conviction, without even wanting it. There's one thing all men and women have in common. We all sin in our dreams with people who wouldn't remotely interest us in our waking lives. Isn't that true?"

"That's enough, Hande," said Kadife.

"But isn't it?"

"No, it isn't," said Kadife. She turned to Ka. "Two years before all this happened, Hande was engaged to a very handsome Kurdish teenager. But the poor boy got mixed up in politics and they killed him—"

"That has nothing to do with my reluctance to bare my head," Hande said angrily. "The true reason is that I can't concentrate, I can't imagine myself without a head scarf. Whenever I try to concentrate, either I turn into an evil stranger like the 'agent of persuasion' or I turn into a woman who can't stop thinking about sex. If I could close my eyes just once and imagine myself going bareheaded through the doors into school, walking down the corridor, and going into class, I'd find the strength to go through with this, and then, God willing, I'd be free. I would have removed the head scarf of my own free will, and not because the police have forced me. But for now I just can't concentrate, I just can't bring myself to imagine that moment."

"Then stop making so much of that moment," said Kadife. "Even if you collapse then and there, you'll still be our beloved Hande."

"No, I won't," said Hande. "That's what's caused me the most anguish since I left you and decided to bare my head—knowing that you despise me." She turned to Ka. "Sometimes I can conjure up a girl walking into school with her hair flying all around her, I can see her walking down the hall and entering my favorite classroom—oh, how I miss that classroom!—I can even imagine the smell of the hallway and the clamminess of the air. Then I look through the pane of glass that separates the classroom from the hallway and I see that this girl is not me but someone else, and I start to cry."

Everyone thought Hande was about to start crying again.

"I'm not all that afraid of becoming someone else," said Hande. "What scares me is the thought of never being able to return to the person I am now—and even forgetting who that person is. That's what makes people commit suicide." She turned to Ka. "Have you ever wanted to commit suicide?" Her tone was flirtatious.

"No, but after hearing about the women of Kars, one can't help asking oneself difficult questions."

"If a lot of girls in our situation are thinking about suicide, you could say it has to do with wanting to control our own bodies. That's what suicide offers girls who've been duped into giving up their virginity, and it's the same for virgins who are married off to men they don't want. For girls like that, a suicide wish is a wish for innocence and purity. Have you written any poems about suicide?" She instinctively turned to İpek. "Have I gone too far now; am I really bothering your friend? All right, then. If he would just tell me where they've come *from,* these poems that have come to him in Kars, I promise to leave him alone."

"When I sense a poem coming to me, my heart is full of gratitude to the sender because I feel so very happy."

"Is that the same person who breathes the soul into your poetry? Who is that person?"

"I can't be sure, but I think it is God who is sending me the poems."

"Is it that you can't be sure of God, or simply that you can't be sure it's God who is sending them?"

"It's God who sends me poems," Ka said fervently.

"He's seen the rise of political Islam," said Turgut Bey. "Maybe they've even threatened him, scared him into becoming a believer."

"No, it comes from inside," said Ka. "I want to join in and be just like everyone else."

"I'm sorry. You're afraid, and I am reprimanding you."

"Yes, of course I'm scared," Ka said, raising his voice. "I'm very scared."

Ka suddenly jumped to his feet, as if someone were pointing a gun at him—or so it seemed to everyone else at the table. "Where is he?" cried Turgut Bey, as if he too sensed there was someone about to shoot them.

"I'm not afraid," said Hande. "I couldn't care less what happens to me."

Like everyone else, she was looking at Ka and trying to figure out where the danger was. Years later, Serdar Bey told me that Ka's face turned ashen at this point, but there was nothing in his expression to suggest fear or dizziness; what Serdar Bey recalled seeing in his face was sublime joy. The maid went further and told me that a light had entered the room and bathed all those present with divine radiance. In her eyes, he achieved sainthood. Apparently someone then said, "A poem has arrived," an announcement that caused more fear and amazement than the imaginary gun.

According to the more measured account in Ka's notes, the tense, expectant air in the room brought back memories of the séances we had witnessed as children a quarter century ago in a house in one of the back streets of Nişantaş. These evenings had been organized by the fat mother of a friend; she'd been widowed at an early age; most of her guests were unhappy housewives, but there was also a pianist with paralyzed fingers, a neurotic middle-aged film star (but only because we kept asking for her), her forever-yawning sister, a retired pasha who was "wooing" the fading star, and also, when our friend could sneak us in, Ka and myself. During the uneasy waiting period, someone would say, "Oh, soul, if you've come back to us, speak!" and after a long silence there would be an almost imperceptible rattling, the scraping of a chair, a moan, and sometimes the sound of someone giving a swift kick to a leg of the table, whereupon someone would announce in a trembling voice, "The soul has arrived." But as he headed for the kitchen, Ka was not at all like a man who'd made contact with the dead. His face was radiating joy.

"He's had a lot to drink," said Turgut Bey, and then, to İpek, who was already running after Ka, "Yes, go and help him, daughter."

Ka hurled himself onto a chair next to the kitchen. He took out his notebook and his pen. "I can't write with you all standing about watching me," he said.

"Let me take you to another room," said İpek.

Ka followed İpek through the kitchen, which was full of the sweet smell of the syrup Zahide was pouring over the bread pudding; they passed through a cold room into another room half in darkness.

"Do you think you can write here?" İpek asked, as she turned on a lamp.

Around him Ka saw a tidy room with two perfectly made beds. There was a low table and a nightstand on which the sisters had arranged various tubes of cream, lipsticks, small bottles of cologne, books, a zippered pouch, and a modest collection of other substances in bottles that had once held alcohol and cooking oil. An old Swiss chocolate box lay open on the table, filled with brushes, pens, charms against the evil eye, necklaces, and bracelets.

Ka sat on the bed, beside the frozen windowpane. "I can write here," he said. "But don't leave me alone."

"Why not?"

"I don't know," he said. Then he added, "I'm worried."

He set to work on the poem, which began with a description of another chocolate box, one his uncle had brought from Switzerland when Ka was a child. The box was decorated with the same Swiss landscapes he'd been seeing all day in the teahouses of Kars. According to notes Ka would make later on, when he went back to interpret, classify, and organize the poems from Kars, the first thing to emerge from İpek's box was a toy clock; two days later he would discover that İpek had played with this clock as a child. And Ka would use this clock to travel back in time and say a few things about childhood and life itself. . . .

"I don't want you ever to leave me," Ka told İpek. "I've fallen wildly in love with you."

"But you hardly know me," said İpek.

"There are two kinds of men," said Ka, in a didactic voice. "The first kind does not fall in love until he's seen how the girl eats a sandwich, how she combs her hair, what sort of nonsense she cares about, why she's angry at her father, and what sorts of stories people tell about her. The second type of man—and I am in this category—can fall in love with a woman only if he knows next to nothing about her."

"In other words, you've fallen in love with me because you know nothing about me? Do you really think you can call this love?"

"If you fall head over heels, that's how it happens," said Ka.

"So once you know how I eat a sandwich and what I wear in my hair, you'll fall right out of love."

"No, by then the intimacy that's built up between us will deepen and turn into a desire that wraps itself around our bodies, and we'll be bound together by our happy memories."

"Don't get up; sit there on the bed," said İpek. "I can't kiss anyone when my father is under the same roof." She did not reject his first kisses but then she pushed him away. "When my father is in the house, I don't like this."

Ka tried to plant one more kiss on her lips before sitting back down on the edge of the bed. "We're going to have to get married and run away from this place as soon as it's humanly possible. Do you know how happy we could be in Frankfurt?"

There was a silence. Then: "How can you fall in love with me without even knowing me?"

"Because you're so beautiful . . . because I've already seen in my dreams how happy we will be together . . . because I can tell you anything without the slightest bit of shame. In my dreams I can never stop imagining us making love."

"What did you do while you were in Frankfurt?"

"I'd think a lot about the poems I wasn't able to write . . . I masturbated. . . . Solitude is essentially a matter of pride; you bury yourself in your own scent. The issue is the same for all real poets. If you've been happy too long, you become banal. By the same token, if you've been unhappy for a long time, you lose your poetic powers. . . . Happiness and poetry can only coexist for the briefest time. Afterward either happiness coarsens the poet or the poem is so true it destroys his happiness. I'm terribly afraid of the unhappiness that could be waiting for me in Frankfurt."

"Then stay in Istanbul," said İpek.

Ka looked at her carefully. "Is Istanbul where you want to live?" he asked in a whisper. His greatest wish just then was for İpek to ask something from him.

İpek sensed this too. "I don't want anything," she said.

Ka knew he was pushing her. Something told him he wasn't going to be in Kars for very long—that before long he would be unable to breathe here—so he had to push as if his life depended on it. For a few moments they listened to snatches of a distant conversation; then a horse and carriage passed under the window and they listened to the wheels rolling over the snow. İpek was standing in the doorway, slowly and meticulously removing the hair from the brush in her hand.

"Life here is so poor and hopeless that people, even people like you, forget what it's like to want something," said Ka. "One cannot think of life here, only death. . . . Are you coming with me?" İpek didn't answer. "If you're going to give me a negative answer, don't answer me at all," Ka said.

"I don't know," said İpek, her eyes on the brush. "They're waiting for us in the other room."

"There's some sort of intrigue going on in there, but I have no idea what it's about," said Ka. "Why don't you explain it to me?"

The lights went off. When İpek didn't move, Ka wanted to embrace her, but he was so wrapped up in fearful thoughts about returning to Frankfurt alone that he didn't move either.

"You're not going to be able to write a poem in this pitch darkness," said İpek. "Let's go."

"What is the thing you want most from me? What can I do to make you love me?"

"Be yourself," said İpek. She stood up and headed for the door.

Ka had been so happy sitting on the edge of the bed that it took a great effort to stand up. He sat down again in the cold room next to the kitchen, and in the flickering candlelight he recorded the poem entitled "The Chocolate Box" in his green notebook.

When he rose again, he found İpek just in front of him; he rushed forward to embrace her and bury himself in her hair, but his thoughts got in the way; it was almost as if they too were stumbling in the dark.

There, glowing in the candlelight from the kitchen, were İpek and Kadife. With their arms around each other's necks, they were embracing like lovers.

"Father sent me to find you," said Kadife.

"That's fine, dear."

"Wasn't he able to write his poem?"

"I did write it," said Ka, coming out of the shadows. "But now I was hoping to help you."

He went into the kitchen; in the light of the candle, he saw no one. He quickly filled a glass with raki and drank it neat. When the tears began to stream down his face, he poured himself a glass of water.

When he left the kitchen, he found himself plunged into a menacing darkness. Then he saw a distant candle on the dinner table and headed toward it. The people sitting there turned to look at Ka and the gigantic shadow he cast on the wall.

"Were you able to write your poem?" asked Turgut Bey. He prefaced the question with a few moments of silence, as if to convey a slight air of mockery.

"Yes."

"Congratulations." He pressed a raki glass into Ka's hand and began to fill it. "What's it about?"

"Everyone I've interviewed since coming here, everyone I've talked to. I agree with them all. The fear I used to feel in Frankfurt when I was walking in the street, that fear is now inside me."

"I understand you perfectly," said Hande, with a very knowing air.

Ka smiled gratefully. Don't bare your head, my little beauty, he wanted to say.

"If, when you say you believe everyone you've heard here," said Turgut Bey, "you mean to tell me that you believed in God while you were in the company of Sheikh Efendi, then let me make one thing clear. Sheikh Efendi does not speak for the God we worship in Kars!"

"So who does speak for God here?" Hande asked.

Turgut Bey didn't get angry at her. Stubborn and quarrelsome though he was, he was too softhearted to be an implacable atheist. Ka also sensed that much as Turget Bey worried about his daughters' unhappiness, he worried even more that his habits and his world might disintegrate. This wasn't a political anxiety but the anxiety of a man who more than anything feared losing his place at the table, whose only pleasure was spending his evenings with his daughters and his guests, arguing for hours about politics and the existence or nonexistence of God.

The electricity came back on, and suddenly the room was bright. They were so accustomed by now to the random coming and going of the lights that no one bothered anymore with the rituals of power outage Ka remembered from his Istanbul childhood—no one cheered when the lights returned or asked whether the washing machine might be stuck in the middle of a cycle; there was none of the joy he had once felt in saying, "Let me be the one to blow out the candles"—instead, everyone simply acted as though nothing had happened. Turgut Bey turned the television back on and, having taken possession of the remote control, began to surf the channels. Ka whispered to the girls that Kars was an extraordinarily quiet city.

"That's because we're afraid of our own voices," said Hande.

"That," said İpek, "is the silence of snow."

Feeling defeated, they stared grimly at the ever-changing television screen. As he held hands with İpek under the table, it occurred to Ka that if he spent his days doing nothing much at all, and his evenings holding hands with İpek and watching satellite television, he would live in bliss until the end of his life.

CHAPTER FIFTEEN

There's One Thing We All Want out of Life

AT THE NATIONAL THEATER

Exactly seven minutes after deciding that he and İpek could live happily ever after in Kars, Ka was racing through the snow to the National Theater, his heart pounding as if he were heading alone into a war zone. Everything had changed during that seven-minute interval, with a speed possessed of its own logic.

It had begun when Turgut Bey switched back to the broadcast of the performance at the National Theater, where it was clear from the roar of the audience that something extraordinary had just happened. Although this awakened in them a longing for excitement, a desire to step outside their little provincial routines if only for one night, it also made them anxious that something might be very wrong. With the camera showing only part of the hall, they were all very curious to know what was going on. As they watched the restless audience clap and shout, they sensed a certain tension between the notables sitting in the front rows and the youths sitting at the back.

Onstage was a goalkeeper who had once been a household name all over Turkey, talking about a tragic match fifteen years earlier in which the English had managed to score eleven goals. He had barely finished the sad tale of the first goal when the emcee appeared on-screen; realizing that they were pausing for a commercial break, just as they did on national television, the goalkeeper stopped speaking. The emcee grabbed the microphone and after rattling off two advertisements (the Tadal Grocery Store on Fevzi Paşa Avenue was proud to announce that the spiced beef from Kayseri had finally arrived, and the Knowledge Study Center had opened registration for their university preparation course), he reminded the audience of the delights still to come; when he announced Ka's name again he looked mournfully into the camera.

"Missing this chance to see our great poet, who traveled all the way from Frankfurt to visit our border city, is a great sadness."

"Well, that does it," said Turgut Bey at once. "If you don't go now, you'll give terrible offense."

"But they never even asked me if I'd like to take part," said Ka.

"That's the way things are done here," said Turgut Bey. "If they'd invited you, you'd have declined. But now you *will* go, because you don't want it to seem as if you look down on them."

"We'll watch you from here," said Hande, with an enthusiasm that no one could have predicted.

At that moment, the door opened. It was the boy who was the night receptionist. "The director of the Institute of Education has just died in hospital."

"Poor fool," said Turgut Bey. Then he fixed his eyes on Ka. "The Islamists have embarked on a cleanup operation. They're taking care of us one by one. If you want to save your skin, I would advise you to increase your faith in God at the earliest opportunity. It won't be long, I fear, before a moderate belief in God will be insufficient to save the skin of an old atheist."

"I think you're right," said Ka. "As it happens, I've already decided to answer the call that's been coming from deep within me my whole long life and open my heart to God."

They all caught his sarcastic tone—for what it was worth. Knowing he was very drunk, they all suspected that this witticism might well have been prepared in advance.

Then Zahide breezed in with a huge pot and an aluminum ladle that glistened in the lamplight. Smiling at the table like a proud mother, she said, "One more portion of soup left; let's not waste it. Which girl would like it?"

İpek had been advising Ka not to go to the National Theater for fear of what might happen there, but now she turned around to smile with Kadife and Hande at the Kurdish maid.

If İpek says, "I do!" thought Ka, it means we're getting married and going back together to Frankfurt. In that case, I'll go to the National Theater and read "Snow."

"I do!" said İpek, holding out her bowl somewhat joylessly.

As he hurried through the giant snowflakes, Ka remembered that he was an outsider in Kars, and for a moment he felt sure he'd forget this city just as soon as he left it—but the feeling didn't last long. Now suddenly he had intimations of destiny. He could see that life had a secret geometry on which his rational mind had no purchase, but even as he was over-come with a desire to subdue his reason and find happiness, he also sensed that—for the moment, at least—his desire for happiness was not strong enough.

He looked ahead, at the line of waving campaign banners stretching as far as the National Theater: there wasn't a soul beneath them anywhere on the wide snow-covered avenue. As he gazed at the grand old buildings on either side, admiring their handsome doors, their generously propor-tioned eaves, their beautiful friezes, and their dignified but timeworn facades, Ka had a strong sense of the people (Armenians who traded in Tiflis? Ottoman pashas who collected taxes from the dairies?) who had once led happy, peaceful, and even colorful lives here. Gone now were all the Armenians, Russians, Ottomans, and early Republican Turks who had made this city a modest center of civilization, and since no one had come to replace them the streets were deserted. But unlike those in most deserted cities, these empty streets did not inspire fear. Ka marveled at the snow-laden branches of the oleanders and the plane trees, at the ici-cles hanging down from the sides of the electric poles feeding the pale orange light of the streetlamps, and the dying neon bulbs behind the icy shop windows. The snow was falling into a magical, almost holy silence, and aside from his own almost silent footsteps and rapid breathing, Ka could hear nothing. Not a single dog was barking. He had arrived at the end of the earth; the whole world was apparently mesmerized by the falling snow. As he watched the snowflakes fall through the halo of light, he saw how some fell heavily earthward while others wheeled around to fly back up into the darkness.

Standing under the eaves of the Palace of Light Photo Studio, with the help of the red light from its ice-covered signboard, he studied a snowflake that had landed on the sleeve of his coat.

There was a gust of wind. Something moved; as the red light on the

sign hanging over the Palace of Light Photo Studio went out, the oleander tree opposite seemed to go out with it. He looked toward the
National Theater and saw crowds around the entrance; just beyond them
he could see a police minibus. There were more crowds gathering outside
the coffeehouses across the road.

The moment he stepped into the theater, the wave of noise and
motion coming from the audience overwhelmed him. The air was thick
with alcohol fumes, cigarette smoke, and exhaled breath. They were
standing shoulder to shoulder in the aisles; in one corner was a tea stand
selling sodas and sesame rolls. From the door to the toilets came the
whiff of something like a corpse; Ka spotted a group of whispering
youths. On one side he saw uniformed policemen in blue, and farther
ahead he passed a few in plainclothes listening to their police radios. Holding her father's hand, a child studied the dried chickpeas she'd dropped
into his soda bottle, totally oblivious to the noise behind her.

Someone was waving vigorously from the side aisle, but Ka was not
sure whether this person was waving at him.

"I recognized you from all the way over there—just by your coat!"

When he saw Necip's face emerge from the crowd, Ka felt his heart
leap. They embraced warmly.

"I knew you would come," said Necip. "I'm so glad to see you. Do
you mind if I ask you one thing right now? I have two very important
things on my mind."

"So do you want to ask me one thing or two things?"

"You're very intelligent, so intelligent you know that intelligence is
not everything," said Necip. He took Ka over to a corner where it was
calmer. "Did you tell Hicran—Kadife—that I was in love with her, and
that she was my whole life?"

"No, I didn't."

"You left the teahouse with her. Didn't you mention me at all?"

"I said you were a student at the religious high school."

"And then what? Didn't she say anything?"

"No, she didn't."

There was a pause.

"I know the real reason why you didn't mention me again," said
Necip, with some effort. He gulped. "Kadife is four years older than me,
so she probably hasn't even noticed me. Maybe you discussed private
matters with her. Maybe even secret political matters. I'm not asking you
to tell me one way or the other. I'm concerned about one thing only and

this thing is extremely important for me. The answer you give will affect the rest of my life. Even if Kadife hasn't yet noticed me—and it might take her years, and by then she could be married—your answer now could lead me to spend the rest of my life loving her or it could lead me to forget her from this moment on. So please, without hesitation, give me your answer now."

"I'm still waiting for your question," said Ka, sounding rather official.

"Did you talk about superficial things at all? Things like the nonsense on television, or little meaningless bits of gossip, or the little things money can buy? Do you know what I mean? Is Kadife the sort of serious person who has no time for such superficialities, or have I fallen in love with her for nothing?"

"No, we didn't talk about anything superficial," said Ka.

He could see that his answer was devastating; in the teenager's face he could see evidence of a superhuman effort to recover his strength.

"But you did decide that she is an extraordinary person."

"Yes."

"Could you yourself fall in love with her? She is very beautiful, after all. She's beautiful and she's independent—more than any other Turkish woman I've ever seen."

"Her sister's even more beautiful," said Ka, "if beauty's what we're talking about."

"What are we really talking about, then?" asked Necip. "What does God in his wisdom intend by making me think so much about Kadife?"

With a childishness that amazed Ka, he opened his large green eyes, one of which would be shattered in fifty-one minutes.

"I don't know," said Ka.

"Yes, you do, you're just not telling me."

"I don't know."

"Oh, a writer should be able to talk about everything that's important," said Necip, in a nudging voice. "If I were a writer, I'd want to talk about everything that people didn't talk about. Can't you tell me everything, just this once?"

"So ask."

"There's one thing we all want out of life, one main thing, isn't there?"

"That's right."

"So what is it, would you say?"

Ka smiled and said nothing.

"For me, it's very simple," Necip said with pride. "I want to marry

Kadife, live in Istanbul, and become the world's first Islamist science-fiction writer. I know none of these things are possible, but I still want them. If you can't tell me what you want, it's OK, because I understand you. You are my future. And my instinct also tells me this: When you look at me, you see your own youth, and that's why you like me."

A happy, cunning smile began to take shape on his lips, which made Ka uneasy. "So are you supposed to be like the person I was twenty years ago?" he asked.

"Yes. There's going to be a scene exactly like this in the science-fiction novel I'm going to write one day. Excuse me, may I put my hand on your forehead?" Ka tilted his head slightly forward. With the ease of a well-practiced gesture, Necip put his palm on Ka's forehead.

"Now I'm going to tell you what you were thinking twenty years ago."

"Is this what you were doing with Fazıl?"

"We think the same thing at the same time. But with you and me, there's a time difference. Now listen to me, please: On a winter day, when you were a lycée student, it was snowing, and you were lost in thought. You could hear God inside you, and you were trying to forget him. You could see that the world was one, but you thought that if you could close your eyes to this vision, you could be more unhappy and also more intelligent. And you were right. Only people who are very intelligent and very unhappy can write good poems. So you heroically undertook to endure the pains of faithlessness, just to be able to write good poems. But you didn't realize then that when you lost that voice inside you, you'd end up all alone in an empty universe."

"All right. You're right, I was thinking this," said Ka. "So tell me, Is this what you're thinking right now?"

"I knew you were going to ask me this," said Necip in an uneasy voice. "Don't you want to believe in God? You do, don't you?" His hand was so cold it was making Ka shiver, but now Necip took it off Ka's forehead. "I could tell you a lot more about this. There's another voice inside me that tells me, 'Don't believe in God.' Because when you devote so much of your heart to believing something exists, you can't help having a little suspicion, a little voice that asks, 'What if it doesn't?' You understand, don't you? Just at those times when I realized my belief in my beautiful God sustained me, I would sometimes ask myself, just as a child would wonder what would happen if his parents died, 'What if God didn't exist, what would happen then?' At those times a vision would appear before my eyes: a landscape. Because I knew this landscape was made by God's love, I felt no fear and looked at it; I wanted to look at it carefully."

"Tell me about this landscape."

"Are you going to put it into a poem? If you do, you don't need to mention my name. I only want one thing from you in exchange."

"Yes?"

"In the last six months, I've written Kadife three letters. I couldn't bring myself to mail any of them. It's not because I'm ashamed: I didn't send them because I knew they would be opened and read at the post office. Half the people of Kars are working as undercover policemen. Half the people in this hall are too. They follow us everywhere we go. Even our people are following us."

"Who are *our* people?"

"All the young Islamists of Kars. They were very curious to know what I was going to say to you. They came here to make trouble, because they knew the military and the secularists were going to turn this evening into a public demonstration. They're going to put on that old play we've heard so much about; it's called *Head Scarf*. And we hear they're going to use it to belittle our head-scarf girls. To tell you the truth, I can't stand politics, but my friends are right to be enraged by this. But they're suspicious of me, because I'm not as fired up as they are. I can't give you those letters. I mean, not right now, with everyone watching. But I want you to give them to Kadife."

"No one's looking now. Give them to me quickly, and then tell me about that landscape."

"The letters are here, but I don't have them on me. I was afraid they'd search me at the door. My friends might have searched me too. If you go through that door next to the stage, you'll see a toilet at the far end of the corridor. Meet me there in exactly twenty minutes."

"Is that when you'll tell me about the landscape?"

"One of them is coming toward us now," said Necip, looking away. "I know him. Don't look in his direction, just act like we're having a normal casual conversation."

"All right."

"Everyone in Kars is very curious to know why you've come here. They think you're on a secret government mission or else you've been sent here by the Western powers. My friends sent me over to ask you if these things are true. Are the rumors true?"

"No, they're not."

"What shall I tell them? Why have you come?"

"I don't know."

"You do know, but once again you're too ashamed to admit it." There was a silence. "You came here because you were unhappy," said Necip.

"How can you tell?"

"From your eyes; I've never seen anyone look so unhappy. . . . I'm not at all happy right now either, but at least I'm young. Unhappiness gives me strength. At my age, I'd rather be unhappy than happy. The only people who can be happy in Kars are the idiots and the villains. But by the time I'm your age, I want to be able to wrap my life in happiness."

"My unhappiness protects me from life," said Ka. "Don't worry about me."

"Oh. You're not angry at me for what I said, are you? There's something so nice in your face I feel I can tell you whatever comes into my head, even if it's really stupid. If I said things like this to my friends, they'd mock me without mercy."

"Even Fazıl?"

"Fazıl's different. If someone does something bad to me, he goes after them, and he always knows what I'm thinking. Now you say something. Someone's watching us."

"Who's watching us?" Ka asked. He looked at the crowds milling behind the seating area: a man with a pear-shaped head, two pimply youths, beetle-browed teenagers in ragged clothes; they were all facing the stage now, and some were swaying like drunks.

"Looks like I'm not the only one who's had too much to drink tonight," Ka muttered.

"They drink because they're unhappy," said Necip. "But you got drunk so you could resist the hidden happiness rising inside you."

As he uttered these words, he plunged back into the crowd. Ka wasn't sure he'd heard him correctly. But despite the noise and commotion around him, his mind was still; he felt relaxed, as if he were listening to his favorite music. Someone waved at him, drawing his eye to a few empty seats reserved for the performing artists; someone from the theater troop—a well-mannered but rather rough-looking stagehand—showed him where to sit.

Years later, in a video I found in the archives of Kars Border Television, I was able to see what Ka then saw onstage. It was a send-up of a well-known bank advertisement, but as it had been years since Ka had watched Turkish television, he could not tell whether they were making fun or just imitating. Even so, he could tell that the man who had gone into the bank to make a deposit was an outrageous dandy, a parody of a Westerner. When it performed in towns even smaller and more remote than Kars, in teahouses never frequented by women or government officials, Sunay Zaim's Brechtian and Bakhtinian theater company made this piece much more obscene, with the bank-card-carrying dandy played as a raving queen who reduced audiences to helpless laughter. In the next sketch, featuring a mustachioed man dressed up as a woman pouring Kelidor shampoo and conditioner onto her hair, it took Ka some time to work out that the actor was Sunay Zaim himself. Just as he did in those remote teahouses when he decided to bring some relief to his poor and angry all-male audiences with an "anticapitalist catharsis," he treated tonight's audience to a string of obscenities as he pretended to stick the long shampoo bottle into his back passage. Later still, Sunay's wife, Funda Eser, did a spoof of a much-loved sausage advertisement. Weighing a coil of sausages in her hand in a decidedly lewd fashion, she asked, "Is it a horse or a donkey?" and then she ran offstage before taking things further.

Vural, the famous goalkeeper from the sixties, returned to the stage to continue his account of the infamous soccer match in Istanbul when the English got eleven goals past him, as well as the details of various allegations of match-fixing and of the love affairs he'd had with famous film stars during the same period. It was a rich assortment of masochistic pleasures that his stories gave the audience, and everyone had a chance to smile at the misery of the Turk.

———◆———

CHAPTER SIXTEEN

Where God Does Not Exist

NECIP DESCRIBES HIS LANDSCAPE
AND KA RECITES HIS POEM

Twenty minutes later, Ka went down the chilly corridor to the men's room, where Necip was standing among the men facing the urinals. For a time they stood together at the back of a line for the locked stalls in front of them, acting as if they'd never met. Ka took this opportunity to admire the molding of the high ceiling, garlands of roses and leaves.

When their turn came, they went into the same stall. Ka noticed that a toothless old man was watching them. After bolting the door from the inside, Necip said, "They didn't see us." He gave Ka a warm but quick embrace. Using a small protrusion as a foothold to hoist himself up the wall, he reached up and retrieved several envelopes from atop the water tank. Back on the floor, he gently blew the dust off the envelopes.

"When you give these letters to Kadife, I want you to say just one thing," he said. "I've given this a great deal of thought. From the moment she reads these letters, I will neither hope nor expect to have anything to do with Kadife for the rest of my life. I want you to tell her this. Make it clear to her, so that she understands exactly what I mean."

"If she is to find out that you're in love with her at the very moment she discovers that there isn't any hope in it, why tell her at all?"

"Unlike you, I'm not afraid of life or my passions," said Necip. Worried that he might have upset Ka, he added, "These letters are all I care about: I can't live without being passionately in love with someone or something beautiful. Now I have to find love and happiness elsewhere. But first I have to get Kadife out of my head." He gave the letters to Ka. "Shall I tell you who it is I plan to love with all my heart after Kadife?"

"Who?" Ka asked, as he put the letters into his pocket.

"God."

"Tell me about that landscape you see."

"First open that window! It's smells really bad in here."

Ka fiddled with the rusty latch until he got it open. For a time they stood there dumbstruck, as if witnessing a miracle, watching the endless stream of snowflakes sailing silently through the night.

"How beautiful the universe is!" Necip whispered.

"What would you say is the most beautiful part of life?" Ka asked.

There was a silence. "All of it!" said Necip, as if he were betraying a secret.

"But doesn't life make us unhappy?"

"We do that to ourselves. It has nothing to do with the universe or its creator."

"Tell me about that landscape."

"First put your hand on my forehead and tell me my future," said Necip. His eyes opened wide, one of them to be shattered twenty-six minutes later, along with his brain. "I want to live a long full life, and I know many wonderful things are going to happen to me. But I don't know what I'll be thinking twenty years from now, and that's what I'm curious about."

Ka pressed the palm of his right hand against Necip's smooth forehead. "Oh my God!" He pulled his hand away mockingly, as if he'd touched something burning hot. "There's a lot going on in there."

"Tell me."

"In twenty years' time—in other words, when you're thirty-seven years old—you will have understood at last that all the evil in the world—I mean the poverty and ignorance of the poor and the cunning and lavishness of the rich—and all the vulgarity in the world, and all the violence, and all the brutality—I mean all the things that make you feel guilty and think of suicide—by the time you're thirty-seven you'll know that all these things are the result of everyone's thinking alike," Ka said. "Therefore, just as so many in this place have done idiotic things and died in the guise of decency, you'll discover that you can actually become a good person while appearing to be shameless and evil. But you know this may have terrible consequences. Because what I feel under my trembling hand is . . ."

"What's that?"

"You're very bright, and even at this age you know what I'm talking about. That's why I want you to tell me first."

"Tell you what?"

"The reason why you feel so guilty about the misery of the poor. I know you know what it is, but you must say it."

"You're not saying—God forbid—that I will no longer believe in God?" said Necip. "If that's what you mean, I'd rather die."

"It's not going to happen overnight, the way it did to that poor director in the elevator! It's going to happen so slowly you'll hardly even notice. And because you'll have been dying so slowly, having been in this other world so long, you'll be just like the drunk who realizes he's dead only after he's had one raki too many."

"Is that what you're like?"

Ka took his hand off Necip's forehead. "No, I'm just the opposite. I must have started believing in God years ago. This happened so slowly, it wasn't until I arrived in Kars that I noticed it. That's why I'm so happy here, and why I'm able to write poems again."

"You surely seem happy right now, and wise," said Necip, "so I'm wondering if you can answer this question: Can a human being really know the future? And even if he can't, can he find peace by convincing himself that he does know the future? This is perfect for my first science-fiction novel."

"Some people do know the future," said Ka. "Take Serdar Bey, owner of the *Border City Gazette*—he printed the story of this evening way in advance." Ka fished his copy of the paper from his pocket and together they read, "The entertainments were punctuated by enthusiastic clapping and applause."

"This must be what they mean by happiness," said Necip. "We could be the poets of our own lives if only we could first write about what shall be and later enjoy the marvels we have written. In the paper it says you read your most recent poem. Which one is that?"

Someone banged on the door of the stall. Ka asked Necip to tell him quickly about "that landscape."

"I'll tell you now," said Necip, "but you have to promise not to tell anyone else. They don't like my fraternizing with you."

"I won't tell anyone," Ka said. "Tell me what you see."

"I love God a lot," said Necip, in an agitated voice. "Sometimes, when I ask myself what would happen if, God forbid, God didn't exist—

I do this sometimes without even meaning to—a terrifying landscape appears before my eyes."

"Yes."

"I see this landscape at night, in darkness, through a window. Outside there are two blind white walls, as tall as the walls of a castle. Like two castles back to back! There is only the narrowest passageway between them, which stretches into the distance like a road, and when I look down this road I am overcome with fear. The road where God does not exist is as snowy and muddy as the roads in Kars, but it's all purple! There's something in the middle of the road that tells me 'Stop!' but I still can't keep myself from looking right down to the end of the road, to the place where this world ends. Right at the end of this world, I can see a tree, one last tree, and it's bare and leafless. Then, because I'm looking at it, it turns bright red and bursts into flame. It's at this point that I begin to feel very guilty for being so curious about the land where God does not exist. Then, just as suddenly, the red tree turns back to black. I tell myself, I'd better not look again, but I can't help it, I do look again, and the tree at the end of the world starts burning red once more. This goes on until morning."

"What is it about this landscape that scares you so much?"

"I can't help thinking that it's the devil making me think such a landscape could be of this world. But if I can make something come to life before my eyes, the source must be my own imagination. Because if there really were a place like this on earth, it would mean that God—God forbid—didn't exist. And since this can't be true, the only possible explanation is that I myself don't believe in God. And that would be worse than death."

"I understand," said Ka.

"I looked it up in an encyclopedia once, and it said that the word *atheist* comes from the Greek *athos*. But *athos* doesn't refer to people who don't believe in God; it refers to the lonely ones, people whom the gods have abandoned. This proves that people can't ever really be atheists, because even if we wanted it, God would never abandon us here. To become an atheist, then, you must first become a Westerner."

"I wanted to be a Westerner *and* a believer," said Ka.

"A man could be at the coffeehouse every evening laughing and playing cards with his friends, he could have so much fun with his classmates that there is never a moment when they aren't exploding into laughter, he could spend every hour of the day chatting with his intimates, but if that man has been abandoned by God, he'd still be the loneliest man on earth."

"It might be of some consolation to have a true love," said Ka.

"But only if she loved you as much as you loved her."

There was another knock on the door, and Necip put his arms around Ka, kissing him like a child on both cheeks before he left the stall. Ka caught a glimpse of the man who had been waiting, now running into the other toilet, so he bolted the door again, lit a cigarette, and watched the wondrous snow still falling outside. He thought about Necip's landscape—he could remember his description word for word, as if it were already a poem—and if no one came from Porlock he was sure he would soon be writing that poem in his notebook.

The man from Porlock! During our last years in school, when Ka and I would stay up half the night talking about literature, this was one of our favorite topics. Anyone who knows anything about English poetry will remember the note at the start of Coleridge's "Kubla Khan." It explains how the work is a "fragment of a poem, from a vision during a dream"; the poet had fallen asleep after taking medicine for an illness (actually, he'd taken opium for fun) and had seen, in his deepest sleep, sentences from the book he'd been reading just before losing consciousness, except that now each sentence and each object had taken on a life of its own in a magnificent dreamscape to become a poem. Imagine, a magnificent poem that had created *itself,* without the poet's having exerted any mental energy! Even more amazing, when Coleridge woke up he could remember this splendid poem word for word. He got out his pen and ink and some paper and carefully began to write it down, one line after the other, as if he were taking dictation. He had just written the last line of the poem as we know it when there came a knock at the door. He rose to answer it, and it was a man from the nearby city of Porlock, come to collect a debt. As soon as he'd dealt with this man, he rushed back to his table, only to discover that he'd forgotten the rest of the poem, except for a few scattered words and the general atmosphere.

As no one arrived from Porlock to break his concentration, Ka still had the poem clear in his mind when he was called onstage. He was taller than everyone else there. He also stood out on account of his German charcoal-gray coat.

There had been a great deal of noise from the audience, but now they fell silent. Some of them—the unruly schoolboys, the unemployed, the Islamist protestors—fell silent because they were no longer quite sure what they should be laughing at or objecting to. The important officials in the front rows, the men who'd been following Ka all day long, the deputy governor, the assistant chief of police, and the teachers all knew he was a poet. The tall thin emcee seemed unnerved by the silence, so he asked Ka a canned question from one of those arts programs on television. "So you're a poet," he said. "You write poems. Is it difficult to write poems?" By the end of this awkward interview—and every time I watch the tape, I wish I could forget it—the audience had no idea whether Ka found it hard writing poems, but they did know he had just arrived from Germany.

"How do you find our beautiful Kars?" the host now asked.

After a moment of indecision, Ka said, "Very beautiful, very poor, and very sad."

At the back of the hall, two students from the religious high school burst out laughing. Someone else cried out, "It's your own soul that's poor!" Encouraged by this taunt, six or seven others stood up and started shouting. Some were heckling Ka, and who knows what the others were saying? Long after the events in question, during my own visit to Kars, Turgut Bey told me that when Hande heard Ka say this on television, she began to cry. "In Germany, you were representing Turkish literature," said the emcee, trying to press on.

"Why doesn't he tell us why he's here?" someone shouted.

"I came here because I was desperately unhappy," said Ka. "I'm much happier here. Listen, please, I'm going to read my poem now."

For a few moments there was confusion. Then the shouting stopped, and Ka began to speak. Only years later, when the videotape of that evening passed into my hands, was I able to watch my friend's moving performance; it was the first time I had ever seen him read a poem to a large audience. He moved forward cautiously, silently, like someone with a great deal on his mind, but there wasn't a hint of pretension in his bearing. Aside from one or two moments when he paused as if slightly uncertain as to what came next, he recited the poem right through to the end without trouble.

When Necip realized that Ka's description of "the place where God does not exist" matched his own description of his "landscape" word for word, he rose from his seat, but he did not break Ka's concentration as he described the falling snow. There was a smattering of applause. Someone in the back stood up and shouted and was soon joined by a few others. It was hard to know whether they were responding to the poem or simply bored.

Unless you count his fleeting appearance a short while later—his falling silhouette, set against a green backdrop—this was the last image of my friend of twenty-seven years.

CHAPTER SEVENTEEN

My Fatherland or My Head Scarf

A PLAY ABOUT A GIRL WHO
BURNS HER HEAD SCARF

After Ka had finished reading his poem, the emcee bowed with an exaggerated flourish and, making the most of every word in the title, announced the evening's main event, *My Fatherland or My Head Scarf.*

From the middle and back rows where the boys from the religious high school were seated came a few shouts of protest, one or two whistles, and a fair amount of booing; a couple of the officials sitting up front clapped approvingly. The rest of the packed hall waited to see what would happen next, their curiosity tempered with a fair amount of awe. The light sketches the troupe had performed earlier in the evening—Funda Eser's shameless parodies of familiar commercials, her rather gratuitous belly dancing, her impression with Sunay Zaim of an aging woman prime minister and her corrupt husband—had caused remarkably little offense, going down rather well even among the officials in the front.

Most of the audience would also enjoy the next offering, though they soon had enough of the taunts and endless disruptions from the religious high school students. At times you couldn't hear a thing being said onstage. But this desperately old-fashioned, primitive, twenty-minute play had such a sound dramatic structure that even a deaf-mute would have had no trouble following it.

1. A woman draped in a jet-black scarf is walking down the street; she is talking to herself and thinking. Something is troubling her.
2. The woman takes off her scarf and proclaims her independence. Now she is scarfless and happy.

3. The woman's family, her fiancé, her relatives, and several bearded Muslim men oppose her independence and demand that she put her scarf back on, whereupon in a fit of righteous rage the woman burns it.

4. The neatly bearded, prayer-bead-clutching religious fanatics, outraged by this show of independence, turn violent.

5. Just as they are dragging the woman off by her hair to kill her, the brave young soldiers of the Republic burst onto the scene and save her.

From the mid-thirties through the early years of the Second World War (when it was known as *My Fatherland or My Scarf*), this short play was performed frequently in lycées and town halls all over Anatolia, and it was very popular with westernizing state officials eager to free women from the scarf and other forms of religious coercion. But after the fifties, when the ardent patriotism of the Kemalist period had given way to something less intense, the piece was forgotten. When I caught up with her years later in a sound studio, Funda Eser, who played the woman that night in Kars, told me of her great pride in re-creating the same role her own mother had played at Kütahya Lycée in 1948, and of her disappointment that the events following her own performance denied her the righteous exultation her mother had enjoyed. Ravaged though she was by drugs, fatigue, and fear, and vapid though her face had become in the manner so common in actors, I nevertheless pressed her to tell me exactly what had happened that evening. Having also interviewed quite a few other witnesses, I can describe it now in some detail.

Most of the locals in the National Theater were shocked and confused by the first scene. When they had heard that the play was entitled *My Fatherland or My Head Scarf,* they assumed it would be a consideration of contemporary politics, but aside from one or two octogenarians who remembered the original from the old days, no one expected to see an actual woman onstage wearing a head scarf. When they did, they took it to be the sort of head scarf that has become the respected symbol of political Islam. And as they watched this mysterious covered woman wandering up and down the stage, it was not immediately clear that she was meant to be sad: Many in the audience saw her as proud, almost arrogant. Even those officials well known for their radical views on religious dress felt respect for this woman. And so when one alert student from the religious high school guessed who was hiding underneath the head scarf, it was to the great annoyance of the front rows that he hooted with laughter.

In the second scene, when the woman made her grand gesture of independence, launching herself into enlightenment as she removed her scarf, the audience was at first terrified. Even the most westernized secularists in the hall were frightened by the sight of their own dreams coming true. Fear of the political Islamists was so great they had long ago accepted that their city must remain as it had always been. I say dreams, but not even in their sleep could they have imagined the state forcing women to remove their head scarves as it had done in the early years of the Republic; they were prepared to live with the practice, "so long as the Islamists don't use intimidation or force to make westernized women wear scarves as we've seen in Iran."

"But the truth of the matter is this: All those fervent secularist Kemalists in the front rows weren't really Kemalists after all, they were cowards!" This was what Turgut Bey told Ka after it was all over. It wasn't just religious extremists who objected to a covered woman baring her head; everyone else in the room was frightened that this spectacle might enrage the unemployed men witnessing it—not to mention the youthful horde milling at the back of the hall. And so when one of the teachers in the front row did rise from his seat to applaud Funda Eser as she shed her scarf with elegance and determination, a handful of youths in the back jeered this poor and forlorn teacher with catcalls. Mind you, according to some witnesses, the teacher was not making a political statement about modern womanhood but rather succumbing to dizzy admiration of Funda's plump arms and famously beautiful throat.

As to the Republicans in the front rows, they weren't too happy with the situation either. Having expected a bespectacled village girl, pure-hearted, bright-faced, and studious, to emerge from beneath the scarf, they were utterly discomfited to see it was the lewd belly dancer Funda Eser instead. Was this to say that only whores and fools take off their head scarves? If so, it was precisely what the Islamists had been saying all along. Several seated near him recall the deputy governor shouting, "This is wrong, all wrong!" While a number of others joined the chorus— perhaps to curry favor—Funda Eser persevered. Still, most people in the front rows, however anxious, continued to watch with quiet appreciation as this enlightened Republican secular girl stood up for the freedoms they all hoped to enjoy, and while a few protests did issue from the religious high school boys, no one felt intimidated by them. Certainly not the deputy governor, flanked on all sides by other top officials who saw little to fear in the antics of a few boys from the religious high school who ought to have known better. This retinue included Kasım Bey, the courageous assistant chief of police, who in his day had made life so difficult for the Kurdish PKK; a number of army officers in civilian clothing, accompanied by their wives; the branch manager of the ordinance survey office, joined by his wife, two daughters, four sons in suits and ties, and three nephews; and the city's cultural director, whose main job was to seize banned tapes of Kurdish music and send them to Ankara.

It could be said that all these officials put their faith in the plain-clothes officers planted throughout the hall, the uniformed officers lined up along the walls, and the soldiers they'd heard were waiting backstage. Their only real concern was the fact that the performance was being broadcast live; although it was only going out locally, these grandees could not help feeling as if all of Ankara—indeed, all of Turkey—were watching them. The great and the good in the front rows, like all those behind them, could not quite forget that the scenes playing out before their eyes were simultaneously appearing on television; this alone can explain why the vulgarities and political provocations and nonsense they witnessed seemed to the audience more elegant and magical than they really were. Some were so concerned to know whether the cameras were still running that they were turning their heads every other moment just to check; like the ones in the back continually waving at the camera, and the others periodically shouting "Oh, my God, they can see me on television!" the front row found this prospect so unnerving that they could barely move, even though they were sitting in the most secluded corner of the hall. As to those citizens not in attendance, the city's first live broadcast did not inspire in most a desire to see the stage on-screen; rather, it made them long to be in the theater, watching the television crew in action.

By now Funda Eser had removed her scarf and tossed it like so much laundry into a copper basin. She then sprinkled it with gasoline—carefully, as if adding detergent—and plunged her hands into the basin as though stirring the wash. By a strange coincidence, they'd put the gasoline into an emptied bottle of Akif liquid detergent, a brand much favored by Kars housewives at the time, and this was why everyone in the auditorium— everyone in Kars, for that matter—took it that the freedom fighter girl had changed her mind: seeing her plunge her hands into the washbasin, they all relaxed.

"That's the way to do it!" someone shouted from the back. "Scrub out all that dirt!" There was a ripple of laughter, annoying some of the high government officials in front; still, everyone in the hall thought they were watching a woman doing laundry. "So where's the Omo?" someone shouted.

He was one of the religious high school boys: although their noise was beginning to annoy some people, no one was very angry. Most of the audience, including the officials up front, were just hoping that this dated, provocative piece of Jacobin theater would end without incident. Quite a few of those I interviewed years later, from the most august official to the poorest Kurdish student, told me that most of the Kars residents in the National Theater had come to the performance hoping for one thing: to be transported from their everyday lives for a few hours and maybe even to enjoy themselves.

Funda Eser was doing her laundry with just as much relish as the happy housewife in the commercials; like all happy housewives, she refused to rush. But when the time came to remove the black scarf from the basin and shake out the wrinkles to prepare it for the clothesline, she unfurled it like a flag before the audience. While everyone was still exchanging glances, struggling to work out what was going on, she produced a lighter from her pocket and lit one of the scarf's corners. For a moment, there was silence. Everyone heard the breath of the flame as the burning scarf cast the entire hall in a strange and fearsome light.

Quite a few leaped to their feet in horror.

No one had expected this. Even the most steadfast secularists were badly shaken. When the woman threw the burning scarf onto the stage, for many the first concern was the theater's 110-year-old fixtures; the filthy patched-velvet curtains, dating back to the richest days of the city, seemed in particular danger of catching fire. But the greatest cause for alarm was, rightfully, the sense that the trouble had only started. Now anything could happen.

From the religious boys at the back there arose a terrible din of boos, catcalls, and angry whistles.

"Down with the enemies of religion!" one shouted. "Down with atheists! Down with infidels!"

The front rows were still in shock. Although the one courageous teacher stood up again to cry, "Be quiet and watch the show!" no one paid him the least bit of attention. With the realization that the booing and shouting and chanting were not going to stop and that things were getting seriously out of control, a ripple of panic spread across the hall. Dr. Nevzat, the branch health director, was first to head for the exit; he was followed by his sons in their suits and ties, his daughter, her hair neatly pulled into two braids, and his wife, in her very best outfit, a crepe dress in all the colors of a peacock. Sadık Bey, one of the rich leather manufacturers from the old days, who had come back to Kars to oversee some work, and his classmate from primary school, Sabit Bey, now a lawyer affiliated with the People's Party, also rose to their feet. Ka saw dread in the faces of everyone in the front rows, but, uncertain what to do, he stayed in his seat: His main concern was that in the confusion he might forget the poem still only in his mind, waiting to be recorded in his green notebook. At the same time, he wanted to leave the theater, to join İpek.

At that moment, Recai Bey, head manager of the telephone company, a gentleman respected throughout Kars for his erudition, made his way toward the smoke-filled stage. "My dear girl!" he cried. "We have all enjoyed your tribute to the ideals of Atatürk. But we've had enough now. Look, the audience is upset; we're in danger of inciting a riot."

By now the scarf had stopped burning and Funda Eser was standing amid the smoke, reciting the same monologue I would later find in the 1936 Townhall edition of *My Fatherland or My Scarf,* the passage of which its author would profess to being most proud. Four years after the events I describe in this book, I had an opportunity to meet the author, then ninety-two years old but still very energetic; during our interview, while most of his energy was consumed in scolding his naughty grandchildren (or great-grandchildren) who wouldn't sit still, he nevertheless found the strength to tell me how sorry he was that of all his works (including *Atatürk Is Coming, Atatürk Plays for High Schools,* and *Our Memories of Him*), it was *My Fatherland or My Scarf* that would be forgotten. Unaware of its revival in Kars, or indeed of the events it precipitated, he went on to tell how, during the thirties, this play had had the same remarkable effect on lycée girls and state officials alike—it had moved them to tears and standing ovations wherever it was performed.

But now, no one could hear anything above the booing and catcalls and angry whistles from the religious high school boys. Despite the guilty, fearful silence at the front of the auditorium, few could hear what Funda Eser was saying: that when the angry girl tore the scarf off her head, she was not just making a statement about people or about national dress, she was talking about our souls, because the scarf, the fez, the turban, and the headdress were symbols of the reactionary darkness in our souls, from which we should liberate ourselves and run to join the modern nations of the West. This provoked a taunt from the back rows that the entire auditorium heard very clearly.

"So why not take everything off and run to Europe stark naked?"

The comment brought laughter even from the front rows and some applause around the hall. But finally those in front were disconcerted and scared. Like many others, Ka chose this moment to stand up. Noise was coming from every mouth by now, and the voluble shouting persisted in the back rows; some who had headed for the door were now looking back over their shoulders. Funda Eser continued reciting the poem almost no one could hear.

CHAPTER EIGHTEEN

Don't Fire, the Guns Are Loaded!

A REVOLUTION ONSTAGE

From this point on, things happened very quickly. Two "religious fanatics" sporting round beards and skullcaps appeared onstage. These actors carried ropes and knives and left no doubt that they were there to punish Funda Eser for burning her scarf and defying God's law.

Once they'd captured her, Funda Eser writhed in a highly provocative manner as she struggled to break free. By now she had given up all pretense of being a heroine of the enlightenment; she had switched to that role she always found more comfortable, the woman about to be raped. But her practiced self-abasing entreaties did not arouse the men in the audience as much as she expected. One of the bearded fanatics (rather clumsily made up, having played the father in the previous scene) yanked at her hair and threw her to the ground; the other laid a dagger on her throat in a manner suggesting a Renaissance tableau of the Sacrifice of Isaac; it illustrated perfectly the fears of a reactionary religious backlash felt in westernized circles in the early years of the Republic. The older officials in the front rows and the conservatives in the back were the first to become alarmed.

For exactly eighteen seconds, Funda Eser and the "fundamentalists" held their grand pose without moving a muscle, though quite a few of the people I interviewed were sure that the trio had remained immobile for much longer. The crowd was out of control. It was not just the play's affront to covered women that bothered the religious high school boys, nor was it simply the caricature of fanatics as ugly, dirty dolts. They also suspected that the whole thing had been deliberately staged to provoke them. So every time they heckled the players, every time they threw half

153

an orange or a cushion onto the stage, they were one step closer to a trap that had been laid just for them, and it was the knowledge of their help-lessness that made them even angrier.

This was why the most politically astute member of the group, a short broad-shouldered boy named Abdurrahman Öz (in fact, his father, who came from Sivas to collect his body three days later, would give a differ-ent name), did everything he could to settle and quiet his companions, but to no avail. Egged on by the clapping and booing from other parts of the auditorium, the angry students assumed that there were others in the anxious crowd who felt as they did. Even more important, the young Islamists, who were weak and disorganized compared with their peers in the areas surrounding Kars, had found the courage for the first time ever to speak with one voice, and they were pleased to see how much they could scare the officials and army officers in the front rows. They were all the more heartened to know that their show of solidarity was being broadcast to the entire city. They were not just shouting and stamping, they were also enjoying themselves—this is one thing that everyone later forgot.

Having seen the video many times, I can also say that a number of the ordinary citizens were even laughing at times at the students' slogans and curses, and if at other moments they also clapped and booed with the stu-dents, it was because they were just a bit bored, though still determined to make the most of a theatrical evening that had turned out to be rather puzzling. One witness even said later, "If the people in the front had not overreacted to this feeble commotion, it would have prevented every-thing that followed." Others insisted, "The rich men and high-ranking officials in the front rows who panicked during those eighteen seconds already knew what was going to happen; otherwise they would not have gathered up their families and headed for the door. Ankara," they said, "had planned the whole thing in advance."

Fearful of losing the poem in his head, Ka also left the auditorium. At the same moment, a man came onstage to rescue Funda Eser from the two round-bearded reactionaries: this man was Sunay Zaim. He was wearing an army uniform from the thirties with a fur hat in the style of Atatürk and the heroes of the War for Independence. As he strode pur-posefully across the stage (no one could have known he had a slight limp), the two "fundamentalists" took fright and threw themselves at his feet. The brave old teacher stood up once more and applauded Sunay's heroism with all his might. One or two others shouted, "Bless you! Bravo!" Standing in the center of the spotlight, he seemed to all of Kars to be a wondrous creature from another planet.

Everyone noticed how handsome and enlightened he looked. The long and punishing years spent touring Anatolia may have left him lame, but they had not diminished his attraction; he still had the hard, decisive, tragic air and faintly feminine good looks that had made him such a sensation among leftist students when he played Che Guevara, Robespierre, and the revolutionary Enver Pasha. Instead of bringing the index finger of his white-gloved hand to his lips, he rested it elegantly on his chin and said, "Quiet!"

There was no need for this line, which wasn't in the script: everyone in the auditorium was already silent. Those who'd stood up were back in their seats.

"They're in torment!"

Probably this is only half of what Sunay Zaim meant to say, because no one had the faintest idea of who was meant to be in torment. In the old days, this would have been a reference to the people or the nation, but his audience was not sure if this man was referring to them or to Funda Eser or to the entire Republic. Still, the feeling evoked by the remark was palpable. The entire audience fell into an uneasy hush.

"O honorable and beloved citizens of Turkey," said Sunay Zaim. "You've embarked on the road to enlightenment, and no one can keep you from this great and noble journey. Do not fear. The reactionaries who want to turn back time, those vile beasts with their cobwebbed minds, will never be allowed to crawl out of their hole. Those who seek to meddle with the Republic, with freedom, with enlightenment, will see their hands crushed."

Everyone in the hall heard the taunt from the boy two seats away from Necip. Again, a deep silence fell over the crowd; there was awe mixed with their fear. They all sat still as candles, as if hoping to hear one or two sweet nothings, a few clues to help them make sense of the evening when they went home, with perhaps a story or two.

At that moment, a detachment of soldiers appeared on either side of the stage. Three more came in through the main entrance and down the aisle to join them. The people of Kars, unaccustomed to the modern device of sending actors among the audience, were first alarmed and then amused.

A bespectacled messenger boy came running onto the stage, and when they saw who it was, they all laughed. It was Glasses, the sweet and clever nephew of the city's principal newspaper distributor; everyone knew him as a constant presence in the shop, which was just across the street from the National Theater. Glasses ran over to Sunay Zaim, who bent down so the boy could whisper into his ear.

All of Kars could see that the news made Sunay Zaim very sad.

"We have just learned that the director of the Institute of Education has passed away," Sunay Zaim told the audience. "This lowly murder will be the last assault on the Republic and the secular future of Turkey!"

Before the audience had had a chance to digest the news, the soldiers onstage cocked their rifles and took aim straight at the audience. They opened fire at once; the noise was thunderous.

It was unclear whether this was another theatrical ruse or an honor guard requested by the company to mark the sad news. A number of Kars residents—out of touch as they were with modern theatrical conventions—took it for yet another bit of experimental staging.

A roar rose as a strong vibration was felt through the hall. Those frightened by the noise of the weapons thought the vibration had issued from the agitation in the audience. Just as one or two were standing up, the bearded "fundamentalists" onstage ducked for cover.

"No one move!" said Sunay Zaim.

Once again, the soldiers cocked their guns and took aim at the crowd. At the exact same time, the short fearless boy two seats away from Necip stood up and shouted, "Damn the godless secularists! Damn the fascist infidels!"

Once again, the soldiers fired.

As the shots rang in the air, another strong vibration was felt through the hall.

Just then, those in the back rows saw the boy who had uttered the taunt collapse into his chair before rising up again, now with his arms and his legs jerking wildly. Among those who had been enjoying the antics of the religious high school students and laughing all evening at everything they couldn't understand, several took this as yet another joke, and when the student's jerking continued—violent as the throes of death—they laughed a bit more.

It was only with the third volley that some in the audience realized that the soldiers were firing live rounds; they could tell, just as one could on those evenings when soldiers rounded up terrorists in the streets, because these shots can be heard in one's stomach as well as in one's ears. A strange noise came from the huge German-manufactured Bohemian stove that had been heating the hall for forty-four years; the stovepipe had been pierced and was now spewing smoke like an angry teapot at full boil. As someone from the back rows stood up and made straight for the stage with blood streaming from his head, there came the smell of gunpowder. The audience looked ready to erupt in panic, and yet everyone was sitting in silence, still as statues. As in a bad dream, everyone felt very alone. Even so, the literature teacher Nuriye Hanım, who attended the National Theater every time she visited Ankara and was full of admiration for the beauty of the theatrical effects, rose to her feet for the first time to applaud the actors. At precisely the same time, Necip rose to his feet, like an agitated student trying to catch his teacher's attention.

The soldiers launched their fourth volley. According to the inspector colonel sent by Ankara to oversee the inquiry, who would spend many weeks in secrecy compiling his meticulous report, this fourth volley killed two people. He named one of them as Necip, adding that one bullet had entered his forehead and the other his eye, but having heard a number of rumors to the contrary, I can't say for sure that this was when Necip died. Those in the front and middle rows would agree on one point: After the third volley, Necip saw the bullets flying through the air and, though realizing what was happening, utterly misjudged the soldiers. Two seconds before being hit, he had risen to his feet to speak the words heard by many though not registered on the tape.

"Stop! Don't fire; the guns are loaded!"

His words gave utterance to what everyone in the hall knew in his heart but still could not bring his mind to accept. Of the five shots in the first volley, one hit the plaster laurel leaves above the box where, a quarter century earlier, the last Soviet consul in Kars had watched films in the company of his dog. This bullet went wide because the soldier who had fired the shot—a Kurd from Siirt—had no wish to kill anyone. Another shot fired with similar care, though somewhat less skillfully, had hit the ceiling, sending a cloud of 110-year-old lime and paint dust snowing down on the anxious crowd below. Another bullet flew over the nest where the TV camera was perched to hit the wooden balustrade that marked off the standing room from which poor romantic Armenian girls who could afford only the cheapest tickets had once watched theater troupes, acrobats, and chamber groups from Moscow. The fourth flew into the outer reaches of the hall, beyond range of the camera; through the back of a seat it went into the shoulder of a dealer in spare parts for tractor and agricultural equipment named Muhittin Bey, who was sitting with his wife and his widowed sister-in-law and, having seen the shower of lime dust, had stood up to see whether something had fallen from the ceiling. The fifth bullet hit a grandfather sitting just behind the Islamist students; he had come from Trabzon to see his grandson, who was doing his military service in Kars; after the bullet shattered the left lens of his spectacles, it entered his brain, but the old man, luckily asleep at the time, died silently, never knowing what had happened to him. The bullet then exited from his neck and, passing through the back of his seat, pierced a bag belonging to a twelve-year-old Kurdish egg and bread vendor. The boy had been passing between the seats to give a customer his change and so was not holding the bag at the time, and the bullet was recovered later inside one of his boiled eggs.

I am relating these details to explain why it was that most people in the audience stayed so still when the soldiers opened fire. When bullets from the second volley hit a student in the temple, the neck, and in the upper chest, just above the heart, most assumed that he was putting on another show, an encore to his terrifying but entertaining show of courage moments earlier. One of the two remaining bullets went into the chest of a relatively subdued religious high school student sitting in the back (it was later revealed that his aunt's daughter was the city's first suicide girl); the last struck two meters over the projection booth, hitting the face of the clock, which, having stopped working sixty years earlier, was now covered with dust and spiderwebs. According to the colonel in charge of the inquiry, the fact that one of the bullets from the second volley had hit the clock was proof that one of the marksmen chosen that evening at sunset for the assignment had violated the oath he'd sworn with his hand on the Koran: Clearly he had gone out of his way to avoid killing someone. As for the fiery Islamist student killed in the third volley, the colonel would mention in a parenthesis the careful consideration that had been given to the lawsuit that the family had brought against the state, in which it had been alleged that the lad had been not just a student but also a hardworking devoted employee of the Kars branch of MİT; but in the end the colonel found insufficient grounds for the award of damages. Of the last two bullets in this same volley, one hit Reza Bey, who had built the fountain in the Kaleiçi district and who was much loved by all the conservatives and Islamists in the city; the other struck the servant he used as his walking stick.

And so it is finally not easy to explain how so many in the audience could have remained still, watching these two lifelong friends moaning and dying on the floor as the soldiers onstage cocked their rifles for the fourth time. Years later, a dairy owner who still refused to let me use his name explained it this way: "Those of us who were sitting in the back knew something terrible had happened. But we were afraid that if we moved from our seats to get a better look, the terror would find us, so we just sat there watching without making a sound."

Even the colonel was unable to determine where all of the bullets from the fourth volley had gone. One had wounded a young salesman who had come to Kars from Ankara to sell parlor games and encyclopedias on the installment plan (he would bleed to death in the hospital two hours later). Another bullet had blown a huge hole in the lower facing wall of the private box where, in the first decade of the twentieth century, Kirkor Çizmeciyan, a wealthy leather manufacturer, had sat with his family, dressed from head to toe in fur. According to one tall tale, the bullet that hit one of Necip's green eyes and the other that hit his wide smooth forehead did not kill him instantaneously; some eyewitnesses claimed that for a moment the teenager had looked at the stage and cried, "I can see!"

By the time the shouting and screaming had stopped, almost everyone—including those rushing for the door—crumpled. Even the TV cameraman was forced to throw himself against a back wall: His camera, which had been panning right and left all evening, now stood still. The only thing the viewers at home could see was the crowd on the stage and the silent respectable notables in the front rows. Even so, most city residents had heard enough shouting, screaming, and gunfire to realize that something very strange was going on at the National Theater. As for those who had grown bored with the play toward midnight and begun to doze off in front of their televisions, by the last eighteen seconds of the gun battle even their eyes were glued to the screen—and to Sunay Zaim. "O heroic soldiers, you have done your duty," he said. Then, with an elegant gesture, he turned to Funda Eser, still lying on the floor, and made an exaggerated bow. Taking the hand of her savior, the woman rose.

A retired civil servant in the front row stood up to applaud. A few others sitting nearby joined in. There was scattered applause from the back, from people presumably in the habit of clapping at anything—or perhaps they were scared. The rest of the hall was silent as ice. Like someone waking up following a long bender, a few even seemed relaxed and allowed themselves weak smiles. It was as if they'd decided that the dead bodies before their eyes belonged to the dream world of the stage; a number of those who had ducked for cover now had their heads in the air but then cowered again at the sound of Sunay's voice.

"This is not a play; it is the beginning of a revolution," he said reproachfully. "We are prepared to go to any lengths to protect our fatherland. Put your faith in the great and honorable Turkish army! Soldiers! Bring them over."

Two soldiers escorted the two round-bearded "fundamentalists." As the other soldiers cocked their guns and descended into the auditorium, a strange man rushed forward onto the stage. It was clear from the unbecoming speed of his approach and his awkward body language that he was neither a soldier nor an actor. But he still had everyone's attention. Quite a few people were hoping he would reveal that it was all one great big joke.

"Long live the Republic!" he cried. "Long live the army! Long live the Turkish people! Long live Atatürk!" Slowly, very slowly, the curtains began to close. He took two steps forward, as did Sunay Zaim; the curtain closed behind them. The strange man was carrying a gun manufactured in Kırıkkale; he was wearing civilian clothes with military boots. "To hell with the fundamentalists!" he cried, as he walked down the steps into the auditorium. Two armed guards appeared to follow him. But the three strangers did not head to the back of the hall (where the soldiers were busy arresting the boys from the religious high school); without paying any attention to their terrified audience, they kept shouting slogans as they rushed for the exits and disappeared into the night.

The three men were in tremendously high spirits. Only at the very last minute, after lengthy discussion and bargaining, had it been agreed that they too could take part in the performance that was to begin "the little revolution of Kars." They'd met with Sunay Zaim on the night of his arrival, and he had resisted the proposal for an entire day, fearing that the involvement of shady armed adventurers would ruin the artistic integrity of his play; but in the end he could not resist the argument that he might need a man experienced with guns to control any lowlifes in the audience who were unlikely to appreciate the nuances of "modern art." It was later said that he felt great remorse at his decision during the hours that followed, and great pangs of passion in the face of the bloodshed caused by this band in tramp's clothing; but as is so often the case, most of this was only rumor.

When I visited Kars years later, I had a tour of what had once been the National Theater. Half the building had been torn down; the other half had been turned into a warehouse for the Arçelik dealership. The owner, Muhtar Bey, was my guide; and it was, I think, to deflect my questions about the evening of the performance and the ensuing terror that he told me how Kars had been witness to an endless string of murders, massacres, and other evils dating all the way back to the time of the Armenians. If I wanted to bring some happiness to the people of Kars, he said, I should, upon returning to Istanbul, ignore the sins of the city's past and write instead about the beautiful clean air and the inhabitants' kind hearts. As we stood in the dark and mildewy auditorium-turned-warehouse surrounded by the ghostlike forms of refrigerators, stoves, and washing machines, he pointed out the sole remaining trace of that last performance: the huge gaping hole made by the bullet that had hit the outside wall of Kirkor Çizmeciyan's private box.

CHAPTER NINETEEN

And How Beautiful Was the Falling Snow

THE NIGHT OF THE REVOLUTION

The leader of the boisterous trio that ran shouting into the auditorium waving pistols and rifles at the cowering audience, only to vanish into the night, was a writer and an old Communist whose alias was Z Demirkol. During the seventies he belonged to various pro-Soviet Communist organizations, and although he worked as a journalist and poet, he was best known as a bodyguard. He was a rather large man. He'd escaped to Germany after the military takeover in 1980; after the Berlin Wall came down, he received a special pardon and returned to Turkey to help defend the secular state and the Republic against Kurdish separatist guerillas and Islamist fundamentalists. The two men behind him had once been Turkish nationalist militants, former comrades of Z Demirkol himself in nighttime street battles in Istanbul during his Marxist years between 1979 and 1980, but now they had put all this behind them, galvanized by their adventurism and their mission to protect the nation state. Some cynics claimed that the threesome had been agents of the state from the very beginning anyway. When they rushed down from the stage and bolted out of the National Theater, no one thought much about them; it was just assumed they were part of the play.

When Z Demirkol saw how much snow there was on the ground, he jumped up and down like a child; firing two shots in the air, he cried, "Long live the Turkish people! Long live the Republic!" The crowd gathered at the entrance retreated to the sides. A few stood watching the men and smiling fearfully; some looked embarrassed, as if they were about to apologize for not staying longer. Z Demirkol and his friends ran up Atatürk Avenue, still shouting slogans and calling to one another like giddy drunks. A few old people struggling through the snow and a few of the fathers guiding their families home decided, after a few moments of indecision, to applaud them.

The happy trio caught up with Ka at the corner of Little Kâzımbey Avenue. They could see that he had seen them coming; he had stepped back under the oleander trees, as if to let a car pass.

"Mr. Poet!" cried Z Demirkol. "You've got to kill them before they kill you. Do you understand?"

Ka still had had no opportunity to write down the poem to which he would later give the title "The Place Where God Does Not Exist," and it was at this moment that he forgot it.

Z Demirkol and his friends continued running straight up Atatürk Avenue. Not wishing to follow them, Ka turned right into Karadağ Avenue, realizing that the poem had vanished, leaving not a fragment in its wake.

He felt the sort of guilt and shame he had once known as a young man leaving political meetings. Those political meetings had disturbed him not only because he was an upper-middle-class boy but because the discussions were so full of childish posturing and exaggeration. Hoping to find a way to bring back his forgotten poem, he decided to continue walking instead of going straight back to the hotel.

A few people alarmed at what they'd just seen on television were at their windows. It's difficult to say how much Ka was aware of the terrors at the theater. The volleys had begun before he left, but it's possible he too thought they were part of the performance, and that Z Demirkol and his friends were part of it as well.

His mind was fixated on his forgotten poem. But sensing another coming in its stead, he willed it into the back of his mind to give it time to ripen.

He heard two gunshots in the far distance, muffled by the snow.

And how beautiful was the falling snow! How large the snowflakes were, and how decisive. It was as if they knew their silent procession would continue until the end of time. The wide avenue was buried knee-deep; it climbed up a slope to disappear into the night. How white and how mysterious! There wasn't a soul in the three-story Armenian building that now housed the city council. The icicles from one of the oleander trees reached down as low as the snow blanket draping an invisible car; the snow and ice had merged to form a tulle curtain. Ka passed an empty one-story Armenian house, its windows boarded up. As he listened to his footsteps and the sound of his own short breaths, he could feel the call of life and happiness as if for the first time, yet he also felt strong enough to turn his back on it.

Across the street from the governor's residence, the little park with the statue of Atatürk was empty. Ka could see no sign of life in the residence itself, which dated back to the Russian period and was still the city's grandest building. Seventy years earlier, after the First World War, when both the Ottoman and Imperial Russian armies had withdrawn and the Turks of Kars had established an independent state, this building housed both the administrative center and the assembly. Just across the street was the old Armenian building that had been attacked by the English army because it was the same doomed republic's presidential palace. The governor's residence was well guarded, so Ka avoided the building by turning right again and looping back toward the park. A little farther down the road, in front of another old Armenian building just as peaceful and beautiful as the rest, a tank moved past an adjoining empty lot, slow and silent, as if in a dream. Ahead, an army truck was parked near the religious high school. There was almost no snow on it, so Ka deduced it had only just arrived. There was a gunshot. Ka turned back. The sentry station in front of the governor's residence was full of policemen trying to warm themselves, but with the windows iced over no one saw Ka walking by down Army Avenue. He knew now that if he could remain within the silence of the snow until he reached his hotel room, he'd be able to preserve not just the new poem in his head but the memory that had emerged with it.

Halfway down the slope he heard a noise on the opposite pavement and slowed down. Two people were trying to kick in the door to the telephone office. The headlights of a car beamed through the snow, and then Ka heard the satisfying rattle of snow chains. As a black unmarked police car pulled up in front of the telephone office, Ka saw two men in the front seat; he remembered seeing one of them in the theater only minutes earlier, just as he'd begun to think about leaving; that man now remained seated as his partner, in a woolen beret and armed, stepped out of the car.

There followed a discussion among those assembled outside the door of the telephone office. They were standing under the streetlamp and Ka could hear their voices, so it was not long before he had realized that the men were Z Demirkol and his friends.

"What do you mean, you don't have a key?" one of them was saying.

"Aren't you the head manager of the telephone office? Didn't they send you here to cut the lines? How could you have forgotten your key?"

"We can't cut off the phones from this office. We'll have to go to the new center on Station Avenue," said the head manager, Recai Bey.

"This is a revolution and we want to get into this office," said Z Demirkol. "If we decide to go to the other office later, we'll do it, understand? Now, where's the key?"

"My child, this snow will be gone in two days and then the roads will be open, and when they are the state will call us all to account."

"So you're afraid of the state? Well, hear this: We *are* the state you fear!" Z Demirkol bellowed. "Are you going to open the door for us or what?"

"I can't open that door for you without a written order."

"We'll see about that," said Z Demirkol. He took out his gun and fired two shots in the air. "Take this man and spread him against the wall," he said. "If he makes any more trouble we'll execute him."

No one believed him, but Demirkol's two assistants dutifully took Recai Bey and spread him against the wall. Not wishing to damage any windows, they pushed him slightly to their right. Because the snow was very soft in that corner, the manager tripped and fell. The men apologized and helped him back to his feet. They removed his tie and used it to bind his arms behind him. Meanwhile, they announced that this was a cleanup operation and all enemies of the fatherland would be eliminated from the streets of Kars by morning.

When Z Demirkol gave the order, they cocked their rifles and, like a firing squad, lined up in front of Recai Bey. Just then there were gunshots in the distance. (These came from the dormitory garden of the religious high school, where soldiers were firing shots in the air to frighten the students.) They all fell silent and waited. For the first time all day, the snow was abating. The silence was extraordinarily beautiful—bewitching, even. After a few moments, one of the men said that the old man (who wasn't old at all) was entitled to a last cigarette. They put a cigarette into Recai Bey's mouth and lit it for him; perhaps having grown a bit restless while the manager was smoking, they started kicking the door of the phone office and ramming it with the butts of their rifles.

"I can't bear to see you destroy state property," said the manager from the wall. "Undo my hands and I'll let you in."

Once the men were inside, Ka went on his way. He continued to hear the odd gunshot, but he now paid no more attention than he paid to the howling dogs. His whole mind was fixed on the beauty of the silent night. For a time, he tarried before an empty old Armenian house. Then he stopped at an Armenian church to pay his respects; the trees in its gardens were dripping with icicles and looked like ghosts. The yellow street-lamps cast such a deathly glow over the city that it looked like a strange sad dream, and for some reason Ka felt guilty. Still, he was mightily thankful to be present in this silent and forgotten country, now filling him with poems.

A little farther on, he happened on an agitated mother standing at a window and telling her son to come home; the boy was saying he was just going out to see what was going on. Ka passed between them. At the corner of Faikbey Avenue, he saw two men about his age coming rushing out of a shoemaker's shop; one was rather large, the other slim as a child. Twice a week for the past twelve years, each of these two lovers had been telling his wife that he was going to stop in at the coffeehouse, and they would then meet secretly in this shop that stank of glue; but hearing on the upstairs neighbor's television set that a curfew had been announced, the couple panicked. Ka turned into Faikbey Avenue; two streets down, opposite a shop he remembered from his morning walk—he had stopped at the trout counter just outside its doors—he saw a tank. Like the street, the tank seemed suffused with a magical silence; it was so still and deathly that he thought it must be empty. But the door opened, and a head popped out to tell him to go home at once. Ka asked the head if it could direct him to the Snow Palace Hotel, but before the soldier could answer Ka noticed across the street the darkened offices of the *Border City Gazette* and knew he could work out the way to go.

The lights in the hotel lobby were blazing; walking into that warmth was like coming home. A number of guests were in pajamas and puffing on cigarettes, watching the lobby television, and it was clear from their expressions that something extraordinary had happened, but like a child eager to avoid a dreaded subject, Ka refused to notice. After letting his eyes skate swiftly over the scene, he proceeded lightheartedly into Turgut Bey's apartment. The whole group was still at the table and still watching television. When Turgut Bey saw Ka, he jumped to his feet, scolding him for being so late and telling him how worried they'd all been. He went on to say a few other things, but by now Ka's gaze had met İpek's.

"You read your poem beautifully," İpek said. "I felt very proud."

Ka knew at once that he would remember this moment until he died.

He felt such joy that, even with the other girls' tedious questions and Turgut Bey's exhausted hectoring, he had to fight back tears.

"It looks as if the army is up to something," said Turgut Bey. To judge from his voice he was in a foul temper, unable to decide whether this was good or bad.

The table was in disarray. Someone had stubbed out a cigarette in an orange peel—most probably it was İpek. Ka remembered seeing Aunt Munire, a distant young relative of his father's, doing the same thing when he was a child, and although she had never once forgotten to say *madam* when speaking to Ka's mother, everyone despised her for her bad manners.

"They've just announced a curfew," said Turgut Bey. "Tell us what happened at the theater."

"I have no interest in politics," said Ka.

Although everyone and especially İpek was aware that this was another voice inside him speaking, Ka still felt sorry.

All he wanted to do now was to sit quietly and look at İpek, but he knew it was out of the question; the house, ablaze with revolutionary fever, made him uncomfortable. It wasn't just the bad memories of the military takeovers during his childhood; it was the fact that everyone was talking at once. Hande had fallen asleep in the corner. Kadife went back to the television screen that Ka refused to watch, and Turgut Bey seemed at once pleased and disturbed that these were interesting times.

For a while Ka sat next to İpek and held her hand; he asked her without success to come up to his room. When it became too painful to keep his distance, he went upstairs alone and hung his coat with great care on the hook behind the door. There was a familiar smell of wood in his room. As he lit the small lamp at the head of the bed, a wave of sleep passed over him; he could barely keep his eyes open; he felt himself floating, as if the whole room, the whole hotel, were floating with him. This is why the new poem, which he jotted down in his notebook line by line as it came to him, portrayed the bed, the hotel in which he lay, and the snowy city of Kars as a single divine unity.

The title he gave this poem was "The Night of the Revolution." It began with his childhood memories of other coups, when the whole family would wake up to sit around the radio, listening to military marches; it went on to describe the holiday meals they'd had together. This was why he would later decide this poem was not about a coup at all and assign it to the branch of the snowflake entitled Memory. One of its important ideas was the poet's ability to shut off part of his mind even while the world is in turmoil. If this meant that a poet had no more connection to the present than a ghost did, such was the price a poet had to pay for his art! After he finished his poem, Ka lit a cigarette and went to the window.

CHAPTER TWENTY

A Great Day for Our Nation!

WHILE KA SLEPT AND WHEN HE
WOKE THE NEXT MORNING

Ka slept for exactly ten hours and twenty minutes without stirring once. In one of his dreams he watched the snow falling. Just before, through the gap in the half-drawn curtains, the snow had begun to fall again onto the white street below, and it looked exceptionally soft where the lamp lit the pink signpost of the Snow Palace Hotel; perhaps it was because this strange and magically soft snow absorbed the sound of the gunfights all over Kars that night that Ka was able to sleep so soundly.

Only two streets away, a tank and two army trucks attacked the religious high school dormitory. There was a skirmish—not in front of the main iron door, where the fine Armenian craftsmanship is visible to this day, but by the wooden door leading to the common rooms and the senior dormitory; hoping to frighten the boys, the soldiers who gathered in the snow-covered garden fired straight up into the night sky. All the hardened political Islamists in the student body had attended the performance at the National Theater, and because they had been arrested on the spot, the only boys in the dormitory were either raw recruits or else had no interest in politics; but the scenes on television had made them rather giddy, and so—barricading the door with tables and desks and shouting slogans like "God is great!"—they'd holed up to wait. One or two of the crazy ones, having stolen a few knives and forks from the kitchen, decided to throw the utensils at the soldiers from the bathroom window and began to horse around with the sole gun in their possession; so the standoff ended in gunfire, with one beautiful slip of a boy—

nothing but innocence in his face—falling to his death, a bullet in his forehead.

Most of the city was still awake, their eyes glued not to the windows and the streets below but to their television sets. The live broadcast had continued Sunay Zaim announced that this was not a play but a "revolution"; as the soldiers were rounding up the troublemakers and carrying out the dead and wounded, there appeared onstage a man well known to all of Kars. This was Umman Bey, the deputy governor; in a formal and uneasy voice that nevertheless inspired confidence, he expressed perhaps for the first time a certain impatience about this live broadcast and announced a curfew over all of Kars until noon the following day. When he left the stage, no one else appeared, and so for the next twenty minutes the only things the city's people could see on their screens were the curtains of the National Theater; there was then a break in transmission, after which the same old curtains reappeared on everyone's screen. Sometime later, the people of Kars would see the curtains were opening again, very slowly, as the whole performance was rebroadcast from the very beginning.

Seated in front of their sets, struggling to work out what was going on, most began to fear the worst. The very tired or half drunk found themselves revisiting earlier times of civic turmoil; others feared a return to death, disappearance, and the rule of night. Those with no interest in politics saw the rebroadcast as an opportunity to make some sense of what had happened that night—just as I would attempt to do many years later—and so they concentrated once more on watching the television.

As the people of Kars were watching Funda Eser's rendition of the prime minister bowing tearfully to every dark desire of her American clientele, and later, as she concluded her spoof of a famous commercial with a riotous belly dance, a specially trained security team raided the branch headquarters of the People's Freedom Party in the Halıl Paşa Arcade, arresting the Kurdish janitor (the only person there at that hour), searching the cabinets and the file drawers, and confiscating every bit of paper they could find. The same police unit rounded up the party's executive committee—they knew from an earlier raid all the identities and addresses—and, charging them with subversion and Kurdish nationalism, took them all into custody.

These were not the only Kurdish nationalists in Kars. The three corpses discovered early that morning in a burned-out Murat taxi not yet covered with snow on the road to Digor were—according to official reports—Kurdish nationalist guerillas. The police claimed that the three young men had been trying to infiltrate the city for months, but, panicked at events of the previous evening, they decided to jump into a taxi and escape into the mountains. When they discovered the road closed they lost hope; in an ensuing quarrel, one of them detonated a bomb, killing all three. The mother of one boy, a cleaner at the hospital, later submitted a petition alleging that unidentified armed agents had rung the doorbell and taken her son away, and the taxi driver's older brother filed his own charge to the effect that his brother was no nationalist, not even a Kurd. Both petitions, however, were ignored.

By this time, everyone in Kars had become aware of the coup under way—if it wasn't a coup, one look at the two tanks wandering the city like ponderous dark ghosts was enough to confirm that *something* very odd was happening—but as they were also watching the performance on their television screens, and as the snow continued to fall apparently without end, their windows like a scene from an old fairy tale, the tanks provoked little fear. Politically active people were the only ones who were at all anxious.

Consider, for example, Sadullah Bey. A journalist held in the highest esteem by the Kurds of Kars and a well-known collector of folklore, he'd seen his share of military takeovers, so the moment he heard of the curfew, he began to prepare for the days in prison he knew lay ahead. After packing his bag with essentials—the blue pajamas he couldn't sleep without, the medicine for his prostate problem, his sleeping pills, his wool cap and socks, the photograph of his daughter in Istanbul (with his smiling grandson on her lap), and the painstaking notes he had taken for a book on Kurdish dirges—he sat down for a glass of tea with his wife, they watched Funda Eser do her second belly dance, and they waited. When the doorbell rang much later, in the middle of the night, he bade his wife farewell, picked up his suitcase, and headed for the door; seeing no one, he stepped out into the street—where in the sulfur light of the streetlamps he let his mind return to the glorious winters of his childhood, when he would skate across the frozen Kars River, when the silent streets were covered with this same beautiful snow—and as he stood there, someone pumped two bullets into his head and his chest, killing him on the spot.

Months later, when most of the snow had melted, the remains of a number of others similarly murdered that night were discovered, but—like the Kars press in the wake of the coup—I don't want to upset my readers any more than necessary, so I won't go into details. As for the rumors that the unknown perpetrators were Z Demirkol and his friends, I can only say that—at least in respect to whatever may have occurred in the early hours of the evening—these allegations are untrue. Although it took longer than expected, they did manage to sever the phone lines and safeguard the Kars Border Television transmission in support of the revolution; by night's end, all their energy was channeled into what had by then become their main obsession: finding a "deep-voiced folksinger to celebrate the heroes of the borderlands." After all, this would never measure up as a real revolution until all the radio and television stations in the city were broadcasting celebratory folk songs.

After asking at the barracks, the hospitals, the science high school, and the teahouses, they finally found a folksinger among the firemen on duty at the fire station; he was sure they would either arrest him or riddle him with bullets, but they whisked him down to the television studio.

When Ka woke the next morning, it was the fireman's sonorous voice he heard coming from the television in the lobby through the walls, the plaster partitions, and the half-drawn curtains. Through those same curtains also came an extraordinarily strong and wonderfully strange shaft of snow light. He'd slept soundly, even awoke relaxed, but he'd not risen from the bed before feeling a pang of guilt so strong it sapped all his strength and certainty. He rallied by pretending he was just an ordinary hotel guest, in another city and another bathroom; after he had washed, shaved, and changed, he picked up his door key by its heavy copper fob and went down to the lobby.

When he saw the folksinger on the screen and the other guests conversing in whispers as they watched, Ka had a measure of the silence that now engulfed the city; his mind returned to the previous evening, and only now did he begin to piece together all the things his mind had put away until this moment. He smiled coolly at the boy behind the reception desk; like a harried traveler vexed with the city's violent political infighting and determined to leave at the first opportunity, he headed straight for the adjoining dining room and ordered breakfast. In the corner an enormous teapot was steaming above a samovar; on the serving table was a plate of Kars cheese sliced very thin and a bowl of olives that, having long since lost their shine, looked rather deadly.

Ka sat down at a table next to the window. Through the gaps in the tulle curtain he gazed out at the snow-covered scene in all its beauty. The peacefulness in the empty street took Ka back to the curfews of his childhood and his youth. The census days, the days devoted to checking the electoral roll, the days given over to hunting for enemies of the state, the days when the military marched in and everyone would gather around their televisions and radios—he recalled them all, one by one. As the other guests sat listening to the martial strains on the radio, as they listened to the news bulletins of martial law, the curfew, and the list of prohibitions, all Ka wanted was to go outside and play in the empty streets. As a child he'd loved those martial-law days like holidays, when his aunts, his uncles, and his neighbors would come together in a common cause. It was perhaps to hide the fact that they felt happier and more secure during military coups that the middle- and upper-middle-class families of Ka's childhood in Istanbul were in the habit of quietly ridiculing the silly actions that inevitably attended any military takeover—the whitewashing of the city's cobblestones to make the whole city look like a barracks, or the rough-handed soldiers and policemen who'd seize anyone with long hair or a beard. While the Istanbul rich had a terrible fear of soldiers, they also knew the deprivations under which they lived—the harsh discipline and the low wages—and on this account they despised them.

The street outside looked as if it had been abandoned for centuries, so when Ka looked down to see an army truck turning into it, this sight too took him back to his childhood; like the boy he'd once been, he sat there transfixed.

A man who looked like a cattle dealer entered the room, came over to Ka, threw his arms around him, and kissed him on both cheeks.

"Congratulations! This is a great day for our nation!"

Ka remembered how the grown-ups in his life would congratulate each other after military coups, in much the same way that they congratulated one another during the old religious holidays. He returned the compliment, muttering a few words.

The door to the kitchen swung open and Ka felt all the blood in his body rise to his head: İpek was walking into the room. They came eye to eye, and for a moment Ka had no idea what to do. He decided he should stand up, but just then İpek smiled at him and turned to the man who had just sat down. She was carrying a tray with a cup and a plate.

Now İpek was setting the cup and the plate on the man's table, like a waitress.

Ka's spirits sank. He hated himself for failing to greet İpek as he should have done, but there was something going on here, and he knew at once that he wouldn't be able to hide from it. Everything he'd done the day before was all wrong. He hated himself for abruptly proposing to a woman he hardly knew; he hated himself for kissing her (as fine as that had been), and for losing control, and for holding her hand at the supper table; and most of all, he hated himself for behaving like a common Turkish man and getting drunk and without the slightest shame letting everyone know that he was sexually attracted to her. He had no idea what to say; his only hope was that İpek would keep playing the waitress forever and ever.

The man who looked like a cattle dealer shouted, "Tea!" in a coarse voice. İpek turned smoothly toward the samovar, the empty tray in her hand. After she had given the man his tea, she approached Ka's table; Ka felt the pulse of his heartbeat even in his nose.

"So what happened?" İpek asked, with a smile. "Did you sleep well?"

This reference to the night before, to yesterday's happiness, made Ka uneasy. "It looks like this snow isn't going to stop," he said haltingly.

They observed each other in silence. Ka knew he had nothing to say; anything he might come up with right now would be false. So, staring into her big, hazel, slightly cast eyes, he told her wordlessly that he had no choice but to remain silent. İpek sensed now that Ka's frame of mind was very different than the day before; he had, in fact, become a very different person. Ka could tell İpek sensed a darkness inside him and accepted it. This, he thought, would bind him to her for life.

"This snow is going to last for some time," she said carefully.

"There's no bread," said Ka.

"Oh, I'm so sorry." She went straight over to the table next to the samovar, put down the tray, and began slicing bread.

Ka had asked for bread because he couldn't bear the tension. Now, as he gazed at her back, he assumed a pensive pose. "Actually, I could have sliced that bread myself."

İpek was wearing a white pullover, a long brown skirt, and a thick belt of a type Ka remembered as being fashionable in the seventies; he hadn't seen such a belt since. Her waist was slim, her hips were perfect. She was just the right height for him. He even liked her ankles, and he knew that if he ended up returning to Germany without her, he would dwell for the rest of his life on painful memories of how happy he'd been here, holding hands, exchanging half-playful, half-serious kisses, and telling jokes.

Ka saw İpek's bread-slicing arm fall still, and before she turned around, he looked away. "Shall I put cheese and olives on your plate?" she asked. Her tone was formal, Ka realized, because she wanted to remind him there were people watching them.

"Yes, please," Ka answered, and as he spoke he looked around the room. When their eyes met again, her expression was enough to tell him that she knew he'd been staring at her the whole time her back was turned. Ka was unnerved by İpek's familiarity with the subtleties of male–female relations, that diplomacy at which he had always felt himself clumsy. And he was already worried that she might be his only chance for happiness.

"The bread came in on an army truck just a few minutes ago," İpek said, giving Ka a smile that broke his heart. "I'm looking after the kitchen; Zahide Hanım couldn't make it here this morning because of the curfew. . . . I was worried when I saw the soldiers."

Because the soldiers could have been coming for Kadife or Hande. Or even her father.

"They've sent hospital janitors to wipe up the blood in the National Theater," İpek whispered. She sat down at the table. "They've raided the university hostels, the religious high school, and the party headquarters." In the course of these raids, there'd been more deaths, she said. Hundreds had been arrested, although some were already released that morning. She told him all this in the particular hushed tone people save for political emergencies. It took Ka back twenty years; he remembered how he and his friends would sit in the university canteen exchanging tales of torture and brutality in whispers that were angry and woeful but also strangely proud. At times like these he had felt most guilty; all he'd wanted was to forget about Turkey and everything in it and go home and read books.

Now, to help İpek close the subject, he felt the impulse to say something like "This is terrible, absolutely terrible!" but though the words were in his mouth, he refrained from comment, knowing he would sound pretentious no matter how hard he tried; instead, he sat there, sheepishly eating his bread and cheese.

While he ate, İpek continued whispering—they'd loaded the dead boys from the religious high school onto army trucks and sent them out to the Kurdish villages for their relatives to identify them, but the trucks had got stuck in the snow; the authorities had granted a daylong amnesty for everyone to surrender all weapons; Koran instruction had been suspended and so had all political activity—and as she told him all this he looked at her arms, he looked into her eyes, he admired the fine color of her long neck, and he admired the way her brown hair brushed against her nape. Did he love her? He tried to imagine them together in Frankfurt, walking down the Kaiserstrasse, going home after an evening at the cinema. But dark thoughts were taking over his soul. All he could see was that this woman had cut the bread into thick slices just as they did in the poorest houses, and, even worse, that she had arranged these thick slices in a pyramid, in the manner of fishermen's soup kitchens.

"Please, talk to me about something else now," Ka said carefully.

İpek had been telling him about a man two houses down who'd been arrested on his way through the back gardens after someone denounced him, but now she gave him a knowing look and stopped. Ka saw fear in her eyes.

"I was very happy yesterday, you know. For the first time in years I was writing poems," he explained. "But I can't bear to hear these stories now."

"The poem you wrote yesterday was very beautiful," said İpek.

"Can I ask you to do something for me, before this despair overtakes me?"

"Tell me what I can do."

"I'm going up to my room now," said Ka. "Come up in a little while and hold my head between your hands? Just for a while—no more than that."

Before he had even finished speaking, he could tell from İpek's frightened eyes that she wasn't going to oblige, so he got up to leave. She was a provincial, a stranger to him, and he had asked her for something no stranger could understand. He could have spared himself this woman's uncomprehending look; he ought to have known better than to make this asinine request. As he ran up the stairs, he was full of self-reproach for having made himself believe he loved her. Throwing himself on the bed, he mused about what a fool he'd been to leave Istanbul for Kars in the first place, and then he concluded it had been a mistake even to leave Germany and return to Turkey. He thought of his mother, who had so wanted him to have a normal life and tried so hard to keep him away from poetry and literature; if she could have known his happiness depended on a woman from Kars who helped out in the kitchen and cut bread in thick slices, what would she have said? What would his father have said to learn that Ka had knelt before a village sheikh and talked with tears in his eyes about his faith in God? Outside, the snow had started falling again; the snowflakes he could see from his window were large and dreary.

There was a knock and he rushed to the door, suddenly full of hope. It was İpek, but wearing a very different expression: An army truck had just arrived with two men, one of them a soldier, and they'd asked for Ka. She'd told them he was here and that she would let him know they were waiting for him.

"All right," said Ka.

"If you want, I can give you that two-minute massage you wanted," İpek said.

Ka pulled her inside, closed the door, kissed her once, and sat her down at the head of the bed. He lay down, putting his head on her lap. They stayed like this for a time, saying nothing as they gazed out the window at the crows walking over the snow on the roof of the 110-year-old building that now housed the police headquarters.

"That's fine, I've had enough now, thank you," said Ka. Carefully lifting his charcoal-gray coat off the hook on the door, he left the room. As he went down the stairs, he smelled the coat to remind himself of Frankfurt; for a few minutes he could see the city in full color and wished he were there. The day he bought the coat at the *Kaufhof*, he'd been helped by a fellow whom he saw again two days later when he came to collect the coat, which had to be shortened. His name was Hans Hansen. It may have been because his name sounded so German and because he had blond hair that Ka also remembered thinking about him when he woke up in the middle of the night.

CHAPTER TWENTY-ONE

But I Don't Recognize Any of Them

KA IN THE COLD ROOMS OF TERROR

The men sent to pick up Ka came in one of those old army trucks—rarely seen these days, even in Turkey. A young hook-nosed, fair-skinned, plainclothes policeman met him in the lobby and sat him down in the middle of the front seat, taking the space by the door for himself as if to block Ka's possible escape. But his manner was polite enough; he addressed Ka as *sir* and this, Ka decided, meant he was not a policeman after all but an MİT agent, perhaps under instructions not to harm him.

They moved slowly through the city's empty white streets. The dashboard of the army truck was covered with indicator dials, but none of them was working; because the cab was high off the ground Ka could see into the handful of houses whose curtains were open. Television sets were on everywhere, and for the most part the city of Kars had drawn its curtains and turned in on itself. It was as if they were driving through another city altogether; as the windshield wipers went about their monotonous work, it seemed to Ka that the dreamlike streets, the old Baltic-style houses, and the beautiful snow-covered oleander trees had cast a spell bewitching even the driver and his hook-nosed companion.

They stopped in front of police headquarters. By now they were very cold, so they lost no time getting inside. It was much more crowded and frenetic than it had been the day before, and even though he'd been expecting this, Ka still felt uneasy. The animated disorder was typical of so many Turkish offices. It made Ka think of courthouse corridors, gates to football stadiums, bus stations. But there was also a whiff of iodine and hospitals, terror and death. Somewhere very close to where he was standing, someone was being tortured; the very thought made him feel guilty. Fear gripped his soul.

As he climbed the same stairs he had climbed with Muhtar the day before, instinct told him to follow the example of the men in charge, so he did his best to adopt an air of authority. Passing open doors, he heard the rapid *tap-tap-tap* of old typewriters. Everywhere men were barking into police radios or calling for the tea boy. On benches outside closed doors he saw lines of young men awaiting interrogation; they were hand-cuffed to one another, and it was obvious they had been badly roughed up; their faces were covered with bruises. Ka tried not to look them in the eye.

They took him into a room rather like the room he'd sat in with Muhtar, and here they informed him that despite his statement to the effect that he had not seen the face of the man who murdered the direc-tor of the Institute of Education and so was unable to identify the assailant from the photographs they'd shown him the day before, they now hoped he would be able to recognize the culprit among the religious high school boys in the cells downstairs. From this Ka deduced that MİT had taken charge of the police following the "revolution" and that rela-tions between the two groups were tense.

A round-faced intelligence agent asked Ka where he'd been around four o'clock the previous afternoon.

For a moment Ka's face turned gray. "They told me it would also be a good idea to pay a visit to His Excellency Sheikh Saadettin—" he began, but his interrogator cut him short.

"No, before that!" he said.

When Ka remained silent, the round-faced agent reminded him of his meeting with Blue. He did it in such a way as to suggest that he already knew all about it and even regretted having to cause Ka such embarrass-ment. Ka struggled to see this as a sign of good intentions. An ordinary police officer would have accused him of trying to conceal the meeting and then would have relished humiliating him, bragging that the police know everything.

In an almost apologetic voice, this agent explained that Blue was a dangerous terrorist as well as a formidable conspirator; he was a certified enemy of the Republic and in the pay of Iran. It was certain that he had murdered a television emcee, so a warrant had been issued for his arrest. He'd been sighted all over Turkey. He was organizing the fundamental-ists. "Who arranged your meeting?"

"A boy from the religious high school—I don't know his name," said Ka.

"Please see if you can identify him now," said the agent. "Look at them very carefully. You're going to be using the observation windows in the doors to their cells. Don't be afraid; they won't recognize you."

They took Ka down a wide staircase to the basement. A hundred-odd years ago, when this fine long building housed an Armenian hospital, the basement was used for wood storage and as a dormitory for the janitors. Much later, during the 1940s, when the building was turned into a state lycée, they had knocked down the interior walls and turned the space into a cafeteria. Quite a few Kars youths who would go on to become Marxists and sworn enemies of the West during the 1960s had swallowed their first fish oil tablets in this place; they'd washed them down with powdered yogurt milk sent by UNICEF, a vile-smelling drink that turned their stomachs. Now this spacious basement amounted to a corridor and four cells.

With a careful confidence bespeaking practiced routine, a policeman placed an army cap on Ka's head. The hook-nosed MİT agent who'd picked him up at the hotel gave him a knowing look and said, "These people are terrified of army caps."

When they reached the two cells on the right, the policeman shoved open the little observation windows and bellowed, "Attention! Officer!" Ka peered in through the window, no bigger than his hand.

The cell itself was about the size of a large bed; Ka could see five people inside. Perhaps there were more; it was hard to tell because they were sitting on top of one another. They were all propped up against the filthy wall on the far side, and although they'd done no military service they knew now to stand, however awkwardly, at attention, their eyes shut. (It seemed to Ka that a few had their eyes half open and were looking at him.) It was less than a day since the "revolution" had begun, but already their heads were shaven and their faces and eyes swollen from beatings. There was more light in the cells than in the hallway, but to Ka's eyes all the boys looked alike. His head began to spin as pain and fear and shame engulfed him. He was glad not to see Necip among them.

After Ka had failed to identify any of the boys in the second and third cells, the hook-nosed MİT agent said, "There's nothing to be afraid of. After all, when the roads open again you're going to pick up and leave."

"But I don't recognize any of them," Ka said, with faint stubbornness.

After that he did recognize a few; he had a very clear memory of one boy he'd seen heckling Funda Eser and another who'd been chanting slogans. If he denounced these boys now, it would be proof of his willingness to work with the police, and so, if he later saw Necip, it would be easier to pretend he hadn't. (It wasn't as if these boys were charged with anything serious.)

But he didn't denounce anyone. One youth whose face and eyes were streaked with blood looked up at Ka and pleaded, "Sir, please don't tell our mothers."

It looked as if these boys had been beaten in the heat of the coup's early hours: the police had not used any instruments, just their boots and fists. Ka looked into the fourth cell and once again failed to see anyone resembling the man who had assassinated the director of the Institute of Education. Once he was sure that Necip was not sitting among these terrified boys, he began to relax.

By the time they went upstairs, it was clear how eager the round-faced agent and his superiors were to find the director's assassin so they could parade him as the first achievement of the "revolution"; Ka suspected that they planned to hang the culprit then and there. Now a retired major entered the room. Despite the curfew he had somehow managed to find his way to police headquarters to ask that his grandson be released from detention. The major begged them not to torture the boy, who had no grievances against the state and had been sent to that religious high school only because his impoverished mother had fallen for those lies they told about how all the students were given free woolen coats and suits; in fact, the family were staunch supporters of Atatürk—

The round-faced man cut off the retired major in midsentence. "My dear sir, no one here gets treated badly," he said. He took Ka to one side. There was, he said, a chance that the murderer and Blue's men (Ka had the feeling that the culprit was thought to be one of them) might be with those they'd detained from the veterinary school.

So Ka ended up back in the army truck with the hook-nosed agent who'd first picked him up at the hotel. En route, as he admired the beauty of the empty streets and smoked a cigarette, he was thankful to have made it out of police headquarters. A small part of him was secretly relieved that the military had taken charge and the country wasn't bending to the will of the Islamists. But with most of his heart he vowed to himself that he would refuse to cooperate with both the police *and* the army. Just then a new poem came rushing into his mind; it was so powerful, so strangely exhilarating, that Ka now found himself turning to the hook-nosed intelligence agent and asking, "Might it be possible to stop off at a teahouse along the way?"

You couldn't walk two feet in this city without passing a teahouse full of unemployed men; although most establishments were closed this morning, one teahouse on Kanal Street was managing to do business without attracting the attention of the army jeep standing by the curb. Inside, a young apprentice was awaiting the end of the curfew, and three other young men were sitting at another table. They all stirred to see a man in an army cap and a plainclothes officer coming through the door.

Without missing a beat, the hook-nosed man drew a gun from his coat and, with a professionalism Ka could not help but admire, lined the young men up with their faces to the huge Swiss landscape hanging on the wall; just as effectively, he searched them and checked their identity cards. Ka was sure he was just going through the motions, so he sat down at the table next to the cold stove and with no difficulty set down the poem in his head.

He would later give this poem the title "Dream Streets"; although it opens on the snowy streets of Kars, the thirty-six-line poem also contains numerous references to the streets of old Istanbul, the Armenian ghost town of Ani, and the wondrous, fearsome, empty cities Ka had seen in his dreams.

When Ka finished his poem, he looked up at the black-and-white television to see that the morning folksinger had gone; in his place they were rebroadcasting the first moments of the drama at the National Theater. Vural the goalkeeper had just begun to recount his past loves and lost goals; by Ka's calculations it would be twenty minutes before he could watch himself reading his poem. This was the poem that had been erased from his mind before he'd had a chance to write it down: he was determined to record it.

Four more people entered the teahouse through the back door; the hook-nosed MİT agent drew his gun and lined them up against the wall also. The teahouse owner, a Kurd, tried to explain to the agent, whom he addressed as "my commander," that these men had not in fact broken the curfew, having really come in from the courtyard via the garden, but the agent decided to check their stories anyway. After all, one of them didn't have his identity card on him, and he was quaking with fear. The agent announced that he would take the man home by the same route he had come and called in his chauffeur to watch the youths still lined up against the wall.

Ka, putting his poetry notebook back into his pocket, followed the two men through the back door into the icy snow-covered courtyard; they went over a low wall, down three icy steps, and were lunged at by a barking dog on a chain before entering a ramshackle concrete building similar to most other buildings in Kars. In the basement was a foul smell: mud and dirty bedclothes. The man at the front slipped past a humming furnace into an area furnished with boxes and vegetable crates; there in a shabby bed slept an exceptionally beautiful fair-skinned woman; Ka could not keep from turning to look. Now the man without the identity card produced a passport for the MİT agent; the furnace was making such a clatter that Ka couldn't hear their words, but as he peered through the semidarkness he could see that the man had now produced a second passport.

It turned out they were a Georgian couple who had come to Turkey hoping to find work and make some money. The unemployed youths whose identity cards the MİT agent had checked back at the teahouse had been full of complaints about these Georgians. The woman was tubercular but still working as a prostitute; her customers were the dairy owners and leather merchants who came down to the city to do business. As for the husband, like so many other Georgians he was willing to work for half pay in the markets and so was taking work away from Turkish citizens whose job opportunities were already scarce. This couple was so poor and so stingy they wouldn't even pay for a hotel; instead, they paid the janitor from the water department five dollars a month to let them live in this furnace room. They were said to be saving up to buy a house when they returned to their own country, after which they planned never to work again for the rest of their lives. The boxes were filled with leather goods they had bought cheaply with an eye to selling them back in Tiflis. They had already been deported twice but both times found their way back to the furnace room. Having taken over, it was now up to the army to do what the corrupt municipal police had failed to accomplish: tackle these parasites and clean the city up.

Back at the teahouse, the owner was only too happy to be serving guests and listening to this table of feeble unemployed youths, who, with a little prompting from the MİT agent, began to speak, if somewhat haltingly, about what they hoped for from the military coup. Mixed in with their complaints about rotten politicians was quite a bit of hearsay good enough to count as denunciation: the unlicensed slaughter of animals, the scams run in the warehouses where state-owned commodities were stored, the crooked contractors who were smuggling Armenian illegals in on meat trucks and housing them in barracks, working the men all day long, only to pay them nothing. These unemployed youths gave no hint of understanding that the military had stepped in to take a position against Kurdish nationalism and keep "religious fanatics" from winning the municipal elections. Instead, they seemed to think that last night's events marked the beginning of a new age, in which immorality and unemployment would no longer be tolerated; it was as if they thought the army had stepped in expressly to find them jobs.

In the army truck once again, Ka observed the hook-nosed MİT agent taking out the Georgian woman's passport; sensing the agent's purpose was to look at her photograph, Ka felt strangely embarrassed.

The moment they stepped into the veterinary school, Ka could see how relatively benign things had been at police headquarters. As he walked down the corridors of this ice-cold building, he realized that he was in a place where no one gave a moment's thought to other people's pain. This was where they'd brought the Kurdish nationalists they'd rounded up, along with left-wing terrorists who proudly took responsibility for bombings, not to mention all those listed in the MİT files as supporters of these people. The police, the soldiers, and the public prosecutors all took a very dim view of any participant at events these groups had organized; the same went for anyone who aided or abetted the Kurdish guerillas who came down from the mountains to infiltrate the city. For people like these there was no mercy, and the interrogation methods were far harsher than those used against those suspected of links to political Islam.

A tall, powerfully built policeman took him by the arm and walked him down the corridor lovingly, as if Ka were an old man unsteady on his feet; together they visited three classrooms where terrible things were going on. I will follow Ka's lead here; just as he chose not to record them in his notebook, I will try not to dwell on them either.

After looking for three or four seconds at the suspects in the first classroom, Ka's first thought was of the shortness of mankind's journey from birth to death. One look at these freshly interrogated suspects was enough to conjure up fond wishful dreams of distant civilizations and countries he'd never visited. And so it was Ka knew with absolute certainty that he and all the others in the room were fast approaching the end of their allotted time; their candles would soon burn themselves out. In his notebook, Ka would call this place the yellow room.

In the second classroom he had a shorter vision. He remembered these men from a teahouse he'd passed the day before during his strolls around the city; their eyes were now blank with guilt. They had drifted off into some faraway dreamworld, or so it now seemed to Ka.

They moved on to the third classroom, where in the mournful darkness that overtook his soul Ka felt the presence of an omniscient power whose refusal to disclose all he knew made a torment of life on earth. Ka's eyes were open, but he could not see what was in front of him; all he could see was the color inside his head. Because the color was something close to red, he would call this the red room. Here the thoughts he'd had in the first two rooms—that life was short, that mankind was awash in feelings of guilt—came back to haunt him, but even with this fearsome landscape before him, he managed to stay calm.

As they left the veterinary faculty, Ka was aware that his companions were losing faith in him and beginning to wonder about his motives when he failed, yet again, to make an identification. But he was so relieved not to have seen Necip that when the MİT agent suggested that they examine the corpses, Ka agreed at once.

In the morgue, located in the basement of the Social Insurance Hospital, they showed him their most suspicious corpse first. This was the slogan-chanting Islamist militant who'd taken three bullets of the soldiers' second volley, but Ka had never seen him before. He approached this corpse with caution, and it seemed to him the dead youth was giving him a sad and respectful greeting. The corpse laid out on the second slab of marble seemed to be shivering from the cold: This was the body of the little grandfather. They showed it to Ka because they hadn't yet established that this man had come from Trabzon to see a grandson who was doing his military service in Kars, and because his small frame suggested he might be the assassin they were seeking. As he approached the third corpse, Ka was already thinking happy thoughts about seeing İpek again. This corpse had a shattered eye. For a moment it seemed this was a feature of all the corpses in this room. Then as he drew closer to the dead boy's white face, something inside him shattered too.

It was Necip, his lips still pushed forward as if to ask one more question. Ka felt the cold and the silence of the hospital. That same childish face, the same little pimples he'd seen earlier, the same aquiline nose, the same grimy school jacket. For a moment Ka thought he was going to cry, and this made him panic. The panic distracted him long enough for him to restrain the tears. There, in the middle of the forehead on which he'd pressed the palm of his hand only yesterday, was a bullet hole. But the most deathly thing about Necip was not the bullet hole, not his pale, bluish complexion, but the frozen stiffness with which he lay on the slab. A wave of gratitude swept over Ka; he was so glad to be alive. This distanced him from Necip. He leaned forward, separated the hands he'd been clasping behind his back, placed them on Necip's shoulders, and kissed him on both cheeks. The cheeks were cold but had not yet hardened. His remaining green eye was still half open, and it was looking right at Ka. Ka straightened himself up and told the agent that this was a friend who had stopped him in the road the day before to describe his efforts as a science-fiction writer and had later taken Ka to see Blue. He kissed him, he explained, because this teenager had had a pure heart.

———◆◆◆———

CHAPTER TWENTY-TWO

A Man Fit to Play Atatürk

SUNAY ZAIM'S MILITARY AND THEATRICAL CAREERS

After Ka had identified Necip's corpse at the Social Services Hospital morgue, an official hastily drew up a report, signed it, and passed it on to be certified. Then Ka and the MİT agent got back into their army truck and set off down the road. A pack of timid dogs walked alongside them; the only other signs of life were election banners and antisuicide posters. As they continued on their way, Ka's mind registered the restless children and anxious fathers twitching their closed curtains to catch a glimpse of the passing truck, but he looked right past them. All he could think about, all he could see, was Necip's face and Necip's stiff body. He imagined İpek consoling him when he got back to the hotel, but after the truck had gone through the empty city center, it continued straight down Atatürk Avenue to stop just beyond a ninety-year-old Russian building two streets away from the National Theater.

This was one of the beautiful run-down single-story mansions that Ka had been so happy to see on his first night in Kars. After the city had passed over to the Turks and joined the Republic, the mansion passed into the hands of one Maruf Bey, a well-known merchant who sold wood and leather to the Soviet Union. For forty-three years, he and his family had lived magnificently here, conveyed in horse-drawn sleighs and carriages, with their every need met by cooks and servants. After the Second World War, at the start of the Cold War, the government rounded up the well-known merchants who did business with the Soviet Union, charged them with spying, and carted them off to prison, from which it was clear they would never return.

And so, for the next twenty years, Maruf Bey's mansion sat empty, first because of having no owner and then because of a dispute over its ownership. In the mid-seventies a club-wielding Marxist splinter group had seized the building as its headquarters, where they planned a number of political assassinations (including that of Muzaffer Bey, the lawyer and former mayor, who had survived the attempt but was wounded); after the 1980 coup the building was empty for a time, and then the enterprising appliance dealer who owned the small shop next door converted half the old mansion into a warehouse, while a visionary tailor—who had returned to his hometown three years earlier with an impossible dream, having made his money in Istanbul and Arabia—turned the other half into a sweatshop.

When Ka walked into the former tailor shops, he saw button machines and big old-fashioned sewing machines and giant pairs of scissors still hanging from nails on the wall; in the soft orange glow of the old rose-patterned wallpaper they resembled strange instruments of torture.

Sunay Zaim was still dressed in the ragged coat, pullover, and army boots he'd been wearing two days earlier, when Ka had first seen him; he was pacing up and down the room with an unfiltered cigarette wedged between his fingers. When he saw Ka, his face lit up as if on seeing a dear old friend, and he hurried across the room to embrace him and kiss him on both cheeks. Ka almost expected him to say, "Congratulations on the military takeover!" as the cattle dealer at the hotel had done; something in his excessive friendliness put Ka on his guard. He would describe his dealings with Sunay in a favorable light: They were just two men from Istanbul who, having been thrown together in a remote and impoverished city, had found a way to work together under difficult conditions. But he was only too well aware of Sunay's part in helping to create those difficult conditions.

"Not a day passes when the eagle of dark depression doesn't take flight in my soul," said Sunay, infusing his words with a mysterious pride. "But I cannot catch myself. So hold yourself in. All's well that ends well."

In the white light pouring through the great windows, Ka surveyed the spacious room. The large stove and the friezes in the corners of the high ceilings bore witness to a glorious past; now the place was crawling with men carrying walkie-talkies, and there were two huge guards clocking Ka's every movement. On the table by the door leading into the corridor was a map, a gun, a typewriter, and a pile of dossiers; Ka deduced that this was the center of operations for the revolution, and that Sunay was the most powerful man present.

"There were times in the eighties, and these were the worst of times," said Sunay as he paced back and forth, "when we would arrive in some wretched, godforsaken town in the middle of nowhere—still not knowing if we would find a place to stage our plays or even a hotel room to rest our weary heads—and I would go out in search of an old friend, only to discover that he had long since left that small town, and it was at such times that depression—grief—would overtake me. To keep it at bay, I would rush about the streets of the city, knocking on the doors of the local doctors and lawyers and teachers in search of someone, somewhere, who might be interested in hearing the news we had brought from the frontiers of modern art and contemporary culture. When I found no one living at the only address I had to hand, when the police informed us that they would not, after all, give us permission to put on a performance, or when—and this was always my last hope—I took my humble request to the mayor, only to learn that he too was unwilling to accommodate us, I began to fear that darkness might engulf me. At moments like this the eagle in my chest would come to life; it would spread its wings and—just before it smothered me—it would take flight.

"It didn't matter where we performed—we could be in the most wretched teahouse the world has ever seen; we could be in a train station, thanks to some stationmaster who had his eye on one of our actresses; we could be in a fire station or an empty classroom in the local primary school or a humble shack or a restaurant; we could be playing in the window of a barbershop, on the stairs of a shopping arcade, in a barn, or on the pavement—but no matter where we were, I would refuse to succumb to depression."

The door to the corridor opened and Funda Eser came in to join them; Sunay switched from *I* to *we*. Ka saw nothing contrived in the shift to plural, this couple was so close. Funda Eser moved her great bulk across the room with considerable grace; after giving Ka a quick handshake she whispered something into her husband's ear and, looking very preoccupied, left the room.

"Yes, those were our worst years," said Sunay. "Social unrest and the combined stupidities of Istanbul and Ankara had taken their toll, and our fall from favor was well documented in the press. I had seized the great opportunity that comes only to those graced with genius—yes, I had—and on the very day that I was going to use my art to intervene in the flow of history, suddenly the rug was pulled out from under me and I found myself dragged through the worst imaginable mud. Although it failed to destroy me, my old friend depression now returned to haunt my soul. But no matter how long I languished in the mire, no matter how much filth, wretchedness, poverty, and ignorance I saw around me, I never lost my belief in my guiding principles, never doubted that I had reached the summit. . . . Why are you so frightened?"

A doctor in a white coat and carrying a bag appeared at the door. With a hurried air that seemed only half genuine, he pulled out a blood-pressure cuff and wrapped it around Sunay's arm, and as he did so Sunay gazed at the white light pouring through the windows, his air so tragic Ka thought he might still be thinking about his fall from favor in the early eighties. For his part, Ka remembered Sunay more for his roles in the seventies; it was these roles that had made him famous.

The seventies was the golden age of leftist political theater, and if Sunay stood out in this still rather small theatrical society, it was not only for being a hardworking and accomplished actor who could rise to the challenge of a demanding role—no, what audiences most admired were his leadership qualities. Young Turkish audiences warmed to his interpretations of powerful leaders like Napoleon, Lenin, and Robespierre, and Jacobin revolutionaries like Enver Pasha, as well as local folk heroes with whom they could identify. When he raised his commanding voice to rail against oppression; when, after a stage beating at the hands of wicked oppressors, he raised his proud head to cry, "The day will come when we will call them to account!"; when, on the worst day of all (the day he knew, when everyone knew, that his arrest was imminent), he gritted his teeth and, wishing his friends luck, told them that no matter what suffering lay ahead, he remained certain they would and could bring happiness to the people through the exercise of merciless violence—it was at that moment the lycée students and progressive university students in the audience would always respond with tearful and thunderous applause. Especially impressive was his decisiveness in the final acts of these plays, when power had passed into his hands and the time had come to mete out punishments to the wicked oppressors—here, many critics saw the influence of his military training. He'd studied at Kuleli Military Academy. He'd been expelled in his final year for slipping over to Istanbul in a rowboat to perform in various Beyoğlu theaters and also for staging a secret performance of a play called *Before the Ice Melts*.

When the military took over in 1980, all left-wing plays were banned, and it was not long afterward that it was decided to commission a big new television drama about Atatürk in honor of the hundredth anniversary of his birth. In the past, no one had thought a Turk was equal to the challenge of playing this blond, blue-eyed, westward-looking national hero; the predominant view was that great national films called for great international stars like Laurence Olivier, Curt Jurgens, or Charlton Heston. But this time *Hürriyet,* the biggest Turkish newspaper, entered the fray to promote the view that for once a Turk be allowed to play the role. It even went so far as to provide ballots that readers could cut out and send in with their suggestions. Sunay was among those nominated by this popular jury; in fact, being still well known for his fine work during the democratic era, he was the clear front-runner from the very first day. He had, after all, been playing Jacobins for years. Turkish audiences had no doubt but that the handsome, majestic, confidence-inspiring Sunay would make an excellent Atatürk.

Sunay's first mistake was to take this public vote seriously. He went straight to the papers and the television networks, making grand pronouncements to all who would listen. He had himself photographed relaxing at home with Funda Eser. He spoke openly about his domestic life, his daily routines, and his political views, remaking himself in Atatürk's image: he was at pains to show that, like Atatürk, he was a secularist. He also dramatized the fact that they enjoyed the same pastimes and pleasures (raki, dancing, fine clothes, and good breeding). He took to posing with volumes of Atatürk's classic work, *Orations,* and claiming that he was rereading his oeuvre from start to finish. (When one unsupportive columnist who entered the fray early on ridiculed him for reading not the original version of *Orations* but an abridged pure Turkish edition, Sunay took the original version out of the library and posed with it too, but all his efforts to get the new photograph published in this columnist's paper proved fruitless.) Undaunted, Sunay continued to appear at grand openings, concerts, and important soccer matches, and wherever he went he answered the questions of every third-rate reporter about Atatürk and art, Atatürk and music, Atatürk and Turkish sport. With an eagerness to please rather unbecoming in a Jacobin, he even did interviews with the anti-Western religious newspapers. It was during one such interview that he said, in answer to a question that was in fact not unduly provocative, "Perhaps one day, when the public deems fit, I might be able to play the Prophet Muhammad."

With this luckless remark, the trouble really began. The small Islamist periodicals went on the rampage. God forbid, they wrote, any mortal should presume to play the Great Prophet. The swarm of angry columnists who began with accusations of "showing disrespect for the Prophet" were soon accusing him of "taking active steps to discredit the Prophet." When even the army proved reluctant to silence the political Islamists, it fell to Sunay himself to put out the fire. Hoping to assuage their fears, he took to carrying around a copy of the Koran and telling the conservative Islamists how much he loved this book, which in so many ways was really rather modern. But this only created an opportunity for Kemalist columnists who had taken offense at his preening as "the people's choice" for the role of Atatürk: Never once, they wrote, had Atatürk tried to curry favor with religious fanatics. The newspapers supporting the military coup kept running the picture of Sunay in a spiritual pose with a copy of the Koran, the caption underneath reading, "A man fit to play Atatürk."

The Islamist press lashed back, running pictures of Sunay drinking raki with captions like "He's a raki drinker, just like Atatürk!" and "Is this man fit to play the Great Prophet?" This sort of war would flare up between the Islamist press and the secular press every couple of months, but now Sunay was the focus.

For a week, you couldn't open a paper without seeing Sunay. One picture had him guzzling beer in a commercial he'd made years earlier, others showed him getting a beating in a film he'd made in his youth, defiantly raising his fist before a flag emblazoned with a hammer and sickle and watching his wife kiss the male leads in various plays.

There was page after page of innuendo: claims that his wife was a lesbian, that he was still as much a Communist as ever, and that he and Funda had done dubbing for contraband porn films. And for the right money, Atatürk was not the only role he could play. After all, it was East German funding that had made it possible for him to perform Brecht; and after the coup, Sunay had insulted the state by telling "women from a Swedish association that torture was endemic to Turkey."

Finally, a high-ranking officer summoned Sunay to command headquarters to inform him rather curtly that in the view of the entire army he should withdraw from the race. This was not the same good-hearted officer who had invited several uppity Istanbul journalists to Ankara to scold them for criticizing the army's involvement in politics, only to offer them chocolates afterward, but another less jovial officer from the same public relations branch. He didn't soften one bit when he saw Sunay quaking with remorse and fear; rather, he ridiculed Sunay for propounding his own political views in the guise of the "man chosen to be Atatürk" and alluded to Sunay's short visit two days earlier to the town of his birth, during which he had played the "people's politician." (Cheered on by convoys of cars and crowds of tobacco manufacturers and unemployed men, Sunay had climbed up to the statue of Atatürk in the town's main square and inspired even more applause by squeezing Atatürk's hand; when a reporter from a popular magazine then asked him whether he thought he might leave the stage one day to enter politics, Sunay answered, "If the people want me.") The prime minister's office announced that the Atatürk film was to be postponed indefinitely.

Sunay was experienced enough to endure this defeat; his undoing came with what followed. During his monthlong Atatürk campaign he'd done so much television that people had come to associate his voice with Atatürk, and that meant no one would give him dubbing work. The television advertisers who had once been so happy to have him play the reasonable father with a knack for buying only the best and healthiest products turned their backs on him; they thought their viewers would find it strange to see a failed Atatürk brandishing a brush and holding a can of paint or explaining why he was so satisfied with his bank. But the very worst were those who believe everything they read in the papers, because now they believed with a passion that Sunay might be both an enemy of Atatürk and an enemy of religion: Some even believed he said nothing when his wife kissed other men. Or if they didn't believe it, there was still a lot of muttering about no smoke without fire.

The chief effect of all these reversals was the dwindling in number of those coming to see them perform. Quite a few people stopped Sunay in the street to say, "I expected better of you!" A young religious high school student, convinced Sunay had stuck his tongue out at the Prophet (and wanting badly to get in the papers), stormed into the theater waving a knife and spat in the face of several people. All this happened in the space of five days; Sunay and Funda then disappeared.

The gossip got even wilder. One rumor had it that they'd joined the Brechtian Berliner Ensemble, ostensibly to teach drama though really they were learning how to be terrorists. According to another account, the French Ministry of Culture had given them a grant and refuge at the French Mental Hospital in Şişli. In fact, they had decamped to the house of Funda Eser's artist mother on the shores of the Black Sea.

A year later, they finally found work as activity directors at an undistinguished hotel in Antalya. They spent mornings playing volleyball in the sand with German grocers and Dutch office workers; in the afternoon they dressed up as the shadow-theater characters Karagöz and Hacivat and performed in butchered German for the amusement of the children; in the evenings they sailed onstage dressed as a sultan and the belly-dancing darling of his harem. This was the beginning of Funda Eser's belly-dancing career, which she would continue to develop during their tours of the provinces over the next ten years. For three months Sunay managed to play the clown, until a Swiss barber crossed the line, interrupting their act with his jokes about Turks with harems and fezzes, which continued the next morning on the beach, where he began to flirt with Funda. Sunay beat him up, in full view of a shocked and terrified crowd of tourists.

After that, it seems the couple worked as freelance emcees, dancers, and theatrical entertainers at weddings and dance halls throughout the Antalya area. Even when he was introducing cheap singers, fire-eating jugglers, and third-class comedians, Sunay would make short speeches about Atatürk, the Republic, and the institution of marriage. Funda Eser would do a belly dance, and then the couple, now assuming an austere and highly disciplined air, would do something like the murder of Banquo, stopping after eight or ten minutes for a round of applause. It was during these evenings that the seeds were planted for the touring theater group they would later take all over Anatolia.

While having his blood pressure checked, Sunay had one of his bodyguards bring over a walkie-talkie; after issuing a few orders into it and reading a message a factotum had abruptly pushed in front of him, his face crumpled with revulsion. "They're all denouncing each other," he said. He went on to say that during his years of touring the remote towns of Anatolia, he had come to the conclusion that all the men in the country were paralyzed by depression.

"For days on end, they sit in those teahouses; day after day they go there and do nothing," he said. "You see hundreds of these jobless, luckless, hopeless, motionless poor creatures in every town; in the country as a whole there must be hundreds of thousands of them, if not millions. They've forgotten how to keep themselves tidy, they've lost the will to button up their stained jackets, they have so little energy they can hardly move their arms and legs, their powers of concentration are so weak they can't follow a story to its conclusion, and they've even forgotten how to laugh at a joke, these poor brothers of mine." Most of them were too unhappy to sleep; they took pleasure in knowing that the cigarettes they smoked were killing them; they began sentences, only to let their voices trail off as they remembered how pointless it was to carry on; they watched TV not because they liked or enjoyed the programs but because they couldn't bear to hear about their fellows' depression, and television helped to shut them out; what they really wanted was to die, but they didn't think themselves worthy of suicide. During elections, it was out of a desire for self-punishment that they voted for the most wretched parties and the most loathsome candidates; it was, Sunay insisted, because the generals responsible for the military coup spoke with honest realism about the need for punishment that these men preferred them to politicians endlessly promising hope.

Funda Eser, who had come back into the room, added that there were also many unhappy women who'd all worn themselves out having too many children, curing tobacco, weaving carpets, and working for pitiful wages as nurses while their husbands were who-knows-where. These women who shouted and wailed at their children all day long were the ones who kept life going; if you took them away, it would be the end of the line for the millions of joyless, jobless, aimless men you now saw all over Anatolia. They all looked the same, these men, unshaven, their shirts dirty; without the women looking after them they would end up like the beggars who froze to death on street corners during cold snaps, or the drunks who staggered out of taverns to fall into open sewers, or the senile grandfathers sent to the grocery store in their pajamas and slippers to buy a loaf of bread, only to lose their way. These men were all too numerous, "as we've seen in the wretched city of Kars"; although they owed their lives to their women, the love they felt for their wives made them so ashamed they tortured them.

"I gave ten years to Anatolia because I wanted to help my unhappy friends out of their misery and despair," said Sunay. There was no self-pity in his voice. "They accused us of being Communists, perverts, spies working for the West, and Jehovah's Witnesses; they said I was a pimp and my wife a prostitute; time and time again they threw us into jail, beating and torturing us. They tried to rape us; they stoned us. But they learned to love my plays and the freedom and happiness my theatrical company brought them. So now, as I am handed the greatest opportunity of my life, I shall not weaken."

Two men entered the room; as before, one of them handed Sunay a walkie-talkie. The channel was open and Ka could hear people talking;

they'd surrounded one of the shanties in the Watergate district, and after someone inside fired at them, they'd gone in to find one of the Kurdish guerillas and a family. On the same frequency, a soldier was giving orders; his subordinates addressed him as "my commander." A short while later, the same soldier addressed Sunay, first to give him advance notice of their plans and then to seek his views, now sounding more like an old school-mate than the leader of a revolution.

"There's a little fellow who's a brigade officer here in Kars," Sunay said, when he noticed Ka's interest. "During the Cold War, the military command had the very best forces massed farther inland, in Sarıkamış, in anticipation of a Soviet incursion. At most the people here would be staging diversions during the first attack. These days, they're mostly here to guard the border with Armenia."

Sunay now told him how, the first night, after he and Ka had come in on the same bus from Erzurum, he'd gone into the Green Pastures Café and run into Colonel Osman Nuri Çolak, a friend for thirty-odd years. The man was an old classmate from the Kuleli Military Academy. In those days, he was the only other person in Kuleli who knew Pirandello's name and could list Sartre's plays.

"Unlike me, he couldn't get himself expelled for lack of discipline, nor could he embrace the military wholeheartedly. This is why he never became a general staff officer. (There were people who whispered that he was too short to be a general anyway.) He's an angry, troubled man, but not, I think, because of professional problems—it's because his wife took their children and left him. He's tired of being alone, bored with having nothing to do here, and worn out by the small-town gossip, although of course he's the one who does most of the gossiping. Those unlicensed butchers I raided after declaring the revolution, the disgraceful stories about the Agricultural Bank loans and the Koran courses—he was the first to tell me about them; he was drinking a bit too much. He was over-joyed to see me but full of complaints about loneliness. And then, by way of apology but also with a note of boastfulness, he told me he was the highest-ranking officer in Kars that night, so he was going to have to get up early the next morning. The commander of his brigade had gone to Ankara with his wife to see doctors about her rheumatism, the deputy colonel had been called to an urgent meeting in Sarıkamış, and the governor was in Erzurum. He was the one with all the power! And as the snow had not yet stopped, it was clear from the experience of years past that the roads would be closed for days. I saw at once that this was the opportunity I had been awaiting all my life, so I ordered my friend another double raki."

According to the report submitted by the inspector major sent from Ankara, this man Ka had heard moments earlier on the walkie-talkie was indeed Colonel Osman Nuri Çolak (or Crooked Arm, as Sunay, his old friend from military school, preferred to call him); the major also reported that the colonel had initially taken this strange proposal for a military coup as nothing more than a joke, a whim of the raki table invented just for fun, but he nevertheless played along with the gag, adding that the job could be done with two tanks. That he would later actually execute the plan owed more to his wish not to blacken the name of courage in the face of Sunay's insistence—and his belief that, when it was all over, Ankara would be pleased with the outcome—than it did to any grudge or grievance or hope for personal glory. (According to the major's report, he had, however, sadly compromised his principles when in the turmoil he went into the Republic district and raided the home of an Atatürk-loving dentist to settle an argument about a woman.)

The colonel had used half a squadron to search houses and schools, and four trucks, and two T-1 tanks—these had to be driven with great care because spare parts were scarce—but that was the only military equipment he had used. If we don't count the "unexplained deaths" ascribed to "special teams" like Z Demirkol and his friends, most of what happened was typical of extraordinary circumstances like these. In other words, it was various hardworking officials at MİT and police headquarters who did most of it—after all, they had the files on everyone in the whole city and employed a tenth of the population as informers. In fact, these same officials were so elated to hear the spreading rumor of the demonstration that the secularists were planning to make at the National Theater that they sent out official telegrams to friends away from the city on leave, advising them to return at once lest they miss the fun.

From what he could hear coming in on the walkie-talkie, Ka gathered that the skirmish in the Watergate district had reached a new stage. When three gunshots sounded, first over the radio frequency and then were heard traveling through the air, muffled by the snowy plain, Ka decided that the sound of gunshots carried better when amplified by a walkie-talkie.

"Don't be cruel," Sunay said into the walkie-talkie, "but let them feel the power of the revolution and the state and let them see how determined we are." He'd raised his left hand and, propping his chin between thumb and forefinger, assumed a pose of deep thought, a gesture so distinctive that Ka now had a memory from the mid-seventies of Sunay posed this way while uttering the exact same words in a history play. He wasn't as handsome as he'd been in those days; he looked tired, pale, and worn.

Sunay picked up a pair of 1940s army-issue field glasses that were sitting on his table. Then he picked up the thick but ragged felt coat he'd worn throughout his ten-year tour of Anatolia and, putting on his fur hat, took Ka by the hand and led him outside. The cold took Ka by surprise; it made him think how weak and thin are men's dreams and desires, how insubstantial the intrigues of politics and everyday life compared with the cold winds of Kars. He noticed that Sunay's left leg was far more damaged than he'd thought. As they set off down the snow-covered pavement, he marveled at the emptiness of the bright white streets, and when it occurred to him that they might be the only ones walking outside in the entire city, he felt a surge of joy. While the beautiful snow-covered city with its empty old mansions could not help but make a man fall in love with life and find the will to love, there was more to Ka's feeling than that; he was also enjoying this proximity to real power.

"This is the most beautiful part of Kars," said Sunay. "This is my theatrical company's third visit to Kars in ten years, and each time this is where I come when the light fades, to sit under the poplars and the oleander trees, to listen to the melancholy cries of the crows and the magpies, while I gaze at the castle, the bridge, and the four-hundred-year-old *hamam.*"

They were now standing on the bridge over the frozen Kars River. Sunay gazed out over the shanties scattered on the hill rising above the left bank and pointed at one of them. Just below that house, just above the road, Ka saw a tank and, a little farther on, an army truck.

"We can see you," Sunay said into the walkie-talkie, as he peered through the field glasses. A few moments later, they heard two gunshots—first through the walkie-talkie, then through the air above the valley into which the river flowed. Was this some manner of greeting? Just ahead, at the entrance to the bridge, two bodyguards awaited them. They gazed at the wretched shantytown—a hundred years after Russian cannon destroyed the villas of the Ottoman pashas, the poor had come here to stake their claim—and they looked at the park on the opposite bank that had once been the heart of the bourgeoisie of Kars and at the city rising behind it.

"It was Hegel who first noticed that history and theater are made of the same materials," said Sunay. "Remember: Just as in the theater, history chooses those who play the leading roles. And just as actors put their courage to the test onstage, so too do the chosen few on the stage of history."

The entire valley rattled with explosions. Ka deduced from this that the machine gun atop the tank was now in use. The tank's cannon had also fired shots, but these had missed. The later explosions were caused by hand grenades. A black dog was barking. The shanty door opened and two people came out, their hands in the air. Ka could see tongues of flame licking at the broken windowpanes. All the while, the dog barked happily, darting back and forth, his tail wagging as he went over to join the people crouching on the ground. Ka saw someone running in the distance, and then he heard the soldiers open fire. The man in the distance fell to the ground, and all noise stopped. Much later, someone shouted, but by then Sunay's attention was elsewhere.

Followed by the bodyguards, they turned their back on the scene outside to reenter the tailor shop. The moment Ka looked again at the exquisite antique wallpaper in the old mansion, he knew he could not contain the new poem now waiting within him, so he retreated to a corner.

This poem, to which he would give the title "Suicide and Power," contains bold references to his walk with Sunay; he describes the thrill of power, the flavor of the friendship he's struck up with this man, and his guilt about the girls committing suicide. Later he would decide that in this "sound and considered" poem, the events he had witnessed in Kars had found their most powerful and authentic expression.

CHAPTER TWENTY-THREE

God Is Fair Enough to Know
It's How You Live Your Life

WITH SUNAY AT MILITARY HEADQUARTERS

When Sunay saw that Ka had completed his poem, he rose from his cluttered worktable and limped across the floor to offer his congratulations. "The poem you read at the theater yesterday was very modern too," he said. "What a shame that audiences in our country are not sophisticated enough to understand modern art. This is why my shows always include belly dancing and the confessions of Vural the goalkeeper. I give the people what they want, and then I give them an unadulterated dose of real-life drama. I would far rather mix high and low art for people than be in Istanbul doing bank-sponsored boulevard comedies. Now tell me as a friend, why didn't you identify any of the suspicious Islamists they showed you at police headquarters or the veterinary school?"

"Because I didn't recognize any of them."

"When they saw how fond you were of that youth who took you to see Blue, the soldiers wanted to arrest you too. They were already suspicious—you'd come all the way from Germany in this time of revolution, and you'd witnessed the assassination of the school director. They wanted to put you through an interrogation—torture you a little—just to see what they could turn up. I'm the one who stopped them. I'm your guarantor."

"Thank you."

"The thing no one can understand is why you kissed that boy who took you to Blue."

"I don't know why," said Ka. "He was very honest, and he spoke from the heart. I thought he was going to live for a hundred years."

"This Necip you're so sorry about. Would you like to know what kind of boy he really was? Let me read you something."

He produced a piece of paper with the following information: One day last March, the boy had run away from school; he was associated with a group that had smashed the windows of the Joyous Beer Hall for selling alcohol during Ramadan; he'd been doing odd jobs at the branch head-quarters of the Prosperity Party for a while but he'd stopped, either because his extreme views caused alarm or because he'd suffered a break-down that frightened everyone (there was more than one informer at party headquarters); he was an admirer of Blue and had been making overtures to him during the eighteen months Blue was visiting the city; he had written a story judged to be incomprehensible by the staff of MİT and got it printed by a religious newspaper with a circulation of seventy-five; on a few occasions a retired pharmacist who wrote columns for the same paper kissed him in a rather odd way, so Necip and his friend Fazıl had conspired to murder the man (this was according to their dossier— the original of the letter explaining their act they'd planned to leave at the scene of the murder had been stolen from the archives); on various occa-sions this Necip been seen walking down Atatürk Avenue, laughing with his friends, and on one of these occasions, in the month of October, he'd made a rude gesture at a unmarked police car that had just driven past them.

"MİT is doing important work here," said Ka.

"His Excellency Sheikh Saadettin's house is bugged, so they also know that the first thing you did when you met him was to kiss his hand. They know you confessed in tears to him that you believed in God— what they can't understand is why. There are quite a few left-wing poets who've panicked and changed sides, deciding they might as well find reli-gion before these people come into power."

Ka felt himself flush. When he saw that Sunay had read it as a sign of weakness, his shame only increased.

"I know the things you saw this morning upset you deeply. The police treat our young very badly; we have in our midst a number of animals who beat up young boys just for the fun of it. But let's leave that matter to one side for now."

He offered Ka a cigarette.

"Like you, I spent the years of my youth roaming the streets of Nişantaş and Beyoğlu. I was mad about films from the West and couldn't see enough of them, I read everything Sartre and Zola had ever written, and I believed that our future lay with Europe. To see that whole world destroyed, to see our sisters forced to wear head scarves, to see poems banned for being antireligious, as has happened already in Iran—this is one spectacle I don't think you would be prepared to take lying down. Because you're from my world. There's no one else in Kars who's read the poetry of T. S. Eliot."

"Muhtar, the candidate for the Prosperity Party, has read Eliot," said Ka. "He has a great interest in poetry."

"We don't even have to keep him locked up anymore," said Sunay with a smile. "He's signed a statement declaring his withdrawal from the race. He gave it to the first soldier who knocked on his door."

They heard an explosion. The windowpanes rattled and the frames shook. Turning in the direction of the noise, the two looked through the windows giving onto the Kars River, but all they could see were snow-covered poplars and the icy eaves of the undistinguished abandoned building opposite. Apart from the guard outside their door, there was no one on the street. Even at midmorning, Kars was heavy with gloom.

"A good actor," said Sunay in a light theatrical tone, "is a man who represents the sediment, the unexplored and unexplained powers that have drifted down through the centuries; he takes the lessons he has gleaned and hides them deep inside him; his self-mastery is awesome; never does he bare his heart; no one may know how powerful he is until he strides onto the stage. All his life, he travels down unfamiliar roads to perform at the most out-of-the-way theaters in the most godforsaken towns, and everywhere he goes he searches for a voice that will grant him genuine freedom. If he is so fortunate as to find that voice, he must embrace it fearlessly and follow the path to the end."

"In a day or two, when the snow melts and the roads reopen, Ankara is going to come down hard on the people responsible for this carnage," said Ka. "Not because they can't bear bloodshed; they'll be angry because this time they weren't the perpetrators. The people of Kars will hate you, and they'll feel the same about this strange production of yours. What will you do then?"

"You saw the doctor. I have a weak and diseased heart, and I've come to the end of my allotted time. They can do what they want with me; I don't care," said Sunay. "Listen to this: They're saying that if we caught someone important—say, the man who shot the director of the Institute of Education—hanged him right away, and broadcast the hanging on live TV, we'd have everyone in the city sitting still as a candle."

"They're already quiet as candles," said Ka.

"We've heard they're about to use suicide bombers."

"If you hang someone, all you'll do is increase the terror."

"Are you afraid of the shame you'll feel when the Europeans see what we've done here? Do you know how many men they hanged to establish that modern world you admire so much? Atatürk had no time for bird-brained fantasists; he had people like you swinging from ropes from the very first day.

"Get this into your head too," said Sunay. "Those religious high school boys you saw in the cells today have your face permanently etched in their memories. They'll throw bombs at anyone and anything; they don't care as long as they are heard. And furthermore, since you read a poem during the performance, they'll assume you were in on the plot. No one who's even slightly westernized can breathe free in this country unless they have a secular army protecting them, and no one needs this protection more than intellectuals who think they're better than everyone else and look down on other people. If it weren't for the army, the fanatics would be turning their rusty knives on the lot of them and their painted women and chopping them all into little pieces. But what do these upstarts do in return? They cling to their little European ways and turn up their affected little noses at the very soldiers who guarantee their freedom. When we go the way of Iran, do you really think anyone is going to remember how a porridge-hearted liberal like you shed a few tears for the boys from the religious high school? When that day comes, they'll kill you just for being a little westernized, for being frightened and forgetting the Arabic words of a simple prayer, even for wearing a tie or that coat of yours. Where did you buy that beautiful coat by the way? May I wear it for the play?"

"Of course."

"Just to keep you from getting any holes in your nice coat, I'll give you a bodyguard. In a little while I'm going to make an announcement on television. The curfew ends at midday, so stay off the streets."

"I can't believe there's an Islamist here in Kars who's so dangerous I can't go outside."

"What's done is done," said Sunay. "Above all, they know that the only way they'd ever get to run this country is by terrorizing us. Over time, our fears turn out to have been well founded. If we don't let the army and the state deal with these dangerous fanatics, we'll end up back in the Middle Ages, sliding into anarchy, traveling the doomed path already traveled by so many tribal nations in Asia and the Middle East."

His perfect posture, his commanding voice, his long and frequent gazes at an imaginary point high above the heads of his audience—Ka remembered seeing Sunay striking these same poses onstage twenty years earlier. But it didn't make him laugh. He felt as if he too were an actor in the same outmoded play.

"What do you want from me?" Ka asked. "Spell it out."

"If it weren't for me, you'd have a hard time keeping your head above water in this city. No matter how much you toady to the Islamists, you'd still get holes in your coat. I'm the only friend you have here; I'm the only one in Kars who can protect you—without my friendship you'd soon be trembling in one of those cells beneath police headquarters, waiting to be tortured. As for your friends at the *Republican,* it's not you they put their faith in, it's the army. Know where you stand."

"I do know."

"Then confess to me what you hid from the police this morning. Tell me of the guilt you hide deep in your heart."

"I think I may be starting to believe in God here," Ka said, with a smile. "It's something I may be hiding even from myself."

"You're deceiving yourself! Even if you did believe in God, it would make no sense to believe alone. You'd have to believe in him the same way the poor do; you'd have to become one of them. It's only by eating what they eat, living where they live, laughing at the same jokes, and getting angry whenever they do that you can believe in their God. If you're leading an utterly different life, you can't be worshiping the same God they are. God is fair enough to know it's not a question of reason or logic but how you live your life. But that's not what I was asking you about just now. In half an hour I'm going on television to address the people of Kars. I want to bring them good tidings. I'm going to say that we've caught the assassin who shot the director of the Institute of Education. There's a high probability that the same man shot the mayor. May I say that you identified this person for us this morning? Then you can go on television and tell the whole story."

"But I didn't identify anyone."

With an anger that owed nothing to theatricality, Sunay grabbed Ka's arm and marched him out of the room and down a wide corridor; he then put him in a bright white room that looked onto the inner courtyard. One look at this room was enough to repel him; it wasn't the filth but the sordid atmosphere. There were stockings hanging on a line strung between the window latch and a nail on the wall. Ka saw in the corner an open suitcase containing a hair dryer, a pair of gloves, shirts, and a huge bra that might have fit Funda Eser. Funda Eser herself was sitting in a chair beside the suitcase; the table before her was piled high with paper and cosmetics she'd pushed aside to make room for a bowl—was it stewed fruit, Ka wondered, or soup? She was reading as she ate.

"We're here in the name of modern art. . . . We're as attached to each other as a fingernail is to flesh," said Sunay, as he squeezed Ka's arm even harder. Ka wasn't sure what he was trying to say, and Sunay seemed unsure whether this was life or a play.

"Vural the goalkeeper has gone missing," said Funda Eser. "He went out this morning and hasn't come back."

"He's passed out somewhere," said Sunay.

"But where?" said his wife. "Everything's closed. No one's allowed out in the street. The soldiers have started a search. I'm afraid he's been kidnapped."

"I hope to God he *has* been kidnapped," said Sunay. "If they would skin him alive and cut out his tongue, we'd all be better off."

For all their coarse manners and rough language, there was something so pleasant about their convivial banter, about the depth of their mutual understanding, that Ka could not help feeling a certain respect, even a little envy. The moment he came eye to eye with Funda Eser he instinctively bowed so low that he almost touched the floor.

"Madam, you were a veritable sensation last night," he said, in an affected voice that did, nevertheless, contain traces of heartfelt admiration.

"Shame on you," she said, with faint embarrassment. "In our company it's not the players who make the masterpiece, it's the audience."

She turned to her husband. The two began to converse, flitting from one subject to the next as a king and his queen might do, pressed by many important matters of state. Ka listened with a mixture of appreciation and amazement as husband and wife fretted over which costume was right for his impending television appearance (civilian clothes? military uniform? black tie?); they went on to discuss the script for his speech (Funda Eser had written part of it) and the statement taken from the owner of the hotel where they'd stayed during previous visits (nervous about the soldiers continually coming by for another search and anxious to curry favor, he'd formally denounced two young guests who looked suspicious); finally, they pulled out a cigarette pack on which someone had scribbled the afternoon schedule for Border City Television (four or five reruns of the gala at the National Theater, three of Sunay's speech, folk songs about heroism and the borderlands, a travelog about the beauties of Kars, and a Turkish film called *Gulizar*). They read it through, and it met with their approval.

"And now," said Sunay, "what are we to do with this poet of ours, whose intellect belongs to Europe, whose heart belongs to the religious high school militants, and whose head is all mixed up?"

"It's clear from his face," said Funda Eser, smiling sweetly. "He's a good boy. He's going to help us."

"But he's been shedding tears for the Islamists."

"He's in love, that's why," said Funda Eser. "Our poet has been awash in emotions these last two days."

"Ah, is our poet in love?" said Sunay Zaim, with exaggerated gestures. "Only the purest poets allow love into their hearts in times of revolution."

"He's not pure poet, he's pure lover," said Funda Eser.

As husband and wife carried the scene forward with their usual flawless technique, Ka felt both furious and stupefied. Afterward they returned to the atelier and drank tea together at the big table.

"I'm telling you this so you'll see why helping us is the wisest thing to do," said Sunay. "Kadife is Blue's mistress. It's not politics that draws Blue to Kars, it's love. They didn't arrest him because they wanted to know which young Islamists he was working with. Now they're sorry, because last night, just before the raid on the religious high school dormitory, he vanished like smoke. All the young Islamists in Kars are in his thrall. He's somewhere in the city, and he will definitely want to see you again. It could be difficult for you to tip us off: I suggest that we plant one or two microphones on you and perhaps a transmitter in your coat—you'd have the same protection then as the late director of the Institute of Education, so you'd have little worry for your safety. After you leave the meeting, we can go in and capture him." By the look on Ka's face, Sunay could tell he had not warmed to this proposal. "I'm not going to insist," he said. "You don't look it, but your behavior today has shown you to be a cautious person. Of course, you are a man who can look after himself, but I'm still telling you that you need to be very careful around Kadife. We suspect she tells Blue everything she hears, and this must include her father's conversations every evening with his dinner guests. It's partly the thrill of betraying her father, but it's also because she's bound by love to Blue. How do you explain the strength of this passion?"

"Do you mean for Kadife?" Ka asked.

"No," said Sunay impatiently. "I mean this passion for Blue. What does this murderer have that makes everyone fall for him? Why is his name legend throughout Anatolia? You've spoken to him. Can you solve this mystery for me?"

Funda Eser had picked up a plastic comb and was passing it through her husband's pale hair with such tender care that Ka, distracted, fell silent.

"I'd like you to hear the speech I'm going to make on television," said Sunay. "Come with me in the army truck, and we can drop you off at the hotel along the way."

The curfew was due to end in forty-five minutes. Ka politely declined the offer and asked whether he might have permission to go back to the hotel on foot. It was granted.

It was a relief to walk down the wide empty pavements of Atatürk Avenue—to feel the silence of the snow-packed side streets, to gaze once again at the beautiful snow-covered Russian houses and the oleanders— but he soon realized he was being followed. He crossed over to Halitpaşa Avenue and then turned left on Little Kâzımbey. The detective behind him was huffing and puffing as he hurried through the snow to catch up. Running after him was the same friendly black dog with the white spotted forehead that Ka had seen around the train station the night before. Ka hid in the doorway of one of the workshops in the Yusufpaşa district, hoping to give him the slip, but all at once he found himself face-to-face with his pursuer.

"Are you following me for intelligence purposes or for my protection?"

"God only knows, sir. Whichever sounds better to you is fine by me."

But the man looked so tired and worn out that Ka doubted he could even protect himself. He looked at least sixty-five years old, his face was lined and wrinkled, his voice was thin, and the light had gone from his eyes; he gazed at Ka timidly, as fearfully as most people gaze at the police. Like all the plainclothes agents in Turkey, he was wearing Sümerbank shoes, and when Ka saw the soles were beginning to come apart, he took pity on him.

"You're a policeman, aren't you? If you have your identity card, let's get them to open up the Green Pastures Café and sit down for a while."

They did not have to knock on the restaurant door for long before it opened. Ka and the detective, whose name was Saffet, sat drinking raki and sharing cheese pastries with the black dog as they listened to Sunay's speech. It wasn't any different from the speeches of the leaders of military coups during Ka's childhood. In fact, by the time Sunay had explained how Kurdish and Islamist militants in the pay of "our enemies abroad" and degenerate politicians who would stop at nothing to win votes had pushed Kars to the brink of destruction, Ka was a little bored.

While Ka was drinking his second raki, the detective, pointing respectfully at Sunay, directed his attention back to the television. His face had changed somehow. No longer a third-rate detective, he had assumed the air of a long-suffering citizen submitting his petition. "You know this man, and what's more he respects you," the detective said plaintively. "I hope you will be able to help me with my humble request. If you would present it to him, you could rescue me from this hellish life. Please, ask him to remove me from this poison investigation and reassign me."

At Ka's questioning look, he rose to his feet and went over to bolt the café door. Then he sat back down at the table to tell the tale of the "poison investigation." The wretched detective had difficulty expressing himself, and the raki had gone straight to Ka's already addled head, so he had a hard time following the confusing story.

It began at Modern Buffet, a snack bar in the city center not far from the military and intelligence headquarters. Many soldiers went there for sandwiches and cigarettes; lately, however, there were suspicions that the cinnamon sharbat sold there had been laced with poison. The first victim was an infantry officer trainee from Istanbul. Two years earlier, on the morning of a much dreaded, exceptionally arduous maneuver, this officer came down with a fever that made his whole body shiver so wildly he couldn't even stay on his feet. He was carted off to the infirmary, where they soon established that he had been poisoned, whereupon the officer, thinking he was about to die, blamed the spicy sharbat he had drunk at the snack bar on the corner of Little Kâzımbey and Kâzım Karabekir avenues—just for the sake, he added angrily, of trying something new.

At first this seemed like a simple case of accidental food poisoning, so it was soon forgotten, but there was reason to think again when, not long afterward, two other officers with similar symptoms turned up at the same infirmary. Like the first, they were shaking so much they could barely talk and couldn't stand up for long before falling to the ground; both blamed the same hot cinnamon sharbat that they'd drunk out of simple curiosity. It then emerged that a Kurdish granny was producing this refreshment in her home in the Atatürk district; everyone loved it, so her grandsons had decided to sell it at their snack bar. This information came to light during the secret interrogation conducted at Kars military headquarters immediately following the denunciations. But when secret samples of the old granny's sharbat were tested at the veterinary school, no trace of poison could be found.

The investigation was closed when the general happened to mention it to his wife; to his alarm and dismay, he discovered that she'd been drinking several cups of the sharbat every day, hoping it might be good for her rheumatism. Quite a few officers' wives, in fact, and quite a few officers had been knocking back huge quantities of this beverage—all claiming it was for health reasons, though really it was out of simple boredom. Further investigation revealed the officers and their wives were not alone in succumbing to this fad; soldiers on leave were going there as well, as were their visiting families, partly because this snack bar was so central one inevitably passed it about ten times a day but mostly because the sharbat was the only new thing in Kars.

When the general added his new findings to the investigation, he was so concerned about the possible implications that he handed the matter over to MİT and the army inspectorate. The more ground the army gained in its savage conflict with the Kurdish PKK guerillas, the lower became the morale of the weak, despairing, and unemployed Kurdish youths who'd fallen in with them; this situation had led some of these youths to nurture strange and frightful dreams of revenge, as was reported by quite a few of the detectives who spent their days dozing in the city's coffeehouses. They'd overheard youths discussing bomb and kidnap plots, possible attacks on the statue of Atatürk, a scheme to poison the city's water supplies, and another to blow up its bridges. This was why the officials had taken the cinnamon sharbat scare so seriously, but owing to the acute sensitivity of the issue, they'd been unable to interrogate or torture the snack bar's owners. Instead, they assigned a number of detectives attached to the governor's office to infiltrate not just the Modern Buffet but the kitchen of the old granny, by now over the moon with delight at all the business she was doing.

The detective assigned to the snack bar subjected the granny's cinnamon drink to yet another examination, and he also inspected the glasses, the heat-resistant holder on the crooked handles of the tin ladles, the change box, a number of rusty holes, and the employees' hands for any sign of a strange powder. A week later, he too had all the symptoms of poisoning; he was shaking and coughing so much he had to leave work.

The detective who'd been planted in the granny's kitchen was far more industrious, however. Every night he would sit down and write a full report, listing not just the people who'd passed through the kitchen that day but also every item of food the old lady purchased (carrots, apples, plums, dried mulberries, pomegranate flowers, dog roses, and marshmallows). His reports soon revealed the recipe for this much-praised and appetizing beverage. The detective who was drinking five or six carafes a day suffered no ill effects whatsoever: Indeed, it was, according to him, a bona fide tonic, a genuine mountain sharbat such as appears in the famous Kurdish epic *Mem u Zin*. The experts sent in from Ankara lost faith in this detective because he was a Kurd. They were able to deduce from his reports that the sharbat was poisonous to Turks but not to Kurds; however, because of the official state position that Kurds and Turks are indistinguishable, they kept this conclusion to themselves.

At this point, a group of doctors sent in from Istanbul set up a special clinic at the Social Insurance Hospital. Soon, however, it was overrun by perfectly healthy Kars inhabitants just looking for free treatment, not to mention some so-called invalids complaining of such common afflictions as hair loss, psoriasis, hernias, and stammers; this stampede cast a long shadow over the seriousness of the investigation.

So it fell once again to the Kars intelligence services to unravel the sharbat plot that was slowly incapacitating the city and had already endangered the health of thousands of soldiers; it was for MİT to capture the perpetrators before the city's spirit was broken. Saffet was just one of several diligent agents assigned to this case. Most had been told simply to follow the people who drank the sharbat the granny boiled with such joy. It was no longer an investigation of the path by which the poison had spread through Kars, but a vain attempt to find a way to distinguish those poisoned by the sharbat from those who were not. To accomplish this task, the detectives were following all the soldier and plainclothes police consumers of the granny's cinnamon drink—sometimes all the way home.

When Ka heard that this exhausting, painstaking mission had worn out not just the detective's shoes but also his spirit, he promised to raise the subject with Sunay, who had yet to reach the end of his televised speech.

The detective was so elated by this promise, he threw his grateful arms around Ka, kissed him on both cheeks, and unbolted the door with his own hands.

CHAPTER TWENTY-FOUR

I, Ka

THE SIX-SIDED SNOWFLAKE

With the black dog following close behind, Ka walked back to the hotel, savoring the empty beauty of the snow-covered streets. He dashed off a note to İpek—*Come at once!*—and asked Cavit, the receptionist, to take it in to her right away. Then he went upstairs and threw himself down on his bed. As he waited he thought of his mother, but soon his thoughts turned instead to İpek, who had still not arrived. It was not long before he felt racked with such pain as to make him decide he had been a fool to fall in love—or to come to Kars at all. He had been waiting for some time and still there was no sign of her.

Thirty-eight minutes after Ka returned to the hotel, İpek walked into his room. "I had to go to the coal seller," she said. "I knew there would be a line once the curfew ended, so I went out through the back courtyard at ten to twelve. After twelve I spent some time wandering around the market. If I'd known you were here, I would have come straight back."

İpek brought such life into the room, Ka's mood soared—so wildly he was terrified of doing something to destroy this moment of bliss. He gazed at İpek's long shiny hair. Her hands never stopped moving. In no time at all, her left hand traveled from her hair to her nose, to her belt, to the edge of the door, and on to her beautiful long neck, before it was back straightening her hair again, only to be found a moment later fingering her jade necklace. (She must have just put it on. Only now did Ka notice it.)

"I'm terribly in love with you, and I'm in pain," Ka said.

"Don't worry. Love that blooms this fast is just as fast to wither."

Ka threw his arms around her and tried to kiss her. İpek kissed him

211

back; she was as calm as he was frenzied. He felt her small hands on his shoulders, and the sweetness of her kiss sent his head spinning. He knew from the easy way she moved her body that she was ready to make love; he was so happy that his eyes, his mind, and his memory opened fully to the moment and to the world.

"I want to make love, too," said İpek. For a moment she looked straight ahead; then she lifted her eyes with swift determination and met Ka's gaze. "But as I've already said, it can't happen under my father's nose."

"So when is your father going out?"

"He never goes out," said İpek. "I have to go," she said, and she pulled herself away.

Ka stood in the doorway watching İpek until she had disappeared down the stairs at the end of the dimly lit corridor. Then he closed the door, sat down on the edge of the bed, whipped his notebook out of his pocket, and, turning to a clean page, began writing the poem he would call "Privations and Difficulties."

After finishing the poem, Ka continued to sit on the edge of the bed. He realized, for the first time since his arrival in Kars, that apart from chasing İpek and writing poems there was nothing in this city for him to do. The insight made him feel deprived and liberated in equal measure. He felt sure that if he could convince İpek to leave Kars with him, he would find lifelong happiness with her. He knew that the moment was fast approaching when he must persuade her but now that he had a plan—he felt grateful for the snow.

He threw on his coat and went outside, unnoticed by anyone except Saffet. Instead of heading toward the city hall, he turned left on National Independence Avenue and walked down the hill. He went into the Knowledge Pharmacy to buy some vitamin C tablets, turned left off Faikbey Avenue, keeping a straight way and pausing now and then to look into restaurant windows, and turned into Kâzım Karabekir Avenue. The campaign banners he'd seen fluttering above the avenue the day before had all been taken down, and all the shops were open. One stationery and cassette vendor was playing loud music. The pavements were crowded with people who'd come out just to mark the end of the curfew; they walked down as far as the market and then back up the hill, pausing now and then to shiver in front of a shop window. Those who usually came to the city on minibuses serving the outlying areas, frequenting the city center to doze in the teahouses and perhaps stop off at the barber's for a shave, had not come in today, and Ka was pleased to see so many teahouses and barbershops empty. The children in the streets made him forget the fear inside. He watched the children sledding on the bridges, throwing snow-balls, playing and fighting and cursing in the vacant lots, the snow-covered squares, the school playgrounds, and the gardens surrounding the government offices. Only a few wore coats; most were wearing school jackets, scarves, and skullcaps. They were happy about the coup because it had given them a school holiday. Whenever the cold got too much for him, Ka went to join Saffet at the nearest teahouse; he'd go straight to the detective's table, have a glass of tea, and then go outside again.

Now used to Saffet's following him, he no longer found the man frightening. If they really wanted to find out everything he did, they'd use a man he couldn't see. A visible detective's only use was to provide cover for an invisible colleague. That's why Ka panicked when, at one point in his walk, he lost sight of Saffet, and why he went in search of him. He found Saffet, with a plastic bag in his hand, panting on the corner of Faikbey Avenue—the spot where the tank was the night before.

"The oranges were very cheap, I couldn't help myself," said the detective. He thanked Ka for waiting, adding that he had proved himself to be well-intentioned by choosing not to give him the slip. "From now on, why don't you just tell me where you're going? That would save us both a lot of effort."

Ka didn't know where he was going. But after two more glasses of raki in yet another empty teahouse, he realized he wanted to pay another visit to His Excellency Sheikh Saadettin. There was no chance of seeing İpek again in the near future, and he dreaded the torment of letting himself think about her, preferring to bare his soul to the sheikh. He'd begin by telling him about the love of God in his heart, and then they could have a civilized conversation about God's intentions and the meaning of life. But then he remembered that the sheikh's lodge was bugged: When the police heard what had to say, they'd never stop laughing.

Still, when he passed His Excellency's modest residence on Bay-tarhane Street, Ka stopped for a moment to look up at the windows.

Later on his walk, Ka noticed that the doors of the local library were open, so he went inside and walked up the muddy stairs. On the landing was a bulletin board onto which someone had carefully tacked the seven local newspapers. Since, like the *Border City Gazette,* they had all been printed the day before, there was no mention of the revolution but a great deal about the splendid performance at the National Theater and the continuing blizzard.

Although the city's schools were closed, he saw five or six students in the library reading room; there was also a handful of retired government officials; like the students, they had probably come here to escape the cold in their houses. In a corner, among the dog-eared dictionaries and tattered children's encyclopedias, he found several old volumes of *The Encyclopedia of Life,* which had given him so many hours of pleasure as a child. Inside the back cover of every volume was a series of colored transparencies, which, as you leafed through them, revealed the organs and inner workings of a car or ship or the anatomy of a man. Ka went straight for the fourth volume, hoping to find the series featuring the baby nestled like a chick inside an egg within its mother's distended tummy, only to find that the pictures had been torn out; all that remained were frayed edges attached to the back cover.

On page 324 of the same volume, he found an entry that he read with care:

> SNOW. The solid form taken by water when falling, crossing, or rising through the atmosphere. Each crystal snowflake forms its own unique hexagon. Since ancient times, mankind has been awed and mystified by the secrets of snow. In 1555, a priest named Olaus Magnus in Uppsala, Sweden, discovered that each snowflake, as indicated in the diagram, has six corners....

How many times Ka may have read this entry during his stay in Kars, to what degree he internalized its illustration of a snow crystal, is impossible for me to say. Years later, when I went to visit his family home in Nişantaş to spend long hours discussing Ka with his tearful and—as always—troubled and suspicious father, I asked whether I could look at the old man's library. Memory told me that what I was looking for would be not in Ka's room with all the other books from his childhood and youth but in a dark corner of the sitting room on the shelves where his father kept his own collection. Here, among the handsome spines of his father's law books, the collection of novels from the forties—some in Turkish, others in translation—and the row of telephone directories, I found the beautifully bound volumes of *The Encyclopedia of Life.* The first thing I did was turn to the back of the fourth volume to glance at the anatomical illustration of the pregnant woman; then I directed my attention to the book as an object. I was still admiring its perfect condition when there, before my eyes, was page 324. It was almost as if the book had opened of its own accord to that page. By the entry on snow, I found a thirty-two-year-old piece of blotting paper.

After Ka had finished looking at the encyclopedia, he reached into his pocket and, like a student sitting down to do homework, took out his notebook. He began to write a poem, the tenth to have come to him since his arrival in Kars. In the opening lines, he extolled the singularity of snowflakes, going on to describe his childhood memories of the mother with child he had this time failed to find at the back of the fourth volume of *The Encyclopedia of Life;* in the poem's final lines, he mapped out a vision of himself and his place in the world, his special fears, his distinctive attributes, his uniqueness. The title he gave this poem was "I, Ka."

Ka was still writing down the poem when he noticed someone else sitting at his table. Lifting his eyes from the page, he gasped: It was Necip. He felt no terror at this apparition, and neither was he amazed; instead he felt ashamed—here was someone who didn't die so easily and yet Ka had been willing to believe he was dead.

"Necip," he said. He wanted to throw his arms around the boy and kiss him.

"I'm Fazıl," said the youth. "I saw you in the street and followed you." He glanced over at the library table where Saffet was sitting. "Tell me quickly—is it true that Necip's dead?"

"It's true. I saw him with my own eyes."

"Then why did you call me Necip? You're still not sure, are you?"

"No, I'm not."

For a moment Fazıl's face crumpled, but then he pulled himself together.

"He wants me to take revenge. This is why I am convinced he's dead. But when school opens all I want to do is study; I don't want to take revenge. I don't want to get involved in politics."

"Revenge is a terrible thing."

"Even so, I would do it if I thought I had to," said Fazıl. "I've been told you discussed this with him. Did you give those letters to Hicran—I mean Kadife?"

"I did." Fazıl's gaze made him uncomfortable. Should I correct that? he asked himself. Say *I was intending to* instead? But it was already too late. For some reason, his lie made him feel more secure. The pain on Fazıl's face was hard to bear.

Fazıl covered his face with his hands and cried a little. But he was so angry the tears wouldn't come. "If Necip is dead, who is the person I should be taking revenge on?" When Ka said nothing, Fazıl looked him straight in the eye. "You know who it is," he said sternly.

"I was told that sometimes the two of you thought the same thing at the same time," said Ka. "If you can still do that, you know who it is."

"But what he thinks, the thing he wants me to think, causes me terrible pain," said Fazıl. For the first time, Ka saw in his eyes the same light he'd seen in Necip's. It was like sitting across from a ghost.

"So what is it that he's forcing you to think?"

"Revenge," said Fazıl. He cried a little more.

Ka could tell right away that Fazıl's own thoughts were of something other than revenge. And Fazıl said so himself when he saw Saffet the detective rise from his table to join them.

"Please, may I see your identity card?" said Saffet the detective, giving him a fierce look.

"They have my school identity card at the circulation desk."

Ka watched the fear that swept over Fazıl as he realized he was talking to a plainclothes policeman. They all walked over to the circulation desk. The detective snatched the identity card from the hand of the terrified woman on duty, and when he saw that Fazıl was a student at the religious high school, he shot Ka a look that said *I might have known* and, like an old man confiscating a child's toy, he put the identity card into his pocket.

"If you want this religious high school ID of yours back, you'll have to come to police headquarters and ask for it."

"With all due respect," said Ka, "this boy has gone to great lengths to stay out of trouble, and he's only just heard that his best friend is dead. Couldn't you give him his card back now?"

Having tried so hard to ingratiate himself earlier in the day so that Ka might put in a good word for him, Saffet now refused to budge.

Hoping he might persuade Saffet to entrust the card to him later on, when no one was watching, Ka arranged to meet Fazıl at five o'clock at the Iron Bridge. Fazıl left the library at once. By now all the other people in the reading room were on tenterhooks, thinking that they too were going to have their identity cards checked. But Saffet was not paying attention; he went straight to his table, where he returned to a 1960s volume of *Life* magazine to read about the sad Princess Sureyya, who had been spurned by her husband the shah after failing to give him a child, and to look at the last picture taken of Adnan Menderes, the former prime minister, before he was hanged.

Calculating now that he would not be able to get Saffet to give him Fazıl's identity card, Ka too left the library. When he returned to the enchanted white street to see swarms of joyous children throwing snowballs, he forgot all his fears. He felt like running. In Government Square he saw a gloomy line of shivering men clutching burlap sacks and packets wrapped in newspaper, tied up with string. These cautious citizens of Kars had decided to take the coup seriously and were turning over all the weapons in their houses to the state. The authorities didn't trust them and had refused to let them inside the provincial headquarters, but they were still lined up like cold little lambs at the main entrance. When it was first announced that all weapons were to be turned in, most Kars residents had gone straight out into the snow in the dead of night to hide their guns in the frozen ground where no one would think to look for them.

While he was walking down Faikbey Avenue, Ka ran into Kadife and felt his face go red. He'd just been thinking of İpek, and because he associated one sister with the other he now thought Kadife extraordinarily beautiful. He had to exercise great self-control to keep himself from embracing her.

"I must have a very quick word with you," said Kadife. "But there's a man following you, so I can't say anything while he's looking. Could you go back to the hotel and come to Room Two-seventeen at two o'clock? It's the last room at the end of your corridor."

"Are you sure we can speak openly there?"

"If you don't tell anyone we've spoken"—Kadife opened her eyes wide—"and I mean not even İpek, no one will ever know." She gave him a stern and businesslike handshake. "Now look behind you as casually as you can and tell me if I have one or maybe even two detectives following me."

Ka nodded, smiling slightly. He was surprised at his own coldbloodedness. Although the thought of meeting Kadife secretly in a room confused him, he had no trouble putting it out of his mind.

He knew at once that he didn't want to see İpek again before his meeting with Kadife, not even by chance, so he decided to continue his walk to kill time. No one seemed to be complaining about the coup; instead, the mood was much as he remembered from the coups of his childhood: There was a sense of new beginnings and of a change from the vexing routines of everyday life. The women had gathered up their handbags and their children and gone out to pick through the fruit in the stalls and at the greengrocer's in search of a bargain; the men with their thick mustaches stood on street corners, smoking filterless cigarettes and gossiping as they watched the crowds go by; the beggar he'd seen feigning blindness twice the day before was no longer in his station under the eaves of an empty building between the garages and the market. The vendors who had been selling oranges and apples out of pickup trucks parked right in the middle of the street were gone. The traffic, normally light, was lighter still, but it was hard to say whether this was owing to the coup or to the snow. There were more plainclothes policemen out on the streets (one had been made a goalkeeper by the boys playing soccer at the bottom of Halitpaşa Avenue). The two hotels next to the garages that served as brothels (the Hotel Pan and the Hotel Freedom) were, like the cockfight ring and the unlicensed butchers, not to be permitted to pursue their black arts "indefinitely." As for the explosions they'd heard coming from the shanty areas, especially at night, the people of Kars were accustomed to this, so their calm was generally undisturbed. Ka found the general lack of interest liberating. This is why he went into the snack bar on the corner of Little Kâzımbey Avenue and Kâzım Karabekir Avenue, and ordered himself a cinnamon sharbat, and he drank it with relish.

CHAPTER TWENTY-FIVE

This Is the Only Time We'll
Ever Be Free in Kars

KA WITH KADIFE IN THE HOTEL ROOM

When he stepped into Room 217 sixteen minutes later, Ka was so worried someone might have seen him that he tried to joke with Kadife about the cinnamon sharbat, its sour taste still in his mouth.

"For a while there were rumors of angry Kurds poisoning that sharbat to kill military personnel," said Kadife. "It's even said that secret investigators were sent in to solve the mystery."

"Do you believe these rumors?" Ka asked.

"When educated, westernized outsiders come to Kars and hear these conspiracy theories," said Kadife, "they immediately try to disprove them by going to the snack bar and ordering a *salep,* and then the fools end up poisoning themselves because the rumors are true. Some Kurds are so unhappy they know no God."

"Then why, after all this time, hasn't the state stepped in?"

"Like all westernized intellectuals, you put your trust in the state without even realizing it. MİT knows everything that goes on in Kars, and they know about the sharbat, too, but they don't stop it."

"So does MİT know we're here together in this room?"

"Don't worry, right now they don't," said Kadife with a smile. "One day they'll find out, but until that day comes we're free here. This is the only time we'll ever be free in Kars. Appreciate it, and take off your coat."

"This coat protects me from evil," said Ka. Seeing fear in Kadife's face, he added, "And it's cold in here."

The room in which they were meeting was half of an old storage room. One narrow window looked onto the inner courtyard, and there was room only for the single bed on which they were now sitting, Ka perched uncertainly at one end of it, Kadife at the other. The room had that stifling dusty smell that you find only in unaired hotel rooms. Kadife leaned over to fiddle with the dial on the radiator, but when it refused to budge she gave up. When she saw Ka had jumped nervously to his feet, she tried to conjure up a smile.

For a moment it seemed to Ka that Kadife was taking great pleasure from this assignation. After so many years of solitude, he too was pleased to be alone in a room with a beautiful girl, but he sensed she had no time for such soft thoughts; the light shining in her eyes spoke of something darker and more destructive.

"Don't worry, right now the only agent they have following you is that poor man with the bag of oranges. You can take this to mean that the state isn't afraid of you, it just wants to frighten you a little. Who was following me?"

"I forgot to look," said Ka, with embarrassment.

"What?" Kadife shot him a poisonous look. "You're in love, aren't you. You're madly in love." But she quickly pulled herself together. "I'm sorry, it's just that we're all so scared," she said, and once again the expression on her face changed abruptly. "You must make my sister happy. She's a very good person."

"Do you think she'll love me back?" Ka asked, in a near whisper.

"Of course she will—she must; you're a very charming man," said Kadife. When she saw how much she'd shocked him, she added, "What's more, you're a Gemini like İpek." She then explained that while Gemini men are best suited to Virgo women, the double personality of Geminis, which makes them both light and shallow, can either delight a Gemini woman or disgust her. "But you both deserve to be happy," she added consolingly.

"When you've discussed me with your sister, has the question of her coming back with me to Germany ever come up?"

"She thinks you're very handsome," said Kadife, "but she doesn't trust you. Trust takes time. Impatient men like you don't fall in love with a woman, they take possession of her."

"Is this what she said to you?" said Ka, raising his eyebrows. "Time is a scarce commodity in this city."

Kadife glanced at her watch. "First let me thank you for coming here. I've summoned you to discuss something very important. Blue has a message he wants to give you."

"If we meet again, they'll follow me and arrest him on the spot," said

Ka. "Then they'll torture us all. They've been in his house. The police hear everything he says."

"Blue knew they were listening," said Kadife. "He sent you this message before the coup, and he also sent a message for you to pass on to the West. He sent it to make a philosophical point. Stop sticking your nose into this suicide business—that's what he wanted you to tell them. But now everything's changed; there's something more important. He wants to cancel that message and give you a new one."

The more Kadife insisted, the more uncertain Ka became. "It's not possible to go from one point to another in this city without anyone seeing you," he said finally.

"There's a horse-drawn carriage. Twice a day it stops just outside the kitchen door to drop off gas canisters, coal, and bottled water. It then goes on to make deliveries all over the city, and it's draped in canvas to protect its goods from snow and rain. The driver can be trusted."

"Am I to hide under the canvas like a thief?"

"I've done it plenty of times myself," said Kadife. "It's lots of fun to go right across the city without anyone knowing. If you agree to this meeting, I promise I'll do everything in my power to help you with İpek. I want you to marry her."

"Why?"

"What woman wouldn't want her older sister to be happy?"

In his entire life, Ka had never known a pair of siblings who didn't feel deep hatred for each other; even if they seemed to get along, there was something oppressive about their solidarity, something to indicate that they were just going through the motions. But that wasn't why Ka dismissed Kadife's claim; what inclined him to doubt her was the way her left eyebrow shot up almost of its own accord and the way she pouted her half-open lips like a child about to cry—or, rather, like a Turkish film actress simulating innocence. Nevertheless, when Kadife looked at her watch again and said that the horse-drawn carriage was arriving in seventeen minutes, and if he promised immediately to accompany her to see Blue, she would tell him everything, Ka agreed without hesitation. "But first you have to tell me why you're willing to put this much trust in me."

"You're a dervish; Blue says so. He believes God has graced you with lifelong innocence."

"Okay, then," said Ka hurriedly. "Is İpek also aware of this special gift from God?"

"Why should she know? This is Blue's view."

"Please tell me everything İpek thinks about me."

"Actually, I've already told you everything." Seeing that she was breaking Ka's heart, Kadife thought for a few moments, or else made as if to think—Ka was too upset by now to tell the difference—and then she said, "She thinks you're fun. You've just arrived from Germany and whatnot. You have so much to talk about."

"What do I have to do to convince her to trust me?"

"It may not happen in the first instant, but within ten minutes of meeting a man, a woman has a clear idea of who he is, or at least who he might be for her, and her heart of hearts has already told her whether or not she's going to fall in love with him. But her head needs time to understand what her heart has decided. If you ask me, there's very little a man can do at this point except wait for time to take its course. If you really love her, all you have to do is tell her all the beautiful things you feel about her: why you love her, why you want to marry her."

Ka said nothing. When Kadife saw him gazing out the window like a dejected child, she told him she could already imagine Ka and İpek living happily together in Frankfurt—and how happy her sister was to put Kars behind her! She could even see the two of them smiling on some Frankfurt street as they walked to the cinema of an evening. "Just give me the name of a cinema you might go to if you were in Frankfurt," she said. "Any name."

"Filmforum Hochts," said Ka.

"Don't they have theaters with names like the Alhambra, the House of Dreams, or the Majestic in Germany?"

"They do. The Eldorado!"

As they watched the snowflakes swirling aimlessly above the courtyard, Kadife told him about a part she'd been offered when she was in the university drama society; it was a German-Turkish production in which the cousin of a classmate had some involvement. They'd wanted someone to play a covered girl and she refused; now she was hoping that İpek would find happiness with Ka in that same German-Turkish world, because really her sister was meant to be happy; the problem was she didn't realize it, and so until now she'd been unhappy. Being unable to have a child had destroyed her too, but her main source of anguish was in not understanding why—being beautiful, refined, thoughtful, and straightforward—why she should be so unhappy. Sometimes she even wondered whether her unhappiness was not owing precisely to her having so many fine qualities (here Kadife's voice began to crack). She went on to say that throughout her childhood and her teenage years, she had looked up to her sister, trying to be as good and as beautiful as she was (here her voice cracked again), but when she compared herself to İpek she felt evil and ugly; her sister was aware of this and so had tried to hide her beauty, hoping to make things easier for Kadife.

By now she was crying. Between tearful gasps, she told him in a trembling voice about when she was in middle school. ("We were in Istanbul then, and not so poor," said Kadife, whereupon Ka took the opportunity to point out that they weren't so poor now either, but Kadife promptly closed this parenthesis by snapping, "But we live in Kars!") Anyway, one morning when she arrived late for her first class, Mesrure Hanım, her biology teacher, asked, "Is your brilliant sister late too?" and then she added, "I'll let you off this time because I'm so fond of your sister." But of course, İpek wasn't late.

The horse-drawn carriage entered the courtyard. It was a typical old rig, with red roses, white daisies, and green leaves painted on its wooden sides. The tired old horse stood behind a cloud of frozen breath, the edges of its nostrils covered with ice. The driver was broad-shouldered and slightly humpbacked; a light blanket of snow covered his hat and coat. When Ka saw another blanket of snow on the tarpaulin, his heart began to beat faster.

"Please don't be afraid," said Kadife. "I'm not going to kill you!"

Ka saw a gun in Kadife's hand, but he didn't seem to realize that she was pointing it at him.

"I'm not having a nervous breakdown, if that's what you're thinking," said Kadife. "But if you try anything funny, believe me, I'll shoot you. . . . We don't trust journalists who go to Blue looking for quotes—or anyone else for that matter."

"But you invited me," said Ka.

"You're right, but even if you don't think so, the MİT people could have guessed we were planning this visit and might be listening in. I'm suspicious because you wouldn't take off your beloved coat just a moment ago. Now take it off and leave it on the bed—quick!"

Ka did as she asked.

Kadife passed her little hands, which were as small as her sister's, over every corner of his coat. Finding nothing, she said, "Please don't take this the wrong way, but now you have to take off your jacket, your shirt, and your undershirt. These people strap microphones to people's backs and chests. There are probably about a hundred people wandering around Kars with these microphones on them any time of the day or night."

Ka removed his jacket and lifted up his shirt and his undershirt, like a child showing his stomach to a doctor.

Kadife gave him a look. "Now turn around," she said. There was a silence. "That's fine, then. My apologies for the gun. . . . But when people are wearing a wire, they won't let us do a search; they won't keep still at all." She was still holding the gun. "Now listen to me," she said, in a menacing voice. "You are to tell Blue nothing about our conversation or our friendship." She sounded like a doctor scolding a patient after an examination. "You are not to mention İpek or let him know you're in love with her. Blue doesn't take kindly to filth like that. If you insist on talking about it, and he doesn't burn you for it, rest assured that I will. He reads minds better than a genie; he might try to coax you into saying something. If he does, you're to act as if you've seen İpek once or twice but that's it. Understood?"

"Understood."

"Make sure you show Blue respect. Whatever you do, don't try to put him down by playing the conceited, foreign-educated, European sophisticate. And if you let this sort of foolishness slip out by accident, don't even think of smiling. Don't forget: The Europeans you admire and imitate so slavishly couldn't care less about you . . . and they're scared to death of people like Blue."

"I know."

"I'm your friend, be frank with me," said Kadife, assuming a pose from a second-rate Turkish film.

"The driver's removed the tarpaulin," said Ka, looking out the window.

"You can trust this driver. His son died last year in a clash with the police. Enjoy the journey."

Kadife was first to go downstairs. When she reached the kitchen, Ka saw the horse-drawn carriage move under the arch that divided the old Russian courtyard from the street, and then he went downstairs as planned. When he saw no one in the kitchen, he had a moment of panic, but then he saw the driver standing in the doorway that led into the courtyard. Without a word, he lay down next to Kadife among the empty propane canisters.

The journey, which he knew at once he would never forget, lasted only eight minutes, but to Ka it seemed much longer. As he wondered where in the city they were, he listened to the people of Kars commenting on the creaking carriage moving past them, and he listened to Kadife's steady breathing as she lay quietly next to him. A gang of boys caught the tail of the carriage and were pulled along with them for a little while. He liked the sweet smile Kadife gave him; it made him as happy as those boys.

———— ••••• ————

CHAPTER TWENTY-SIX

It Is Not Poverty That Brings Us So Close to God

BLUE'S STATEMENT TO THE WEST

As the wheels of the horse-drawn carriage rolled over the snow, rocking Ka like a baby, the first lines of a new poem came to him; but when the carriage mounted a pavement he was jolted back to the present. They creaked to a stop and a silence followed, long enough for Ka to receive a few more lines of the poem. Then the driver lifted the tarpaulin and Ka saw they were in an empty snow-covered courtyard lined with auto repair and welding shops and also harboring a broken tractor. In the corner was a dog on a chain; when they emerged from under the tarpaulin, he greeted them with a few barks.

They went through a walnut door. As they continued through a second door, Ka could see Blue gazing down at the snow-covered courtyard; once again, Ka was struck by the red highlights in his brown hair, the freckles on his face, and his midnight-blue eyes. When he walked into yet another threadbare room filled with a number of familiar items (the same hair dryer as yesterday, the same half-open suitcase, and the same plastic ashtray with the Ottoman figures running along the edges and the logo ERSIN ELECTRIC) it didn't take Ka long to guess that Blue had moved the night before. But from his cold-blooded smile Ka could tell that he'd already adjusted to the new situation and was pleased with himself for having eluded the authorities.

"One thing's for sure," said Blue. "You can't write anything about the suicide girls now."

"Why not?"

"Because the military doesn't want anything written about them either."

"I'm not a spokesman for the military," Ka said carefully.

"I know that."

For a long tense moment, the two stared at each other.

"Yesterday you told me that you had every intention of writing about the suicide girls in the Western press," said Blue.

Remembering his little lie, Ka felt embarrassed.

"Which Western newspaper did you have in mind?" Blue now asked. "At which of the German papers do you have contacts?"

"The *Frankfurter Rundschau*," said Ka.

"Who?"

"It's a liberal German newspaper."

"What's his name?"

"Hans Hansen," Ka said, and hugged his coat.

"I have a statement for Hans Hansen. I intend to speak up against the coup," said Blue. "We don't have much time. I want you to start writing it down this instant."

Ka opened to the back page of his poetry notebook and began to take notes. Blue began by saying that at least eighty people had been killed so far (the actual death toll, including those shot at the theater, was seventeen); numerous schools and houses had been raided, and tanks had destroyed nine shanties (the real figure was four); after claiming that some students had died under torture, he alluded to some street skirmishes that Ka had not heard anyone else mention; passing rather quickly over the sufferings of the Kurds, he slightly exaggerated those visited on the Islamists; it was, he now said, to provide a pretext for this coup that the state had arranged for the mayor and the director of the Institute of Education to be assassinated. The reason for all this, he said, was to prevent the Islamists from winning the elections. The banning of all political parties and associations proved his point, he said.

As he went into more detail, Ka looked straight into Kadife's eyes; she hung on Blue's every word. In the margins of these pages he would later tear out of his poetry notebook, he made a number of drawings and doodles that proved he was thinking about İpek: a slender neck, a head of hair, a child's house with childish smoke rising out of a child's chimney. . . . Many years before, Ka had explained to me that when a good poet is confronted with difficult facts that he knows to be true but also inimical to poetry, he has no choice but to flee to the margins; it was, he said, this very retreat that allowed him to hear the hidden music that is the source of all art.

Ka appreciated some of Blue's pronouncements enough to record them in his notebook word for word.

Contrary to what the West seems to think, it is not poverty that brings us so close to God; it's the fact that no one is more curious than we are to find out why we are here on earth and what will happen to us in the next world.

Instead of explaining the source of this curiosity and revealing mankind's purpose on earth, Blue's final words posed a challenge to the West:

Will the West, which takes democracy, its great invention, more seriously than the word of God, come out against this coup that has brought an end to democracy in Kars? [He stopped here to make a grand gesture.] Or are we to conclude that democracy, freedom, and human rights don't matter, that all the West wants is for the rest of the world to imitate them like monkeys? Can the West endure any democracy achieved by enemies who in no way resemble them? I have something to say to all the other nations that the West has left behind: Brothers, you're not alone.

He paused for a moment. "Can you be sure that your friend at the *Frankfurter Rundschau* is going to print all this?"

"He takes offense when people discuss the West as if it's a single person with a single point of view," Ka said carefully.

"But that's how it is," Blue said, after another pause. "There is, after all, only one West and only one Western point of view. And we take the opposite point of view."

"The fact remains that they don't live that way in the West," said Ka. "It's not as it is here; they don't want everyone thinking alike. Everyone, even the most ordinary grocer, feels compelled to boast of having his own personal views. If we used the term *Western democrats* instead of *the West,* you'd have a better chance of pricking people's consciences."

"Fine, do what you think best. Must we make more corrections to get this published?"

"Although this began as a news item, it's become more interesting, more like a proclamation," said Ka. "They might want to put your name to it . . . and maybe even include a few biographical details—"

"I've prepared those already," said Blue. "All they need say is that I'm one of the most prominent Islamists in Turkey and perhaps the entire Middle East."

"Hans Hansen is not going to print this as it stands."

"What?"

"If the social-democratic *Frankfurter Rundschau* were to print a statement from a single Turkish Islamist, it would seem as if they were taking sides," Ka said.

"I see. When something doesn't serve Mr. Hans Hansen's interests, he has a way of slithering away," said Blue. "What do we need to do to convince him?"

"Even if the German democrats come out against a military coup in Turkey—and it has to be a real coup, not a theatrical one—they'll still be very uneasy if the people they're defending are Islamists."

"Yes, these people are all terrified of us," said Blue.

Ka could not tell if he was boasting or merely feeling misunderstood. "Well," he said, "if you included the signatures of a liberal ex-Communist and a Kurdish nationalist, you'd have no trouble getting this announcement into the *Frankfurter Rundschau*."

"Come again?"

"If we could find two other people in this city to come in on this, we could get started on a joint announcement immediately," Ka said.

"I'm not going to drink wine just to make Westerners like me," said Blue. "I'm not going to flutter around imitating them just so they can stop fearing me long enough to understand what I'm doing. And I'm not going to abase myself at the door of this Westerner, this Mr. Hans Hansen, just to make the godless atheists of the world feel pity for us. Who is this Mr. Hans Hansen anyway? Why is he laying down so many conditions? Is he a Jew?"

There was a silence. Sensing Ka's rebuke, Blue glared at him with hatred. "The Jews are the most oppressed people of our century," he said, by way of recovery. "Before I change a word of my statement, I want to know more about this Hans Hansen. How did you meet him?"

"Through a Turkish friend who told me that the *Frankfurter Rundschau* was going to publish a news analysis on Turkey and that the commentator wanted to speak to someone familiar with the background."

"So why didn't Hans Hansen take his questions to this friend of yours? Why did he need to speak to you as well?"

"That particular Turkish friend didn't have as much background knowledge of these things as I did."

"Let me guess what these things might be," said Blue. "Torture, brutality, foul prison conditions, and various other things that make us look even worse."

"Perhaps around that time some religious high school students in Malatya had killed an atheist," said Ka.

"I don't remember hearing about any such event," said Blue. He was watching Ka carefully. "It is deplorable when Islamists go on television to boast about killing just one poor atheist, but it is just as appalling when Orientalists seek to vilify the Islamists by running news reports that augment the death toll to ten or fifteen. If Mr. Hans Hansen is one of these people, let's forget him."

"All Hans Hansen did was ask me a few questions about the EU and Turkey. I answered his questions. A week later he called me up and invited me to his house for dinner."

"Just like that—without giving any reason?"

"Yes."

"That's very suspicious. What did you see while you were in his house? Did he introduce you to his wife?"

Ka looked at Kadife, seated beside the fully drawn curtains and staring at him intensely.

"Hans Hansen has a lovely happy family," said Ka. "One evening, after the paper was put to bed, Mr. Hansen picked me up from the *Bahnhof*. A half hour later, we arrived at a beautiful bright house set inside a garden. They were very kind to me. We ate roast chicken and potatoes. His wife boiled the potatoes first and then roasted them in the oven."

"What was his wife like?"

Ka conjured up the image of Hans Hansen, the *Kaufhof* salesman who had sold him his precious coat. "Hans Hansen is blond and handsome and broad-shouldered; his wife, Ingeborg, and his children have the same blond beauty."

"Did you see a cross on the wall?"

"I don't remember. I don't think so."

"There was a cross, but you probably didn't notice," said Blue. "Contrary to what our own Europe-admiring atheists assume, all European intellectuals take their religion and their crosses very seriously. But when our guys return to Turkey, they never mention this, because all they want to do is use the technological supremacy of the West to prove the superiority of atheism. . . . Tell me what you saw, what you spoke about."

"Although he works on the foreign news desk of the *Frankfurter Rund-*

schau, Hans Hansen is a lover of literature. The conversation soon turned to poetry. We talked about poems, countries, stories. I lost all sense of time."

"Did they pity you? Did their hearts go out to you because you were a miserable Turk, a lonely destitute political exile, the sort of Turkish nobody that drunken German youths beat up just for the fun of it?"

"I don't know. No one was putting pressure on me."

"Even if they did put pressure on you and tell you how they pitied you, it is human nature to seek pity. There are thousands of Turkish-Kurdish intellectuals in Germany who've turned that pity into a livelihood."

"Hans Hansen's family—his children—they're good people. They were refined, kindhearted. It's possible that they were too refined to let me know how much they pitied me. I liked them a lot. Even if they did pity me, I wouldn't hold it against them."

"In other words, this situation didn't crush your pride."

"It's possible that it did hurt my pride, but I still had a lovely evening. The lamps on the side tables cast an orange glow that I found very comforting. The knives and forks were a make I'd never seen before, but they weren't so unusual that you felt uneasy using them. The television was on all evening, and from time to time they'd glance in its direction, and this too made me feel at home. Sometimes, when they saw I was having a hard time understanding their German, they'd switch to English. After we finished eating, the children asked their father for help with their homework; when they sent their children to bed, they kissed them. By the time the meal was over, they had made me feel so welcome that I helped myself to a second slice of cake and no one noticed—or if they did notice, they acted as if it were the most natural thing in the world. I thought about all this a great deal afterward."

"What sort of cake was it?" asked Kadife.

"It was a Viennese torte with figs and chocolate."

There was a silence.

"What color were the curtains?" Kadife asked. "What sort of design did they have?"

"They were off-white or cream-colored," said Ka. He tried to look as if he were struggling to conjure up a distant memory. "I seem to remember their having little fishes on them, and flowers, and moons, and fruits of every color."

"In other words, the sort of material you buy for children?"

"Not really. The atmosphere in this house was very serious. Let me say this: They were a happy family, but that didn't mean they were flashing smiles every other minute, as we do here even when there's nothing to smile about. Maybe this is why they were happy. For them life was a serious business to be dealt with responsibly. It wasn't a dead-end struggle or a painful ordeal the way it is here. But their gravity of purpose permeated every aspect of their lives. Just as the moons and fishes and suchlike on their curtains helped lift their spirits."

"What color was the tablecloth?" asked Kadife.

"I can't remember," said Ka, pretending to dredge his memory for more details.

"And how many times did you go there?" asked Blue with faint annoyance.

"I had such a lovely time that night that I was very much hoping for a second visit. But Hans Hansen never invited me again."

The dog on the chain in the courtyard was barking louder now. Ka saw melancholy in Kadife's face as Blue glared at him with angry contempt.

"There were many times when I thought I should call them," he continued obstinately. "Sometimes I wondered whether Hans Hansen might have called at a time I wasn't home to invite me to supper again, and whenever I had this thought it was hard to keep myself from leaving the library and running home. I so longed for another look at that beautiful dresser with the mirror behind the shelves, and those chairs—I've forgotten what color they were; they may have been lemon yellow. I dreamed of sitting at their table again as they cut bread on the wooden board and they would turn to ask me, 'Is this how you like it?'—as you know, the Europeans don't eat as much bread as we do. There were no crosses on their walls, just beautiful scenes from the Alps. I would have given anything to see all this again."

Ka now saw that Blue was eyeing him with open revulsion.

"Three months later, a friend brought me news from Turkey," said Ka. "It concerned a horrifying new wave of torture, brutality, and destruction, and I used this as an excuse to call Hans Hansen. He listened to me carefully and again he was very refined and courteous. A small item appeared in the paper. I didn't care about the torture and death that was reported. All I wanted was for Hans Hansen to call me. But he never called me again. From time to time I played with the idea of writing him a letter, to find out what I had done wrong, to ask him why he'd never invited me back to his house."

Ka allowed himself a smile, even as Blue grew more visibly tense.

"Well, now you have a new excuse to call him," he said contemptuously.

"But if you want your statement to appear in his newspaper, you're going to have to meet German standards and prepare a joint document," Ka said.

"Who is this Kurdish nationalist who's going to help me with this joint document, and where am I going to find a liberal ex-Communist?"

"If you're worried that they might turn out to be working for the police, you can suggest the names yourself," said Ka.

"Without a doubt, an atheist Kurdish nationalist is worth more to the Western journalist than an Islamic Kurdish nationalist. There are many Kurdish youths up in arms over what's happened to the religious high school boys. A young student might just as well represent the Kurds in our statement."

"Fine. If you can arrange for a young student," said Ka, "I can guarantee that the *Frankfurter Rundschau* will accept him."

"Yes, of course," said Blue sarcastically. "You're our ambassador to the West."

Ka did not rise to the bait. "As for the Communist-turned-new-democrat, your best man is Turgut Bey."

"My father?" said Kadife, with alarm.

When Ka said yes, Kadife warned him that her father never went outside the hotel. They all began to talk at once. Blue insisted that, like all old Communists, Turgut Bey was not really a democrat; he was most probably quite pleased about the coup because it was hammering the Islamists, but he didn't want to give the left a bad name, so he was pretending the coup was wrong.

"My father's not the only pretender!" said Kadife.

From the trembling in her voice and the way Blue's eyes flashed with anger, Ka could tell that they had arrived at the threshold of an argument these two had had many times before, like so many couples worn down by constant quarreling, with hardly the strength to hide their differences from outsiders. Kadife had that determined look of a mistreated woman who's decided she's going to answer back, no matter what the cost, while Blue's expression was a mixture of pride and extraordinary tenderness. But then, in the space of a moment, everything changed. What he now saw in Blue's eyes was resolve.

"Like all atheist poseurs and Europe-loving leftist intellectuals, your father is a pretender with a contempt for the people."

Kadife picked up the ERSIN ELECTRIC ashtray and shot it at Blue. She may have missed on purpose: The ashtray hit the picture of Venice hanging on the wall behind him before falling noiselessly to the floor.

"And furthermore," said Blue, "your father likes to pretend that his daughter is not the secret mistress of a radical Islamist."

Kadife beat her two hands lightly against Blue's chest and then burst into tears; Blue sat her down on the chair in the corner. They were carrying on in such a contrived way that Ka could not help feeling it was all so much theater staged expressly for his benefit.

"Take back what you said," Kadife said.

"I take back what I said," said Blue. It was the voice you'd use to comfort a crying child. "And to prove this to you, I'm prepared to ignore the impious jokes your father makes morning and night and sign a joint bulletin with him. But since it's just possible that this representative of Hans Hansen we have here"—he paused to smile at Ka—"since it's just possible he might be trying to lure us into a trap, I'm not going to come to your hotel. Do you understand, darling?"

"But my father never leaves the hotel," said Kadife. To Ka's dismay, she was talking like a spoiled little girl. "The poverty of Kars ruins his mood."

"Then you must convince your father for once to go out, Kadife," said Ka, in a commanding tone he had never used with her before. "The city won't depress him now—it's all covered with snow." He looked straight into her eyes.

This time Kadife read his meaning. "All right," she said. "But before he leaves the hotel, someone has to convince him to put his name to the same document with an Islamist and a Kurdish nationalist. Who's going to do this?"

"I will," said Ka, "and you can help me."

"Where are they going to meet?" Kadife asked. "What if this nonsense ends with my poor father getting arrested? What if he has to spend the rest of his life in prison?"

"This isn't nonsense," said Blue. "If there are one or two news items in the European press, Ankara will whisper into a few ears and stop them."

"This is not about planting a news item in the European press, it's about getting your name in print, isn't it?" Kadife asked.

When Blue met this question with a sweetly tolerant smile, Ka felt a certain respect for him. It was only now he realized that the little Islamist papers in Istanbul would seize upon any mention in the *Frankfurter Rund-*

schau and proudly exaggerate it. This would make Blue famous throughout Turkey. There was a long silence. Kadife took out a handkerchief and wiped her eyes. Ka imagined that as soon as he was gone, these lovers would quarrel and make love. Did they want him to leave? High in the sky, a plane was passing. They all raised their eyes to the upper panes of the window, staring at the sky and listening.

"Actually, planes never fly over here," said Kadife.

"Something very strange is going on, something extraordinary," said Blue, chuckling at his own paranoia. He took offense when Ka chuckled too. "They say that even when the temperature is way below minus twenty, the government will never admit it's ever any colder." He glared at Ka defiantly.

"All I ever wanted was a normal life," said Kadife.

"You've thrown away your chance for a normal life," said Blue. "This is what makes you such an exceptional person."

"But I don't want to be exceptional. I want to be like everyone else. If it weren't for the coup, who knows? I might even decide to be like everyone else and pull off my scarf."

"All the women here wear scarves," said Blue.

"That's not true. Most educated women of my background and education don't cover their heads. If it's a question of being ordinary and fitting in, I've certainly distanced myself from my peers by wearing a head scarf. There's a prideful element in this that I'm not at all happy about."

"Then go ahead and uncover your head tomorrow," said Blue. "People will see it as a triumph for the junta."

"Everyone knows that, unlike you, I don't live my life wondering what people think of it," said Kadife. Her face was pink with excitement.

Blue responded with another sweet smile, but this time Ka could tell that it took every bit of strength he had. And Blue knew that Ka had seen this: It created an awkward intimacy between them and made Ka feel as if he had invaded the couple's privacy. As he listened to Kadife harangue her lover, and as he caught the undertones of desire, it seemed to him that she was dragging out their dirty linen deliberately—not just to tax Blue but also to embarrass Ka for having witnessed it. And, one might well ask, why did he choose this moment to remember the love letters from Necip to Kadife that he had been carrying around in his pocket since last night?

"As for girls who've been roughed up and thrown out of school for wearing head scarves, we can be sure there'll be no mention of them in these articles." Her tone matched the blind fury in her eyes. "They'll pass right over the women whose lives have been ruined and instead we'll get pictures of the cautious provincial Islamist simpletons who presume to speak in their name. Whenever you do see a picture of a Muslim woman, it's because her husband is a politician and she happens to be standing next to him during a religious festival. For this reason I'd be more upset to appear in those papers than not to appear. I pity these men wasting so much effort to gain exposure themselves while we endure so much to protect our privacy. That's why I think it's important to mention the girls who've committed suicide. Come to think of it, I have the right to tell Hans Hansen a thing or two myself."

"That would be excellent," said Ka, without thinking. "You could sign as the representative of the Muslim feminists."

"I have no wish to represent anyone," said Kadife. "If I'm going to stand up to the Europeans, it will be on my own, to tell my own story—my whole story, with all my sins and my foibles. You know how sometimes you'll meet someone you've never met before, someone you're sure you'll never see again, and you're tempted to tell him everything, your whole life history? The way it seemed the heroes told their stories to the authors of the European novels I read when I was a girl. I wouldn't mind telling my story like that to four or five Europeans."

There was an explosion that sounded very close by; the whole house shook and the windows clattered. A second or two later, both Blue and Ka rose to their feet.

"Let me take a look," said Kadife finally, seeming the most cold-blooded of the three.

Ka peeked timidly through the curtains. "The carriage isn't there," he said.

"It's dangerous for him to stand too long in this courtyard," said Blue. "When you leave, you'll be going through the side entrance."

Ka took this to mean *Why don't you leave now?* yet he remained still in his seat and waited, as he and Blue exchanged hateful looks. Ka remembered the fear he'd felt at university whenever he'd cross paths in dark empty hallways with armed students of the extreme nationalist variety, but at least in those days there'd been no sexual undercurrent to the exchange.

"I can be a little paranoid sometimes," said Blue. "But this doesn't mean you're not a spy for the West. You may know you're not a spy, and you may have no desire to be one, but it doesn't change the situation.

You're the stranger in our midst. You've sown doubt in this lovely and devout girl, and the strange things going on around her are the proof. And now you've aired all your smug Western views, probably even having a few laughs deep down inside at our expense. I don't mind, and neither does Kadife, but by inflicting your own naïve ideas on us, by rhapsodizing about the Western pursuit of happiness and justice, you've clouded our thinking. I'm not angry at you, because, like all good people, you are not aware of the evil inside you. But having heard it from me, you can't claim to be an innocent from now on."

CHAPTER TWENTY-SEVEN

Be Strong, My Girl; Help
Is on the Way from Kars

KA URGES TURGUT BEY TO SIGN THE STATEMENT

Ka left the house unseen by anyone in the courtyard or the car repair shops and walked straight to the market. He went into the same little stocking-stationery-audiocassette shop where he'd heard Peppino di Capri singing "Roberta" the day before; taking out Necip's letters to Kadife, he handed them page by page to the pale beetle-browed teenage assistant in charge of the photocopy machine. But to do this Ka first had to open the envelopes. Once the letters were copied, he put each of the originals into a new envelope made from the same cheap, faded paper stock as the letters and, imitating Necip's hand as best he could, addressed them to Kadife Yıldız.

Ever ready to fight for his happiness, to tell any lie, play any trick to make his dream come true, he hurried back to the hotel, musing upon a vision of İpek he had conjured in his mind. It was snowing again, the same huge snowflakes as before. Everyone in the streets seemed as tired and tense as they would on any ordinary evening. At the corner of Palace Path Road and Halitpaşa Avenue, a mud-splattered coal wagon drawn by a tired horse was stuck between the snowbanks. The wipers on the truck standing behind it were barely able to keep the windshield clear. He looked at the passersby clutching their plastic bags and imagined them all running home to their happy safety; although he sensed in the air a melancholy that called to mind the gray winter evenings of his childhood, he remained full of resolve, determined to start life anew.

He went straight up to his room. He hid the photocopies of Necip's letters in the bottom of his suitcase before he'd even removed his coat and hung it up. He washed his hands with excessive care. Then, without quite knowing why, he brushed his teeth (something he usually did in the evening); sensing that a new poem was on its way, he spent a long while looking out the window, making good use of the heat rising from the radiator; in the place of a poem came a stream of childhood memories: the fine spring morning he had accompanied his mother to Beyoğlu to buy buttons and a "dirty man" had trailed after them; the day his mother left with his father for a tour of Europe and the taxi taking them from Nişantaş to the airport disappeared around the corner; the hours spent dancing with a tall long-haired green-eyed girl at a party in Büyükada, his neck so stiff for days thereafter that he could barely move (he'd fallen for her but had no idea how to get in touch again). None of these memories were in any way related, apart from the commonality of love; Ka knew very well that life was a meaningless string of random incidents.

He bounded downstairs as eagerly as a man just arrived somewhere he'd been planning to visit for years; with a sangfroid he was shocked to discover in himself, he knocked on the white door that divided the lobby from the owner's apartment. The Kurdish maid answered, and her expression, half conspiratorial, half respectful, was straight out of Turgenev. He went into the room where they'd eaten dinner the night before to find Turgut Bey and İpek sitting side by side on the long divan facing the back door; they were watching television.

"Kadife, where have you been? It's about to begin," said Turgut Bey.

The pale snowlight pouring through the windows of the Russian house gave this spacious high-ceilinged room an aspect that was very different from the night before.

When father and daughter saw it was Ka who had joined them, they bristled for a moment like a couple whose privacy has just been invaded by a stranger. But then Ka was cheered to see something light up in İpek's eyes. He sat down on a chair that faced both them and the television and allowed himself to notice once again how much more beautiful İpek was in life than in his memories. This intensified his fear, though before long he had convinced himself that they were destined to live happily ever after.

"Every afternoon at four my daughters and I sit down on this divan and watch *Marianna*," said Turgut Bey. There was a note of embarrassment in his voice, but something else as well that said, Don't expect me to apologize.

Marianna was a Mexican soap opera that was broadcast five times a week on one of the big Istanbul channels to the intense delight of the entire country. The heroine who gave her name to the series was a small, bubbly, charming girl with large green eyes and skin so fair as to suggest an affluent background; she was, however, from the very lowest class. The innocent long-haired Marianna had been orphaned early in childhood and had spent most of her life in impoverished solitude (hardly a day passed without a new setback), and whenever she fell in love with someone who refused to love her back or was the victim of some misunderstanding or false accusation, Turgut Bey and his daughters would nestle up against one another like cats; with the two girls' heads propped against their father's chest and shoulders, they would all shed a few tears.

Perhaps out of his embarrassment to be seen so caught up in a silly soap opera, Turgut Bey now offered a running commentary on the underlying reasons for Marianna's and Mexico's persistent poverty; he applauded Marianna for her own war against the capitalists and as the show began he even addressed the screen: "Be strong, my girl; help is on its way from Kars." When he said this, his teary-eyed daughter smiled very faintly.

Ka's lips curled into a smile too, but then he caught İpek's eye and, seeing that she didn't like this smile, assumed a more serious expression.

During the first commercial break, Ka broached the subject of the joint statement with swift confidence and managed in no time to arouse Turgut Bey's interest. The old man was flattered to be taken so seriously. He asked whose idea this was and how his name had come to be suggested.

Ka said it was a decision he'd reached himself after consulting with the liberal press in Germany. Turgut Bey asked about the circulation of the *Frankfurter Rundschau* and whether Hans Hansen called himself a humanist. To prepare Turgut Bey for Blue, Ka described him as a dangerous religious fanatic who had nonetheless grown to understand the importance of democracy. But Turgut Bey seemed unperturbed; people gave themselves to religion because they were poor, he said; he went on to remind Ka that even if he didn't believe in what his daughter and her friends were doing, he respected them. It was in much the same spirit that he respected the Kurdish nationalist, whoever he might be; were he himself a Kurdish youth living in Kars today, he'd be a fierce Kurdish nationalist too. Turgut Bey said all this in the same jocular tone in which he offered his support to Marianna. "It's wrong to say this in public, but I am against military coups," he declared. Ka calmed him down by reminding him that this bulletin was not going to be printed in Turkey anyway and went on to say that the best place for this meeting to happen in safety was the shed at the top of the Hotel Asia. He could get there via the back door of an adjacent shop giving onto the same courtyard, and no one would be the wiser.

"We must show the world that there are true democrats in Turkey," said Turgut Bey. He spoke fast because the soap opera was about to resume. Just before Marianna reappeared, he looked at his watch and said, "Where's Kadife?"

Ka joined father and daughter to watch *Marianna* in silence.

At one point Marianna climbed a flight of stairs with her lover; once she was sure no one could see them, she wrapped her arms around him. They didn't kiss, but what they did Ka found even more moving: They embraced each other with all their might. During the long silence that followed, it occurred to Ka that the entire city was watching this same scene. All across Kars, housewives just returning from the market were tuning in with their husbands; girls in middle school were watching with their retired and aging relatives. With everyone watching, Ka realized, it wasn't just the wretched streets of Kars that were empty, it was every street in the entire country; at that same moment he also understood that his intellectual pretensions, political activities, and cultural snobberies had brought him to an arid existence that cut him off from the feelings this soap opera was now provoking in him—and worst of all it was his own stupid fault. Ka was sure that, after they'd finished making love, Blue and Kadife had curled up in a corner and wrapped their arms around each other to watch *Marianna* too.

When Marianna turned to her lover and said, "I've waited all my life for this day," Ka saw it as no coincidence that she was echoing his own thoughts. He tried to catch İpek's eye. She was resting her head on her father's chest, and her large, sad, lovelorn eyes were glued to the set, lost in the desires the soap opera had awakened.

"But I'm still so worried," said Marianna's handsome clean-shaven lover. "My family won't allow us to be together."

"As long as we love each other, we have nothing to fear," said the good-hearted Marianna.

"Watch out, my girl, this man is your worst enemy!" Turgut Bey shouted at the screen.

"I want you to love me without fear," said Marianna.

Looking deep into İpek's mysterious eyes, Ka now succeeded in getting her to notice him, but she quickly averted her gaze.

At the commercial break, İpek turned to her father and said, "Daddy dear, if you ask me it's too dangerous for you to go to the Hotel Asia."

"Don't worry," said Turgut Bey.

"You're the one who's been telling me for years that it brings you bad luck to go out into the streets of Kars."

"Yes, but if I don't attend this meeting, it has to be for a matter of principle and not because I'm scared," said Turgut Bey. He turned to Ka. "The question is this: Speaking as the Communist modernizing secularist democratic patriot I now am, what should I put first, the enlightenment or the will of the people? If I believe first and foremost in the European enlightenment, I am obliged to see the Islamists as my enemies and support this military coup. If, however, my first commitment is to the will of the people—if, in other words, I've become an unadulterated democrat—I have no choice but to go ahead and sign that statement. Which of the things I've said is true?"

"Take the side of the oppressed and go sign that statement," said Ka.

"It's not enough to be oppressed, you must also be in the right. Most oppressed people are in the wrong to an almost ridiculous degree. What shall I believe in?"

"Ka doesn't believe in anything," said İpek.

"Everyone believes in something," said Turgut Bey. "Please, tell me what you think."

Ka did his best to convince Turgut Bey that if he signed the statement he would be doing his bit to help Kars move toward democracy. Sensing a strong possibility that İpek might not want to go to Frankfurt with him, he started to worry that he might fail to convince Turgut Bey to leave the hotel. To express beliefs without conviction was liberating. As he nattered on about the statement, about issues of democracy, human rights, and many other things that were news to none of them, he saw a light shining in İpek's eyes that told him she didn't believe a thing he was saying. But it wasn't a shaming, moralistic light he saw; quite the contrary, it was the gleam of sexual provocation. Her eyes said, I know you're spouting all these lies because you want me.

So it was that, just minutes after discovering the importance of melodramatic sensibilities, Ka decided he'd discovered a second great truth that had eluded him all his life: There are women who can't resist a man who believes in nothing but love. Overcome with excitement at this new discovery, he launched into a further monologue about human rights, freedom of thought, democracy, and related subjects. And as he mouthed the wild simplifications of so many well-intentioned but shameless and slightly addled Western intellectuals and the platitudes repeated verbatim by their Turkish imitators, he thrilled to the knowledge that he might soon be making love to İpek and all the while stared straight into her eyes to see the reflection of his own excitement.

"You're right," said Turgut Bey, when the commercials had come to an end. "Where's Kadife?"

As the show resumed, Turgut Bey grew nervous—part of him wanted to go to the Hotel Asia and part of him didn't. Like a sad old man lost in a sea of dreams and ghosts, he talked about the political memories that came to him when he was watching *Marianna,* and about his fear of winding up back in prison, and about man's responsibilities. Ka could see perfectly well that İpek was annoyed at him for making her father anxious, but she also admired the speed with which he had convinced the old man to leave the hotel. Ka didn't mind that she kept averting her eyes, and when at the end of the soap opera she turned to her father, wrapped her arms around him, and said, "Don't go if you don't want to; you've already suffered enough to help others, Father," he was not offended.

Ka saw a cloud pass over İpek's face, but now a joyful new poem had come into his head. In the chair next to the kitchen, where, only moments earlier, Zahide Hanım sat with tears streaming down her face as she watched *Marianna,* Ka now sat, beaming with optimism as he began to write.

It was only much later that he decided to call this poem "I Am Going to Be Happy," perhaps choosing this title to torment himself. Ka had just completed it, not a single missing word, when Kadife came rushing into the room. Turgut Bey flew to his feet, threw his arms around her, kissed her, and asked where she'd been and why her hands were so cold. A single tear rolled down his cheek. Kadife said she'd been to see Hande. She'd stayed later than expected, not wanting to miss any of *Marianna,* and so having decided to watch at Hande's till the end. "So how's our girl doing?" asked Turgut Bey (he was referring to Marianna). But he did not wait for Kadife's answer before turning to the other subject. A great cloud of apprehension descended over him as he summarized what he'd heard from Ka.

It was not enough for Kadife to pretend she was hearing all this for the first time; when she caught sight of Ka at the other end of the room, she pretended to be surprised. "I'm so happy you're here," she cried, as she hastened to cover her hair. But her scarf was not yet back in place when she sat down in front of the television to advise her father. Kadife was so convincing in her feigned surprise at seeing him that when she went on to encourage her father to attend the meeting and sign the joint statement, Ka thought this too must be an act. Since Blue's motive was to produce a statement that the foreign press would be willing to print, his suspicion may have been correct, but Ka could tell from the fear in İpek's face that something else was going on here too.

"Let me go with you to the Hotel Asia," said Kadife.

"I'm not about to let you get into trouble on my account," said Turgut Bey, affecting a gallant air straight out of the soap operas they watched and the novels they had read together once upon a time.

"Please, Daddy, if you get involved in this business, you could be exposing yourself to unnecessary risks," said İpek.

While İpek spoke to her father, Ka took stock: It seemed that—as with everyone else in the room—everything she said had a double meaning; as for this game she was playing with her eyes—averting her gaze one moment, staring at him intensely the next—he could only assume that this was just another way of transmitting the same mixed message. Only much later would he realize that—apart from Necip—everyone he met in Kars spoke in the same code, and so harmoniously that they seemed almost a single chorus; he would go on to ask himself whether it was poverty that somehow brought it out in them or fear, solitude, or the very simplicity of their lives. Even as İpek said, "Daddy, please don't go," she was teasing Ka; even as Kadife spoke of the statement and her bonds to her father, Ka could see she was revealing her bonds to Blue.

It was with all this in mind that Ka entered into what he would later call "the most profoundly duplicitous conversation of my life." He had a strong feeling that if he could not get Turgut Bey to leave the hotel now, he would never have a chance to sleep with İpek, and since the challenge he saw in İpek's eyes only confirmed the notion, he told himself that this was his last chance in life for happiness. When he began to speak, he used the same words and ideas that had ruined his life. But as he tried to convince Turgut Bey to leave the hotel—because it was important to act for the common good, to take responsibility for his country's poor and share in their struggles, because he was on the side of the civilizers and so obliged to stand up against the forces of darkness, even if the gesture itself seemed insignificant—Ka found that he even believed some of what he was saying. He remembered how he had felt as a young leftist, when he'd been so determined not to join the Turkish bourgeoisie, when all he wanted was to sit in a room reading great books and entertaining great thoughts. So it was with the elation of a twenty-year-old that he repeated those thoughts and ideals that had so upset his mother, who had been right in wishing he would never become a poet, and which had condemned him to exile in a rathole in Frankfurt. Meanwhile he was well aware what the passion of his words said to İpek: This is how passionately I want to make love to you. He was thinking that at last those fine words of youth that had ruined his life would serve a purpose; thanks to them, he would be making love to the object of his desires, knowing at this same moment that he'd lost his faith in them; he now knew that the greatest happiness in life was to embrace a beautiful, intelligent girl and sit in a corner writing poetry.

Turgut Bey announced that he was leaving at once for the Hotel Asia. He went to his room to change, accompanied by Kadife.

Ka walked over to İpek, still in the spot where she'd been watching television with her father. She looked almost as if she were still leaning on the old man. "I'll be waiting for you in my room," Ka whispered.

"Do you love me?" asked İpek.

"I love you very much."

"Is it true?"

"It's very true."

For a while, neither spoke. İpek turned to gaze out the window, and so did Ka. It had started snowing again. The streetlamps in front of the hotel had come on, but darkness had not yet descended, so even as they lit up the frenzy of the giant snowflakes, they seemed superfluous.

"Go to your room," said İpek. "As soon as they leave, I'll come up."

CHAPTER TWENTY-EIGHT

The Difference Between Love
and the Agony of Waiting

KA WITH İPEK IN THE HOTEL ROOM

İpek did not come straight up and the waiting was torture, the worst Ka had ever known. It was this pain, this deadly wait, he now remembered, that had made him afraid to fall in love. Upon arriving in his room he'd thrown himself on the bed, only to stand up again at once to straighten out his clothes; he washed his hands and felt the blood draining from his arms, his fingers, his lips; with trembling hands he combed his hair and then, seeing his reflection in the windowpane, he messed it up again. As all this had taken very little time, he directed his anxious attention to the scene through his window.

He'd hoped to see Turgut Bey leaving the hotel with Kadife. Perhaps they'd gone past while he was in the bathroom. But if this were the case, İpek should have come by now. Perhaps she was back in the room he'd seen the night before, painting her face and dabbing her neck with perfume. What a waste of the little time they had together! Didn't she understand how much he loved her? Whatever she was doing, it couldn't justify the pain he felt at this moment; he was going to tell her so when she finally arrived, but would she come at all? With every passing moment, he became more convinced that İpek had changed her mind.

He saw a horse-drawn carriage come up to the hotel; aided by Zahide Hanım and Cavit the receptionist, Turgut Bey and Kadife climbed in and the carriage's oilskin drapes closed around them. But the carriage remained still. Ka watched the blanket of snow on the awning get thicker and thicker; the streetlamps made each snowflake look bigger than the one before. It was as if time had stopped, Ka thought; it was driving him mad. Just then Zahide came running out the door and handed something

Ka couldn't see into the carriage. As the carriage began to move, Ka's heart began to beat faster.

But still İpek didn't come.

What was the difference between love and the agony of waiting? Like love, the agony of waiting began in the muscles somewhere around the upper belly but soon spread out to the chest, the thighs, and the forehead, to invade the entire body with numbing force. As he listened to sounds from other parts of the hotel, he tried to guess what İpek was doing. He saw a woman passing in the street, and even though she didn't look a bit like İpek, he thought it must be she. How beautiful the snow looked as it fell from the sky! When he was a child, they'd been sent down to the school cafeteria for their injections; as he stood there waiting, hugging his arms as cooking fumes tinged with iodine swirled around his head, his stomach had ached like this and he wanted to die. He wanted to be home, in his own room. Now he wanted to be in his own miserable room in Frankfurt. What a huge mistake he'd made by coming here! Even the poems had stopped coming. It hurt so much he couldn't even look at the snow falling onto the empty street. And yet it felt good to be standing at this warm window; this was still better than dying, and if İpek didn't come soon, he would die anyway.

The lights went off.

This was a sign, he thought, sent specially to him. Perhaps İpek hadn't come because she knew there was about to be a power outage. He looked down at the dark street for a sign of life, something that might explain İpek's absence. He caught sight of a truck—was it an army truck? No, just his mind playing tricks on him. So were the footsteps he thought he heard on the stairs. No one was coming. He left the window and lay on the bed on his back. The pain that had begun in his belly had now spread to his soul; he was alone in the world with no one to blame but himself. His life had come to nothing; he was going to die here, die of misery and loneliness. This time he wouldn't even find the strength to scurry like a rat back into that hole in Frankfurt.

The thing that grieved and distressed him the most was not his terrible unhappiness; it was knowing that, had he acted a bit more intelligently, his entire life might have been much happier. The worst thing was knowing that no one even noticed his fear, his misery, his loneliness. If İpek had any idea she'd have come right up without delay! If his mother had seen him in this state . . . she was the only one in the world who would have felt for him; she would have run her fingers through his hair and consoled him.

The ice on the windows gave an orange glow to the light from the streetlamps and the surrounding houses. Let the snow keep falling, he thought; let it fall for days and months on end; let it cover the city of Kars so completely that no one will ever find it again. He wanted to fall asleep on this bed and not wake up until it was a sunny morning and he a child again, with his mother.

There was a knock at the door. By now, Ka told himself, it could only be someone from the kitchen. But he flew to the door, and the moment he opened it he could feel İpek's presence.

"Where have you been?"

"Am I late?"

But it was as if Ka hadn't even heard her. He was already embracing her with all his strength; he'd put his head against her neck and buried his face in her hair, and there he stayed without moving a muscle. He felt such joy that the agony of waiting now seemed absurd. But the agony had worn him out all the same; that, he thought, was why he could not relish her presence fully. That is why he demanded that İpek explain her delay: Even knowing he had no right to do so, he kept complaining. But İpek insisted that she had come up as soon as her father had left—yes, it was true that she had stopped off in the kitchen to give Zahide one or two instructions about dinner, but that couldn't have taken more than a minute. So Ka showed himself to be the more ardent and fragile of the two; even at the very beginning of their relationship, he had let İpek have the upper hand. And even if his fear of seeming weak had moved him to conceal the agony she'd put him through, he would still have to grapple with feelings of insecurity. Besides, didn't love mean sharing everything? What was it if not the desire to share your every thought? He related this chain of thought to İpek as breathlessly as if revealing a terrible secret.

"Now put all that out of your head," said İpek. "I came here to make love to you."

They kissed, and with a softness that brought Ka comfort, they fell onto the bed. For Ka, who had not made love in four years, it felt like a miracle. So even as he succumbed to the pleasures of the flesh, his conscious mind was reminding him what a beautiful moment this was. Just as with his first sexual experiences, it was not the act as much as the thought of making love that occupied him. For a while, it protected Ka from overexcitement. Details from the pornographic films to which he'd become addicted in Frankfurt rushed through his head, creating a poetic aura that seemed beyond logic. But he wasn't imagining these pornographic scenes to arouse himself; he was celebrating the fact that he could at last enact such fantasies as had played incessantly in his mind. So it was not İpek herself who was arousing Ka but a pornographic image; and the miracle was less her presence than the fact that he could imagine his fantasy here in bed with her. It was only when he began to pull off her clothes with an almost savage clumsiness that he began to look at the real İpek. Her breasts were enormous; the skin on her neck and her shoulders was wonderfully soft, its scent strange and foreign. He watched the snow-light playing on her; now and again something sparkled in her eyes that frightened him. Her eyes were very sure of themselves: Ka worried that İpek was not as fragile as he wanted her to be. This is why he pulled her hair to cause her pain, why he took such pleasure from her pain that he yanked her hair again, why he subjected her to a few other acts also inspired by the pornographic film still playing in his head, and why he treated her so roughly—to the accompaniment of an internal musical sound track as deep as it was primitive. When he saw that she enjoyed his being rough, his triumph gave way to brotherly affection. He wrapped his arms around her; no longer wishing to save just himself from the miseries of Kars, he wanted to save İpek too. But when he decided her reaction was commensurate with his ardor, he pulled himself away. In a corner of his mind he was able to control and coordinate these sexual acrobatics with surprising finesse. But when his mind was somewhere far off he could seize the woman with a passion verging on violence; at such a moment he wanted to hurt her.

According to the notes Ka made about his lovemaking—notes I feel I must share with my readers—his passion was finally reciprocated, and they fell upon each other with such intensity as to leave the rest of the world behind. The same notes also reveal that İpek let out a mournful cry when it was over. Ka's native paranoia came rushing back as he wondered whether this was the reason they'd given him a room in the most remote corner of the hotel; the pleasure they'd taken in causing each other pain now gave way to the old loneliness. It seemed to him that this remote room on this remote corridor had split away from the hotel and floated off to the most remote corner of this empty city. And the quiet of this empty city was as if the world had come to an end, and it was snowing.

For a long time they lay side by side in bed, gazing silently at the snow. From time to time, Ka turned his head to watch the snow falling in İpek's eyes.

CHAPTER TWENTY-NINE

It's Not Just You I've Lost

IN FRANKFURT

Four years after Ka's visit to Kars and forty-two days after his death, I went to see the small Frankfurt apartment in which he had spent the last eight years of his life. It was a snowy, rainy, windy February day. When I arrived in Frankfurt on the morning flight from Istanbul, the city looked even drearier than it had in the postcards Ka had been sending me for sixteen years. Except for the dark cars rushing past in the streets, the trams that appeared out of nowhere like ghosts only to vanish a moment later, and the umbrella-wielding housewives hurrying along the pavements, the streets were empty. It was the middle of the day, but looking into the dark, dense mist I could still see the deathly yellow glow of streetlamps.

Still, it cheered me to see—in the streets surrounding the central train station, along the pavements lined with restaurants and travel agencies and ice-cream parlors and sex shops—signs of the deathless energy that sustains all big cities. After I had checked into my hotel and phoned the young Turkish-German literature enthusiast who had (at my request) arranged for me to give a talk at the city hall, I went to the Italian café at the station to meet with Tarkut Ölçün. In Istanbul, Ka's sister had given me his number. This tired well-meaning man in his sixties was Ka's closest acquaintance during his years in Frankfurt. He had given a statement to the police during the inquiry following Ka's death; he was the one who had contacted Ka's family in Istanbul and helped arrange for the body to be flown back to Turkey. At the time I was still hoping to find the typescript of the poetry collection on which Ka said he had been laboring ever since returning from Kars four years earlier and had only just completed, so I asked his father and sister what had happened to his belongings. They'd not been strong enough to make the trip to Germany, so they asked me to gather up Ka's things and clear out his apartment.

Tarkut Ölçün had come to Germany in the first wave of immigration in the early sixties. For years he'd worked as a teacher and a social worker, serving a number of Turkish associations and charities. When he brought out pictures of his German-born son and daughter, he told me proudly that he'd sent them both through university; although Tarkut was a figure of some standing in Frankfurt's Turkish community, in his face I still saw the loneliness and defeat so commonly seen in first-generation immigrants and political exiles.

The first thing Tarkut Ölçün gave me was the small bag Ka had been carrying when he was shot. The police had made Tarkut sign for it before they handed it over. I opened it at once and frantically rummaged through it. Inside I found the pajamas Ka had bought in Nişantaş eighteen years earlier, a green pullover, shaving articles, a toothbrush, a pair of socks, a change of underwear, and a number of literary magazines I had sent him from Istanbul. There was no sign of his green poetry notebook.

Later, as we sat drinking our coffee and gazing into the crowded station where two aging Turks were laughing and talking as they mopped the floor, Tarkut said, "Orhan Bey, your friend Ka Bey was a solitary man. No one in Frankfurt apart from me knew much about what he was doing." But he still promised to tell me everything he knew.

We walked around to the back of the station, wending our way past the old army barracks and the hundred-year-old factory buildings to the building near Goethestrasse where Ka had spent his last eight years. The apartment overlooked a small square with a playground, but the landlord was not there to open the front door or let us into Ka's apartment. The paint on the old door was flaking, and as we stood waiting in the wet snow I recognized many of the things Ka had described to me in his letters and his infrequent phone calls (given as he was to paranoia, Ka suspected someone was listening in on all his calls to Turkey, so he didn't like using the phone). I looked at the small neglected park and the grocery store on the other side, and as my eyes wandered beyond them to the dark windows of the shops that sold alcohol and newspapers, I felt I was looking at my own memories. The swings and seesaws in the playground, like the benches where Ka had spent summer evenings drinking beer with the Italian and Yugoslavian workmen who were his neighbors, were now covered with a light blanket of snow.

We went back to the station square, following the route to the city library Ka had taken every morning during his last years. He had enjoyed walking through the crowds of people rushing to work. So we followed his footsteps into the station and down through an underground arcade, coming aboveground again to follow the tram route past the sex shops, souvenir stores, patisseries, and pharmacies of Kaiserstrasse as far as Hauptwache Square. Tarkut Ölçün saw many Turks and Kurds he knew in the *döner* shops, kebab restaurants, and fruit and vegetable shops we passed along the way, and as he waved to them he told me how when these same people had seen Ka walking to the city library every morning at exactly the same time, they'd cry out, "Good morning, Professor!" When we arrived in Hauptwache Square, he pointed out the big store on the opposite side of the square—the *Kaufhof.* I told him it was here that Ka had bought the overcoat he wore in Kars, but I declined his offer to take me inside.

Ka's final destination, the Frankfurt city library, was a modern and anonymous building. Inside were the types you always find in such libraries: housewives, old people with time to kill, unemployed men, one or two Turks and Arabs, students giggling over their homework assignments, and all other manner of stalwarts from the ranks of the obese, the lame, the insane, and the mentally handicapped. One drooling young man raised his head from his picture book to stick out his tongue at me. My guide was not particularly interested in books so I left him in the coffee shop downstairs and went to the shelves of English poetry. Here I searched the checkout slips on the inside back covers for my friend's name; whenever I opened a copy of Auden, Browning, or Coleridge to find his signature, I shed tears for him and for the years he'd wasted away in this library.

I cut short my search, which had plunged me into melancholy, and walked back with my friendly guide along the same avenues without saying a word. We turned left somewhere in the middle of the Kaiserstrasse, just before a place that was called the World Sex Center or something equally absurd, and from here we walked down one street to Münchnerstrasse, where I saw more Turkish-owned produce stores and restaurants, as well as an empty hairdresser's. By now I had guessed what I was about to be shown, so my heart was pounding, and as my eyes moved from the fresh leeks and oranges displayed outside the fruit and vegetable shops to the one-legged man begging nearby, and on to the headlights flashing across the stifling windows of the Hotel Eden, I looked into the charcoal twilight and there, shining in bright pink solitary splendor, I found the neon letter *K.*

"This is where it happened, I'm afraid," said Tarkut Ölçün. "They found Ka's body right here."

I stared helplessly at the wet pavement. Two boys came flying out of a fruit and vegetable shop pushing and shoving each other; as they ran off, one of them stepped on the patch of wet pavement where Ka had lain dying with three bullets in his body. The red lights of a truck parked just ahead were reflected in the asphalt. Ka had spent several minutes writhing on this very pavement and then died before the ambulance arrived.

For a moment I lifted my head to find the patch of sky he saw as he was dying: between the old dark buildings, the streetlamps, and the power lines, there was a sliver of sky. Ka had been shot around midnight. Tarkut Ölçün told me there would still have been a smattering of prostitutes walking up and down the street. The actual red-light district was one street up, along the Kaiserstrasse, but on busy nights and weekends, or during one of the trade fairs, the ladies would spread out along this street too. "They didn't find anything," he said, when he saw me looking left and right as if in search of a clue. "And the German police aren't like our Turkish police. They do their job well."

When I started canvassing the occupants of the shops in the immediate vicinity anyway, this good-natured man decided to help. The girls at the hairdresser's recognized him; after exchanging a few niceties, he asked whether they'd seen anything, but of course they were not in the shop at the time of the murder and had in fact heard nothing about the incident. "The only thing Turkish families teach their daughters here is how to be hairdressers," he told me, when we were outside again. "There are hundreds of Turkish hairdressers in Frankfurt."

The Kurds in the fruit and vegetable shop, by contrast, were only too well aware of the murder and the police inquiry that had followed. This could explain their evident displeasure at meeting us.

With the same dirty cloth he had when we entered, the waiter in the Holiday Kebab House had been wiping off the Formica tabletops at twelve on the night in question when he'd heard the gunshots; he waited a short time before going outside to become the last person Ka would see.

After leaving the kebab restaurant, we walked swiftly into the first passageway we came to and ended up in the back courtyard of a dark building. I followed Tarkut Bey down two flights of stairs, through a door, and into a forbidding space the size of a hangar, which had once served as a warehouse. This underworld area was as wide as the street above. It now served as a mosque—between fifty and sixty worshipers were saying their evening prayers on the carpeted area in the middle—and was lined with shops as dark and dirty as the ones you'd find in any underground arcade in Istanbul. I saw a glitterless jewelry store and a fruit and vegetable shop almost small enough to qualify as a dwarf; the butcher's next door was crowded, but the man in the grocery store sat idly watching the TV set in the coffeehouse as he sat surrounded by coils of garlic sausage. In that corner stood cases of Turkish fruit juice, Turkish macaroni, Turkish canned goods, and religious literature, and I noticed that the café was even more popular than the mosque. The air was thick with cigarette smoke. The men at the tables looked tired—most had their eyes glued to the Turkish film on television, but now and then someone shuffled over to the makeshift fountain; after filling it with water from a plastic bucket, he would perform his ablutions before joining the worshipers outside.

"On Fridays and holidays, you can see two thousand people here," Tarkut Bey told me. "The overflow goes all the way up the stairs to the back courtyard." I went over to the stall that sold books and magazines and—for no particular reason—bought a copy of *Communication*.

Afterward we repaired to the old Munich-style beer parlor directly overhead. "That mosque belongs to the Süleymans," Tarkut Ölçün said, pointing at the ground below us. "They're theocrats, but they won't have anything to do with terrorism; they're not like the National Advocates or the Cemalettin Tigers. They don't want to take up arms against the Turkish state, either." Perhaps troubled by the suspicion he could read in my face and the attention with which I was poring over *Communication,* as if looking for clues, he now told me everything he knew about Ka's murder and what he had later discovered from the police and the press.

At half past eleven, exactly forty-two days before my visit, Ka had returned from Hamburg, where he had taken part in a poetry evening. The journey had taken six hours, but when he got into the station he did not take the south exit straight back to his apartment in Goethestrasse; instead, he took the north exit onto the Kaiserstrasse and spent the next twenty-five minutes wandering among tourists, drunks, solitary men, and the prostitutes who were waiting for customers. He'd been walking around for half an hour when he turned right at the World Sex Center; he was shot crossing Münchnerstrasse. He was probably on his way to the Big Antalya Greengrocer to buy some tangerines to take home. This was the only fruit and vegetable shop in the area still open at this hour, and the shop clerk recalled that Ka had often stopped in to buy oranges. Faced with his claim of total ignorance about Ka's murder, the police were suspicious enough to take the clerk in for questioning, but they released him the next day, having discovered nothing.

The police had been unable to find anyone who'd seen Ka's assailant. The waiter from the Holiday Kebab House had heard gunshots, but with the television and the customers making so much noise he couldn't even say how many he'd heard. And it was impossible to see through the fogged-up windows of the beer parlor that sat right atop the mosque. A prostitute on the next street down who'd been smoking a cigarette between tricks reported having seen a short dark "Turkish-looking" man in a black coat running in the direction of the Kaiserstrasse around midnight, but she was unable to provide the police with a good description. A German who happened to be standing on the balcony of his apartment when Ka fell to the ground had called the ambulance, but he'd not seen anyone either. The first bullet had gone in through the back of Ka's head and out his left eye. The other two bullets had shattered major blood vessels around his heart and his liver, piercing both the front and the back of his charcoal-colored coat, which was drenched in blood.

"He was shot from the back, so it was probably premeditated," the garrulous old detective in charge had concluded. The murderer may even have followed Ka all the way from Hamburg. The police considered a variety of motives, everything from sexual jealousy to the sort of political vendetta carried out so frequently in the Turkish community. Ka had had no connection to the world below the neighborhoods around the station. When the police showed his photo to people who worked in the immediate vicinity, some remembered seeing him in the sex shops from time to time and others recalled that he had used the small cubicles in the back for viewing porno films. But there were no eyewitnesses, true or false, and there was no pressure from on high to find the killer. Neither was there an outcry in the press, so eventually the police had suspended their inquiries.

When he interviewed Ka's acquaintances, the garrulous detective sometimes seemed to have lost sight of the point of the investigation and wound up doing most of the talking. It was from this fatherly Turkophile that Tarkut Ölçün had first heard about the two women who had entered Ka's life eight years before his visit to Kars. One was German and the other Turkish; I carefully recorded their names in my notebook. In the four years since his return from Kars, Ka had had no relations with any women at all.

Tarkut and I went back out into the snow; as we returned to Ka's house, neither of us spoke. This time we were able to see the large and affable, if also discontented, landlord. He let us into the building, which was cool and smelled of soot, and took us up to the penthouse apartment, which, he told us in a querulous voice, he was about to rent out again; any of this filth we didn't clear out, he was going to throw away, and having said that, he left. Tears came to my eyes the moment I stepped into the small, dark, low-ceilinged rooms in which Ka had spent his last eight years. The distinct smell took me back to our childhood; it was the smell I associated with his school satchel and his room at home and the pullovers his mother had knitted. I thought it must be a Turkish brand of soap I'd never known by name and never thought to ask about.

During Ka's early years in Germany he had worked as a porter, a mover, and a house painter, and he'd also given English lessons to Turks; once he was officially declared a political exile and granted asylum benefits, he cut his links with the Turkish Communists who ran the neighborhood centers and who had, until then, made sure he was gainfully employed. His fellow exiles had found Ka too remote and too bourgeois. During his last twelve years, Ka supplemented his income by doing poetry readings in town libraries, cultural foundations, and Turkish associations. Only Turks attended, and the audiences rarely exceeded twenty; even so, if he could do three of them in a month, it was an extra five hundred marks, which, combined with his asylum benefit, would have allowed him to live comfortably. But it was clear now that such months had been few and far between. The chairs in his apartment were broken, the ashtrays chipped, and the electric stove covered with rust. Still affronted by the threat the landlord made when he let us in, I wanted to stuff Ka's belongings into an old suitcase and a couple of plastic bags and leave. I wanted to take everything: the pillow on the bed that still smelled of his hair, the belt and the tie I remembered him wearing in high school, the Bally shoes that (according to his letters) he had continued using as house slippers once his toes had poked through the leather, the dirty glass in which he kept his toothpaste and brush, his library of some three hundred and fifty books, the TV set, the video machine he'd never mentioned to me, his threadbare jacket and worn-out shirts, and the pajamas he'd brought with him from Turkey sixteen years earlier. But when I looked at the worktable and failed to find the thing I coveted most, the thing I now realized I had flown to Frankfurt to retrieve, I lost my courage.

In his last letter from Frankfurt, Ka had happily announced that after four years of hard work he had finally completed a new book of poetry. The title was *Snow*. Most of the poems were based on childhood memories that had come to him in flashes during his visit to Kars, and he had carefully recorded these inspirations in a green notebook. In an earlier letter written almost immediately upon leaving Kars, he had told me he had come to believe that the emerging book had a "deep and mysterious" underlying structure; he had spent his last four years in Frankfurt filling in the blanks in this hidden design. For this grueling purpose, he'd had to withdraw from the world, abstaining from its pleasures like a dervish. In Kars he had felt like a medium, as if someone were whispering the poems into his ear; back in Frankfurt, he could hardly hear them at all.

Still, he labored to reveal what he had become convinced was the hidden logic of this testament to the visions and inspirations he had experienced in Kars. In his last letter, he said that with the arduous task now complete, he was going to try out the poems at readings in several German cities. Aside from the longhand version he kept in the green notebook he had no other copy, he told me, but he would have a manuscript typed up and duplicated once he was sure everything was in its rightful place. He was planning to send one copy to me and one to his Istanbul publisher. Would I please write a few words for the back cover and send them on to the publisher, our mutual friend Fahir?

The view from Ka's desk of the snowcapped rooftops of Frankfurt was now darkening as night fell over the city. The desk itself, covered with a green tablecloth, was surprisingly tidy for a poet's. On the right were the diaries in which Ka described his visit to Kars and the poems that had come to him there; on the left was a pile of books and magazines he was in the process of reading. Equidistant from the unmarked center line of the table stood a bronze lamp and a telephone.

I searched the desk drawers for the notebook; I fanned through the books, the diaries, and the collection of newspaper clippings without which no political exile's room seems complete; with rising panic I went on to search his wardrobes, his bed, the cabinets in his kitchen and his bathroom, his refrigerator, his little laundry basket, and every other corner of the house where a man might think to hide a notebook. Refusing to accept that it might be lost, I then checked all the same places again while Tarkut Ölçün stood smoking a cigarette and watching the snow fall over Frankfurt. If the notebook wasn't in the small bag he'd taken with him to Hamburg, it had to be here in his apartment. Ka had always refused to make copies of his poetry until every last word was in place; he thought it was bad luck. But he'd told me himself that the book was finished and ready to go, so where was it?

Two hours later, still refusing to accept the loss of the green notebook in which Ka had recorded his Kars poems, I had convinced myself that it was here, somewhere, right under my nose, and that it was only on account of having let myself become so upset that I had missed it. When the landlord knocked impatiently again, I scooped up all the notebooks in Ka's drawers and threw them into a plastic bag, along with every handwritten note I could find. I gathered up the porno tapes piled higgledy-piggledy around the VCR—proof he'd never received visitors here—and threw them into a shopping bag from the *Kaufhof*. Like a man about to set out on a long journey who takes along some very ordinary memento of the life he's left behind, I searched the room for a simple keepsake to remember my friend by. But I couldn't make up my mind; before I knew it I was stuffing a plastic bag with the ashtray and the cigarettes sitting on his desk, the knife he'd used as a letter opener, the clock on his bedside table, the threadbare waistcoat he had worn over his pajamas for twenty-five years, and which still carried Ka's smell, and the photograph of him and his sister standing on Dolmabahçe wharf. By now I had become the curator of my own passion. Recognizing my last chance, I gathered up almost everything else; and almost everything had value, from his dirty socks to his handkerchiefs (never used), from the kitchen spoons to the empty cigarette packets in the wastebasket. During one of our last meetings in Istanbul, Ka had asked about my plans for a new novel, and I had told him about *The Museum of Innocence*, an idea I was still keeping from everyone.

The moment I returned to my hotel room, having parted from my guide, I resumed my analysis of Ka's belongings. By now I had decided to be clinical and put memories of my friend to rest for the night, before despair could destroy me. The first task I set myself was to review the porn tapes. My room didn't have a VCR, but from the notes in Ka's own hand on the cassette sleeves, it was clear that he had a special affection for an American star called Melinda.

I proceeded next to read the notebooks in which Ka had written about the poems that had come to him in Kars. Why had he never mentioned this love affair, the terrors he had witnessed? I was to find the answer in a file retrieved from one of Ka's drawers: When I opened this folder, almost forty love letters fell into my lap; all were addressed to İpek, none had been sent. Every one began exactly the same way—*My darling, I have thought long and hard about whether I should write to tell you this*—but then each went on to describe a different experience of his in Kars, each time adding a heart-wrenching new detail to my understanding of his love affair with İpek; there were also scattered insights into his everyday life in Frankfurt (the lame dog he'd seen in Von Bethmann Park and the zinc tables in the Jewish Museum, both of which distresses he had written of in letters to me as well). He'd not folded any of these love letters, and this revealed to me a degree of indecision about sending them that would not admit even the commitment of an envelope.

Just say the word and I'll come to you, he has written in one letter, though in another he declares he would never return to Kars *because I would never allow you to misunderstand me again.* One letter refers to a poem, not enclosed, and another invites one to imagine a preceding letter from İpek: *I'm so sorry you took my letter amiss.* That evening, I laid out all Ka's belongings, on the bed and on every other surface in the room, examining every item with a forensic eye, and so it is with certainty that I can say Ka never received a single letter from İpek. Why did he pretend to answer one, even knowing that he would never send her a single letter either?

Here, perhaps, we have arrived at the heart of our story. How much can we ever know about the love and pain in another's heart? How much can we hope to understand those who have suffered deeper anguish, greater deprivation, and more crushing disappointments than we ourselves have known? Even if the world's rich and powerful were to put themselves in the shoes of the rest, how much would they really understand the wretched millions suffering around them? So it is when Orhan the novelist peers into the dark corners of his poet friend's difficult and painful life: How much can he really see?

All my life I've felt as lost and lonely as a wounded animal [Ka wrote]. Perhaps if I hadn't embraced you with such violence, I wouldn't have angered you so much, and I might not have undone the work of twelve years, ending up exactly where I started. But here

I am, abandoned and wasting away; I carry the scars of my unbearable suffering on every inch of my body. Sometimes I think it's not just you I've lost, but that I've lost everything in the world.

Could the mere act of my reading these words ensure that I understood them?

Late that night, made pleasantly tipsy by the whiskeys I'd taken from the minibar, I went back to the Kaiserstrasse to investigate Melinda.

She had enormous olive-colored eyes with a slight cast to them. Her skin was fair, her legs were long, her lips, which an Ottoman court poet might have likened to cherries, were small but full. She was quite well known. The video section of the World Sex Center was open twenty-four hours a day, but it took me only twenty minutes to locate six films bearing her name. I smuggled these videos back to Istanbul, and only after having watched them did I begin to have some sense of what Ka might have been feeling. Whatever sort of man it was she was kneeling before—he could be the coarsest, ugliest fellow in the world—Melinda always responded to his moans of ecstasy in the same way: Her pale face softened with a compassion unique to mothers. No matter how provocative in costume (whether as an impatient businesswoman, a frolicsome stewardess, or a housewife tired of her ineffectual husband), she was always fragile and vulnerable when naked. As I would later come to see on making my own visit to Kars, there was something of İpek in her manner, her large eyes, and her curvaceous body.

I know I risk offending those poor souls who insist on seeing poets as saintly or metaphysical when I suggest that my friend spent the last four years engrossed by this adult entertainment. But as I wandered the World Sex Center hunting for videos of Melinda, it seemed to me that Ka had just one thing in common with these hordes of miserable men, lonely as ghosts. It was the habit of answering his guilt by retreating into the shadows when he would watch these films. In the cinemas around New York's 42nd Street, Frankfurt's Kaiserstrasse, and the back streets of Beyoğlu, the lonely, lost men who watch their films with shame and self-loathing, struggling to avoid one another's eyes at intermissions, these men, in defiance of all national stereotypes and anthropological distinctions, in fact look exactly the same. I left the World Sex Center with my black plastic bag full of Melinda videos and walked back through the giant snowflakes down the empty streets to my hotel.

I had two more whiskeys at the makeshift bar in the lobby, and while

I waited for them to take effect I looked outside at the falling snow. I decided that if I did manage to get tipsy again I'd take a break from Melinda and Ka's notebooks. But the moment I reached my room, I picked up one of Ka's notebooks at random, lay down on the bed without pausing to undress, and began to read. On the third—or was it the fourth?—page I found the snowflake reproduced below.

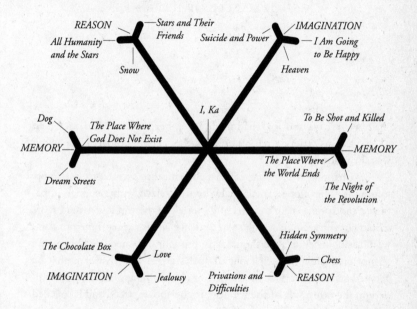

CHAPTER THIRTY

When Can We Meet Again?

A SHORT SPELL OF HAPPINESS

After Ka and İpek had made love, they stayed in bed with their arms around each other; for a time, neither moved. The world was shrouded in silence.

Ka's happiness was so great that the embrace seemed to last a very long time. This alone explains why he was seized with a sudden impatience and sprang from the bed to go look out the window. Later on, he would come to see their long shared silence as his happiest memory and would ask himself why he should have brought this unequaled bliss to an abrupt end, pulling himself out of İpek's arms. The answer is that he allowed panic to overtake him. It was as if something were about to happen on the other side of the window, in the snowy street, and he needed to be there before it did.

But there was nothing to see outside the window, apart from the falling snow. The electricity was still off, but there was a candle burning in the icy window of the kitchen downstairs, casting an orange light on the thick snow outside. Much later, it would occur to Ka that he had cut short the happiest moment of his life because he couldn't bear to be so happy. But in the beginning, as he lay in bed with İpek's arms around him, he didn't even know how happy he was; he felt at peace with the world, and this sense of peace seemed so natural that he had a hard time remembering why so much of his life up until this point had been sorrow and tumult. The peace he felt was like the silence that presaged a poem, but on those times before a poem came to him he would see the meaning of life stripped bare, a vision that also brought him joy. There was no such moment of enlightenment in this happy memory of İpek; it had about it a simple childish purity, like that of a child with the words to explain the meaning of the world on the very tip of his tongue.

One by one, he recalled the facts about snow he had read in the library that afternoon; he had gone to prepare himself just in case another poem on the subject came to him. But his head was empty of poetry. Although his poems had come to him one by one, he now saw that they all fit together as neatly as the six-pointed snowflake in the encyclopedia. It was at this moment he had the first intimation that his poems were all part of a grand design.

"What are you doing over there?" İpek asked.

"I'm looking at the snow, dear."

It seemed to him that İpek somehow knew he could see more than just beauty in the geometry of the snowflakes, but at the same time he knew this could not be so. Part of him knew she was not altogether happy to see his attention drawn elsewhere. Up to now he had been the pursuer, and his evident desire had made him feel uncomfortably vulnerable, so Ka was pleased to see the tables turned: From this he deduced that making love had gained him a slight advantage.

"What are you thinking?" asked İpek.

"I'm thinking about my mother," said Ka, at first not knowing why he said this, for though she had just died, his mother was actually far from his thoughts. Later, returning to this moment, he would explain it by saying, "My mother was on my mind throughout my visit to Kars."

"So what are you remembering about your mother?"

"I am remembering how we were standing at the window one winter night, looking out at the snow, and she ran her hands through my hair."

"Were you happy when you were a child?"

"People don't know when they're happy, at least not at the moment. I decided years later that I'd been happy as a child, but the truth is, I wasn't. On the other hand, I was not unhappy in the way I was during the years that followed. I just wasn't interested in happiness at first."

"When did you start becoming interested?"

Ka longed to say *never* but he didn't, partly because it wasn't true and partly because it seemed too aggressive. He was still tempted, if only because it might impress İpek, but there were weightier things on his mind now than the desire to make an impression.

"A moment arrived when I was so unhappy I could barely move, and that's when I began to think about happiness," Ka told her. Was this the right thing for him to say? The silence made him uneasy. If he told her how unhappy he'd been in Frankfurt, how in the world would he convince her to go back there with him? As a wild and nervous wind scattered the snowflakes outside, the panic that had driven Ka from the bed now returned with a vengeance, and more fiercely than ever his stomach ached with love and the agony of waiting. The happiness he'd felt only moments earlier now gave way to the awful certainty that he was going to lose it. In the place of happiness, doubts mounted. He wanted to ask İpek, Are you coming with me to Frankfurt? but he was already afraid of not getting the answer he wanted.

He returned to bed, pressed himself up against İpek's back, and embraced her with all his strength. "There's a store in the market," he said. "It was playing a very old song called 'Roberta,' by Peppino di Capri. Where do you think they found it?"

"There are still a few old families hanging on in Kars," said İpek. "Eventually the parents die and the children sell off their belongings and leave, and so all sorts of things turn up in the market that seem very out of place in the poor city we see today. There used to be a junk dealer who'd come from Istanbul every spring, buy everything cheap, and cart it off. But now even he's stopped coming."

For a moment Ka thought he had recaptured his earlier unequaled bliss, but it just wasn't the same as before. Once again, he succumbed to the fear that it might be lost to him forever; everything before his eyes increased his panic; he was never going to convince İpek to return to Frankfurt with him, that much was clear.

"So, darling, I think it's time for me to get up."

Even when she used the word *darling*, even when she kissed him sweetly, Ka still could find no peace.

"When can we meet again?"

"I'm worried about my father. The police might have followed him."

"I'm worried about that, too," said Ka. "But first I'd like to know when we can meet again."

"I'm not coming to your room if my father's in the hotel."

"Oh, everything's changed now," Ka said. But as he watched the silent ease with which İpek dressed in the dark, he was hit by the fear that nothing had changed at all. "Why don't I move to another hotel? Then we could see each other right away," he said.

There was a devastating silence. Now a new wave of panic overtook him, and a helpless jealousy ran through him. He allowed himself to wonder whether İpek might have another lover. Part of him was still sane enough to remember that this sort of jealousy was commonplace in the early stages of an untested love affair, but a stronger voice inside him told him to wrap his arms around her with all the strength he could muster and devote every ounce of his energy to overcoming the obstacles still standing between them. He knew it was a matter of urgency, but he also knew that if he acted too hastily it might make things awkward for him. Uncertain, he stayed silent.

CHAPTER THIRTY-ONE

We're Not Stupid, We're Just Poor

THE SECRET MEETING AT THE HOTEL ASIA

When Zahide rushed out to the horse-drawn carriage that was to take Turgut Bey and Kadife to the secret meeting at the Hotel Asia, the light was failing and so Ka, watching from the window, could not quite make out what the faithful servant had in her hands. In fact, it was an old pair of woolen gloves.

Uncertain as to what he should wear to the meeting, Turgut Bey had taken the two jackets he had from his teaching days—one black, one gray—and spread them out on the bed with the felt hat he saved for national holidays and inspection visits and the checked tie he had not worn for years except to amuse Zahide's grandson. He would have spent a good deal more time poring over the other elements of his wardrobe and the contents of his drawers, but, seeing him acting like a dreamy girl wondering what her father would let her wear to the ball, Kadife stepped in to make the final selection. After buttoning his shirt for him, she helped him on with his jacket and his coat; then came the pair of white dog-leather gloves that she struggled to pull onto his small hands.

At this moment Turgut Bey remembered his old woolen gloves. Stubbornly insisting that these were the ones he had to wear, he sent İpek and Kadife rushing around the house frantically to search every wardrobe and every chest from top to bottom; upon finally finding them, they saw how many holes the moths had made, and they threw the gloves aside. But once he was ensconced in the carriage, Turgut Bey insisted yet again that he wasn't leaving the house without them; years ago, he explained, when his left-wing activities had landed him in prison, his dear departed wife had brought him these gloves, knitted especially for him. Kadife, who knew her father better than he knew himself, saw the matter for what it was: If the old man was insisting on these gloves as a talisman, he must be very scared indeed.

After the gloves had arrived and the carriage set off into the snow, Kadife asked her father to tell her more about his prison days; she listened to his stories (how he'd cried whenever he received letters from his wife, how he'd taught himself French, how he'd worn these very gloves to bed on winter nights) as intently as if she were hearing them for the first time, occasionally interrupting to say, "What a brave man you are, Father!" And then he did what he always did when he heard his daughters utter these words (which over the last few years, he'd hardly heard at all): Fighting back tears, Turgut Bey enfolded Kadife in his arms and, shuddering, kissed her cheeks.

When the horse-drawn carriage reached the Hotel Asia, they saw that the lights were still burning in the street outside.

As he stepped out of the carriage, Turgut Bey said, "Look at all these new shops. Let's see what they have in the windows." Kadife knew he was dragging his feet out of fear, so she was careful not to hurry him. Turgut Bey proposed they stop for a cup of linden tea—if a detective was following them, he said, they might as well give him a run for his money—so they made their way into a teahouse, where they sat silently watching a race on television. Just as they were leaving, Turgut Bey spotted his old barber, so they turned around and went back inside, so as not to be seen going to the meeting.

"Do you think we're too late now? Do you think we'll offend them if we don't go at all?" The fat barber at a nearby table seemed to be eavesdropping, so Turgut Bey spoke to Kadife in whispers. He took her arm, but instead of heading straight for the back courtyard, he now went into a stationery store, where he picked out a navy-blue pen. When they finally reached the back courtyard of Ersin Electric and Plumbing Supplies and turned toward the dark door that was the back entrance to the Hotel Asia, Kadife saw the blood drain from her father's face.

Not a thing was stirring at the back entrance to the hotel. They stuck close together; no one was following them. They took a few steps inside, but in the darkness Kadife had to grope her way to the stairs that led to the lobby. "Don't let go of my arm," said Turgut Bey.

The lobby was in semidarkness, its high windows hidden behind heavy drapes. There was a weak, dirty lamp on the reception desk, which barely illuminated the face of the unshaven, unkempt clerk standing behind it. In the darkness beyond the desk they could make out a few other shadowy figures wandering about the lobby and gliding up and down the stairs. These were either plainclothes police or black marketeers who dealt in livestock or lumber or undocumented workers smuggled across the border. Eighty years earlier, this hotel had been popular with Russian businessmen; after the revolution, most of its custom came from Istanbul Turks and aristocratic English double agents heading into Armenia to spy on the Soviet Union; now it was full of women who'd come over from Georgia and the Ukraine to work as prostitutes and petty smugglers. By and large it was men from the villages around Kars who rented rooms for these women; they'd live there together during the day, almost as married couples, and after the men had gone back to their villages on the last minibus of the day, the women would come downstairs to drink coffee and cognac in the dark recesses of the bar.

As Turgut Bey and Kadife made their way among the wooden chairs once draped with red tapestry, they found themselves face-to-face with one of these tatty blondes; Turgut Bey turned to Kadife and whispered, "The Grand Hotel, where Ismet Pasha stayed when he was negotiating the Treaty of Lausanne, was just as cosmopolitan as this," and with that he took the navy-blue pen out of his pocket. "I'm going to do just what Ismet Pasha did in Lausanne: I'm going to sign the statement with a brand-new pen." For the longest time, he wouldn't move; it wasn't clear to Kadife if he was stalling or listening for noise on the stairs. And when they finally arrived at Room 307, Turgut Bey said, "Let's just sign this thing and leave."

It was so crowded inside that Kadife at first thought they'd come to the wrong room. Seeing Blue sitting glumly near the window with two other Islamist militants, she took her father across the room and sat him beside them. A naked lightbulb hung from the ceiling; on the table was a lamp in the shape of a fish, but the room was still inadequately lit. The fish was made of Bakelite; propped on its tail fins, it held the lightbulb in its mouth, and a state-owned microphone was hidden in one of its eyes.

Fazıl was in the room too; the moment he saw Kadife, he jumped to his feet, and when the others rose to pay their respects to Turgut Bey, he remained standing. He looked stunned, as if someone had cast a spell on him. A few in the room thought he was about to speak, but Kadife didn't even notice him. Her eyes were on Blue and Turgut Bey, whose eyes were on each other, and the atmosphere was tense.

Blue had decided the West would take the statement more seriously if the Kurdish nationalist who signed it was also an atheist. But the thin pale teenager who'd reluctantly agreed to sign had a difference of opinion with his Kurdish nationalist associates as to the wording. Now the three of them were waiting sullenly for their turn to speak. Since the associations of angry, hopeless, jobless youths known to admire the Kurdish guerillas from the mountains tended to convene in the houses of individual members, and since association directors were often being arrested, beaten, and tortured following frequent raids on meetings, it was hard to find these youngsters after the coup. But the three young Kurds had an even more pressing problem: The mountain warriors might find their very presence in this room suspect. They might decide that these young men had it too easy in these warm city rooms and accuse them of accommodation with the Turkish Republic. In fact, the charge that the associations were not sending their fair share of guerilla recruits up to the mountains had demoralized the handful of members who had not yet been arrested.

Also at the meeting were two old-wave socialists, both in their thirties. The possibility of a joint statement to the German press had been conveyed to them by the Kurdish youths, who'd gone to the socialists to brag a little and also to ask for advice. Socialist militancy had once cast a long shadow over Kars, but now it was spent; these days no socialist would dare set an ambush, kill a policeman, or start a mail-bomb campaign without first seeking the support of the Kurdish guerillas, and the result was an epidemic of premature decrepitude and widespread depression in their once-formidable ranks. Now here were these old militants who'd come uninvited to the meeting, having heard there were still a lot of Marxists in Europe. At the far end of the room, just beside the oldest socialist, who looked bored, sat a relaxed, clean-faced comrade, who was in high spirits, knowing he would relay the details of the meeting to the local MİT branch. His intentions weren't malign; he did this to help the associations head off police harassment. He would inform the state of any activities he didn't like—most of which seemed unnecessary in retrospect anyway—but in his heart of hearts, he was proud that there were rebels out there fighting for the cause, so proud, in fact, that he would brag about the shootings, the kidnappings, the beatings, the bombings, and the assassinations to anyone who would listen.

At first no one spoke, so sure were they that the room was bugged and that there were several informers present. Or if they spoke, it was with a nod in the direction of the window to note that it was still snowing, or to admonish someone for stubbing out cigarettes on the floor. The silence lasted until a Kurdish granny unnoticed until that moment stood up and told the story of her grandson's disappearance (they had come in the middle of the night and taken him away). Even only half listening to this disappearance story, Turgut Bey felt uneasy. He was as appalled to hear of the abduction and murder of Kurdish teenagers as he was angry to hear them described as innocents. Holding her father's hand, Kadife tried to make sense of the disgust and contempt in Blue's face. Blue felt he had walked into a trap, but fearing what people would say if he left, he remained, against his better judgment. And then: (1) the Islamist youth who was sitting next to Fazıl, and whose connection to the murder of the director of the Institute of Education would be proved months later, began to argue that the director had been assassinated by a government agent; (2) the revolutionaries in the room made a long announcement about a hunger strike begun by their friends in prison; and (3) the three youths from the Kurdish association read out an even longer statement, in which they threatened to withdraw their signatures from the joint declaration unless the *Frankfurter Rundschau* published it, thus restoring Kurdish culture and literature to its proper place in world history.

When the granny, who had come to submit a petition on behalf of the missing teenager, asked where this German journalist was, Kadife rose to explain: Ka was indeed in Kars, she said, in a reassuring voice, but had stayed away from the meeting lest his presence cast any doubt on the impartiality of the statement. The others being unaccustomed to seeing a woman address a political meeting with such confidence, she quickly gained their respect. On hearing that Kadife would do everything in her power to get her story published in the German papers, the granny threw her arms around Kadife and began to cry, and then gave her a piece of paper on which someone had written her grandson's name.

The well-meaning leftist-militant informer chose this moment to present the first draft, which he had written in longhand in a notebook; as he read it, he did his best to look inscrutable.

Almost everyone warmed to the title at once: "Announcement to the People of Europe about the Events in Kars." Remembering how he felt at that moment, Fazıl would later smile and tell Ka, "This was the first time it ever occurred to me that our small city might one day have a role to play on the world stage." (Ka would later use these very words in his poem "All Humanity and the Stars.")

Only Blue adamantly opposed the title. "We're not speaking to Europe," he said, "we're speaking to all humanity. Our friends should not be surprised to learn we have been unable to publish our statement—not just in Kars and Istanbul but also in Frankfurt. The people of Europe are not our friends, they're our enemies. And it's not because we're *their* enemies, it's because they instinctively despise us."

The leftist in charge of the first draft interrupted to clarify that it wasn't all humanity that despised them, just the European bourgeoisie. The poor and unemployed were their brothers, he reminded them, but no one other than his fellow socialist was persuaded.

"No one in Europe is as poor as we are," said one of the three Kurdish youths.

"My son, have you ever been to Europe?" asked Turgut Bey.

"I haven't had the opportunity yet, but my mother's brother is a worker in Germany."

This provoked some laughter. Turgut Bey straightened his chair. "Although the word means much to me, I have never been to Europe either," he said. "This is not a laughing matter. Please, would all those in the room who have been to Europe raise their hands."

Apart from Blue, who had spent many years in Germany, no one raised his hand.

"But we all know what Europe has come to mean," Turgut Bey continued. "Europe is our future, and the future of our humanity. So if this gentleman"—here he pointed at Blue—"thinks we should say *all humanity* instead of *Europe,* we might as well change our statement accordingly."

"Europe's not *my* future," said Blue with a smile. "As long as I live I shall never imitate them or hate myself for being unlike them."

"It's not just Islamists who take pride in this country, the Republicans feel the same way," said Turgut Bey. "If we say *all humanity* instead of *Europe,* what do we have?"

"Announcement to All Humanity about the Events in Kars," said the man in charge of the statement. "That might be too bold."

There followed a discussion in which they considered replacing *Humanity* with *the West,* but the freckled man beside Blue objected to this too. The Kurdish youth with the shrill voice then suggested the more modest *An Announcement,* and this met with everyone's approval.

Contrary to all expectations, this draft was in fact very short. And although no one took issue with the opening lines—to the effect that a coup had been "staged" at the very moment when it had become clear that Islamist and Kurdish candidates stood to prevail in the upcoming elections—Turgut Bey objected that people here were known to change their minds on a whim, giving their vote to the party that stood for everything they themselves had opposed only a day before, and that it would be better not to imply with any certitude that this or that politician was sure to have won.

In response, the leftist-militant informer in charge of the working draft said, "Everyone knows this coup happened in advance of the elections in order to prevent certain people from winning."

"You have to remember that we're dealing with a theater troupe," said Turgut Bey. "The only reason they've succeeded is that the roads are blocked. Everything will be back to normal in a matter of days."

"If you're not against the coup, why are you here?" asked a boy with a beet-red face seated next to Blue.

It was hard to tell whether Turgut Bey had even heard this disrespectful remark. In any case, Kadife rose to her feet at this same moment (she was the only one in the room to stand up when she was speaking, though no one, certainly not she, saw how strange this was). Her eyes burning with anger, she said that her father, having spent many years in prison for his political beliefs, remained categorically opposed to all forms of state-sponsored oppression.

Turgut Bey quickly removed his jacket and sat her down, saying, "I have come to this meeting because I wish to prove to the Europeans that in Turkey, too, we have people who believe in common sense and democracy."

"If a big German paper gave me two lines of space, this would not be the first thing I'd be aiming to prove," said the red-faced young man contemptuously; he would have said more, had Blue not laid a warning hand on his arm.

It was enough to make Turgut Bey regret having come. He mastered his disappointment by convincing himself he'd just stopped by on his way somewhere else. Assuming the air of someone preoccupied with matters far away from this room, he rose and took a few steps toward the door; but then, noticing the snow accumulating on Karadağ Avenue, he walked over to the window. Kadife took his arm as if to suggest her father might be unable to walk any farther without assistance. For a long time, father and daughter stood there like mournful children trying to forget their troubles, as a horse-drawn carriage made its way down the street.

One of the three boys from the Kurdish association—the one with the shrill voice—succumbed to curiosity and joined them at the window.

The others watched with a mixture of respect and apprehension; as they wondered whether there was about to be a raid, the room grew tense. The various factions were soon so worried that they reached an agreement about the rest of the statement in no time.

The statement declared the military coup to have been the work of a handful of adventurers. It was Blue who suggested this, rejecting a broader definition that might give Westerners the impression that the military had taken over all of Turkey. In the end they agreed to describe it as a "local coup supported by Ankara." Brief references were made to the Kurds who'd been shot or taken one by one from their homes and killed and to the torture and intimidation suffered by the boys from the religious high school. "A wholesale assault on the people" was amended to read "an assault on the people, the spirit, and religion." And they changed the last line, calling finally not just on the people of Europe but on the entire world to unite in protest against the Turkish Republic. As he was reading out this line, Turgut Bey caught Blue's eyes for a moment and saw contentment in them. Again, the old man was sorry he had come.

"Now, if there are no further objections, let's sign this at once," said Blue. "Because there could be a raid at any moment."

By now the statement was a tangle of crossed-out words, arrows, and circled emendations, but this deterred no one from rushing to the middle of the room to jostle for position with one objective: to sign and be off. A few were already heading for the door when Kadife cried, "Stop! My father has something to say!"

This only heightened the panic. Blue ordered the red-faced boy to guard the door. "No one may leave," he said. "Let Turgut Bey make his objection."

"I don't have an objection," the old man said. "But before I put my name to this statement, there's something I want from that teenager over there." He pointed at the red-faced boy, now standing guard at the door. "And not just from him—from everyone in the room. I'm going to ask a question, and I want an answer first from him and then from the rest of you, and if I don't get it, I won't be signing this statement." He turned to Blue to gauge the force of the remark.

"Please, be my guest, ask your question," said Blue. "If it's in our power to answer it, we'll be only too pleased to do so."

"Just a moment ago you laughed at me. So now I want you to tell me this: If a big German newspaper gave you personally two lines of space, what would you say to the West? I want that boy to go first."

The red-faced teenager was strong and powerful, with an opinion on everything, but the question caught him unprepared. Clutching the door handle more tightly than ever, he looked to Blue for help.

"Just say whatever you think you'd say, so we can leave," said Blue, forcing a smile. "If you don't, the police will be here."

The red-faced teenager searched the air as if struggling with an exam question he knew how to answer only yesterday.

Hearing nothing, Blue said, "Fine, then let me answer first. I couldn't care less about your European masters. All I want is to step out of their shadow. But the truth is, we all live under a shadow."

"Don't try to help him, let him speak from his own heart," said Turgut Bey. "You can go last." He smiled at the red-faced teenager, still squirming. "It's a difficult decision. It's a complicated business. It's not the sort of dilemma you can resolve on your way out the door."

"He's looking for excuses!" someone shouted from the back of the room. "He doesn't want to sign the statement!"

They all retreated, each into his own thoughts. A few moved to the window, to watch another horse-drawn carriage swaying back and forth on its way down the street. Later that same night, in describing the "enchanted silence" that had fallen over the room, Fazıl would tell Ka, "It was as if we were all brothers suddenly, as if we were closer to one another than we'd ever been before."

An airplane passing far above them in the night sky broke the silence. Everyone heard it. "That's the second plane today," Blue whispered.

"I'm leaving!" someone shouted. The speaker, a pale-faced man in his thirties in a pale jacket, had gone unnoticed until this moment. He was one of the three workingmen in the room. A cook in the Social Insurance Hospital, he'd come in with the families of the disappeared and he couldn't stop looking at his watch. According to later reports, his older brother, a political activist, had been carted off to the police station for questioning, never to return. It was said that the pale-faced cook wanted to secure a death certificate so he could marry his missing brother's beautiful wife. He'd petitioned the state a year after his brother's disappearance, but the police, the secret services, the public prosecutor's office, and the army garrison all gave him the brush-off; he'd joined the families of the disappeared two months earlier, not out of any desire for revenge but simply because they were the only people willing to listen to him.

"You'll call me a coward behind my back, but you're the cowards.

And these Europeans of yours, they're the biggest cowards of all. You can go ahead and quote me." He kicked the door open and walked out.

Someone now asked just who was this "Hans Hansen Bey." Kadife panicked, but to her great surprise Blue courteously explained that he was a well-intentioned German journalist who took a deep interest in Turkey's problems.

"Beware of Germans with good intentions!" cried someone at the back of the room.

"My friends, let's not hang back like frightened little schoolchildren, waiting for the other kid to speak first," someone else said.

"I'm at the lycée," piped up one of the boys from the Kurdish association. "I knew what I would say before I got here."

His voice couldn't have been calmer, but his face burned with passion. "I've always dreamed of the day when I'd have a chance to share my ideas with the world—and so has everyone else in this room. What I would say is very simple. All I'd want them to print in that Frankfurt paper is this: We're not stupid, we're just poor! And we have a right to want to insist on this distinction."

"Such humble words!"

"Who do you mean, my son, when you say *we*?" asked a man at the back. "Do you mean the Turks? The Kurds? The Circassians? The people of Kars? To whom exactly are you referring?"

"Mankind's greatest error," continued the young Kurd, "the biggest deception of the past thousand years is this: to confuse poverty with stupidity."

"And what exactly does he mean by stupidity? He should explain his terms."

"Throughout history, religious leaders and other honorable men of conscience have always warned against this shaming confusion. They remind us that the poor have hearts, minds, humanity, and wisdom just like everyone else. When Hans Hansen sees a poor man he feels sorry for him. He would not necessarily assume that the man's a fool who's blown his chances or a drunk who's lost his will."

"I can't speak for Hans Hansen, but that's what everyone thinks when they see a poor man."

"Please listen to what I have to say," said the passionate Kurdish youth. "I won't speak long. People might feel sorry for a man who's fallen on hard times, but when an entire nation is poor, the rest of the world assumes that all its people must be brainless, lazy, dirty, clumsy fools. Instead of pity, the people provoke laughter. It's all a joke: their culture, their customs, their practices. In time the rest of the world may, some of them, begin to feel ashamed for having thought this way, and when they look around and see immigrants from that poor country mopping their floors and doing all the other lowest paying jobs, naturally they worry about what might happen if these workers one day rose up against them. So, to keep things sweet, they start taking an interest in the immigrants' culture and sometimes even pretend they think of them as equals."

"It's about time he told us what nation he's talking about."

"Let me add this," said one of the other Kurdish youths. "Mankind refuses to laugh any longer at those who kill and murder and oppress. This is what I learned from my mother's brother when he came to Kars from Germany last summer. The world has lost patience with oppressive countries."

"Are we to assume then that you're making a threat on behalf of the West?"

"As I was saying," the first young Kurd continued, "when a Westerner meets someone from a poor country, he feels deep contempt. He assumes that the poor man's head must be full of all the nonsense that plunged his country into poverty and despair."

"And if he did, he wouldn't be far off the mark, would he?"

"If you're like that conceited poet and think we're all stupid, stand up and state your case. That godless atheist will end up in hell, but at least he showed some courage. He went on live TV and looked the entire country in the eye and told us to our faces we are stupid."

"Excuse me, but people on live TV can't see their audience."

"The gentleman didn't say he 'saw,' he said he 'looked.' "

"Friends! Please! Let's not be a debating society," pleaded the leftist who was taking minutes. "And also, please try to speak more slowly."

"If he's not brave enough to say what nation he's talking about, I refuse to be quiet. Let's be clear that it's treason to give a German paper a quote trashing our nation."

"I'm no traitor. I agree with you," the passionate Kurdish youth said, rising to his feet. "That's why I want to tell this German paper that even if I got a chance to go to Germany one day, even if they gave me a visa, I wouldn't go."

"They'd never give a European visa to a feeble, unemployed nothing like you."

"Forget the visa, our own state wouldn't give him a passport."

"You're right, they wouldn't," said the passionate but humble youth. "But say they did and I went, and the first Western man I met in the street turned out to be a good person who didn't even despise me, I'd still mistrust him, just for being a Westerner, I'd still worry that this man was looking down on me. Because in Germany they can spot Turks just by the way they look. There's no escaping humiliation except by proving at the first opportunity that you think exactly as they do. But this is impossible, and it can break a man's pride to try."

"You started badly, my son, but you've ended up in the right place," said an old Azeri journalist. "But I still think we shouldn't say this to the German press, because it will lay us open to ridicule." He paused for a moment and then asked cunningly, "So what nation was it you were talking about?"

When the teenager from the Kurdish association sat down without speaking further, the old journalist's son cried out, "He's afraid!"

"He's right to be afraid. He's not on the government payroll like you."

Neither the journalist nor his son took offense. Everyone was talking at once, but not in frustration: All the joking and teasing and keeping score had made the atmosphere festive and intimate. Later, on hearing Fazıl's account of the proceedings, Ka would observe in his notebook that this sort of political meeting could go on for hours, and the beetle-browed, mustachioed, cigarette-smoking men who attended them did so precisely to enjoy the pleasure of the crowd, even without realizing that they were having a good time.

"We will never be Europeans!" cried one of the proud young Islamists. "They may try to roll over us with their tanks and spray us with bullets and kill us all, but they can't change our souls."

"You can take possession of my body but never my soul!" said one of the Kurdish youths. He made his contempt clear by reciting the line in the style of a Turkish melodrama.

Everyone laughed. And to show he didn't mind, the boy who'd been speaking started laughing too.

"Now I'm going to say something," said one of the youths sitting near Blue. "No matter how hard our friends here try to draw a line between themselves and the lowlifes who ape the ways of the West, I still sense a certain note of apology. It's as if they're saying, 'I'm so sorry I'm not a Westerner.'" He turned to the man in the leather jacket who was taking notes. "Please, dear sir, ignore these preliminary remarks!" He spoke like a polite thug. "Here's what I'd like you to write: I'm proud of the part of me that isn't European. I'm proud of the things in me that the Europeans find childish, cruel, and primitive. If the Europeans are beautiful, I want to be ugly; if they're intelligent, I prefer to be stupid; if they're modern, let me stay pure."

No one in the room would sign on to that sentiment. The ensuing laughter preserved the new spirit of the gathering, with everything now said giving way to a joke. Then someone went too far—"But you're stupid already!" At the very same moment the oldest of the leftists and his friend in the black jacket both had coughing fits, so fortunately no one was sure who had uttered these insulting words.

The red-faced teenager guarding the door rattled off a poem. "Europe, O Europe,/Let's stop and take a look,/When we're together in our dreams/Let's not let the devil have his way." Fazıl had a hard time hearing the rest over all the coughing, taunting, and sniggering, but he could recount in detail the objections to it; jotted down on the same sheet bearing his record of the various two-line statements for Europe were these snippets of reaction that ended up in "All Humanity and the Stars," the poem Ka was to write shortly afterward.

1. "Let's not be afraid of them, there's nothing there to be afraid of!" One of the old-guard leftist militants now approaching middle age.

2. The old Azeri journalist who could not stop asking, "To what nation are you referring?" said, "Let's not sacrifice our Turkishness or forsake our religion."

3. A defeatist in the crowd slyly asked, "And whatever happened to the millions of Armenians who once lived all across Anatolia, including Kars?" in the course of a long speech about the Crusades, the Holocaust, the American massacre of the Red Indians, and the Algerian Muslims massacred by the French. But feeling pity for this man, the informer-secretary did not write down his name.

4. "No one in his right mind would ever want to translate such a long and idiotic poem, and Hans Hansen would never let it be published in his newspaper." This from one of the three poets in the room. It was their chance to bemoan the luckless isolation of Turkish poets on the international stage.

At the end of his recitation of the poem that everyone denounced as idiotic and primitive, the red-faced youth was drenched in sweat; there was scattered, rather contemptuous applause. Most seemed to agree that it would be unwise to let this poem be published in Germany, as it might give rise to more ridicule. The Kurdish youth whose mother's brother lived in Germany was the most outspoken on this point.

"When they write poems or sing songs in the West, they speak for all humanity. They're human beings—but we're just Muslims. When *we* write something, it's just called ethnic poetry."

"My message is this: Write this down," said the man in the black jacket. "If the Europeans are right and our only future and only hope is to be more like them, it's foolish to waste time talking about what makes us who we are."

"Ah, of all the things said so far, here is the one that will most effectively convince the Europeans that we're idiots."

"Please, once and for all, state clearly which nation it is that's going to look idiotic."

"And here we are acting as if we're so much smarter and worthier than Westerners, but gentlemen, I put it to you that if Germany opened a consulate in Kars today and started handing out free visas, the city would be empty within a week."

"That's a lie. After all, our friend over there just told us he wouldn't go even if they offered him the chance. I wouldn't leave either. I'd do the honorable thing and stay here."

"And many others would stay too, gentlemen, make no mistake. All those who wouldn't go raise your hands so we can see you."

A few gravely raised their hands. A handful of youths saw them but remained undecided. "And why is it that those who would go are seen as dishonorable?" asked the man in the black jacket.

"This is hard to explain to people who don't already understand," said one mysterious fellow.

Fazıl noticed that Kadife had turned away, looking mournfully out the window, and his heart began to thump wildly. Please God, he thought, help me preserve my purity, protect my mind from confusion. It occurred to him that Kadife might like these words. It occurred to him to make this his quote for the German newspaper, but with so many people speaking, there was no chance for him to be heard.

The only one whose voice rose above all this noise was the shrill

Kurdish youth. He proposed to tell the German newspaper about a dream he'd had. Pausing from time to time with a shiver, he explained how in this dream he'd been sitting all alone in the National Theater watching a film. It was a Western film, and everyone in it was speaking a foreign language, but this didn't make him uncomfortable; he somehow understood everything they said. And then, in the blink of an eye, he entered the film itself; it turned out that his seat was not in the National Theater but in the sitting room of a Christian family. There, before his eyes, was a table laden with food; he longed to fill his stomach, but for fear of doing something wrong he kept his distance. His heart began to race: there, before him, was a beautiful blond woman, and the moment he saw her he remembered that he'd been in love with her for years. The woman was warmer and more gentle than he could ever imagine. She complimented him on his clothes and his manners, kissed his cheeks, and ran her fingers through his hair. He felt so very happy. Before he knew it, she sat him on her lap and pointed out the food on the table. Only then did he realize that he was still a child, said the Kurdish youth, with tears welling in his eyes. It was because he was still a child that she found him so charming.

The old journalist broke the silence. "No one could dream a dream like that," he said. "This Kurdish boy made it all up just to mock us to the Germans."

To prove the authenticity of this dream, the teenager from the Kurdish association offered a detail he'd omitted from his earlier account: Every time he'd woken up since the dream, he'd remembered this same blond woman. He'd first seen her five years ago; she was stepping out of a bus, one of a group of tourists who'd come to see the Armenian churches. She was wearing a blue dress with straps that she also wore in his dreams.

This produced more laughter. "We've all seen European women like that," said someone, "and we've all been tempted by the devil." It was an opportunity for a few mischievous anecdotes, off-color jokes, and angry diatribes against Western women. A tall, thin, and rather handsome youth who had stayed in the background until that moment launched into a story about a Westerner and a Muslim who met at a train station. Sadly, the train didn't arrive. At the end of the same platform they saw a beautiful Frenchwoman waiting for the same train. . . .

Anyone who'd ever attended a boys' school or done his military service recognized this for a story about to draw a parallel between sexual prowess and national culture. It contained no rude words; its coarseness was hidden under a veil of insinuations. But in no time at all there fell over the room a mood that would later cause Fazıl to exclaim: "My heart was heavy with shame!"

Turgut Bey rose to his feet. "All right, my boy, that's enough," he said. "Bring me this statement so I can sign it."

He fished out his new pen, and it was done. The noise and the cigarette smoke had worn him out, and Kadife had to help him stand.

"Now listen to me for a minute," she said. "You seem to feel no shame, but my face is red from what I've just heard. I cover my head with this scarf so you won't see my hair, and maybe you think this causes me undue hardship, but—"

"You don't do it for us!" someone said in a respectful whisper. "You do it for God, to proclaim your spirituality!"

"I have a few things to say to the German paper too. Please write them down." She was enough of an actress to know that her audience half hated and half admired her. "A young woman of Kars—no, don't write that; say a Muslim girl who lives in Kars—has covered her head for personal religious reasons but also wears the scarf as an emblem of her faith. One day this girl is overcome by a sudden revulsion and pulls the scarf off her head. (The Westerners would greet this as good news. If we did that, Hans Hansen would certainly want to print our views.) When she pulled off her scarf, this girl said, 'Please God, forgive me, because I have to be alone. This world is so loathsome, and I am so powerless and so full of woe that your—' "

"Kadife," whispered Fazıl. "Please, I beg you, don't bare your head. We're all here right now, all of us, including me and Necip. It would kill us, kill us all."

Everyone in the room seemed confused by these words. "Stop talking nonsense," someone said, and then someone else, "But of course she shouldn't bare her head." But most looked at her expectantly, half hoping she was about to do something shocking and newsworthy and half wondering who had staged this melodrama and who was playing games with whom.

"The two lines I want to give the German paper are as follows," said Fazıl. The buzzing in the room grew louder. "I speak not only for myself but for my friend Necip, who was so cruelly martyred on the night of the revolution: Kadife, we love you very much. If you bare your head, I'll kill myself, so please. Please don't."

According to some reports, Fazıl didn't say *we love you* but *I love you,* though it's possible these witnesses adjusted their memories to explain what Fazıl would do later on.

"No one in this city may talk about suicide!" bellowed Blue, and he stormed out of the hotel room without even pausing to look at Kadife; this brought the meeting to an immediate close and, although they were not particularly quiet about it, they'd cleared the room in a matter of seconds.

CHAPTER THIRTY-TWO

I Have Two Souls Inside My Body

ON LOVE, INSIGNIFICANCE, AND
BLUE'S DISAPPEARANCE

A t a quarter to five, Ka stepped out of the Snow Palace Hotel. Turgut Bey and Kadife had not yet returned from the meeting at the Hotel Asia, and Ka still had fifteen minutes before he was due to meet Fazıl, but he was too happy to sit still. He turned left off Atatürk Avenue and walked as far as the Kars River, slowing down from time to time to gaze into the windows of grocery stores and photographers' and teahouses crowded with men watching television. When he reached the Iron Bridge, he smoked two Marlboros in quick succession; with his head full of visions of living happily ever after with İpek in Frankfurt, he didn't feel the cold at all. Across the river was the park where rich families of Kars used to go to watch the ice skaters; it was now ominously dark.

Fazıl was late to the Iron Bridge rendezvous, and when he emerged from the darkness Ka for a moment mistook him for Necip. Together they went into the Lucky Brothers Teahouse, where Fazıl reported everything he could remember about the meeting at the Hotel Asia. When he got to the part where he declared his feeling that the history of his small city had become as one with the history of the world, Ka silenced him as one might hush another in midsentence upon catching the thread of something important being said on the radio; he then proceeded to write the poem entitled "All Humanity and the Stars."

In the notes he made afterward, Ka described its subject as the sadness of a city forgotten by the outside world and banished from history; the first lines followed a sequence recalling the opening scenes of the Hollywood films he had so loved as a child. As the titles rolled past, there was a faraway image of the earth turning slowly; as the camera came in closer and closer, the sphere grew and grew, until suddenly all you could see was one country, and of course—just as in the imaginary films Ka had been watching in his head since childhood—this country was Turkey; now the blue waters of the Sea of Marmara and the Bosphorus and the Black Sea were visible; as the camera moved in farther you could see Istanbul, and the Nişantaş of Ka's childhood, with the traffic policeman on Teşvikiye Avenue, the Street of Niğar the Poetess, and trees and rooftops (how lovely they looked from above!); then came a slow pan across the laundry hanging on the line, the billboard advertising Tamek canned goods, the rusty gutters and the pitch-covered sidewalls, before the pause at Ka's bedroom window. Then a long tracking shot through the window of rooms packed with books, dusty furniture, and carpets, to Ka at a desk facing the other window; panning over his shoulder, the camera revealed a piece of paper on the desk and, following the fountain pen, came finally to rest on the last letters of the message he was writing, thus inviting us to read:

ADDRESS ON THE DAY OF MY ENTRANCE
INTO THE HISTORY OF POETRY: POET KA,
16/8 NIGÂR THE POETESS STREET,
NİŞANTAŞ, ISTANBUL, TURKEY

As discerning readers will already have guessed, this address, which I think must also appear in the poem itself, is located on the Reason axis but positioned to suggest the power of the imagination.

Fazıl's main preoccupation was clear by the end of his story; he was now very uneasy about having threatened to kill himself if Kadife bared her head. "It's not just because committing suicide is tantamount to losing your faith, it's also because I didn't mean it. Why did I say something I didn't mean?" Fazıl claimed that right after his vow, he had said, "God forgive me, I'll never say that again!" But then, coming eye to eye with Kadife at the door, he had trembled like a leaf.

"Do you think Kadife thought I was in love with her?" he asked Ka.

"*Are* you in love with Kadife?"

"You know the truth already; I was in love with Teslime, may she rest in peace. My friend Necip, may he also rest in peace, was the one who was in love with Kadife. I feel so ashamed of myself for falling in love with the same girl not a day after his death. And I know there can be only one explanation. This scares me too. Tell me why you're so sure that Necip is dead!"

"I looked at the place where the bullet entered his forehead before I laid my hands on his shoulders and kissed him."

"It's possible that Necip's soul is now living inside my body," said Fazıl. "Listen. I stayed away from the gala last night; I didn't even watch it on television. I went to bed early and passed out immediately. Only later did I hear about the terrible things that had happened to Necip while I was asleep. Then the soldiers raided our dormitory, and I had no doubt they were true. By the time I saw you at the library, I knew Necip was dead, because his soul had been in my body since early morning. The soldiers who came to empty the dormitory passed me by, so I spent the night on Sunday Street, at the home of one of my father's friends from army days—he's from Varto. As I lay in his guest bed, my head suddenly started spinning and a deep rich feeling came over me. My friend was at my side again; he was inside me. It's just as they say in the old books: The soul leaves the body six hours after death. According to Suyuti, at that instant the soul is a playful, mercurial thing, and it has to sit in Berzah till the Day of Judgment. But Necip's soul decided to enter my body instead. I'm sure of this. I'm also very much afraid, because this is never mentioned in the Koran. But there's no other way I can explain how I fell in love with Kadife so quickly. So the idea of committing suicide over her wasn't mine either. Do you think it could be true that Necip's soul has taken refuge in my body?"

"If that's what you believe," said Ka carefully.

"You're the only one I'm telling. Necip told you secrets he never told anyone else. I beg you, tell me the truth: Necip never once told me that the doubt of atheism had taken root in him, but he could have mentioned it to you. Did Necip ever tell you that he—God forbid—doubted God's existence?"

"It wasn't the sort of doubt you imagine; what he told me was different. Like imagining your parents might die one day and taking pleasure from that sadness, it was about thoughts that came to him unbidden about what might happen if his beloved God did not exist."

"Now the same thing's happening to me," said Fazıl. "I've no further doubt that Necip's soul has planted these thoughts in me."

"These uncertainties don't equal atheism."

"But I'm already siding with the suicide girls," said Fazıl sadly. "Just a few minutes ago, I said I was ready to commit suicide myself. I don't want to believe that my dear departed friend was an atheist. But now I hear the voice of an atheist inside me, and this makes me very scared. I don't know if it's the same for you, but you've been to Europe; you've met all the intellectuals and all those alcohol and sleeping-pill addicts who live there. So please, tell me again, what does it feel like to be an atheist?"

"Well, they certainly don't fantasize endlessly about suicide."

"I don't fantasize endlessly, but sometimes I do think about it."

"Why?"

"Because of Kadife. I can't get her out of my mind! I close my eyes and there she is, shimmering before me. When I'm studying, watching television, waiting for evening to fall, everything reminds me of Kadife, even if it has nothing to do with her, which causes me great pain. This started happening before Necip died. To tell you the truth, it was not really Teslime; it was always Kadife I loved. But because my friend loved her I hid my feelings. It was actually Necip who provoked it, by talking endlessly about Kadife. When the soldiers raided our dormitory I knew there was a chance they had already killed him and, yes, this thought made me glad. It wasn't because I saw a chance to make my feelings plain; it was because I thought it served him right for provoking this love in me. Necip is dead now, and I am free, but that only means I love Kadife more than ever. I've been thinking of her ever since I woke up this morning; she's consuming my thoughts; it's got so I can't think about anything else and—dear God—I just don't know what to do!"

Fazıl buried his face in his hands and began to sob. Ka lit a Marlboro as a wave of selfish indifference passed through him. But he still reached out to comfort the boy and, for the longest time, stroked his head.

Saffet, the detective assigned to follow him, had been sitting at the other end of the teahouse, watching them with one eye and the television set with the other; now he got up and walked over to the table.

"Tell this boy to stop crying. I didn't take his identity card to head-quarters; I still have it with me." When this failed to stem Fazıl's tears, he put his hand in his pocket and produced the identity card; Ka reached out and took it. "Why is he crying?" asked Saffet, half out of professional curiosity and half out of compassion.

"He's in love," said Ka. The detective immediately relaxed. Ka watched him leave the teahouse and vanish into the night.

Later, Fazıl asked what he had to do to get Kadife's attention, mentioning that all of Kars knew Ka was in love with Kadife's sister. Fazıl's passion seemed so plainly hopeless and impossible that Ka wondered whether his own love for İpek might not be similarly doomed. As Fazıl's sobs faded away, Ka dolefully repeated the advice İpek had given him: "Just be yourself."

"That's not going to be possible as long as I have two souls inside my body," said Fazıl. "Especially with Necip's atheist soul slowly taking over. For years and years, I've thought my friends and fellow classmates were wrong to get mixed up in politics, and now suddenly I want to join the Islamists and do something to protest this military coup. But even there my motivation, I think, is to make Kadife notice me. It scares me to have nothing but Kadife inside my head. It's not just because I don't know her. It's because this proves I'm a typical atheist. I don't care about anything except love and happiness."

When Fazıl broke down into sobs again, Ka thought of telling him that he shouldn't be discussing his infatuation with Kadife in public; he would be in serious trouble if Blue found out about it. If everyone knew about his own relationship with İpek, Ka reasoned, it followed that everyone also knew about Kadife's relationship with Blue. In this case, Fazıl's professed ardor would be a direct challenge to the Kars Islamist hierarchy.

"We're poor and insignificant," said Fazıl, with a strange fury in his voice. "Our wretched lives have no place in human history. One day all of us living now in Kars will be dead and gone. No one will remember us; no one will care what happened to us. We'll spend the rest of our days arguing about what sort of scarf women should wrap around their heads, and no one will care in the slightest because we're eaten up by our own petty, idiotic quarrels. When I see so many people around me leading such stupid lives and then vanishing without a trace, an anger runs through me because I know then that nothing really matters more in life than love. And when I think that, my feelings for Kadife become all the more unbearable—it hurts to know that my only consolation would be to spend the rest of my life with my arms around her."

"Yes," said Ka ruthlessly. "These are the sorts of thoughts you have when you're an atheist."

Fazıl started crying again. Ka either couldn't remember what they said afterward or he chose not to write it down; the notebooks show no record of the end of the conversation. On the television screen a horde of little American children were clowning for the camera. They were knocking over their chairs, an aquarium was bursting, and then they were all crouching on the ground to the sound of canned laughter. Like everyone else in the teahouse, Fazıl and Ka forgot their troubles and sat laughing at the antics of the American children.

When Zahide entered the teahouse, Ka and Fazıl were watching a truck weave stealthily through a forest. She gave Ka a yellow envelope in which Fazıl showed no interest. Ka opened it up and read the note inside; it was from İpek. She and Kadife proposed to meet him in twenty minutes at the New Life Pastry Shop. Fortunately, Zahide had found out from Saffet that he was in the Lucky Brothers Teahouse.

As Zahide was leaving, Fazıl said, "Her grandson is in our class. He's mad about gambling. If there's a cockfight or a dogfight going on, he'll have a bet on it."

Ka handed him his student identity card. "They want me back at the hotel for dinner," he said, as he rose to his feet.

"Are you going to see Kadife?" asked Fazıl, hopelessness in his voice. The pity and annoyance he could see on Ka's face made him blush with shame. As Ka left the teahouse, Fazıl shouted, "I want to kill myself! If you see her, tell her that if she bares her head I'm going to kill myself! But it won't be because she's bared her head, I'll do it just for the pleasure of killing myself in her honor."

Having more than enough time to get to the New Life Pastry Shop, Ka decided to take the back roads. Walking down Kanal Street, he saw the teahouse where he'd written "Dream Streets" that morning; only when he went inside did he realize that he was not destined to write his next poem in this smoky half-empty teahouse; what he wanted was to go straight across the room and out through the back door. He walked into the snow-covered courtyard, stepped over the low wall he could hardly see, now that it was dark, and went past the same barking dog down three steps into the basement.

A weak lamp illuminated the interior. Mixed with the smell of coal and the stench of old bedding there were now also raki fumes. He could see several silhouettes huddled around the humming stove. When he saw it was the hook-nosed MİT agent drinking raki with the tubercular Georgian woman and her husband, he wasn't at all surprised. Neither did they seem surprised to see Ka. Ka noticed that the woman was wearing a fashionable red hat. She offered him boiled eggs with pita bread, and her husband poured him a glass of raki. While Ka was still peeling his boiled egg, the MİT agent told him that this furnace room was not merely the warmest place in Kars, it was heaven itself.

The poem Ka wrote during the ensuing silence, without a single difficulty or missing word, was the one he would later call "Heaven." If he placed it on the Imagination axis of the snowflake, far from the center, way at the top, it was not to suggest that heaven was the future we remember: For Ka, heaven was the place where you kept your memories. Recalling this poem afterward, he would summon one by one a string of recollections: the summer holidays of his childhood, the days he'd skipped out of school, the times he and his sister had gone into their parents' bed, various drawings he'd done as a child, and the time he went on a date with a girl he'd met at a school party and dared to kiss her.

As Ka walked to the New Life Pastry Shop, his mind was busy with İpek. When he arrived, he found the sisters already there. İpek looked so beautiful, and Ka felt such happiness at the sight of her, that tears came to his eyes—although it's possible that his reaction might have had something to do with the raki he'd just drunk on an empty stomach. To sit at a table with two lovely women didn't just make him happy, it made him proud. He thought of those worn-out Turkish shopkeepers in Frankfurt who smiled and waved at him every morning and evening and imagined what they would think to see him now with these two women. Today he had no audience; no one else was here apart from the old waiter who'd been present when the director of the Institute of Education was assassinated. But even as he sat in the New Life Pastry Shop with İpek and Kadife, Ka knew he would always remember this scene; like a photograph taken from outside the shop, it showed him sitting at a table with two beautiful women—never mind that one of them had wrapped her head in a scarf.

The two women were as agitated as Ka was calm. After Ka explained that Fazıl had given him a full report of the meeting at the Hotel Asia, İpek came right to the point.

"Blue left the meeting in a fury. And Kadife now regrets what she said there. We sent Zahide to his hiding place but he wasn't there. We can't find Blue anywhere." When she started speaking, it was in the tone of the elder daughter trying to help a sister in trouble, but soon it was clear that she too was distressed.

"If you find him, what then?"

"We want to be sure they haven't caught him. Above all, we need to know he's still alive," said İpek. She glanced at Kadife, who looked as if she was about to burst into tears. "Please find him and ask him if he has anything he wants to say to us. Tell him Kadife's ready to do whatever he asks."

"You know Kars a lot better than I do."

"It's dark and we're just two women," said İpek. "You've learned your way around the city by now. Go see what you can find out at the Man in the Moon Teahouse and the Divine Light Teahouse—that's where the religious high school boys and the Islamist students go. They're both swarming with undercover police, and those men are terrible gossips. If something bad's happened to Blue, they're sure to be talking about it."

Kadife had taken out her handkerchief and was blowing her nose. Ka thought she was still on the verge of tears.

"Bring us news of Blue," İpek said. "If we stay here any longer, our father will begin to worry. He's expecting you for dinner."

"Don't forget to check out the teahouses on Bayrampaşa Avenue!" Kadife said, as she rose from her chair.

Her voice was about to crack; it seemed to Ka that both girls were terrified and fast losing hope. Ka was uneasy about leaving them in this state, so he walked them halfway back to the Snow Palace Hotel. Fearful as he was of losing İpek, the knowledge of being their accomplice, helping them do something behind their father's back, bound him to them both. As they walked, he imagined one day when he and İpek would be in Frankfurt and Kadife would come to visit, and the three of them would weave in and out of the cafés on Berliner Avenue, stopping from time to time to gaze at a shop window.

But after giving it some thought, he began to doubt he'd be able to accomplish the mission they had set him. He had no trouble finding the Man in the Moon Teahouse, a place so ordinary and uninspiring that Ka soon forgot why he was there; for the longest time he sat alone watching television. There were a few men there who seemed young enough to be students, and although he did try to coax them out with a few remarks about the football match on the screen, none of them responded. Ka's next move was to take out his cigarettes, so that he'd be ready to offer them to anyone who might approach him; he even went so far as to put his lighter on the table. When he realized that no one, not even the cross-eyed man at the counter, was going to talk to him, he went next door to the Divine Light, where he found a handful of youths watching the same football match in black-and-white. If he hadn't gone over to the wall to look at the newspaper clippings and the schedule of all Karsspor matches to be played that season, he would not have remembered that this was the teahouse where, only yesterday, he and Necip had discussed God's existence and the meaning of life. Looking again at the doggerel someone had scribbled on the Karsspor poster, and seeing that another poet had added a few more lines since yesterday, he took out his notebook and began to copy them down:

> *So it's settled: our mother's not coming back from heaven,*
> *Never again will we know her embrace,*
> *But no matter how many beatings she suffers at our father's hand,*
> *She'll still keep warming our hearts and breathing life into our souls,*
> *Because that was fate,*
> *And the shit we're sinking into smells so bad*
> *it even makes the city of Kars look like heaven.*

"Are you writing a poem?" asked the boy at the counter.

"Congratulations," said Ka. "Tell me, do you know how to read writing upside down?"

"No, big brother, I can't even read when it's right side up. I ran away from school, so I never managed to crack the code. But that's all in the past now."

"Who wrote the new poem on the wall here?"

"Half the boys who used to come here are poets."

"Why aren't they here today?"

"Yesterday the soldiers rounded them all up. Some are locked up now, and the rest are in hiding. Ask those men over there if you want; they're undercover agents, so they should know."

The boy pointed toward two young men in the corner in feverish discussion of the football match, but rather than approach them to ask about the missing poets, Ka headed for the door.

He was glad to see that the snow had started falling again. He was sure he'd find no clues to Blue's whereabouts in the teahouses of Bayrampaşa Avenue. Immersed as he was in the dusky melancholy that had begun descending over the city, he still felt happy. A long procession of images paraded before his eyes as he awaited his next poem—a waking dream of ugly unadorned concrete buildings, parking lots buried in snow, teahouses and barbershops and grocery stores all hidden behind their icy windows, courtyards in which dogs had been barking in unison since the days of the Russians, stores selling spare parts for tractors alongside horse-drawn carriage supplies and cheese. He was seized by the certainty that everything he saw—the banners for the Motherland Party, the little window hidden behind those tightly drawn curtains, the slip of paper someone had taped to the icy window of the Knowledge Pharmacy months earlier to announce that the shot for Japanese influenza had finally arrived, the yellow antisuicide poster—every last one of these little details would stay with him for the rest of his life. There arose from these minor things a vision of extraordinary power: So certain was he that "everything on earth is interconnected and I too am inextricably linked to this deep and beautiful world," he could only conclude another poem was on its way, and so he stepped into one of the teahouses on Atatürk Avenue. But the poem never arrived.

CHAPTER THIRTY-THREE

A Godless Man in Kars

THE FEAR OF BEING SHOT

No sooner had Ka left the teahouse for the snow-covered pavement than he came face-to-face with Muhtar. Muhtar wore the absentminded look of a man on a mission; when he first saw Ka through the swarm of giant snowflakes he didn't seem to recognize him, and for a moment Ka was tempted to run away. Then they both rushed forward at once to embrace like long-lost friends.

"Did you pass my message on to İpek?"

"Yes."

"What did she say? Come, let's sit down in that teahouse over there, and you can tell me."

In spite of the military coup, the beating at the police station, and the canceled election, Muhtar did not seem at all downcast.

Once they were seated, he said, "So why do you suppose they didn't arrest me? Because when the snow melts, the roads open, and the soldiers are sent back to their barracks, they'll set a new date for the elections, that's why! Make sure you tell İpek!"

Ka assured him that he would pass on the message. Then he asked if there was any news of Blue.

"I'm the one who first summoned him to Kars. In the beginning he always stayed with me," Muhtar told him proudly. "But after the Istanbul press branded him a terrorist, he didn't want to put the party in a difficult position, so now when he comes to Kars he never gets in touch. I'm always the last to know what he's up to. What did İpek say when you passed on my message?"

Ka told Muhtar that İpek had not seemed particularly interested in his proposal that they remarry. Muhtar impressed upon Ka what a sensitive, refined, and understanding woman his ex-wife was; he made the point as though disclosing very precious information. He went on to reiterate his regret for having treated her so badly during a difficult crisis in his life.

"When you get back to Istanbul, you'll take the poems I gave you and deliver them by hand to Fahir, won't you?" he asked next.

When Ka had given his word, Muhtar rearranged his face to take on the air of a sad and tenderhearted uncle. Ka's embarrassment was already giving way to something halfway between pity and revulsion when Muhtar produced a newspaper from his pocket.

"If I were you, I wouldn't be wandering the streets so casually," Muhtar said pleasantly.

Ka grabbed the next day's edition of the *Border City Gazette,* on which the ink wasn't yet dry. He scanned the headlines—THEATRICAL REVOLU-TIONARIES TAKE CITY BY STORM, HAPPY DAYS RETURN TO KARS, ELECTIONS POSTPONED, CITIZENS APPLAUD THE REVOLUTION—and turned his attention to the front-page article that Muhtar indicated:

A GODLESS MAN IN KARS
QUESTIONS ASKED ABOUT KA,
THE SO-CALLED POET
WHY DID HE CHOOSE TO VISIT OUR
CITY IN SUCH TROUBLED TIMES?

YESTERDAY WE INTRODUCED THE SO-CALLED
POET TO THE PEOPLE OF KARS
TODAY WE REPORT THE SUSPICIONS HE HAS
AROUSED IN OUR READERS

We have been hearing many rumors about the so-called poet who came close to ruining yesterday's joyous performance by the Sunay Zaim Players when he strode onto the stage halfway through the celebrations of Atatürk and the Republic and robbed the audience of their happiness and their peace of mind by bombarding their ears with a joyless, meaningless poem.

Although the people of Kars once lived side by side in happy harmony, in recent years outside forces have turned brother against brother. Disputes between Islamists, secularists, Kurds, Turks, and Azeris drive us asunder for specious reasons and reawaken old accusations about the Armenian massacre that should have been buried long ago.

It is only natural that the people of Kars wonder whether this suspicious character who fled Turkey many years ago and now lives in Germany has chosen to grace us with his company because he is some sort of spy. Can it be true that his efforts to provoke an incident at our religious high school resulted in his making the following statement to youths who engaged him in a conversation two days ago? "I am an atheist. I don't believe in God, but that doesn't mean I'd commit suicide, because after all God—*God forbid*—doesn't exist." Can these be his exact words? And when he said, "An intellectual's job is to speak against holiness," was he denying God's existence and—if so—was he expressing European views on freedom of thought?

Just because Germany is bankrolling you, that doesn't mean you have the right to trample on our beliefs! Is it because you are ashamed of being a Turk that you hide your true name behind the fake foreign counterfeit name of Ka?

Many readers have telephoned our offices to express their regret about this godless imitation-European's decision to stir up dissent in our city in these troubled times. They have voiced particular concern about the way in which he has wandered the shantytowns, knocking on the doors of the most wretched dwellings to incite rebellion against our state and indeed, even in our own presence, vainly attempting to stick his tongue out at our country and even at the great Atatürk, Father of our Republic. The youth of Kars know how to deal with blasphemers who deny God and the Prophet Muhammad (SAS)!

"When I passed by their office twenty minutes ago, Serdar's two sons had only just started printing this edition," said Muhtar. Far from commiserating with his friend's fears, he seemed cheerful, as if he had just introduced a pleasant new topic.

Reading the article more carefully a second time, Ka felt very much alone. Long ago, when he'd first dreamed of a glittering literary future, he had foreseen that the modernist innovations he would bring to Turkish poetry (the very concept now seemed excessively nationalist) would provoke harsh criticism and personal attack; still, he'd assumed that notoriety would at least confer a certain aura. Although he'd enjoyed a modest fame in the years since and had never been subject to harsh criticism, it hurt him to be referred to as a "so-called" poet.

After warning him not to wander the streets like a moving target, Muhtar left him alone at the teahouse. Ka was overtaken by the fear that he could be shot at any moment. He left the teahouse and wandered through the snow, lost in thought; the giant snowflakes that sailed down from the heavens so fast were moving with a speed to suggest bewitchment.

Early in his youth, Ka had firmly believed that there could be no higher honor than to die for an intellectual political cause or for what he had written. By his thirties, he'd seen too many of his friends and classmates tortured for the sake of foolish, even malign principles; then there were those who were shot dead in the attempt to rob banks and those who made bombs that wound up exploding in their hands. Seeing the havoc of his lofty ideas put into action, Ka deliberately distanced himself from them. Finally, the fact of having spent years and years of exile in Germany for political beliefs he no longer held had finally severed the connection between politics and self-sacrifice. Whenever he picked up a Turkish paper in Germany and read that this or that columnist had been shot for political reasons, "most probably by political Islamists," he felt some respect for the victim as a dead man but no particular admiration for him as a murdered writer.

On the corner of Halitpaşa and Kâzım Karabekir avenues, Ka saw a pipe protruding from an icy hole in a windowless wall, imagined it was the barrel of a gun aimed straight at him, and in his mind's eye saw himself dying on the snow-covered pavement. What would they say about him in the Istanbul papers? Most likely the governor's office or the local branch of the secret police would want to downplay the political dimension, and if the Istanbul press didn't pick up on his having been a poet, they might not cover the incident at all. Even if his friends in the poetry world and at the *Republican* did everything in their power to publicize the political angle (and who would write that article? Fahir? Orhan?), it would only serve to diminish his literary significance. Similarly, if someone succeeded in placing a piece that established him as an important poet, his death would be reported on the arts pages, where no one would read about it. Had there really been a German journalist called Hans Hansen, and had Ka really been his friend, the *Frankfurter Rundschau* might have run a story about his murder, but it would be the only Western newspaper to do so. Ka took some consolation in imagining that his poems might be translated into German and published in *Akzent* magazine, but it was still perfectly clear to him that should this article in the *Border City Gazette* prove to be the death of him, the published translations would mean nothing. Finally, what frightened him most was the thought of dying just at the dawn of his hope of living happily ever after in Frankfurt with İpek.

The many writers killed in recent years by Islamist bullets paraded before his eyes: first the old preacher-turned-atheist who had tried to point out "inconsistencies" in the Koran (they'd shot him from behind, in the head); behind him came the righteous columnist whose love of positivism had led him to refer in a number of columns to girls wearing head scarves as "cockroaches" (they strafed him and his chauffeur one morning as he drove to work); then there was the investigative journalist who had tenaciously sought to uncover the links between the Turkish Islamist movement and Iran (when he turned on the ignition, he and his car went sailing into the sky). Even as he recalled these victims with tender sorrow, he knew they'd been naïve. As a rule the Istanbul press, like the Western press, had little interest in these fervent columnists and even less in journalists apt to get shot in the head for similar reasons on a backstreet of some remote Anatolian city. But Ka reserved his bile for a society that so easily forgot its writers and poets: For this reason he thought the smartest thing to do was retreat into a corner and try to find some happiness.

Arriving at the offices of the *Border City Gazette* on Faikbey Avenue, Ka looked up to see the next day's edition taped to the back of the recently deiced window. He read the article about himself again, and then he went inside. The elder of Serdar Bey's two busy sons was securing a pile of freshly printed papers with nylon twine. Ka took off his hat so they could see who he was and brushed off the snow sticking to the shoulders of his coat.

"My father's not here." This was the younger son, coming in from the other room with the cloth he'd been using to polish the press. "Would you like some tea?"

"Who wrote the article about me in tomorrow's edition?"

"Is there an article about you in there?" said the younger son, raising his eyebrows.

"Yes, there is," said the older son, giving him a warm and happy smile. He had the same thick lips as his brother. "My father wrote the whole edition today."

"If you distribute this paper tomorrow morning . . ." said Ka. He paused to think. "It will be bad for me."

"Why?" asked the older son. He had a soft kind face and pure, innocent eyes.

Ka saw that if he talked to them in a nice friendly voice and kept his questions short, the way you do with children, he could find out quite a bit from them. The brothers soon informed him that only three people had purchased the paper so far: Muhtar Bey, a child who'd been sent from the branch headquarters of the Motherland Party, and the retired literature teacher Nuriye Hanım, who made a habit of stopping by every evening. Normally they would have dispatched copies to Istanbul and Ankara, but because the roads were closed these papers would have to wait with today's edition until the snow began to melt. The sons would be distributing the rest of the papers tomorrow morning, and if their father wished it, of course they could print a new edition for tomorrow; their father, they told Ka, had only just left the offices, telling them not to expect him back in time for dinner. Ka told them he wouldn't stay for tea; he bought a copy of the paper and went out into the murderous Kars night.

The boys' untroubled innocence had calmed him somewhat. As Ka walked among the slowly falling snowflakes, he began to feel guilty—had he been wrong to take such fright? But in another corner of his mind he knew he would share the fate of the other luckless writers who had died of multiple gunshot wounds after facing similar dilemmas and choosing, either out of pride or courage, to do nothing, or the many others who, assuming that any package from a stranger had to be an ardent fan's gift of *lokum*, had died eagerly tearing open what would turn out to be a mail bomb.

There was, for example, the poet Nurettin, who admired all things European but took little interest in politics until the day a radical Islamist newspaper unearthed something he'd written years earlier—an essay on art and religion—and distorted it to charge that he'd "insulted our faith"; afraid of looking frightened, Nurettin dusted off his old ideas and passionately reasserted them; the army-backed secular press warmed to his fine Kemalist words and inflated their importance to make him seem the lifelong hero. Then one morning a device in a plastic bag hanging from the front tire of his car blew him into so many bits that his ostentatious throng of mourners had to march behind an empty coffin.

There was the small-town version too, the materialist doctors and the old leftist journalists of the regional papers who, when faced with similar indictments, responded with fiery antireligious rhetoric, just so no one could say they were cowards. Some perhaps even entertained vain hopes of attracting world attention "like Salman Rushdie," but the only ones listening were the angry young fanatics in their own neighborhoods, and they had no time for the fancy bomb plots of their colleagues in the cities, or even for guns. As Ka knew only too well from the small lifeless news items he'd seen poring over the back pages of Turkish newspapers in the Frankfurt city library, they preferred to knife the godless in dark alleyways or strangle them with their bare hands.

Ka was still trying to figure out how to save both his skin and his pride if the *Border City Gazette* gave him a chance to reply—I'm an atheist but I've never insulted the Prophet? I'm not a believer but I'd never dream of disrespecting the faith?—when suddenly he heard someone tramping through the snow behind him; a chill went down his spine as he turned around to see it was the bus company manager he'd met yesterday at the same hour at His Excellency Sheikh Saadettin's lodge. It occurred to him that this man could testify that he wasn't an atheist; immediately the thought embarrassed him.

He continued dragging his feet down Atatürk Avenue, slowing down to negotiate the icy street corners and pausing from time to time to admire the huge snowflakes, the endless repetition of an ordinary miracle. Afterward, he would often think back to the beautiful scenes he had witnessed while wandering the city's snow-covered streets (as three children pulled a sled up a narrow street, the windows of the Palace of Light Photo Studio reflected the green light of the one traffic signal in Kars), and he'd wonder why he carried these sad postcard memories with him wherever he went.

He saw an army patrol truck and two soldiers guarding the door to the old tailor shop that Sunay Zaim was using as his base of operations. Ka told the soldiers huddled on the threshold trying to duck the snow that he wanted to contact Sunay, but they treated him like a lowly peasant who'd come in from an outlying village to petition the chief of staff. Ka had been hoping that Sunay might be able to keep the paper from being circulated.

If we are to make sense of the fury that was soon to overtake him, it's important to understand the sting of this rebuff. His first thought was to run off into the snow and seek refuge in the hotel, but before even reaching the corner, he turned left into the Unity Café. Here he took a table between the wall and the stove and wrote the poem he would later call "To Be Shot and Killed."

As he would explain, in his notes, this poem was an expression of pure fear, so he placed it between the axes of memory and imagination on the six-pronged snowflake and humbly turned his back on the content of its prophecy.

As soon as the poem was finished, Ka left the Unity Café; it was twenty past seven when he reached the Snow Palace Hotel. Stretched out upstairs on his bed, he watched the snowflakes floating through the halos of the streetlamp and the pink letter *K* pulsating in the window across the way and tried to quell his growing panic by conjuring up happy visions of life with İpek in Frankfurt. Ten minutes later, he was overcome by a desire to see her. He went downstairs to find the entire family seated around the dinner table with that evening's guest, and his heart leaped to see İpek's hair shimmering behind the bowl of soup that Zahide had just set before her. When İpek beckoned him to take the place next to her, Ka was proud that everyone at the table knew they were in love, very proud; then, across the table, he saw Serdar Bey, the owner of the *Border City Gazette*.

As Serdar Bey extended his hand, his smile was so friendly that Ka began to doubt what his own eyes had read in the newspaper folded in his pocket. After serving himself soup, he reached under the table and put his hand on İpek's lap; he brought his head closer to hers, smelling her smell and savoring her presence, and then whispered that he was sorry to have no news of Blue for her. He had hardly finished when he came eye to eye with Kadife, sitting next to Serdar Bey; it amazed and infuriated him to realize that İpek had already communicated his news to her.

Although his mind was full of Serdar Bey, he managed to contain his feelings and give his attention to Turgut Bey, who was complaining about the meeting at the Hotel Asia. It had succeeded only in stirring things up, he said; he then added that the police knew all about it. "But I'm not at all sorry to have taken part in this historic occasion," he added. "I'm glad I got to see with my own eyes how low the level of political understanding has sunk. Young and old alike, they're hopeless. I went to this meeting to protest the coup, but now I think the army is right to want to keep them out of politics—they're the dregs of society, the most wretched, muddled, brainless people in the city. I'm glad the army couldn't stand by and let us abandon our future to these shameless looters. I'll say this again, Kadife: Before meddling with national politics, consider this carefully. And think also of that painted aging singer you saw turning the wheel of Fortune," he added mysteriously. "Everyone in Ankara has known for thirty-five

years that she was the mistress of Fatin Rustu Zorlu, the old foreign secretary, the one they executed."

When Ka took out his copy of the *Border City Gazette,* they'd been sitting at the table for twenty minutes, and even with the television blaring
in the background, the room seemed quiet.

"I was going to mention it myself," said Serdar Bey. "But I couldn't
make up my mind; I thought you might take it the wrong way."

"Serdar, Serdar, who gave you the order this time?" said Turgut Bey,
when he saw the headline. "Ka, you're not being fair to our guest. Give it
to him so he can read it and see what a bad thing he has done."

"First, let me make clear that I don't believe a single word I wrote,"
said Serdar Bey, as he took the newspaper from Ka. "If you really
believed I believe it, you'd break my heart. Please realize that it's nothing
personal, and please, Turgut Bey, help me explain why it is that a journalist in Kars might be forced to write such things under orders."

"Serdar's always under orders to sling mud at someone," Turgut Bey
explained. "So let's hear this article."

"I don't believe a single word," Serdar Bey repeated proudly. "Our
readers won't believe it either. That's why you have nothing to fear."

Serdar Bey read out his article in a sarcastic voice, pausing here and
there for dramatic effect. "As you see, there's nothing to fear!" he said,
with a smile.

"Are you an atheist?" Turgut Bey asked Ka.

"That's not the point, Father," said İpek with annoyance. "If this
paper gets distributed, they'll shoot him in the street tomorrow."

"Nonsense," said Serdar Bey. "Madam, I assure you, you have nothing to fear. The soldiers have rounded up all the radical Islamists and
reactionaries in town." He turned to Ka. "I can tell just by your eyes that
you haven't taken offense. You know how much I respect your work and
how I esteem you as a human being. Please don't do me the injustice of
holding me to European standards that were never designed for us! Let
me tell you what happens to fools who wander around Kars pretending
to be Europeans—and Turgut Bey knows this as well as I do—three
days, that's all it takes, three days and they're dead: gone, shot, forgotten.

"The Eastern Anatolian press is in desperate trouble. Our average
Kars citizen doesn't bother to read the paper. Almost all our subscribers
are government offices. So of course we're going to run the sort of news
our subscribers want to read. All over the world—even in America—
newspapers tailor the news to their readers' desires. If your readers want

nothing but lies from you, who in the world is going to sell papers that tell the truth? If the truth could raise my paper's circulation, why wouldn't I write the truth? Anyway, the police don't let me print the truth either. In Istanbul and Ankara we have a hundred and fifty readers with Kars connections. And to please them we're always bragging about how rich and successful they've become there; we exaggerate everything, because if we don't they won't renew their subscriptions. And you know what? They even come to believe the lies we print about them. But that's another matter." He let out a laugh.

"And who ordered you to print this article? Go on, tell him," said Turgut Bey.

"My dear sir! As you know only too well, the first principle of Western journalism is to protect your sources."

"My girls have grown very fond of our guest here," said Turgut Bey. "If you distribute this paper tomorrow, they'll never forgive you. If some crazed fundamentalist shoots him, won't you feel responsible?"

"Are you that afraid?" Serdar smiled as he turned to Ka. "If you're that afraid, stay off the streets tomorrow."

"It would be better that the paper rather than Ka remain unseen," Turgut Bey said. "Don't circulate this edition."

"That would offend my subscribers."

"All right, then," said Turgut Bey. He had an inspiration. "Whoever's ordered a copy, let him have it. As for the others, I suggest you remove the offending article and print a new edition."

İpek and Kadife agreed this was the best solution. "I'm thrilled to see my paper taken so seriously," said Serdar Bey. "But who's going to pay for this new print run? That's the next thing you need to tell me."

"My father will take you and your sons out for an evening meal at the Green Pastures Café," said İpek.

"I accept if you come too," said Serdar Bey. "But let's wait until the roads open and we can be rid of this bunch of actors! Kadife must come too. Kadife Hanım, I am wondering if you could help me with the new article to replace the one we're taking out. If you could give me a quote about this coup, this coup de théâtre, I'm sure our readers would be very pleased."

"No, she can't. That's out of the question," said Turgut Bey. "Don't you know my daughter at all?"

"Kadife Hanım, could you tell me if you think the Kars suicide rate is likely to go down in the wake of our theater coup? I'm sure our readers would like your views on this, especially since they know you were opposed to these Muslim girl suicides."

"I'm not against these suicides anymore."

"But doesn't that make you an atheist?" Serdar Bey asked. Though he may have hoped this would set them off on a fresh discussion, he was sober enough to see that everyone at the table was glaring at him, so he relented.

"All right, then, I promise. I won't circulate this edition."

"Are you going to print a new edition?"

"As soon as I leave this table, before I go home."

"We'd like to thank you, then," said İpek.

A long strange silence followed. Ka found it very soothing. For the first time in years, he felt part of a family; in spite of the trials and responsibilities of what was called family, he saw now that it was grounded in the joys of an unyielding togetherness, a feeling he was sorry to have known so little of in his life. Could he find lasting happiness with İpek? It wasn't happiness he was after—this was very clear to him following his third glass of raki; he would even go so far as to say that he preferred to be unhappy. The important thing was to share the hopelessness, to create a little nest in which two people could live together, keeping the rest of the world at bay. He now thought that he and İpek could create such a space, just by making love for months and months on end. To sit at a table with these two girls, knowing that he'd made love to one of them only that afternoon, to feel the softness of their complexions, to know that when he went to bed tonight, he would not be lonely—as sexual bliss beckoned, he allowed himself to believe the paper would not be circulated, and his spirits soared.

His outsize happiness took the edge off the stories and rumors he then heard; they lacked the thud of bad news. It was more like listening to the chilling lines of an ancient epic. One of the children working in the kitchen had told Zahide that a large number of detainees had been taken to the football stadium. With the goalposts now only half visible, half buried in snow, most had been kept outside all day in the hope that they would fall ill or perhaps even die; it was said a few of them had been taken into the locker rooms and pumped full of bullets as an example to the others.

There were also eyewitness reports, perhaps exaggerated, about the terror Z Demirkol and friends had been visiting on the city throughout the day: they'd raided the Mesopotamia Association, founded by a number of Kurdish nationalist youths to promote "folklore and literature," but none of them happened to be there at the time, so instead they'd taken the old man who made the tea in the office—someone who was utterly indifferent to politics—and beaten him severely.

Then there were the three men—two of them were barbers and the third was unemployed—who'd been implicated in an incident six months earlier in which parties unknown had poured colored sewer water over the statue of Atatürk that stood outside the Atatürk Work Plant; although they'd opened an investigation on these men, they'd never put them behind bars; but after beatings that had gone on all night, they'd taken responsibility for a number of other anti-Atatürk incidents in the city (taking a hammer to the nose of the Atatürk statue that stood in the garden of the Trade and Industry Lycée, writing ugly remarks on the Atatürk poster hanging on the wall at the Gang of Fifteen Café, and entering into a conspiracy to use a hatchet to destroy the Atatürk statue standing outside the government offices).

Just after the coup, they'd shot and killed one of two Kurdish boys they caught writing slogans on the walls of Halitpaşa Avenue; after arresting another boy, they'd beaten him until he fainted. There was also the young unemployed boy they'd taken to the religious high school so he could remove the graffiti from its walls—when he'd tried to escape, they'd shot him in the legs. Thanks to various informers, all those who'd been saying ugly things about the soldiers and the actors and spreading groundless rumors about them in the city's teahouses had been rounded up, but—as was always the case in murderous times like these—there were still plenty of rumors and exaggerations making the rounds, from the Kurdish youths who'd died when bombs exploded in their hands to the head-scarf girls who'd killed themselves to protest the coup, to the truck laden with dynamite that they'd stopped as it approached İnönü police station.

Although Ka pricked up his ears when they mentioned the truck carrying explosives—he'd heard someone else discussing this suicide bomb attack earlier—he did nothing else that night but enjoy every moment that he sat sitting peacefully at İpek's side.

Much later, when Serdar Bey rose to leave and Turgut Bey and his daughters stood up to go bid him farewell before going to their rooms, it crossed Ka's mind to ask İpek to his room. But he was afraid of the shadow that might fall over his happiness if she refused, so he left the room without even hinting at what he wanted.

CHAPTER THIRTY-FOUR

Kadife Will Never Agree to It Either

THE MEDIATOR

K a stood at his window smoking a cigarette. It had stopped snow-ing, and finally, as the pale streetlamps cast their ghostly glow over the empty snow-covered courtyard, the stillness of the scene brought him peace. But the peace he felt had more to do with love than the beauty of the snow. He was so happy he could also admit that his peace derived in part from the easy sense of superiority of knowing he was from Istan-bul and Frankfurt.

There was a knock at the door; Ka was astonished to see it was İpek.

"I can't stop thinking about you, I can't sleep," she said, as she stepped inside.

Ka knew at once that they would make love till morning, even as Turgut Bey slept under the same roof. It was the most sublime surprise to wrap his arms around her without first enduring the agony of waiting. Their long night of lovemaking took Ka to a place beyond the outer reaches of happiness, or at least of what he had thought happiness to be; he was outside time, impervious to passion; his only regret was that it had taken him a lifetime to discover this paradise. He felt more at peace than he ever had before. He forgot the sexual fantasies kept in ready storage at the back of his brain, the pornographic images from magazines. As he and İpek made love, he heard music play inside him, music he'd never heard before, never even imagined, and it was by obeying its harmonies that he found his way forward.

From time to time he fell asleep and dreamed of summer holidays bathed in heavenly light; he was running free, he was immortal; his plane was about to fall out of the sky but he was eating an apple, an apple he would never finish, an apple that would last for all time. Then he would wake to the warm apple aroma of İpek's skin. Guided by snow light and the faint yellow glow of the streetlamps, he would press his eyes against hers and try to see into them; when he saw she was awake and silently watching him, it seemed to him they were like two whales basking side by side in shallow water; it was only then he realized that they were holding hands.

At one such moment, when they had woken up to find themselves gazing into each other's eyes, İpek said, "I'm going to speak to my father. I'm going with you to Germany."

Ka couldn't go back to sleep for a long while after that. Instead, he watched his life play before him like a happy film.

Somewhere in the city, there was an explosion. It was strong enough to shake the bed, the room, and the hotel. They heard distant machine-gun fire. It was muffled by the snow that still covered Kars. They embraced each other and waited in silence.

The next time they woke up, the gun battle had ended. Twice Ka rose from the warm bed and smoked a cigarette as the icy air coming in through the window cooled his perspiring body. No poems came to his mind. He felt happier than he'd ever felt before.

When he was awakened in the morning by a knock at the door, İpek was no longer lying beside him in bed. He had no idea what time it was, or what he and İpek had talked about, or what time the gunshots had ended.

It was Cavit, the receptionist. He'd come up to tell Ka that an officer had appeared at the front desk with an invitation from Sunay Zaim: Ka was to report to headquarters at once; the officer was downstairs waiting to escort him. No matter; Ka took his time shaving.

The empty streets of Kars looked more beautiful, more enchanted, than the previous morning. Somewhere high up on Atatürk Avenue, he saw a house with broken windows, a shattered door, and a front wall riddled with bullet holes.

At the tailor shop, Sunay told him there'd been an attempted suicide-bomb attack. "The poor man got his houses mixed up, and instead of coming here he attacked a building farther up the hill," he explained. "He blew himself up into so many pieces we don't even know yet whether he died for Islam or the PKK."

Ka was struck by the childish gravity of a famous actor taking himself so seriously. Freshly shaved, he looked clean, pure-hearted, bursting with energy.

"We've captured Blue," Sunay said. He looked straight into Ka's eyes. Ka made a valiant effort to conceal his joy at this news.

Sunay wasn't fooled. "He's an evil man," he said. "He's definitely the mastermind behind the assassination of the director of the Institute of Education. He goes around telling everyone that he's against suicide while he's busy turning poor brainless teenagers into suicide bombers. National Security is not in any doubt that he's come here with enough explosives to send the entire city of Kars up in smoke! On the night of the revolution, he managed to lose the men we'd put on his tail. No one had any idea where he was hiding. Of course you know all about that ridiculous meeting yesterday evening at the Hotel Asia."

It was as if they were onstage, playing a scene together; Ka gave Sunay an affected theatrical nod.

"My aim in life is not to punish these heinous creatures, these reactionaries and terrorists in our midst," Sunay said. "There's actually a play I've been longing to do, and that's the real reason I'm here. There's an English writer who goes by the name of Thomas Kyd. They say Shakespeare stole *Hamlet* from him. I've discovered another injustice too, a forgotten play by Kyd known as *The Spanish Tragedy*. It's a blood feud, a tragedy that ends in suicide, and like *Hamlet* there's a play inside the play. Funda and I have been waiting for an opportunity to perform it for fifteen years."

When Funda Eser came into the room, brandishing a long elegant cigarette holder, Ka greeted her with an exaggerated bow which obviously pleased her. With no encouragement from Ka, the couple now launched into talk of *The Spanish Tragedy*.

"We want people to enjoy our play, to be uplifted by it, and toward this end I've simplified the plot," said Sunay. "We plan to perform it tonight at the National Theater in front of a live audience, and of course it will go out on television at the same time so the whole city can see it."

"I'd love to see it too," said Ka.

"We want Kadife to be in it. Funda will play her evil-hearted rival. Kadife will appear onstage wearing a head scarf. Then, in defiance of the ludicrous customs that have given rise to the blood feud, she'll bare her head for all to see." With a broad theatrical flourish, Sunay took hold of the imaginary scarf around his head and made as if to rip it off.

"This is bound to cause more trouble!" said Ka.

"Don't worry, there won't be any trouble at all. Remember, the army's in charge now."

"Anyway, Kadife will never agree to it," Ka said.

"Kadife is in love with Blue," said Sunay. "If Kadife bares her head, I can have Blue released at once. They can run off together to some foreign land and live happily ever after."

Funda Eser's face radiated the compassion of a good-hearted auntie from a nice Turkish melodrama who smiles as she watches the two lovers departing to find happiness in the great beyond. For a moment, Ka imagined his own love affair with İpek bringing the same smile to her lips.

"I'm still very doubtful that Kadife will agree to bare her head on live TV," said Ka.

"You seem to us to be the only one who might be able to talk her into it," said Sunay. "To bargain with us is to bargain with the biggest devil in creation. She knows you are concerned about the head-scarf girls. And you're in love with her sister."

"It's not just Kadife, you'd also have to persuade Blue. But Kadife must be approached first," said Ka, still smarting from the brutal directness of his last remark.

"You can do it any which way you like," said Sunay. "I'll give you whatever authorization proves necessary and your very own army truck. You have permission to negotiate in my name."

There was a silence. Sunay had picked up on Ka's reluctance.

"I don't want to get involved," said Ka.

"Why not?"

"Well, it could be because I'm scared. I'm very happy right now. I don't want to turn myself into a target for the Islamists. When they see her bare her head, those students will think I'm the atheist who arranged the performance. And even if I can manage to escape to Germany, they'll track me down. I'll be walking down a street late one night, and someone will shoot me."

"They'll shoot me first," said Sunay proudly. "But I admire your courage in admitting you're afraid. I'm the coward to end all cowards, believe me. The only ones who survive in this country are the cowards. But there's not a coward in the world who doesn't dream of the day when he might find himself capable of great courage. Don't you agree?"

"As I said, I'm very happy right now. I have no desire to play the hero. Heroic dreams are the consolation of the unhappy. After all, when people like us say we're being heroic, it usually means we're about to kill each other—or kill ourselves."

"Yes," Sunay insisted, "but isn't there a small voice somewhere inside reminding you that this happiness of yours is not destined to last very long?"

"Why do you want to scare our guest?" said Funda Eser.

"No happiness lasts very long," said Ka cautiously. "But I have no desire to do something heroic that will get me killed just because I know how likely it is that I'll be unhappy again at some point in the future."

"If you don't get involved, as you put it, they're not going to wait until you're back in Germany to kill you; they'll kill you right here. Have you seen today's paper?"

"Does it say I'm going to die today?" Ka asked with a smile.

Sunay took out the *Border City Gazette,* turned to the front page, and pointed to the article Ka had read the previous evening.

" 'A godless man in Kars!' " read Funda Eser in a booming voice.

"That's from yesterday's first print run," said Ka evenly. "Later on in the evening, Serdar Bey decided to correct the inaccuracies in this article and print a new edition."

"In the end he was unable to do so. This is the edition that went out this morning. Never take a journalist's promise at face value. But we'll protect you. Those fundamentalists can't do anything against the military, so naturally they'll want to vent their spleen by taking a potshot at a Western spy."

"Are you the one who told Serdar to write this piece?" asked Ka.

Raising his eyebrows and pursing his lips, Sunay glared at him and played the affronted man of honor, but Ka still recognized him as a politician pulling a fast one.

"If you agree to protect me all the way, I'll be your mediator," said Ka.

Sunay gave his word and, still in Jacobin mode, threw his arms around Ka, congratulated him, and gave his assurance that his two men would never leave Ka's side.

"If necessary, they'll even protect you from yourself!" he boomed.

They sat down to work out the details of Ka's mission, with two fragrant cups of breakfast tea to help them along. Funda Eser was all smiles, as if a brilliant famous actress had just joined the company. She spoke for a time about the power of *The Spanish Tragedy,* but Ka's mind was elsewhere: He was looking at the wondrous white light pouring through the high windows of the tailor shop.

His dream ended abruptly when, upon leaving the shop, he met the two burly armed guards who'd be protecting him. He'd hoped at least one of them would be an officer or a plainclothes detective with some modicum of sartorial sense. Once upon a time, there was a famous writer who went on television saying that Turks were fools and he didn't believe in Islam; Ka had once seen him with the two bodyguards the state gave him toward the end of his life: They had excellent manners and wore stylish clothes. They insisted on the sort of exaggerated servility Ka thought befitting famous writers of the Opposition; not only did they carry the man's bag, they even held the door open for him and locked arms with him on staircases, to protect him from any fan or enemy who might pass.

The soldiers sitting next to Ka in the army truck could not have been more different. They acted like jailors, not protectors.

When Ka walked into the hotel, he felt as happy as he had in the early hours of the morning. Although he longed to see İpek, he dreaded having to tell her about his mission; he feared she might take it as a betrayal. However small it might be in the scheme of things, he still worried it could diminish their love. It would be better all around, he thought, if he could find a way to see Kadife alone first. But he ran into İpek in the lobby.

"You're even more beautiful than I remembered!" he told İpek, looking at her in awe. "Sunay Zaim summoned me for a meeting. He wants me to be his mediator."

"What for?"

"They've caught Blue. It happened yesterday, in the evening," said Ka. "Why is your face changing? We're not in any danger. Yes, Kadife will be upset. But in my view, it's a relief, believe me." Very quickly, he told her what Sunay had told him: the noises they'd heard during the night, the gun battle, everything. "You left this morning without waking me. Don't worry, I'll take care of things; no one will come out of this with so much as a bloody nose. We're going to Frankfurt; we're going to be happy. Have you spoken to your father?" He told her he was charged to negotiate a deal, and that was why Sunay would send him to speak to Blue, but first he had to speak to Kadife. He registered the extreme concern in İpek's eyes as a sign that she was worried for him, and this made him glad.

"I'll send Kadife upstairs in a few minutes," she said, and walked away.

When he reached his room, he saw that someone had made the bed. The room in which he had spent the happiest night of his life had changed; the glare from the snow outside had given a new aspect to the bed, the table, and the pale curtains—even the silence in the room seemed different. But there was still the lingering smell of their lovemaking for him to breathe in. He lay down on the bed and, gazing up at the ceiling, thought of all the trouble ahead if he couldn't manage to win Kadife's and Blue's cooperation.

Kadife burst into the room. "Tell me everything you know about Blue's capture," she said. "Did they treat him roughly?"

"If they'd roughed him up, they wouldn't be letting me see him," said Ka. "They're going to take me over in a few minutes. They captured him after the hotel meeting, that's all I know."

Kadife gazed out the window at the snow-covered avenue below. "So now you're the one who's happy, and I'm the one who's sad. How things have changed since our meeting in the storage room."

Ka thought back to their meeting yesterday in Room 217, where Kadife had held a gun on him and made him strip before they left to see Blue; the sweet, distant memory bound them together.

"That's not the whole story, Kadife," Ka said. "Sunay's associates are convinced that Blue had a hand in the assassination of the director of the Institute of Education. What's more, it seems that the dossier connecting him to that Izmir television host has also reached Kars."

"Who are these associates?"

"A handful of people from the Kars MİT, plus one or two soldiers who have links to him. But don't think Sunay is completely in their pocket. He has artistic ambitions too. Here's what he has asked me to propose to you. This evening he means to perform a play at the National Theater, and he wants you to be in it. Don't make a face—listen. There's going to be a live broadcast too, with all of Kars watching again. If you're willing to play this part, and if Blue can convince the religious high school boys to come watch the play and sit quietly, to be polite and clap at the right moments, Sunay will have Blue released. Then this whole thing can be forgotten, and we'll all come out of it without so much as a bloody nose. They've asked me to be the go-between."

"What's the play?"

Ka told her everything he knew about Thomas Kyd and *The Spanish Tragedy*, explaining as well that Sunay had changed the play to make it more relevant. "In the same way that during their long years of touring Anatolia they've made Corneille, Shakespeare, and Brecht more relevant by adding belly dances and bawdy songs."

"I suppose I'm the one who gets the blood feud started by being raped on live television."

"No. You're a proper Spanish lady with a covered head, but then you tire of the blood feud and in a burst of anger you pull off your scarf to become the rebel heroine."

"To play the rebel heroine in Turkey you don't pull off your scarf, you put it on."

"This is just a play, Kadife. And because it's just a play, it shouldn't be a problem to take off your scarf."

"I see now what they want from me. But even if it's a play, even it's a play within a play, I'm still not baring my head."

"Look, Kadife, the snow's going to melt in two days, the roads will open, and the people sitting in jail will pass into the hands of men who know no pity. If that happens, you won't see Blue again in this life. Have you really thought this through?"

"I'm afraid that if I do think about it, I'll agree to it."

"You could wear a wig underneath your scarf. Then no one would see your real hair."

"If I'd wanted to wear a wig, I would have done it a long time ago, like a lot of other women I know, and I'd be back at the university."

"This is not a question of sitting outside the university and trying to save your honor. You'll be doing this to save Blue."

"Well, let's see if Blue will want me to save him by pulling off my scarf."

"Of course he will," said Ka. "You won't hurt his honor by baring your head. After all, no one even knows you two are involved."

Ka could tell at once from the fury in her eyes that he had found her weak spot, but then she gave him a strange smile that filled him with fear. Mixed in with this fear was jealousy. He was afraid that Kadife was about to tell him something damning about İpek.

"We don't have much time, Kadife," he said. He could hear that strange note of dread in his voice. "I know you're bright enough and sensitive enough to get through all this with grace. I'm saying this to you as someone who's spent years as a political exile. Listen to me: Life's not about principles, it's about happiness."

"But if you don't have any principles, and if you don't have faith, you can't be happy at all," said Kadife.

"That's true. But in a brutal country like ours where human life is cheap, it's stupid to destroy yourself for the sake of your beliefs. Beliefs, high ideals—only people living in rich countries can enjoy such luxuries."

"Actually, it's the other way round. In a poor country, the only consolation people can have is the one that comes from their beliefs."

Ka wanted to say, But the things they believe aren't true! but he managed to hold his tongue. Instead he said, "But you're not one of the poor, Kadife. You're from Istanbul."

"That's why I do what I believe in. I don't fake things. If I decide to bare my head, I won't go halfway, I'll really do it."

"All right, then, what would you say to this? Let's say they give up on the idea of a live audience. What if they just televise it, and that's the only performance that the people of Kars ever see. So when they get to the part where you have your moment of fury, all they show is your hand pulling off the scarf. Then they can cut to another woman who looks like you, and we'll simply show her hair swinging free, but from the back."

"That's even more dishonest than wearing a wig," said Kadife. "And in the end, when the coup is over, everyone will think I really did bare my head."

"What's more important, honoring the law of God or worrying what people might say about you? The important thing is, if we do it like this, you won't really have bared your head. But if you are so worried what people will think, it's still not a problem, because once all this nonsense is over, we can make sure everyone knows about the last-minute switch. When it gets around that you were prepared to do all this to save Blue, those boys at the religious high school will be even more in awe of you than they are now."

"Has it ever occurred to you," said Kadife, her tone suddenly very different, "that when you're trying with all your might to talk someone into something, you say things you don't believe at all?"

"That can happen. But it's not that way now."

"But if it were, and you managed to convince this person in the end, wouldn't you feel some remorse for having fooled her? I mean, for having left her out on a limb?"

"This is not about leaving you out on a limb, Kadife. It's about using your head and seeing that this is the only option. Sunay's people are ruthless. If they decide to hang Blue, they won't hesitate—you're not prepared to let them do that, are you?"

"Let's just say I bared my head in front of everyone. That would be admitting defeat. And what proof is there that they'd release Blue? Why should I believe any promise that comes from the Turkish state?"

"You're right. I'm going to have to discuss this with them."

"With whom are you going to speak and when?"

"First I'll meet with Blue and then I'm going back to speak to Sunay."

They were both silent. By now it was clear that Kadife was more or less prepared to go along with the plan. But Ka still needed to be sure, so he made a show of looking at his watch.

"Who has Blue, MİT or the army?"

"I don't know. It probably doesn't make much difference."

"If it's the army, he may not have been tortured," said Kadife. She paused. "I want you to give these to him." She gave Ka an old-fashioned jeweled lighter coated with mother-of-pearl and a pack of red Marlboros. "The lighter belongs to my father. Blue will enjoy lighting his cigarettes with it."

Ka took the cigarettes but not the lighter. "If I give him the lighter, Blue will know I came here to talk to you first."

"Why shouldn't he?"

"Because then he'll know what we've been talking about and he'll want to know what your decision was. I wasn't planning to tell him I'd seen you first, or that you were ready to bare your head, so to speak, in order to save him."

"Is that because you know he'd never agree to it?"

"No. He's an intelligent, rational man, and he'd certainly agree to your doing something like baring your head if it would save him from the gallows; you know this as well as I do. The thing he would never accept is my having asked you first instead of going straight to him."

"But this is not just a matter of politics; it's also personal, something between him and me. Blue would understand this."

"That may be, Kadife, but you know as well as I do that he wants the first word. He's a Turkish man, and a political Islamist. I can't go to him and say, 'Listen, Kadife's decided to bare her head to set you free.' He must believe it's his decision. I'm going to ask him what he thinks of the various options—whether you should wear a wig or if it's better to do that montage with another woman's hair. He must convince himself that this will save your honor and solve the problem. Believe me, he'll never venture into such murky areas where your uncompromising ideas of honor can't be reconciled with his more practical understanding. If you are to bare your head, he certainly won't prefer to see you do it openly without playing some tricks."

"You're jealous of Blue; you hate him," said Kadife. "You don't even want to see him as a human being. You're like all republican secularists, you see someone who isn't westernized and you dismiss him as a primitive underclass reprobate. You tell yourself a good beating is bound to make a man of him. Do you enjoy seeing me bow to the army to save Blue's skin? It's immoral to take pleasure from something like this, but you're not even trying to hide it." Her eyes glittered with hatred. "Anyway, if it has to be Blue's decision, and if you are an enlightened Turkish man, why didn't you go straight to him after you left Sunay? I'll tell you why: You wanted to watch me deciding to bow my own head. This was to make you feel superior to Blue—a man who terrifies you."

"You're right about one thing, he does terrify me. But everything else you said is unfair, Kadife. Say I'd gone to Blue first and then come to you with his decision that you have to bare your head. You would have taken it as an order, and you'd have refused."

"You're not a mediator, you're cooperating with the tyrants."

"My only ambition is to get out of this city in one piece. You shouldn't take this coup any more seriously than I do. You've already done more than enough to prove to the people of Kars what a brave, clever, righteous woman you are. After we get out of this, your sister and I are going to Frankfurt. We hope to find happiness there. I would advise you to do the same—to do whatever you must to find happiness. If you and Blue can manage to get out of here, you could live happily ever after as political exiles in any number of European cities, and I've no doubt your father would want to join you. But before any of this can happen, you've got to put your trust in me."

All this talk of happiness had sent a large tear rolling down Kadife's cheek. Smiling in an odd way that Ka found alarming, she quickly wiped it away with the palm of her hand. "Are you sure my sister is ready to leave Kars?"

"I'm positive," said Ka, though his voice didn't sound sure.

"I'm not going to insist that you give Blue the lighter or tell him that you came to see me first," said Kadife. She was speaking now like a haughty but forbearing princess. "But before I bare my head in front of anyone I must be absolutely sure they'll set him free. I need more than the guarantee of Sunay or one of his henchmen. We all know what the word of the Turkish state is worth."

"You're a very intelligent woman, Kadife. No one in Kars deserves happiness as much as you do," Ka said. He was tempted to add, Except for Necip! But no sooner had he thought this than he forgot it. "If you give me the lighter right now, I can take that to Blue, too. But please, try to trust me."

Kadife bent forward to pass him the lighter, and they embraced with a warmth that neither expected. For a fleeting moment, Ka enjoyed the thrill of touching Kadife's body, which was much lighter and narrower than her sister's, but he stopped himself from kissing her. A moment later, when there was a loud bang on the door, he could not help but think it was a good decision.

It was İpek, come to tell Ka that an army truck was waiting for him. She stood there and gazed softly, searchingly, into their eyes, as if trying to understand what Ka and Kadife had decided. Ka left the room without kissing her. When he reached the end of the corridor, he turned around in guilty triumph to see the two sisters locked in a silent embrace.

CHAPTER THIRTY-FIVE

I'm Not an Agent for Anyone

KA WITH BLUE IN HIS CELL

The image of Kadife and İpek embracing in the corridor lingered in Ka's mind. Sitting beside the driver in the army truck, at the Atatürk and Halitpaşa Avenue intersection, waiting for the only set of traffic lights in the city to change, he was high enough off the road to see into the unpainted second-floor window of an old Armenian house. Someone had opened it to let in some fresh air, and as a light wind swayed the shutters and ruffled the curtains, Ka looked inside and could tell at once that he was witnessing a secret political meeting—in fact, so penetrating was his awareness of what was going on inside, he was like a doctor looking at an X-ray. And so, though a pale and frightened woman soon dashed forward to draw the curtains, he was able to guess with extraordinary accuracy what had transpired in that bright room: Two of Kars's most seasoned Kurdish militants were talking to an apprentice tea-man whose older brother had been killed in the raid the night before; the apprentice was now hunched in a cloud of sweat by the stove, wrapping the body in Gazo-brand bandages, while the militants assured him how easy it would be to enter the police headquarters on Faikbey Avenue and set off a bomb.

Ka had not, however, guessed his own destination. Instead of taking him to police headquarters or turning into the grand old square dating from the early years of the Republic where MİT had its headquarters, the army truck went straight through the Faikbey Avenue intersection and continued along Atatürk Avenue, before it turned finally into the military compound in the center of the city. In the 1960s there'd been a plan to convert this space into a park, but after the military coup in the early seventies, they built a wall around it, and before long it had become a garrison comprising barracks, new command headquarters, training grounds, and bored children riding bicycles among the stunted poplar trees. According to *Free Nation,* the pro-army newspaper, it was thanks to the new occupants that the house in which Pushkin had stayed during his visit to Kars, as well as the Cossack horsemen's stables built by the czar forty years after the poet's visit, had been saved from demolition.

The cell in which they were holding Blue was right next door to these stables. The army truck dropped Ka outside a pleasant old stone building that stood under an oleander tree; its branches, he noticed, were bowing under the weight of the snow. Inside were two gracious men whom Ka correctly took to be MİT operatives; they picked up a roll of Gazo bandages and a tape recorder, awfully primitive-looking considering it was the 1990s, and after they had used the former to secure the latter to his chest, they showed him how to operate the ON/OFF button. When they spoke about the prisoner downstairs, it was as if they were sorry he'd been caught and wanted to help him. At the same time, they made it clear that they expected Ka to get the prisoner's confession, in particular concerning the murders he had committed or had ordered others to commit: It didn't occur to Ka that they might not know his real reason for being here.

In the days of the czar, when the Russian cavalry used this little stone building as its headquarters, you would go down a cold stone staircase to reach a large windowless room in which soldiers were punished for lacking discipline. After the founding of the Turkish Republic, the cell had served as a depot for a time, and then, during the nuclear panics of the Cold War, it was turned into a model fallout shelter; it was still far cleaner and more comfortable than Ka had expected.

The room was well heated by the Arçelik furnace (donated several years earlier by Muhtar, the area's main distributor, in an effort to ingratiate himself), but Blue, who was in bed reading a book, had still found it necessary to cover himself with a clean army blanket. He rose the moment he saw Ka and stepped into his shoes, from which the laces had been removed; assuming an official air but still managing a smile, he shook Ka's hand and, with the decisiveness of one ready to talk business, he pointed to a Formica table pushed up against the wall. When they had claimed their seats at opposite ends of the table, Ka looked across to see an ashtray filled with cigarette butts, so he took the pack of Marlboros out of his pocket and passed them to Blue, commenting as he did so on the comforts of the surroundings. Blue told him that he'd not been tortured; then he struck a match and lit Ka's cigarette before lighting his own.

"So tell me, sir, for whom are you spying today?"

"I've given up spying," said Ka. "These days I'm a mediator."

"That's even worse. Spies traffic in snippets of information that aren't much use to anyone, and mostly they do it for the money. Mediators, on the other hand—well, they're just smart alecks who think they can stick their noses into your private business on the pretense of being 'impartial.' What's your game here? What are you trying to get out of all this?"

"To get out of this dreadful city in one piece."

"As things stand today, only one person in this city is in any position to protect an atheist flown in from the West to spy on us, and that's Sunay."

So Blue had seen the front page of the *Border City Gazette*. How Ka hated that smile forming underneath Blue's mustache! How could this militant Islamist who'd spent half his life railing against the merciless Turkish state, and who was now sitting in a prison cell implicated in two separate murder inquiries, be so calm and cheerful? Now more than ever, Ka could see why Kadife was so madly in love with him. Blue never looked more handsome than today.

"What are you here to mediate?"

"I've come to try to arrange your release," said Ka, and in a very calm voice he relayed Sunay's proposal. He didn't mention the possibility of Kadife's wearing a wig, nor did he discuss the various tricks they might resort to in the event of the live transmission; he reserved these just in case he needed a bargaining chip later. While he was explaining the gravity of the present circumstances and the pressure certain merciless parties were putting on Sunay to hang Blue at the first opportunity, he felt a certain joy, but as this joy was soon followed by a certain guilt, he went on to denounce Sunay as the crackpot to end all crackpots and to assure Blue that as soon as the snow melted everything would go back to normal. Later on, he would ask himself whether he'd said this to please the MİT operatives upstairs.

"What all this means is that my only chance for freedom is to take part in another crack at Sunay's pot, so to speak," said Blue.

"Yes, that's right."

"Well, tell him this: I reject his proposal. And I thank you for taking the trouble to come all this way."

Ka expected Blue would now rise, shake his hand, and see him to the door. But instead there was a silence.

Tipped back on the hind legs of his chair, Blue was now rocking happily back and forth. "But if your mediation efforts come to nothing, and you don't escape this dreadful city in one piece, it won't be because of me, it will be because of your loose-lipped atheist boastfulness. The only time people in this country brag about atheism is when they know the army is behind them."

"I'm not the sort of person who takes pride in being an atheist."

"I'm glad to hear it."

Both men fell silent, smoking their cigarettes. Ka felt he had no choice but to get up and leave. But instead he asked, "Aren't you afraid of dying?"

"If that's a threat, the answer is no, I'm not afraid of dying. If you're asking me as a concerned friend, the answer is yes, I'm very afraid. But whatever I do now, these tyrants will still want to hang me. There's nothing I can do to change that."

Blue gave Ka a damningly sweet smile. The message Ka took was, Look, I'm in a far worse fix than you are, but I'm still taking it better than you!

Shame forced Ka to admit to himself that his panic stemmed from the sweet, aching hope for happiness that he'd been carrying around since falling in love with İpek. Was Blue immune to that sort of hope? I'll count to nine and then I'll get up and leave, he told himself. One, two. . . . By the time he reached five, he'd decided that if he failed to dupe Blue, he'd never be able to take İpek back with him to Germany.

Suddenly inspired, he began to talk, saying whatever came into his head. He began by describing a luckless mediator he remembered from a black-and-white American film he'd seen as a child; he went on to remind Blue that—once things were straightened out—he was sure he'd be able to get their Hotel Asia statement printed in Germany; then he remarked that those who go through life making bad decisions out of some stubborn intellectual passion sometimes live to regret it. He recounted as example the time in a fit of pique he'd quit a basketball team, never to return; the time he would have spent on the court, he elected to idle away at the Bosphorus, watching the sea for hours on end; and once he'd said this he could not stop himself from telling Blue how very much he loved Istanbul, and how beautiful the little Bosphorus town of Bebek could be on a fine spring evening. All the while he struggled to keep Blue's cold-blooded stare from crushing him into silence. It was like the final visit before an execution.

"Even if we broke all precedents and did everything they asked, they'd never keep their word," said Blue. He pointed to the paper and pens sitting on the table. "They want me to write down my whole life story, every crime I've ever committed. If I do, and they decide I'm sincere, they could pardon me under the remorse law. I've always pitied the fools who fell for such lies, only to spend their last days on trial having betrayed themselves. But since I'm going to die anyway, I want to make sure those who follow get to hear a few things about me that are true." On the table there were several sheets already covered with writing, and now he picked up one of them. With the same grave and rather ludicrous expression he'd assumed for giving a quote for Hans Hansen and the German press, he began to read:

"MY EXECUTION

"On the subject of my execution, I would like to make it clear that I have no regrets about anything I have done for political reasons at any time in the past, not excluding today, Thursday, the twentieth of February. My father is a retired clerk, formerly of the Istanbul Regional Treasury Office, and I am his second child. During my childhood and early youth, my father maintained secret links with a Cerrahi lodge and I grew up inside his humble, silent world. In my youth I rebelled against him by becoming a godless leftist, and when I was at university I tagged along with other young militants and stoned the sailors coming off the American aircraft carriers. Around the same time I got married; then we split up and I managed to survive the crisis.

"For years no one noticed me. I was an electronics engineer. Because of the hatred I felt for the West, I admired the revolution in Iran. I returned to Islam. When the Ayatollah Khomeini said, 'The most important thing today is not to pray or fast but to protect the Islamic faith,' I believed him. I took inspiration from Frantz Fanon's work on violence, from the pilgrimages Seyyid Kutub made in protest against oppression, from the same man's ideas on changing places, and from Ali Sheriyat.

"I escaped to Germany after the military coup. Then I returned to Turkey. I was wounded while fighting in Grozny with the Chechens against the Russians, and as a result of that wound, I have a limp in my right leg. When I was in Bosnia during the Serbian siege, I married a Bosnian girl named Merzuka and took her back to Istanbul with me. Because my political obligations and my ideas on pilgrimage meant that I was hardly ever in any given city longer than two weeks, my second wife and I eventually separated.

"After cutting off relations with the Islamist groups that sent me to Chechnya and Bosnia, I set out to explore all four corners of Turkey. In spite of the fact that I believe it is sometimes necessary to kill the enemies of Islam, I have never killed anyone, nor have I ever ordered anyone's death. The man who assassinated the former mayor of Kars was a deranged Kurdish driver who was angry because the mayor was threatening to take all the horse-drawn carriages off the streets. I came to Kars for the girls who were committing suicide. Suicide is the greatest sin of all. I leave behind my poems as my testament, and I would like them to be published. Merzuka has them. And that's all I have to say."

There followed a silence.

"You don't have to die," said Ka. "That's why I'm here."

"Then let me tell you something else," said Blue. Once he was sure he had Ka's full attention, he lit another cigarette. Did he know about the tape recorder whirring silently on his chest, working as unobtrusively as a dutiful housewife?

"When I was living in Munich, there was this cinema I went to a lot. They had discount double features after midnight," Blue said. "And you know that Italian who did *The Battle of Algiers,* about the French oppression of Algeria—one day they showed his latest film, *Burn!* It's set on an island in the Caribbean where they produce sugarcane, and it's about the tricks the colonialists played and the revolutions they staged. First they find a black leader and get him to rise up against the Portuguese, and then they sail in and take over. After failing the first time, the blacks rise up again, this time against the English, but the English defeat them by setting the entire island on fire. The leader of both rebellions is arrested, and soon it is the morning of his execution. Then who should arrive but the man who first discovered him, the man who talked him into the first rebellion and went on to crush the second one for the English. Before you know it, Marlon Brando has gone into the tent in which they're keeping the black captive; he cuts his ropes and sets him free."

"Why?"

Blue bridled at the question. "Why do you think? So he wouldn't hang, of course! Marlon knew very well that if they hanged this man, they'd turn him into a legend, and then the local people would use his name as a battle cry for years to come. But the black leader, knowing exactly why Marlon has cut his ropes, rejects his chance for freedom and refuses to run away."

"Did they hang him?" asked Ka.

"Yes, but they don't show the hanging in the film," said Blue. "Instead they show what happened to Marlon Brando, the agent who, like you, tried to tempt the condemned man with his freedom. Just as he was about to leave the island, one of the locals stabbed him to death."

"I'm not an agent!" Ka said, unable to hide his annoyance.

"Don't be so sensitive about the word *agent*: after all, I see myself as an agent of Islam."

"I'm not an agent for anyone," Ka insisted, still perturbed.

"Do you mean to tell me that no one even bothered to put some amazing drug into this cigarette to make me dizzy and sap my willpower? Ah, the best thing America ever gave the world were these red Marlboros. I could smoke these Marlboros for the rest of my life."

"If you use your head, you can smoke your Marlboros for another forty years."

"This is just what I meant by the word *agent*," said Blue. "An agent's main job is to talk people into changing their minds."

"All I mean is that it's stupid to let yourself be killed by these crazed, bloodthirsty fascists. Don't count on becoming a revolutionary icon either; it's not going to happen. These meek lambs here—they may have strong religious beliefs but at the end of the day it's the state's decrees they obey. And all those rebel sheikhs who rise up because they fear our religion is slipping away, all those militants trained in Iran, even the ones like Saidi Nursi who enjoyed long-lasting fame—they can't even hold on to their graves. As for all those religious leaders in this country who dream of the day their names turn to emblems of faith, the soldiers load their bodies onto military planes and dump them in the sea. But you know all this. Those Hezbollah cemeteries in Batman to which so many came on pilgrimage—one night was all it took to raze them. Where are they now, those cemeteries?"

"In the people's hearts."

"Empty words. Only twenty percent of the people give their votes to the Islamists. And to a moderate Islamist party at that."

"If it's so moderate, why do they panic and send in the military? Please explain that! So much for your impartial mediating."

"I *am* an impartial mediator," said Ka, raising his voice.

"No, you're not. You're a Western agent. You're the slave of the ruthless Europeans, and like all true slaves you don't even know you *are* one. You're just a typical little European from Nişantaş. Not only were you brought up to look down on your own traditions, you also think you live on a higher plane than ordinary people. According to your kind, the road to a good moral life is not through God or religion, or through taking part in the life of the common people—no, it's just a matter of imitating the West. Perhaps from time to time you say a word or two reproaching the tyrannies visited on the Islamists and the Kurds, but in your heart of hearts you don't mind at all when the military takes charge."

"What if I did this for you: Kadife could wear a wig under her head scarf, and that way, when she bared her head, no one would see her real hair."

"You can't make me drink wine!" said Blue. He'd raised his voice, too. "I refuse to be a European, and I won't ape their ways. I'm going to live out my own history and be no one but myself. I for one believe it's possible to be happy without becoming a mock European, without becoming their slave. There's a word Europhiles very commonly use when they denigrate our people: To be a true Westerner, a person must first become an *individual*, and then they go on to say that in Turkey, there are no individuals! Well, that's how I see my execution. I'm standing up against the Westerners as an individual; it's because I *am* an individual that I refuse to imitate them."

"Sunay believes so deeply in this play that I can even do this for you. The National Theater will be empty. The live TV camera will show Kadife's hand pulling off the scarf first. Then we can do some tricky editing, and the hair we show will really belong to someone else."

"I find it rather suspicious that you are prepared to go through such contortions just to save me."

"I'm very happy right now," said Ka, and just saying this made him feel as guilty as if he'd been telling a lie. "I've never been so happy in my entire life. I want to preserve that happiness."

"What is it that's made you so happy?"

Ka did not give the answer that later occurred to him as wise: Because I'm writing poems again. But neither did he say, Because I believe in God. Instead he blurted out, "Because I'm in love!" He added, "And I'm taking my love back to Frankfurt with me." For a moment, he was glad just to be speaking so openly about his love to a virtual stranger.

"And who is this love of yours?"

"Kadife's sister, İpek."

Ka could see confusion in Blue's face. He regretted his joyous outburst, and was silent.

Blue lit another Marlboro. "When a man is so happy that he is willing to share his happiness with someone about to be executed, it is a gift from God. Let's imagine I agreed to your proposals and fled the city to save your happiness, and Kadife found a way to take part in the play using some trickery that saved her honor and also secured her sister's hope for happiness. What guarantee do I have that these people will keep their word and let me go?"

"I knew you would ask this!" cried Ka. He paused for a moment. He brought his finger to his lips and signaled to Blue to stay quiet and watch. He undid the buttons of his jacket and made a great show of turning off the tape recorder taped to his chest. "I'll be your guarantor, and they can release you first," he said. "Kadife can wait before going onstage until she hears of your release and that you have gone back into hiding. But to get Kadife to agree, you will need to write her a letter saying you've approved the plan—I need to deliver it to her personally." He was making all this up as he went along. "And if you would tell me how this release should happen and where they should leave you," he whispered, "I'll make sure they do as you ask. And then you can stay underground until the roads have opened again. You can trust me on this; you have my guarantee."

Blue handed Ka a piece of paper. "Put it in writing: In securing my consent for Kadife to go onstage and bare her head without staining her honor, and to ensure that I am able to leave Kars in one piece, you, Ka, have undertaken to act as mediator and guarantor. If you don't keep your word, if this turns out to be a trap, what sort of punishment should the guarantor expect?"

"Whatever they do to you, they must also do to me!" Ka said.

"OK, write that down."

Now Ka gave Blue a sheet of paper. "I'd like you to write that you have agreed to my plan, that I have your permission to relay the plan to Kadife, and that the final decision is up to her. If Kadife agrees, she must make a written statement to this effect and sign it with the understanding that she must not bare her head until you have been freed in a suitable way. Write all that down. But when it comes to the time and place of your release, I'd rather not be involved. It would be better if you chose someone you trusted. I'd recommend Fazıl, blood brother of the dead boy, Necip."

"Is that the boy who was sending love letters to Kadife?"

"That was Necip, the one who died. He was a very special person, a gift from God," said Ka. "But Fazıl's just as good-hearted."

"If you say so, I believe you," said Blue, and turning to the sheet before him, he began to write.

Blue was done first. When Ka finished writing out his own guarantee, he detected a contemptuous half smile flashing across Blue's face, but he wasn't bothered. He'd set things in motion, he'd removed all the obstacles, he and İpek were now free to leave the city, and he could hardly contain his joy. They exchanged papers in silence. When Blue folded Ka's statement and put it in his pocket without bothering to read it, Ka followed suit; and then, making sure Blue could see what he was doing, he switched the tape recorder back on.

There was a silence. Ka repeated the last thing he had said before turning off the tape recorder. "I knew you would ask this," he said. "But unless the two sides can establish some sort of trust, no agreement is possible. You'll just have to trust the state to keep its word."

They looked into each other's eyes and smiled. Afterward, he would return to this moment many times, and each time he would feel great remorse; happiness had blinded him to the fury in Blue's eyes; looking back, he often thought that if he'd sensed this fury, he might never have asked the question:

"Will Kadife agree to this plan?"

"She'll agree to it," whispered Blue, his eyes still bright with rage.

There was another short silence.

"Seeing that you aim to make a contract with me that binds me to life, you might as well tell me more about this great happiness of yours."

"I've never loved anyone like this in my entire life," said Ka. His words sounded credulous and clumsy, but still he said them. "For me, there's only one chance for happiness, and that's İpek."

"And how do you define happiness?"

"Happiness is finding another world to live in, a world where you can forget all this poverty and tyranny. Happiness is holding someone in your arms and knowing you hold the whole world." He was going to say more, but Blue jumped to his feet.

At this moment the poem Ka would later call "Chess" came rushing into his head. He took a quick look at Blue and then, having left him standing there, took out the notebook in his pocket and began to write. As he jotted down the lines of the poem, which was about happiness and power, wisdom and greed, Blue peered over his shoulder, curious to know what was going on. Ka could sense Blue's eyes on him, and that image too found its way into his poem. It was as if the hand that was writing belonged to someone else. Ka knew Blue wouldn't be able to see it, but that did not stop his wishing Blue could know that Ka's hand was in thrall to a higher power. It was not to be: Blue sat on the edge of the bed, gloomily smoking in the manner of condemned men the world over.

On an impulse he would spend much time trying (and failing) to understand afterward, Ka found himself opening his heart to Blue yet again.

"Before I got here, I hadn't written a poem in years," he said. "But since coming to Kars, all the roads on which poetry travels have reopened. I attribute this to the love of God I've felt here."

"I don't want to destroy your illusions, but your love for God comes out of Western romantic novels," said Blue. "In a place like this, if you worship God as a European, you're bound to be a laughingstock. Then you cannot even believe you believe. You don't belong to this country; you're not even a Turk anymore. First try to be like everyone else. Then try to believe in God."

Ka could feel Blue's hatred. He gathered up a few of the sheets on the table and, announcing that he had to go see Sunay and Kadife without any further delay, pounded on the cell door. When it opened, he turned back to Blue and asked him if he had a special message for Kadife.

Blue smiled. "Be careful," he said. "Don't let anyone kill you."

———••••••———

CHAPTER THIRTY-SIX

You're Not Really Going to Die, Sir, Are You?

BARGAINING IN WHICH LIFE VIES WITH THEATER, AND ART WITH POLITICS

As the MİT operatives upstairs cut through the tape and slowly unwound the bandage with which they had attached the tape recorder to his chest, Ka tried to ingratiate himself by assuming their scornful air of efficiency and making fun of Blue. This may explain why he was not preoccupied with Blue's show of aggression downstairs.

He sent the driver of the army truck back to the hotel with instructions to wait. Flanked by military guards, he walked from one end of the garrison to the other. The officers' quarters looked out over a large snow-covered courtyard where a number of boys were throwing snowballs among the poplar trees. Waiting there was a girl in a red and white wool coat that reminded Ka of the one he'd worn in the third year of primary school; a little farther away, two of her friends were making a snowman. The air was crystalline. The grueling storm was over, and it was beginning to feel a little warmer.

Back at the hotel, he went straight to see İpek. She was in the kitchen, dressed in a smock, the one all lycée girls in Turkey wore once upon a time, and over it an apron. As he gazed at her with happy eyes, he longed to throw his arms around her, but there were other people in the room, so he held himself back and instead told her of the morning's developments. Things were going well, he said, not just for them but also for Kadife. He said that while the newspaper had in fact been circulated without amendment, he was no longer worried about being shot. There was much more to say, but just then Zahide came into the kitchen to make a request on behalf of the two soldiers guarding the door; she asked İpek to invite them inside and give them some tea. In the few moments left to them, İpek arranged to continue their conversation upstairs.

In his room, Ka hung up his coat and sat staring at the ceiling as he waited for İpek. With so much to discuss, Ka knew she would be there soon, and without feigning reluctance, but it wasn't long before he fell prey to a dark pessimism. First he imagined that İpek had been delayed because she'd run into her father; then he began to worry that because of the trouble she didn't want to be with him. The old ache returned, spreading out from his stomach like a poison. If this was what others called love pangs, they held no promise of happiness. He was only too aware that, as his love for İpek deepened, these dark panics descended on him all the faster. But was he right to assume that these attacks, these fearsome fantasies of deception and heartbreak, had anything to do with what others called love? He seemed alone in describing the experience as misery and defeat; unable even to imagine bragging about it as everyone else bragged of love, he could only suppose that his own feelings were abnormal, and this is what bothered him most. Even in the torment of paranoid theories (İpek was not coming; İpek didn't really want to come; all three of them—Kadife, Turgut Bey, and İpek—were having a secret meeting, discussing Ka as an enemy outsider and plotting to be rid of him), a part of him knew these fantasies to be pathological; so, for example, when his stomach began to ache at the terrible visions before his eyes of İpek as another man's lover, another region of his brain would repeat assurances that these were but a symptom of his sickness. Sometimes, to relieve the pain and to erase the evil scenes intruding on his thoughts (in the worst one, İpek refused even to see Ka, much less go to Frankfurt with him), he would by force of sheer will take refuge in reason, the one part of his mind that love had not thrown off balance. Of course she loves me, he would tell himself; if she didn't, why would she be looking so ecstatic? With such thoughtful focus, his evil anxieties would float away, but before long a new worry would inevitably come flying in to undo again his precarious inner peace.

He heard footsteps in the corridor. It couldn't be İpek, he told himself; it was someone else to tell him that İpek wasn't coming. And so, when he opened the door to find İpek there, he was radiating hostility as well as joy. He had been waiting for twelve long minutes. His consolation was to see that İpek had made herself up and was wearing lipstick.

"I've spoken to my father, and I've told him I'm going to Germany," she said.

Ka was still so much in thrall to the dark images in his head that his first response was disappointment; he couldn't give İpek his full attention. This failure to show any pleasure at her news planted some doubts in her own mind—or, more to the point, a disillusionment that proposed a way out. She still knew that Ka was madly in love and already bound to her like a hapless five-year-old who can't bear to be apart from his mother. She also knew that he wanted to take her to Germany not merely to share his happy home in Frankfurt; his far greater hope was that, when they were far away from all these eyes in Kars, he would know for sure that he possessed her absolutely.

"Darling, is something bothering you?"

In later years, when racked with pangs of love, Ka would recall a thousand times how softly and sweetly İpek had asked this question. For now he replied by telling her about the terrible thoughts that had been running through his head. One by one he recounted them for her: the dreaded abandonment, the worst scenes of horror that had played before his eyes.

"If love pangs cause you such dread, I can't help thinking there was a woman earlier in your life who hurt you very badly."

"I've known a bit of suffering in my life, but already I'm terrified of how much you could hurt me."

"I'm not going to hurt you at all," said İpek. "I'm in love with you; I'm going back to Germany with you. Everything will be fine."

She threw her arms around Ka, embracing him with all her strength, and they made love with such ease Ka could hardly believe it. Now he felt no urge to be rough with her; instead, he took pleasure in the strong but tender embrace, glorying in the whiteness of her delicate skin, but they were both aware that their lovemaking was neither as deep nor as intense as the night before.

Ka's mind was on his mediation plans. He believed that if, for once in his life, he could be happy, and if, by using his head, he could manage to get out of Kars not just in one piece but with his lover on his arm, that happiness might last forever. He had been thinking this for some time, as he smiled and gazed out the window, when to his great surprise he realized another poem was beckoning. He wrote it down very fast, just as it came, as İpek watched in loving admiration. He would later recite this poem, called "Love," at six readings in Germany. Those who heard it told me that, although apparently concerned with the familiar tension between peace and isolation, or security and fear, and special relations with a woman (though only one listener thought to ask afterward who this woman might be), the poem in fact emanated from the darkest, most incomprehensible part of Ka's being. As for the notes Ka later made, these were mostly explicit remembrances of İpek, and how he missed her, and scattered remarks about how she dressed and moved. (It may be because I'd read these notes so many times that İpek made such a strong impression on me on our first meeting.)

İpek dressed quickly and left; she had to say goodbye to her sister. But a moment later, Kadife was at his door. Seeing her eyes larger than ever, and her evident anxiety, Ka assured her she had nothing to fear and in particular that no one had laid a hand on Blue. He then told her he'd come to see what a very brave man Blue was by the difficulty he had had in persuading him to agree to the plan.

Then all at once a lie he had sketched out in advance occurred to him in glorious detail. He began by saying that the hardest part had been convincing Blue that Kadife would agree to the plan. He said Blue had been worried that Kadife might be offended, and he couldn't agree before having talked it over with her; here Kadife raised an eyebrow, so Ka retreated a bit, giving his lie a more truthful ring by expressing doubt that Blue had spoken those words in absolute sincerity. Then, not merely to keep the lie afloat but also to help Kadife save face, he added that Blue's reluctance (in other words, the respect he showed for a woman's feelings) was a positive thing—especially for him.

It cheered Ka to be spinning lies for these luckless people who'd allowed themselves to be swept into the asinine political feuds of this stupid city, the city that had taught him so late in life that the only important thing was happiness. But a part of him knew he needed to spin them because Kadife was so much braver than he was, so much readier to make sacrifices, and as he sensed how much unhappiness lay before him, his mood darkened. That's why, before cutting his story short, he told one more white lie: that just as he was leaving, Blue had asked him in a whisper to give Kadife his best.

Ka then proceeded to set out the plan, and when he had finished, he asked her what she thought of it.

"I'll bare my head, but I'll be the one to decide how," said Kadife.

Ka tried to convince her that Blue didn't mind her wearing a wig or something along those lines, but he stopped when he saw he'd angered her. The plan now went like this: First they were to release Blue; Blue was to go into hiding, somewhere he felt safe; only then would Kadife bare her head (in a manner of her own choosing). Could Kadife write out the plan as she understood it on a sheet of paper and sign it at once? Ka handed her the statement Blue had given him, hoping she would use it as a model for her own. But seeing the emotion on Kadife's face at the mere sight of Blue's handwriting, Ka felt an unexpected wave of affection for her. As she read, Kadife did her best to keep Ka from looking on too, and at one point she even sniffed the paper.

Sensing some hesitation, Ka told her he would use the statement to persuade Sunay and his associates that they should set Blue free. The army was probably angry with Kadife, and certainly the head-scarf affair had not won her any friends in high circles, but everyone in Kars respected her courage and her honesty. Ka handed Kadife a fresh sheet of paper and watched as she threw herself into the assignment. He thought about the Kadife with whom he'd discussed astrological signs and walked down Butcher Street on the first evening of his visit; the Kadife now sitting before him looked much older.

As he put her statement into his pocket, he said that, assuming Sunay could be made to agree, their next task would be to find a haven for Blue after his release. Was Kadife prepared to help find Blue a hiding place?

She gave her assent with a grave nod.

"Don't worry," said Ka. "At the end of this we'll all be happy."

"Doing the right thing doesn't always end in happiness," said Kadife.

"The right thing is the thing that makes us happy," said Ka. He imagined a day not far off when Kadife would come to Frankfurt and see the happy life he and her big sister had made for themselves. İpek would take Kadife to the *Kaufhof* and buy her a chic new raincoat; the three of them would go to the cinema together; afterward they would stop off at a restaurant on the Kaiserstrasse for beer and sausages.

They put on their coats, and Kadife followed Ka downstairs to the army truck waiting in the courtyard. The two bodyguards took the backseat. Ka wondered whether he'd been right to worry about being attacked walking the streets alone. From the front seat of an army truck, the streets of Kars didn't look at all frightening. He watched women clutching string bags on their way to the market, children throwing snowballs, and elderly men and women clinging to one another to keep from slipping on the ice, and he imagined himself with İpek at a cinema in Frankfurt, holding hands.

Sunay was with Colonel Osman Nuri Çolak, the coup's other mastermind. What Ka told them was colored by the optimism engendered by his happy daydreams. He said that everything had been arranged: Kadife would take part in the play and bare her head at the appointed moment, and Blue was only too eager to allow this condition of his release. He sensed a quiet understanding between these two men, the sort one found only between two people who spent their youths reading the same books. In a careful but confident voice, Ka explained how delicate the mediation had been. "First I had to flatter Kadife, and then I had to flatter Blue," he said, presenting Sunay with their statements. As Sunay read them, Ka could sense that the actor had been drinking though it wasn't even noon. Moving nearer to Sunay's mouth for a moment, he was sure of it.

"This guy wants us to release him before Kadife goes onstage to bare her head," said Sunay. "He has his eyes open, this one. He's no fool."

"And Kadife wants the same thing," said Ka. "I really tried hard, but this was the best deal I could make."

"We represent the state. Why should we believe either of them?" said Colonel Osman Nuri Çolak.

"They don't trust the state any more than you trust them," said Ka. "If we don't accept some mutual assurances, we won't get anywhere."

"He could be hanged as an example to others and then, when the authorities hear what a drunken actor and a broken-down colonel have done in the name of a military coup, they could use this to destroy us. Hasn't any of this occurred to Blue?" asked the colonel.

"He's very good at acting unafraid to die. I can't tell you what's really going on in his head, but he did imply that hanging him would make him a saint, an icon."

"OK, let's say we release Blue first," said Sunay. "How can we be sure that Kadife will keep her word about appearing in the play?"

"If you bear in mind that Turgut Bey once endured a bitter trial and terrible suffering to preserve his honor, and that Kadife is this man's daughter, it should be clear that we can trust her to keep her word—far more than we can trust Blue. Still, if you told her now that Blue was certain to be released, it's possible that she wouldn't yet know her own mind as to appearing onstage this evening. She does have a temper, and she is given to snap decisions."

"What do you suggest?"

"I know that you staged this coup not just for the sake of politics but also as a thing of beauty and in the name of art," said Ka. "Just to look at his career is to see that Sunay Bey's every political involvement has been for the sake of art. If what you want to do now is see this as an ordinary political matter, you won't want to set Blue free and put yourself in considerable danger. But at the same time, you know only too well that a play in which Kadife bares her head for all in Kars to see will be no mere artistic triumph; it will also have profound political consequences."

"If she's really going to bare her head, we'll let Blue go," Osman Nuri Çolak decided. "But we must make sure everyone in the city sees the play."

Sunay wrapped his arms around his old army comrade and kissed him. When the colonel had left the room, he took Ka's hand and led him deeper into the house. "I'd like to tell my wife all about this!" They approached an unfurnished room, still cold despite an electric heater burning in the corner, and there was Funda Eser, posing dramatically as she read a script. She saw Sunay and Ka looking at her through the open doorway, but she continued reading without losing her composure. Dazzled by the dark rings of kohl around her eyes, her thick rouged lips, the great breasts swelling out of her low-cut dress, and her exaggerated gestures, Ka found it impossible to grasp what she was saying.

"Thomas Kyd's *The Spanish Tragedy*: the rebellious rape victim's tragic speech," Sunay said proudly, "with some alterations inspired by Brecht's *The Good Woman of Szechuan*, though most of the changes are the fruits of my own imagination. When Funda delivers this speech tonight, Kadife will not yet have found the courage to bare her head, but she will be using the edge of her scarf to wipe the tears from her eyes."

"If Kadife Hanım is ready, let's start rehearsals at once."

The desire in her voice not only made clear to Ka how much Funda Eser loved the theater, it also reminded him of the oft-repeated claim of those who'd wanted to deny Sunay the chance to play Atatürk—that Funda was a lesbian. Looking less the soldier of the revolution than the proud theater producer, Sunay was just explaining to his wife that Kadife had not yet resolved all the questions concerning her decision to "accept the role" when an orderly came to report they had just brought in Serdar Bey.

Standing face-to-face with the owner of the *Border City Gazette*, Ka felt himself succumbing to an impulse unknown to him since the time when he still lived in Turkey: For a moment he was tempted to punch Serdar Bey in the face. But now as they welcomed this man to a carefully laid meal, with white cheese soon, he was sure, to be accompanied by raki, it was clear to Ka that such urges had no place at the table of revolutionary leaders, who sat down with an easy confidence known only to those for whom it has become second nature to decide other people's fates.

As they ate and drank, they discussed the affairs of the world with merciless assurance. At Sunay's request, Ka told Funda Eser what he'd just been saying about art and politics. When he saw how much these words excited her, the newspaperman said he wanted to write them down for use in a future article, but Sunay roughly put him in his place. First he had to correct the lies he'd printed about Ka in today's edition. And so it wasn't long before Serdar Bey had promised to print a new and very positive front-page article that would, he hoped, encourage the already forgetful readers of Kars to forget that they'd ever been encouraged to think ill of Ka.

"And the headline must mention the play we're putting on this evening," said Funda Eser.

Serdar Bey promised to publish the article they wanted; they could dictate every detail, even to the point size of the headlines. But as he wasn't very knowledgeable about classical or modern theater, it might be better, he said, if Sunay would describe this evening's play in his own words—that is to say, if Sunay would write the article himself, just to ensure that tomorrow's front page was one hundred percent accurate. He reminded everyone that for most of his working life, he'd been writing about events before they happened: This, it could be said, was his forte. But there were still four hours to work with: They were operating on a special schedule in accordance with martial law, so the edition would not be put to bed until four that afternoon.

"It won't take me much time to give you a rundown of the performance," said Sunay. They hadn't been sitting at the table for long, but he'd already finished a glass of raki, Ka noticed. As Sunay knocked back a second, Ka could see pain and passion flicker in his eyes.

"Write this down, Mr. Journalist!" Sunay bellowed, glaring at Serdar Bey as if delivering a threat. "The headline is as follows: DEATH ONSTAGE." He paused to think. "And then another headline right below, in smaller print: ILLUSTRIOUS ACTOR SUNAY ZAIM SHOT DEAD DURING YESTERDAY'S PERFORMANCE."

He was speaking with an intensity Ka could not help but admire. He listened, unsmiling and utterly respectful, as Sunay continued, speaking only when Serdar Bey needed help to make sense of his words.

From time to time Sunay stopped to ponder what he'd said and clear his head with another raki, so it took him about an hour to complete the article. I was to acquire the final version from Serdar Bey during my visit to Kars four years later.

DEATH ONSTAGE

ILLUSTRIOUS ACTOR SUNAY ZAIM SHOT DEAD DURING YESTERDAY'S PERFORMANCE

YESTERDAY, WHILE APPEARING IN A HISTORIC PLAY AT THE NATIONAL THEATER, KADIFE THE HEAD-SCARF GIRL SHOCKED AUDIENCES FIRST BY BARING HER HEAD IN A MOMENT OF ENLIGHTENMENT FERVOR AND THEN BY POINTING A WEAPON AT SUNAY ZAIM, THE ACTOR PLAYING THE VILLAIN, AND FIRING. HER PERFORMANCE, BROADCAST LIVE, HAS LEFT THE PEOPLE OF KARS TREMBLING IN HORROR.

On Tuesday night, the Sunay Zaim Theater Company stunned the people of Kars with an evening of original revolutionary plays that gave way to a real-life revolution before their very eyes. Last night, during their second gala, the Sunay Zaim Players shocked us yet again. The vehicle on this occasion was an adaptation of a drama penned by Thomas Kyd, a wrongfully neglected sixteenth-century English playwright who nevertheless is said to have influenced the work of Shakespeare. Sunay Zaim, who has spent the last twenty years touring the forgotten towns of Anatolia, pacing its empty stages and bringing culture to its teahouses, brought his love of the theater to a climax in the closing scene. In a moment of excitement induced by this daring modern drama that paid homage to both French Jacobin and English Jacobean drama, Kadife, the stubborn leader of the head-scarf girls, brashly bared her head for all to see and, as the people of Kars watched in amazement, she then produced a gun, the contents of which she proceeded to empty into Sunay Zaim, the illustrious actor who was playing the villain and whose name, like Kyd's, has languished in the shadows for too long. This real-life drama reminded onlookers of the performance two days earlier, in which the bullets flying across the stage turned out to be real, and so it was in the horrified knowledge that these also were real bullets that the people of Kars watched Sunay fall. The death of the great Turkish actor Sunay Zaim was for the audience more shattering than life itself. Although the people of Kars were fully aware that the play was about a person liberating herself from tradition and religious oppression, they were still unable to accept that Sunay Zaim was really dying, even as bullets pierced his body and blood gushed from his wounds. But they had no trouble understanding the actor's last words, and never will they forget that he sacrificed his life for Art.

When Sunay had made his last corrections, Serdar read out the final draft to the assembled guests. "If this meets with your approval, I shall print it word for word in tomorrow's edition," he said. "But in all my years of writing news before it's happened, this is the first time I'll be praying that an article doesn't come true! You're not really going to die, sir, are you?"

"What I am trying to do is push the truths of Art to their outer limits, to become one with Myth," said Sunay. "Anyway, once the snow melts tomorrow and the roads open again, my death will cease to be of the slightest importance."

For a moment Sunay's eye caught Funda's. Seeing how deeply these two understood each other, Ka felt a pang of jealousy. Would he and İpek ever learn to share their souls like this or enjoy such deep happiness?

"Mr. Newspaperman, the time has come for you to leave, dear sir; our work is done, so please prepare the presses," said Sunay. "In view of the historical importance of this edition, I shall see to it that my orderly provides you with a plate of my photograph." As soon as Serdar Bey had left, Sunay dropped the mocking tone that Ka had attributed to too much raki. "I accept Blue's and Kadife's conditions," he said. He then turned to Funda Eser, whose eyebrows rose as he explained that Kadife was willing to bare her head onstage only if they would release Blue first.

"Kadife Hanım is a very brave woman. I am sure we'll come to an understanding once we start rehearsals," said Funda Eser.

"You can go to her together," said Sunay. "But first Kadife must be convinced that Blue has been released and that no one has followed him to his hiding place. This will take time."

Thus ignoring Funda Eser's desire to launch immediately into rehearsals with Kadife, Sunay turned to Ka to discuss how best to organize Blue's release. My sense from studying his notes of this meeting is that Ka was still taking Sunay's promises at face value. In other words, Ka did *not* think Sunay would have Blue followed to a hiding place after his release and recaptured once Kadife had bared her head onstage. It is likely that this concealed plan emerged slowly, and that its masterminds were in fact the secret police, still planting microphones everywhere and struggling to decipher the intelligence furnished by their double agents in the hopes of staying one step ahead of everyone.

Perhaps they were even manipulating Colonel Osman Nuri Çolak to their own advantage. The secret police knew they were outnumbered—as long as Sunay, the disgruntled colonel, and his small gang of like-minded officers were in control of the army, there was no chance of MİT taking charge of the revolution—but nevertheless they had men everywhere doing everything in their power to keep Sunay's "artistic" lunacies in check. Before the article he'd written out at the raki table went to be typeset, Serdar Bey had used his walkie-talkie to read it out to his friends at the Kars branch of MİT, causing great consternation and not a little concern about Sunay's mental health and stability. As for Sunay's actual plan to release Blue, until the very last moment it was generally unknown how much MİT knew.

Today I would say that these details have little bearing on the end of our story, so I shall not dwell overmuch on the minutiae of the plan to release Blue. Suffice it to say that Sunay and Ka decided to leave the job to Fazıl and Sunay's Sivas-born orderly. Sunay dispatched an army truck the moment he got Fazıl's address from the secret police: Ten minutes later, they'd brought him in. This time there was fear in his face and he no longer reminded Ka of Necip. It was quickly decided that he and the orderly should head for the army garrison in the city center; they immediately left the tailor shop by the back door, shaking off the detectives who'd been following them. For while the MİT people by now had grave doubts about Sunay and were eager to keep him from doing any mischief, they were caught so unprepared by the speed of events that they still hadn't posted a guard at every exit.

So the plan moved forward, and Sunay's assurances that there would be no double cross were not contradicted: Blue was removed from his cell and put into an army truck, and the Sivas-born orderly drove straight to the Iron Bridge over the Kars River. With the truck parked on the near bank, Blue followed faithfully the instructions he'd been given; he made straight for a grocery store, its windows plastered with posters featuring special deals on garlic sausages; he then slipped out the back, where a horse-drawn carriage was waiting. Taking cover under the tarpaulin and making himself comfortable among the Aygaz canisters, he was whisked off to a safe house. Ka would hear of all this only after the fact. The sole person who knew where the horse-drawn carriage had taken Blue was Fazıl.

It was an hour and a half before this business was concluded. At about half past three, as the oleander and chestnut trees were losing their shadows, disappearing like ghosts, giving way to the first shades of darkness to descend on the empty streets of Kars, Fazıl came to tell Kadife that Blue had reached his hiding place. From the door leading from the courtyard to the kitchen, he stared at Kadife as if having just come in from outer space, but Kadife, just as she'd always failed to notice Necip, took no note of Fazıl. Instead she ran upstairs joyfully. İpek was just leaving Ka's room, where she'd been for over an hour. It had been an hour of undiluted bliss, and my dear friend's heart was soaring as never before at the prospect of his future happiness—as I shall undertake to explain in the opening pages of the next chapter.

CHAPTER THIRTY-SEVEN

The Only Script We Have This Evening Is Kadife's Hair

PREPARATIONS FOR THE PLAY TO END ALL PLAYS

As I have already mentioned, Ka had always shied away from happiness for fear of the pain that might follow, so we already know that his most intense emotions came not when he was happy but when he was beset by the certainty that this happiness would soon be lost to him. When he rose from Sunay's raki table and returned to the Snow Palace Hotel with his two army bodyguards, Ka still believed that everything was going according to plan, and the prospect of seeing İpek again filled his heart with joy, even as the fear of loss was fast overtaking him.

When my friend later alluded to the poem he wrote on Thursday afternoon around three o'clock, he made it clear that his soul was vacillating between these two antipodes, so I feel it my duty to pass on what he said. The poem, to which Ka gave the title "Dog," seems to have been inspired by another chance encounter with the charcoal-colored stray, this time on his way back from the tailor shop. Four minutes later, he was up in his room writing out this poem, and great as his hopes for happiness might have been at the time, the fear of loss was now spreading through his body like poison: Love equaled pain. The poem refers to his great fear of dogs as a child, to the strays that would bark at him in Maçka Park when he was six, and to a cruel neighbor who was always letting out his dog to chase passersby. Later in life, Ka had come to see his fear of dogs as punishment for his many hours of childhood bliss. But he felt a paradox underlying all this: Heaven and hell were in the same place. In those same streets he had played soccer, gathered mulberries, and collected those player trading cards you got with chewing gum; it was precisely because the dogs turned the scene of these childish joys into a living hell that he felt the joys so keenly.

Seven or eight minutes after hearing of his return to the hotel, İpek went up to his room. Considering that she could not have been certain of his actual return, and bearing in mind that Ka had sent her no message, it was a very modest delay; for the first time ever, they managed to meet without Ka's having read any dark motives into her tardiness, much less the conclusion that she'd abandoned him. The achievement made Ka even happier. What's more, İpek's face was also radiating happiness. Ka confirmed that everything was going to plan, and she did likewise. She asked about Blue, and Ka told her his release was imminent. İpek lit up at this news, just as she had done when he told her all the other things. It was not enough to be convinced that their own fortunes were still on course; they had to believe all the misery around them had been extinguished to keep a shadow from falling over their own happiness.

Despite incessant embraces and impatient kisses, they refrained from getting back into bed to make love. Ka told İpek that once they were in Istanbul he'd be able to get her a German visa in a day; he had a friend at the consulate. They'd need to marry right away to qualify, but they could always have a proper ceremony and celebration later if they wished. They discussed the possibility of Kadife's and Turgut Bey's joining them in Frankfurt once their own affairs in Kars were settled, with Ka even mentioning the names of some hotels where they might stay; and now their heads were so dizzy with wild dreams that they were even a bit ashamed of themselves. İpek changed the tone to tell Ka about her father's anxieties, particularly his fear of suicide bombers, and she warned him that on no account was he to go out into the street again. Then, promising each other that they would leave the city on the first bus once the snow melted, they spent a long time standing at the window, hand in hand, gazing at the icy mountain roads.

İpek said she'd already started packing. Ka told her not to take anything, but İpek had quite a few treasures she'd been carrying around with her since childhood, things so much a part of her that she couldn't imagine life without them. Still in front of the window, they saw the dog that had inspired Ka's poem dash in and out of sight, and Ka took stock of those things İpek insisted she couldn't leave behind: a wristwatch her mother had given her when İpek was a child in Istanbul, all the more precious now that Kadife had lost the one given her on the same day; an ice-blue angora sweater that her late uncle had brought her from Germany, a garment of high quality but so tight-fitting she'd never been able to wear it in Kars; a tablecloth from her trousseau, embroidered by her mother with silver filigree, that Muhtar had stained with marmalade on the very first use—which explained why there hadn't been a second; seventeen miniature perfume and alcohol bottles holding the collection of evil eyes that she'd started for no particular reason many years ago and now saw as bringing her good luck; photographs of herself as a child on her parents' laps (the moment she mentioned these, Ka wanted to see them); the beautiful black velvet evening dress Muhtar had bought her in Istanbul, its back so low he had only allowed her to wear it at home; the embroidered silk satin shawl she'd bought to conceal the plunging neckline, in the hope of one day inducing Muhtar to change his mind; the suede shoes never worn for fear the Kars mud would ruin them; the jade necklace that she was able to show him because she happened to have it with her.

If I say now that I saw the same great jade stone hanging on a black silk cord around İpek's neck exactly four years later, as she sat across from me at a dinner hosted by the mayor of Kars, I hope my readers won't accuse me of having strayed too far from the subject. To the contrary, we are now approaching the heart of the matter: For until that moment I could have said I had seen nothing for which I had been prepared so utterly, and so it must be for all of you following the story I have related in this book: İpek was more beautiful than anyone could have imagined. At this dinner, where I had my first glimpse of her, I must confess to have found myself stunned, bedazzled, and deeply jealous. And as this passion overtook me, my dear friend's lost poetry collection, which mystery I'd been trying to unravel, turned into a story of a very different order. It was at this astounding moment that I must have decided to write the book now in your hands, but at the time my soul remained entirely unaware of the decision. I was beset by all manner of those feelings that women of exceptional beauty never fail to inspire; gazing at this paragon before me, I felt myself crumbling, I felt possessed. When I think back now to the transparent maneuvers of the other Kars residents at that same table—ploys I'd foolishly ascribed to the aim of exchanging a few words with this novelist who had come to town, or of collecting a few tidbits for the next day's gossip—it is clear to me that all their palaver served a single purpose: to draw a veil over İpek's beauty, concealing it not just from me but from themselves. A terrible jealousy was gnawing at me that I feared might turn to love: For a while, just like my dear friend Ka, I too dreamed that I might enjoy the affections of a woman this beautiful. For a moment, I let myself forget my sadness at how Ka's life had come to nothing in the end and found myself thinking admiringly, Only a man with a soul as deep as his could have won the heart of a woman like this! Did I myself have the slightest chance of beguiling İpek and whisking her off with me to Istanbul? I would have proposed to her on the spot or, if she wished, kept her as my secret mistress until the day it all fell apart, but by whatever path I wanted to end beside her! She had a wide, commanding forehead, moist eyes, elegant lips so much like the film star Melinda's I could hardly trust myself to look at them. What, I wondered, did she think of me? Had I ever come up in conversation between her and Ka? Even without another sip of raki, my head was swimming, my heart pounding. Then I noticed Kadife, sitting just a few places away and lancing me with fierce looks. I must return to my story.

As they stood before the window, Ka picked up the jade necklace, draped it around İpek's neck, and, giving her a tender kiss, carelessly recited the words fast becoming an incantation: They would be happy in Germany. Just then İpek saw Fazıl dart into the courtyard; she waited a moment and went downstairs, where she found Kadife standing alone at the kitchen door; it was here she must have heard the good news about Blue's release. The two girls bounded up to their room. I have no idea what they talked about or did. Ka was still in his own room, his heart so full of his new poems and his new faith in love that, for the first time, the part of his mind that had kept track—sometimes meticulously, sometimes fancifully—of their every movement through the Snow Palace Hotel was now at rest, and he let them go.

As I would later discover, it was at about this time that the weather bureau announced the first clear signs of a thaw. The sun had been shining all day, and now the icicles dangling from the trees and eaves had begun to drip and then drop. The rumors started long before any meteorological development now spread throughout the city: The roads were sure to open tonight and the theater coup would come to an end. Those who remembered the evening's events in detail would tell me that it was just following the weather report that Kars Border Television ran the first announcement of the new play that the Sunay Zaim Players would be performing that evening at the National Theater. It was Hakan Özge, the city's favorite young announcer, who advised the people of Kars that the bloody events two days earlier were no cause for concern and in any case no excuse for nonattendance; security forces would be flanking the stage, and as the event was free to the general public, the people of Kars should feel welcome to bring the entire family. The effect of these assurances was to fan popular fears and empty the streets earlier than usual. Everyone was sure of yet another evening of violence and madness at the National Theater, so—apart from the usual assortment of wild-eyed ne'er-do-wells prepared to attend virtually anything just to say they did (their not inconsiderable ranks comprising aimless unemployed youths, bored leftists with a penchant for violence, elderly denture wearers so desperate for entertainment it little mattered to them if anyone got killed in the process, and staunch Kemalists who'd seen Sunay on television and admired his republican views)—most Kars residents decided they would stay home and watch the live broadcast on TV. Meanwhile Sunay and Colonel Osman Nuri Çolak met again; fearing that the National Theater would be empty, they sent out the army trucks to gather up all the religious high school boys and let it be known that every student at every lycée, every resident teacher, and every government official in the city was required to report to the performance in coat and tie.

After the meeting, a number of people saw Sunay passed out in the back of the tailor shop on a small dusty floor mat, surrounded by scraps of cloth, paper wrappers, and empty boxes. It wasn't drunken expedience. For years now, Sunay had been convinced that soft beds would make his body go soft, so he was in the habit of napping on a hard coarse mattress before any performance of great importance to him. Before he could lie down, however, he'd had a row with his wife about the script, which had yet to be finalized, so he put her into an army truck and sent her over to join Kadife at the Snow Palace Hotel and begin rehearsals.

Funda Eser sauntered into the Snow Palace Hotel like a woman to whom all doors are open; she went straight up to the sisters' room, and I am able to report that the warm dulcet tones by which she so effortlessly created an atmosphere of female intimacy offered offstage a more compelling proof of her greatness than the play that night would ever allow her. Certainly her eyes must have been fixed on İpek's crystalline beauty, but her mind was on the role Kadife was to play that evening.

My view is that her own estimation of this role derived from the importance her husband gave it, because during the twenty years she'd been touring Anatolia playing wronged and raped women, she never had another goal in presenting the victim above arousing the men in the audience. Marriages, divorces, the covering of heads or the baring of them—they were all just means to the same ordinary end—to reduce the heroine to such a state of helplessness that no man could resist her—and although it is impossible to say whether she fully understood her roles in dramas celebrating the republican enlightenment, it must be allowed that the male dramatists who invented these stereotypes could not see a heroine expressing a notion any deeper or more refined than eroticism or social duty. Funda Eser used these roles to splendid effect in her life offstage, and to a degree these male dramatists would have scarcely anticipated.

Not long after having entered the sisters' room, therefore, Funda was able to suggest to Kadife that they rehearse the scene in which she was to bare her head and reveal her beautiful hair. Kadife feigned reluctance but not for long; when she loosened her mane Funda let out a loud cry, remarking on how healthy and shiny it was and that she couldn't take her eyes off it. Sitting Kadife in front of the mirror, she picked up an imitation ivory comb and, running it slowly through her hair, explained that the essence of theater was not the words but the images. "Let your hair speak for itself, and let the men go mad!" she said.

By now she had Kadife's head spinning so she kissed the young woman's hair to calm her down. She was clever enough to see that this kiss awakened the dormant evil that Kadife kept hidden, and experienced enough to draw İpek into the game too. Providing a flask from her bag, she began to pour cognac into the tea glasses Zahide had set for them. When Kadife objected, she mocked her, saying, "But tonight you're going to bare your head!" Kadife burst into tears, and Funda planted insistent little kisses on her cheeks, her neck, her hands. Then, to amuse the girls, she recited what she called Sunay's unknown masterpiece, "The Innocent Air Hostess Protests," but this, far from diverting the girls, only made them more anxious. When Kadife said she wanted to study the script, Funda proclaimed, "The only script we have this evening is Kadife's hair," the moment when all the men of Kars gazed dumbfounded at her long, beautiful, radiant mane. The women in the audience would be so moved by love and jealousy they would want to reach out and touch it.

As she spoke this, Funda kept refilling their glasses with cognac. She said that when she looked into İpek's face she saw happiness, and when she looked into Kadife's she saw courage and fury. But she couldn't decide which sister was more beautiful.

Funda Eser continued in this amusing vein until a purple-faced Turgut Bey burst into the room. "They've just announced on television that Kadife, the leader of the head-scarf girls, is going to bare her head during this evening's performance," he said. "Tell me, is this true?"

"Let's go watch television," said İpek.

"Please allow me to introduce myself, sir," said Funda Eser. "I am the life partner of the illustrious actor and newly anointed statesman Sunay Zaim, and my name is Funda Eser. I would like to congratulate you on having raised two such marvelous and outstanding girls. Thanks to Kadife's heroic decision, I can advise you that you have nothing to fear."

"If my daughter does this, the religious fanatics in this city will never forgive her!" said Turgut Bey.

They moved to the dining room so they could all watch the television. Funda Eser took Turgut Bey by the hand and said something to the effect that she could promise, in the name of her husband, the city's supreme ruler, that everything would go according to plan. Hearing noise in the dining room, Ka came to join them, whereupon a happy Kadife informed him that Blue had been released. Without waiting for Ka to ask, she declared she was planning to keep the promise she had made to him that morning, and that she and Funda Hanım were preparing to rehearse the play. As everyone watched television, talking at the same time, Funda Eser applied herself to charming Turgut Bey, lest he stand in the way of his daughter's appearance.

Ka would often think back to this ten-minute interlude as one of the happiest of his life. He was now utterly free of doubt about his destiny of lifelong happiness and dreamily imagining life as part of this jovial family. It was not yet four o'clock, but the dark old wallpaper in the high-ceilinged dining room was already the shade of a childhood memory. Looking into İpek's eyes, Ka could not help but smile.

Seeing Fazıl standing at the door, Ka hastened to push him back into the kitchen and, before the boy could ruin the mood, pump him for information. But Fazıl resisted: He stood fast in the doorway, pretending to stare at the image on the TV screen, but in fact his angry eyes were fixed in astonishment on the animated crowd around it. Seeing Ka was trying to get the boy into the kitchen, İpek stepped over to them.

"Blue wants to talk to you one more time," said Fazıl, and it was clear from the tone of his voice that he was happy to be ruining the party. "He's changed his mind about something."

"About what?"

"He'll tell you himself. The horse and carriage will pick you up in the courtyard in ten minutes," he said, leaving the kitchen to return to the courtyard himself.

Ka's heart began to pound. It wasn't just reluctance to set foot outside the hotel again today; he was also afraid that his own cowardice would betray him.

"Please, whatever you do, don't go!" İpek cried, giving voice to Ka's own thoughts. "After all, they know about the horse and carriage by now. No good can come of this."

"No, I'm going," said Ka.

Why, given his reluctance, did he decide to go? It was an old habit. In school, whenever a teacher asked a question he knew he couldn't answer, he'd always raise his hand. He would go into a store and, finding the perfect sweater, perversely buy something else not nearly as nice for the same money, knowing all the while it made no sense. It may have been a form of anxiety that made him do this, or perhaps it was his fear of happiness. They went up to his room, taking care not to let Kadife notice. How Ka wished that İpek had used a little ingenuity, contrived something imaginative to let her linger peacefully in the room, but as they stood looking out the window, İpek could voice only the same impotent words: "Don't go, darling; don't leave the hotel at all today; don't put our happiness at risk."

Ka listened dreamily, like a sacrificial lamb. Soon the horse-drawn carriage appeared in the courtyard: He was shocked to see how quickly his luck had turned and it broke his heart. Without pausing to give İpek a kiss, but not forgetting to embrace her and say his farewells, he went downstairs; his two bodyguards were in the lobby reading the papers but he managed to slip past them into the kitchen and then out through the back door into the hated horse-drawn carriage, to lie down once again underneath the tarpaulin.

It is tempting to read too much into this moment—we are, after all, fast approaching the point of no return, and the mission on which Ka was now embarked would change his life forever—so I feel obliged to caution readers against viewing Ka's decision to accept Blue's invitation as the pivotal moment in this story. Certainly I am not of this view myself: Ka had not yet run out of chances. He still had time to make a success of his visit to Kars, and he would have other opportunities to right his fortunes and find "happiness"—or whatever it was he meant by that word. But when the events in this story reached their conclusion, and all his bridges were burned, it was this moment that Ka would look back on with stinging regret and undying curiosity as to how things might have turned out if only İpek had managed to keep him in his room. She might have said something to talk him out of going to see Blue, but even having racked his brain hundreds of times during the following four years, he still had no idea what the right words might have been.

As we turn back to the image of Ka hiding under the tarpaulin, we are right to see him as a man who has surrendered to his fate. He was sorry to be there; he was angry at himself and at the world. He was cold, he was afraid of falling ill, and he knew no good could come of this appointment. He paid careful attention to the noises of the street and the things people said as the carriage passed by, just as he had done during his first journey in this conveyance, but this time he was not in the least interested to know where in Kars the carriage was taking him.

When the carriage came to a halt, the driver prodded him and Ka emerged from underneath the tarpaulin; before he could make out where he was, he saw in front of him a decrepit building that, like so many others in Kars, was lurching to one side and shedding flakes of paint. Inside, he made his way up a narrow, crooked staircase to a landing two floors up. (In a happier moment, he would remember seeing a door lined with shoes and a child's bright eyes staring at him through the gap in the door.) The apartment door opened, and he found himself face-to-face with Hande.

"I've made up my mind," said Hande with a smile. "I'm refusing to cut myself off from the girl I really am."

"It's important for you to be happy."

"What makes me happy is being here and doing what I want," said Hande. "It doesn't scare me anymore if I'm someone else in my dreams."

"Isn't it dangerous for you to be here at all?"

"Yes, but it's only in times of danger that a person can really concentrate on life," said Hande. "What I understand now is that I will never be able to concentrate on things I don't believe in, things like baring my head. Right now I'm happy to share a cause with Blue. Could you write poems here?"

Although only two days had passed since their first meeting, Ka's memories of their dinner conversation were now so distant that for a moment he stood there gaping like an amnesiac. How much did Hande wish to draw attention to her intimacy with Blue? The girl opened the door to the next room for Ka to find Blue watching a black-and-white television.

"I knew you'd come," said Blue. He looked pleased.

"I have no idea why I'm here," said Ka.

"You're here because of the turmoil inside you," said Blue. He looked very knowing.

They eyed each other hatefully. It didn't escape either of them that Blue was very pleased about something while Ka was full of sorrow. Hande left the room and closed the door.

"I want you to tell Kadife not to have anything to do with that disaster they plan to stage this evening," said Blue.

"Couldn't you have sent this news with Fazıl?" said Ka. He could tell from the expression on his face that Blue had no idea who Fazıl was, so Ka added, "He's the religious high school boy who sent me here."

"Ha!" said Blue. "Kadife wouldn't have taken him seriously. You're the only one she's going to take seriously. And it's only when she hears this from you that she'll understand how serious I am about my decision. And she'll understand why after she's seen the loathsome way they're promoting this on television."

"When I left the hotel, Kadife was already starting to rehearse," Ka said with pleasure.

"Then you can tell her I couldn't be more opposed to this performance! Kadife didn't decide of her own free will to bare her head, she did it to free *me*. She was negotiating with a state that takes political prisoners as hostages, so she's under no obligation to keep her word."

"I can tell her all this," said Ka, "but I can't predict what she'll do."

"In other words, if Kadife decides to play this her way, you're not responsible; that's what you're trying to tell me, is it?" Ka said nothing. "Then let me make it clear—if Kadife goes onstage this evening and bares her head, you too will be to blame. You've been involved in this deal every step of the way."

For the first time since his arrival in Kars, Ka felt the peace of righteousness: At long last, the villain was talking like a villain, saying all the vicious things that villains say, and this cleared his head. "You're right to think you're a hostage!" he said, in the hopes of calming Blue, as he considered how he might get out of this place without angering him further.

"Give her this letter," said Blue. He handed Ka an envelope. "Kadife may refuse to believe my spoken message. And one day, when you've found your way back to Frankfurt, I trust you'll also find a way to make Hans Hansen publish that statement so many people risked so much to sign."

"Of course."

There was something in Blue's face that hinted at frustration. He'd been far more relaxed that morning as he sat in his cell awaiting execution. Now he'd managed to save himself, he was already looking ahead in anger, aggrieved to know he'd never manage to do anything in life but generate more wrath. Ka was slow to realize that Blue saw what Ka could see.

"It doesn't matter where you live, here or in your beloved Europe; you'll always be imitating them; you'll always be groveling."

"If I'm happy, that's all I care about."

"You can go now!" shouted Blue. "And know this: People who seek only happiness never find it."

———•••••———

CHAPTER THIRTY-EIGHT

I Didn't Bring You Here to Upset You

AN ENFORCED VISIT

Ka was glad to get away from Blue, but at the same time he knew there was now a bond, however damning, between them. It was not a simple bond—there was more to it than fear and hatred—for as Ka shut the door behind him, he realized with some remorse that he was going to miss this man. Hande appeared, all good intentions and deep thoughts, and though Ka tried to dismiss her as utterly guileless and even rather simple, he soon found himself ceding to her the higher ground. Eyes opened wide, Hande asked him to send her best to Kadife and tell her it didn't matter what she decided about baring her head on television (she didn't say *onstage*; she said *television*); Hande's heart would be with her no matter what she did. Once she had said this, Hande told Ka how to leave the building without attracting the attention of the plainclothes police.

Ka fled from the apartment in a panic; on the first-floor landing he felt a poem coming, so he sat down on the first step, in front of the shoes lined up on either side of the entrance, and, taking out his notebook, began to write.

It was the eighteenth poem Ka had written since his arrival in Kars; its subject was the link between love and hate, but if he hadn't explained the allusion in the notes he later wrote, no one could have guessed it. When he was at the Advanced Şişli Middle School, according to his notes, there'd been a boy whose family owned a prosperous construction company. This boy, who had won a Balkan equestrian championship, was very spoiled, but Ka was infatuated with his air of independence. There was another boy too—his mother, a White Russian, had been a lycée classmate of Ka's mother—who'd grown up without a father, sisters, or brothers, and while he was still a student he had started using drugs. Although this enigmatic white-faced boy had never seemed to pay anyone any mind, it turned out he always knew everything to be known about the people around him. Finally, during Ka's military training in Tuzla, there'd been this handsome, laconic, rather aloof wise guy in the neighboring regiment who taunted him tirelessly with small acts of cruelty (like hiding his cap). Ka had been bound to each of these fellows by both unveiled contempt and an adoration he kept secret. The title of the poem—"Jealousy"—referred to the feeling that bound together these two conflicting emotions and that also bound Ka to the task of resolving the contradiction in his mind, but the poem itself revealed an even deeper problem: After a time, these people's souls and voices had taken up residence in Ka's own body.

On leaving the apartment building, Ka still had no idea where he was, but after following a narrow lane he saw he had reached Halitpaşa Avenue. Without knowing why, he turned and cast a final glance at Blue's hiding place before heading off.

As he made his way back to the hotel, Ka missed his bodyguards; he felt unsafe without them. As he walked past the city hall an unmarked car pulled up alongside him; when he saw the door had opened, Ka stopped.

"Ka Bey, please don't be afraid, we're from police headquarters. Please get in, and we'll drive you back to the hotel."

As he was trying to figure out which option was more dangerous—returning to the hotel without police escort or being seen getting into a police car in the middle of the city—another car door swung open. Suddenly a huge brute of a man stood before him—he seemed so familiar, who was it? Yes, someone in Istanbul, a distant uncle, Uncle Mahmut—and this man departed from the polite tone of the previous exchange to push Ka roughly into the car. Inside, it was eerily dark. Once they were under way he delivered two punches to Ka's head. Or did he punch him as he was pushing him into the car? Ka was terrified. One of the men in front—not Uncle Mahmut—was muttering terrible curses. When he was a child, there was a man on Niğar the Poetess Street who cursed that way whenever a ball landed in his garden.

Ka kept calm by convincing himself he was a child. The car seemed convincing too (now he remembered; the unmarked police cars in Kars were little Renaults, not big flashy 1956 Chevrolets like this). They took him on a long and winding tour of the dark, mean streets of Kars, as though to frighten a disobedient kid; it seemed a very long while before the car finally pulled into a courtyard. "Face front," they said. They took him by the arm and led him up two steps. Ka was certain that these men—three of them, counting the driver—were not Islamists (where could Islamists have set hands on a car like this?). And they couldn't be MİT either, because some of those guys were in league with Sunay. A door opened, a door closed, and Ka found himself in another old Armenian house with very high ceilings; the window beside him looked out over Atatürk Avenue. As he scanned the room he saw a television blaring in the corner and a table covered with dirty plates, orange peels, and newspapers; he also saw a magneto that he later realized was used in electric shock torture; beside this were a couple of walkie-talkies, a few guns, a vase, and a mirror in which he saw himself framed. He realized he'd fallen into the hands of the special operations team and thought he was finished, but when he came eye to eye with Z Demirkol, he relaxed: a murderer, to be sure, but a familiar face at least.

Z Demirkol was playing good cop. He told Ka how sorry he was that they'd had to bring him in like this. Ka guessed that Uncle Mahmut was playing bad cop, so he decided to give his full attention to Z Demirkol and his questions.

"What is Sunay planning?"

Ka sweetly surrendered every scrap of information he had, including all there was to know about Kyd's *Spanish Tragedy*.

"Why did they release that crackpot Blue?"

Ka explained that they'd let him go in exchange for Kadife's promise to bare her head on live television. In a moment of inspiration, he used a pedantic chess term: Maybe this was an overambitious "sacrifice" in need of an exclamation mark. But the fact remained that the political Islamists would see this as a demoralizing move.

"How likely is it that the girl will keep her word?"

Ka said that Kadife had agreed to go onstage, but no one was sure whether she would go through with the unveiling.

"Where is Blue's new hiding place?" asked Z Demirkol.

Ka said he had no idea.

They asked why Ka had had no bodyguards when they'd picked him up. Where was he coming from?

"I was taking an evening stroll," said Ka. When he stuck to this answer, Z Demirkol did just what Ka expected; he left the room, leaving Uncle Mahmut to sit down across from Ka with an evil glare. Like the man in the front of the car, he had a large repertoire of exotic curses that he used to adorn his every thought. It didn't matter what he was saying; he could be making a threat or pontificating about national interests or expounding his highly unoriginal political views. He was like a child who can't eat his supper unless it's swimming in ketchup.

"What do you think you achieve by concealing the whereabouts of an Islamist terrorist with blood on his hands who is in the pay of Iran?" asked Uncle Mahmut. "You know what these people will do when they come to power, don't you? What they have planned for oatmeal-hearted pseudo-European liberals like you?" Ka was quick to confirm that he did know, but Uncle Mahmut was not deterred from describing vividly and at length what the Iranian mullahs had done to their former democratic and Communist allies; they stuck dynamite up their asses and blew them sky-high, lined up all the prostitutes and homosexuals and gunned them down, and banned all nonreligious books. When they got their hands on intellectual poseurs like Ka, they immediately shaved their heads, and as for their ludicrous books of poetry . . . As he launched into another well-rehearsed string of unsavory epithets, by now looking very bored, he paused to ask again where Blue was hiding, and where Ka had been that night before they'd picked him up. When Ka offered the same bland answers, Uncle Mahmut, looking bored again, slapped on the handcuffs. "Watch what I do to you now," he said, launching into a perfunctory beating: a few aimless slaps around the head, a few zestless punches.

Reviewing Ka's notes after the fact, I was able to identify five reasons why he did not find this beating unbearable; I hope my readers won't judge me too harshly if I list them here.

1. Ka believed happiness to be comprised of good and evil in equal measures and so could readily see the beating as the suffering he was due for the right to take İpek back to Frankfurt.
2. Ka belonged to the ruling elite, and this, he guessed, afforded him a degree of protection; this special operations team surely had one standard for his like and quite another for the miserable guilty hordes of Kars; and so, not wishing to leave too many traces of their frustration upon him, they would take care to beat him with restraint and certainly wouldn't subject him to serious torture.
3. He thought, rightly, that the beating would only heighten İpek's affection for him.

4. During his visit to police headquarters two days earlier, the look on Muhtar's bloody face was that of a man so guilt-ridden over his country's wretchedness that he could see in all fairness he had a beating coming to him. Infected by this attitude, Ka now stupidly hoped that a good beating would cleanse his own guilt too.

5. Whatever the discomforts of the beating, they could scarcely equal the pride of being a real political prisoner, standing up to his tormentors, and refusing to divulge the whereabouts of a man in hiding.

This last pleasure would have meant far more to him twenty years earlier, but it now seemed somewhat dated and Ka could not help feeling a bit embarrassed. The salty taste of blood gushing from his nose took him back to his childhood. When was the last time he had a bloody nose? As Uncle Mahmut and the others turned their attentions to the television, leaving him to languish in a half-lit corner of the room, Ka thought back to the windows that had snapped shut in his face, and all the footballs that had bounced against his nose, and then he remembered the blows to his nose in a scuffle during his military service. As Z Demirkol and his friends tuned in to that night's episode of *Marianna*, Ka, cradling his bloody nose and his swollen head, was perfectly content to sit like a child in the corner. It occurred to him that they might search him and find Blue's note. A new wave of guilt washed over him as he silently watched *Marianna* with his captors and mused that Turgut Bey and his daughters were at the hotel watching the same program.

During a commercial break, Z Demirkol rose to his feet, picked up the magneto on the table, and asked Ka if he knew what it was for; when Ka said nothing, he answered the question himself, and then, like a father menacingly brandishing a belt, he waited in silence.

"Do you want me to tell you why I love Marianna?" he said, when the soap opera resumed. "Because she knows what she wants. But intellectuals like you, you never have the faintest idea, and that makes me sick. You say you want democracy, and then you enter into alliances with Islamist fundamentalists. You say you want human rights, and then you make deals with terrorist murderers. You say Europe is the answer, but you go around buttering up Islamists who hate everything Europe stands for. You say feminism, and then you help these men wrap their women's heads. You don't follow your own conscience; you just guess what a

European would do in the same situation and act accordingly. But you can't even be a proper European! Do you know what a European would do here? Let's just imagine that your Hans Hansen printed that idiotic statement, and let's say Europe took it seriously and sent a delegation to Kars; the first thing that delegation would do would be to congratulate the army on refusing to surrender the country to the political Islamists. But of course the moment those faggots got back to their Europe they'd start complaining about how there was no democracy in Kars. As for people like you, you love to trash the army even while you depend on it to keep the Islamists from cutting you up into little pieces. But you know all this already. That's why I'm not going to torture you."

Ka took this to signify that "good cop" was back in charge: He hoped this meant his release was near and he'd be able to catch the end of *Marianna* with Turgut Bey and his daughters.

"Before we let you go back to your lover at the hotel, we'd like to disabuse you of a few illusions; we'd like you to know a thing or two about that terrorist you've been making deals with—that murderer whose life you've just saved," said Z Demirkol. "But first get this into your head: You were never in this office. We'll be out of here within an hour. Our new operations center is the top floor of the religious high school. We'll wait for you there. So should you suddenly remember where Blue is hiding, or where you went on your 'evening stroll,' you'll know where to find us.

"You're already aware that this handsome hero with the midnight-blue eyes is wanted for the barbarous murder of a birdbrained television host who stuck out his tongue at the Prophet Muhammad, and that he was also behind the assassination of the director of the Institute of Education. As we all know, you had the pleasure of witnessing this brutal killing firsthand, and you know the rest of it too; you heard it all from Sunay while he was still in his right mind. But there's something else that the diligent agents of MİT have been able to document in some detail. Maybe no one wanted to break your heart by mentioning it, but we think it would be good for you to know."

We have now arrived at the point to which Ka would return again and again over the remaining four years of his life, like a sentimental projectionist who vainly expects a different ending each time he screens the same sad film.

"This İpek Hanım with whom you hope to return to Frankfurt to live happily ever after—she was, once upon a time, Blue's mistress," Z Demirkol said, in a soft voice. "According to the file I have before me, their relationship dates back four years. At the time, İpek Hanım was still married to Muhtar Bey—who as you know is no longer running for mayor, having withdrawn from the race of his own free will just the other day. It seems that this half-witted old leftist—pardon the expression—poet welcomed Blue into his home as an honored guest; of course he was hoping Blue would help him organize the city's Islamist youth, but don't you think it's a shame no one ever told him what a passionate relationship the firebrand was enjoying with his wife while he himself was sitting in his appliance store trying to sell electric stoves?"

This is a prepared speech; he's lying, Ka thought.

"The first person to become aware of the illicit affair—not counting the surveillance staff, of course—was Kadife Hanım. By now İpek Hanım's marital relations were troubled, and so when her sister came home to attend university, she used this as an excuse to move. Blue was still visiting Kars at every opportunity to 'organize Islamist youth,' and naturally he would always stay with his great admirer, Muhtar, so whenever Kadife had classes the two wild-eyed lovers conducted their assignation in the new house. This continued until Turgut Bey came back to Kars, at which point he and his two daughters took up residence in the Snow Palace Hotel. That was when Kadife, the leader of the head-scarf girls, took up her older sister's game. Our blue-eyed Casanova managed to keep both women on a string for some time after that. We have the proof."

With every ounce of his strength, Ka escaped Z Demirkol's gaze, turning his now streaming eyes to the tremulous snow-covered streetlamps of Atatürk Avenue—they were visible from where he was sitting, but he hadn't noticed them until now.

"I'm telling you this only because I want you to see that a heart of oatmeal gets you nowhere and you have no reason to conceal the whereabouts of this murderous monster," said Z Demirkol, who, like all special-team operatives, grew more vituperative the more he talked. "I didn't bring you here to upset you. It occurs to me that when you've left this room, you might be tempted to doubt whether what I've just told you has in fact been fully documented by the surveillance teams who have been bugging the city quite ably for going on forty years; perhaps I just made up a lot of nonsense. Maybe İpek Hanım in her determination to protect your Frankfurt happiness from being darkened by any stain will manage to convince you it's all lies. Your heart is stuffed with oatmeal and may not be strong enough to accept what I'm telling you, but allow me to

chase away any doubt you might have as to its truth. I shall, with your permission, read out a few excerpts of some phone conversations. As I do,
please bear in mind the expense lavished on this long surveillance operation and the time it must have taken the poor secretaries to type up the
transcript.

" 'My darling, my dearest, the days I spend without you I'm hardly
alive!' That, for example, is what İpek Hanım said on a hot summer's day
four years ago—August sixteenth, to be precise—and this probably
alluded to one of their first separations. Two months later, when Blue was
in town to speak at a conference on Islam and the Private Sphere of
Women, he rang her from grocery stores and teahouses all over the
city—eight times in all—and they talked of nothing but how much they
loved each other. Two months after that, when İpek Hanım was still
entertaining the idea of running off with him, she said, and I quote,
'Everyone has only one true love in life, and you are that love in mine.'
Another time, out of jealousy over Merzuka, the wife he kept in Istanbul,
she made clear to Blue that she wouldn't make love to him while her
father was under the same roof. And here's the kicker: In the past two
days alone, she's phoned him three times; she may have made more calls
today. We don't yet have the transcripts of these last conversations, but
that doesn't matter; when you see İpek Hanım, you can ask her yourself.

"I'm so sorry to upset you; I can see I've said enough. Please stop
crying. Let me ask my friends to remove those handcuffs so you can wash
your face. And then, if you want, my associates will take you back to the
hotel."

———•◦•———

CHAPTER THIRTY-NINE

The Joy of Crying Together

KA AND İPEK MEET AT THE HOTEL

K a declined the escort. After wiping the blood from his nose and mouth, he splashed some water over his face and, turning to the murderous villains who'd been holding him captive, bade them good evening, as timid as an uninvited guest who'd nevertheless stayed for supper. Like a common drunk he staggered down the ill-lit Atatürk Avenue, turning for no particular reason into Halitpaşa Avenue; and it was when he passed the little shop where, during one of his first walks through the city, he'd heard Peppino di Capri singing "Roberta" that he began to sob. It was here too that he ran into the slim and handsome villager who'd been his traveling companion three days earlier on the bus from Erzurum to Kars, and who'd been so gracious and uncomplaining when Ka fell asleep, allowing Ka's head to fall onto his shoulder. It seemed all the rest of Kars was inside watching *Marianna,* but as Ka continued down Halitpaşa, he also ran into the lawyer Muzaffer Bey and later, turning into Kâzım Karabekir Avenue, the bus company manager and his elderly friend, both of whom he'd first met in the lodge of His Excellency Sheikh Saadettin. He could tell from the looks these men gave him that tears were still streaming from his eyes. All those times he'd walked up and down these streets, past icy shop windows, teeming teahouses, photography shops exhibiting pictures of Kars in better days, flickering streetlamps, the great wheels of cheese in the windows of grocery stores, he knew—even if he didn't see them on the corner of Kâzım Karabekir and Karadağ avenues—that his plainclothes shadows were there.

Before entering the hotel, he paused to assure the bodyguards everything was on track and did his best to steal up to his room without being noticed. There, he threw himself onto the bed and immediately broke down. When he had managed to calm himself, he settled in to wait, and though it was only one or two minutes before there was a knock on the door, it seemed longer than any time he'd ever passed, waiting as a child, lying in bed, listening to the sounds of the streets.

It was İpek. The boy at reception had told her something strange seemed to have happened to Ka Bey, and she came straight up. When she saw Ka's face she gasped and fell silent. Neither spoke for some time.

"I've found out about your relationship with Blue," Ka finally whispered.

"Did he tell you himself?"

Ka turned off the lamp. "Z Demirkol and his friends hauled me in," he said, still very softly. "They've been taping your phone conversations for four years." He lay down again, weeping silently. "I want to die," he said.

When İpek reached out to run her fingers through his hair, he cried even harder. Despite the loss they were suffering, they'd both relaxed—as people do when they realize they've run out of chances for happiness. İpek stretched out on the bed and wrapped her arms around him. For a while they cried together, and this drew them closer.

As they lay together in the dark, İpek told her story. She said it was all Muhtar's fault; not only had her husband invited Blue into his home; he also wanted his Islamist hero to marvel at what a wondrous creature his wife was. Muhtar was treating İpek very badly at the time and blaming her for their childlessness. And as Ka knew only too well, Blue had a way with words and so knew just how to turn the head of an unhappy woman. No sooner had she succumbed than she found herself frantic to forestall disaster. Her first concern was to keep Muhtar in the dark; she still cared for him and didn't want to hurt him. But when the love affair started to flicker out, her main worry was how to extricate herself.

In the beginning, the thing that made Blue so attractive was his superiority to Muhtar: Muhtar made a fool of himself, talking so ignorantly about political matters that İpek would feel ashamed for him. And even after she and Blue had found each other, poor Muhtar was still praising him, always urging him to visit Kars more often and chiding İpek for not treating him with more hospitality and tolerance. Even when she moved to the new house to live with Kadife, Muhtar had no clue; unless Z Demirkol and his friends set him straight, he would never know.

Sharp-eyed Kadife, on the other hand, had worked it all out by the end of her first day in the city; her only real motivation for associating with the head-scarf girls was to get closer to Blue. İpek, who'd been living with Kadife's jealousy since childhood, was not blind to her interest in Blue; it was only on seeing the fickle Blue returning Kadife's affection that İpek's own feelings cooled. And she saw opportunities: If Kadife was to become involved with him, İpek would be free of him; and once her father moved to Kars too, she was able to keep her faithless lover at bay.

This account effectively reduced the affair with Blue to a mistake already buried in the past, and Ka might have been inclined to believe her had she not quite suddenly succumbed to some childish impulse and blurted out, "The truth is, Blue doesn't really love Kadife, he loves me!"

It was not what Ka wanted to hear, so he asked what İpek now thought about this "filthy man"; refusing to be drawn into this subject, she reiterated that it was all in the past, and her only wish now was to go with Ka to Frankfurt. This was when Ka brought up Z Demirkol's final claim, that she'd been in contact with Blue by phone in just the last few days. İpek insisted there'd been no such conversations, and anyway Blue was too savvy to take a call that might allow his hunters to track his whereabouts.

"We're never going to be happy!" Ka said.

"No, we're going to Frankfurt, and we *are* going to be happy!" said İpek, throwing her arms around him. According to İpek, Ka believed her for a moment, and then tears returned to his eyes.

She held him tighter and tighter, and they cried again.

As Ka would later write, it may have been now, as they were holding each other and weeping, that İpek discovered something for the first time: To live in indecision, to waver between defeat and a new life, offered as much pleasure as pain. The ease with which they could hold each other and cry this way made Ka love her all the more, but even in the bitter contentment of this tearful embrace a part of him was already calculating his next move and remained alert to the sounds from the street.

It was almost six o'clock. Tomorrow's edition of the *Border City Gazette* was ready for circulation; the snowplows were going at a furious pace to clear the road to Sarıkamış; Funda Eser, having worked her charms and spirited Kadife into the army truck, was at the National Theater, where the two women were rehearsing the play with Sunay.

It took Ka half an hour to get around to telling İpek of the message he was carrying from Blue to Kadife. Throughout this time of holding each other and crying, they'd come close to making love, but fear, indecision, and jealousy intervened to hold him back. Instead, Ka asked when İpek had last seen Blue; over and over he accused her of speaking to him every day; and then compulsion overtook him and he accused her of seeing him every day as well, of still being his lover.

Ka would later recall that while İpek initially balked at his questions and accusations, angry at his refusal to believe her, later, when she came to see that the emotional undercurrents were more powerful than the words themselves, she began to answer him with more affection, and soon she herself would find the affectionate rejoinder soothing; there was even a part of her that embraced the hurt Ka's questions and accusations were causing her. During his last four years, which he dedicated to remorse and regret, Ka would admit to himself that those given to verbal abuse are often obsessed by a need to know how much their lovers loved them—it had been that way with him throughout his life. Even as he taunted her in his broken voice that she wanted Blue, that she loved him more, his concern was to see not so much how İpek answered him as how much patience she would expend for his sake.

"You're only trying to punish me for having had a relationship with him!" said İpek.

"You only want me because you're trying to forget him!" said Ka. Looking into her face, he saw with horror that he'd spoken the truth, but this time he did not lose his composure. His outburst had renewed his strength. "Blue has sent Kadife a message from his hiding place," he said. "He now says he wants Kadife to continue with her work: She must refuse to go onstage and bare her head. He's quite adamant."

"Let's not tell Kadife any of this," said İpek.

"Why not?"

"Because that way we'll have Sunay's protection all the way through. And it's best for Kadife too. I want to put some space between Blue and my sister."

Ka said, "You mean you want to break them up." He could see from İpek's eyes that she had ceased to humor his jealousy and he had fallen in her estimation, but he couldn't stop himself.

"I broke off with Blue a very long time ago."

Still unconvinced by İpek's protestations, Ka held back this time and decided not to speak his mind. But not a moment later he found himself staring sternly out the window and telling her exactly what he was thinking. Anger and jealousy now ruled him, and seeing this only inflamed his misery. With tears in his eyes, he waited to hear what İpek would say next.

"I was very much in love with him," İpek said. "But that's mostly in the past now, and I think I'm over it. I want to come with you to Frankfurt."

"Just how much did you love him?"

"A lot," said İpek, and settled into a determined silence.

"I want you to tell me how much." Although he had lost his cool, Ka sensed that İpek was wavering. She wanted to tell the truth, but she also wanted to assuage his pain by sharing it; she wanted to punish Ka as he deserved, but at the same time she was sad to see him suffer.

"I loved him more than I'd ever loved anyone before," İpek said finally, averting her eyes.

"Maybe that's because the only other man you'd been with was your husband, Muhtar."

He regretted these words even as he said them, not only because they were hurtful but because he knew İpek would say something even more hurtful in reply.

"It's true," she said. "Like most Turkish girls, I've not had much opportunity to get to know a lot of men. You probably met quite a few independent women in Europe. I'm not going to ask you about any of them, but surely they taught you that new lovers wipe out old ones."

"I'm a Turk," said Ka.

"Most of the time, being a Turk is either an excuse or a pretext for evil."

"That's why I'm going back to Frankfurt," Ka said listlessly.

"I'm coming with you and we're going to be happy there."

"You want to come to Frankfurt because you hope you can forget him there."

"If we go to Frankfurt together it won't be long, I'm sure, before I love you. I'm not like you; it takes me longer than two days to fall in love with someone. If you're patient, if you don't break my heart with your Turkish jealousies, I'll love you deeply."

"But right now you don't love me," said Ka. "You're still in love with Blue. What is it about this man that makes him so special?"

"I'm glad you've asked, and I believe you really do want to know, but I'm worried about how you'll take my answer."

"Don't be afraid," said Ka, again without conviction. "I love you with all my heart."

"First, let me say that the only man I could ever live with is the man who could listen to what I am about to say and still find it in him to love me." İpek paused for a moment; she turned her eyes away from Ka to gaze at the snow-covered street. "He's very compassionate, Blue, very thoughtful and generous." Her voice was warm with love. "He doesn't want anyone to suffer. He cried all night once, just because two little puppies had lost their mother. Believe me, he's not like anyone else."

"Isn't he a murderer?" Ka asked hopelessly.

"Even someone who knows only a tenth of what I know about him will tell you what stupid nonsense that is. He couldn't kill anyone. He's a child. Like a child, he enjoys playing games and getting lost in his daydreams and mimicking people; he loves telling stories from the Shehname and Mesnevi—behind that mask, he's a very interesting person. He's very strong-willed and decisive; in fact, he's so strong, and so much fun— Oh, I'm sorry, darling, don't cry, please; you've cried enough."

Ka stopped crying for a moment, long enough to tell İpek that he no longer believed they'd be able to go to Frankfurt together. There followed a long eerie silence, punctuated only by Ka's sobs. He lay down on the bed, his back to the window, and curled up like a child. After a time, İpek lay down next to him, her arms around his back.

Ka wanted to say, Leave me alone. Instead he whispered, "Hold me tighter."

His tears had made the pillow wet: He liked the way it felt against his cheek. He liked İpek's arms around him. He fell asleep.

When they woke up it was seven o'clock. At that moment they both felt that happiness was still within reach, but, unable to look each other in the face, they were both searching for an excuse to get away.

Ka began to speak, but İpek said, "Forget it, darling, just forget it."

For a moment he couldn't work out what she was trying to tell him. Was it all hopeless, or did she know they'd be able to put the past behind them?

He thought İpek was leaving. He knew very well that if he returned to Frankfurt alone there would be no more solace even in his melancholy old daily routines.

"Don't go yet. Let's sit here a little longer."

After a strange, discomfiting silence, they embraced once again.

"Oh, my God!" cried Ka. "My God, what's to become of us?"

"Everything will turn out fine," said İpek. "Please believe me. Trust me. Come, let me show you the things I'm packing for Frankfurt."

Ka was relieved just to get out of the room. He held İpek's hand as they walked downstairs. When they reached Turgut Bey's office, he let it go, but still he noticed that people in the lobby saw them as a couple, and that pleased him. In her room, İpek opened a drawer and took out the ice-blue sweater she'd never been able to wear in Kars; after unfolding it and shaking out the mothballs she stood in front of the mirror, holding it up to her chest.

"Put it on," said Ka.

İpek pulled off her thick woolen pullover and exchanged it for the ice-blue garment; it was very tight and as she fitted it over her blouse Ka was once again overcome by her beauty.

"Will you love me for the rest of your life?" Ka asked.

"Yes."

"Now put on the dress that Muhtar would let you wear only at home."

İpek opened the wardrobe and took the black velvet dress off its hanger; unfastening it with great care, she prepared to put it on.

"I like it when you look at me like that," she said, as their eyes met in the mirror.

He gazed at her long beautiful back, at the tender spot just below the hairline, and, farther down, at the shadow of her backbone and the dimples that formed on her shoulders as she gathered up her hair to pose for him. Overwhelming pleasure, and jealousy too. He felt happy—and very evil.

"Oooh, what's with this dress?" said Turgut Bey, as he walked into the room. "So tell me, where's the ball?" But his face was joyless. Ka took it for paternal jealousy, and that made him feel good.

"Since Kadife left for the theater, the television announcements have become much more aggressive," said Turgut Bey. "If she appears in this play, she'll be making a big mistake."

"Daddy dearest, can you please explain to me why we should be against Kadife baring her head?"

They entered the sitting room to stand in front of the television set that had been on all the time. An announcer soon appeared, proclaiming that with this evening's live performance, there would come an end to the tragedy that had visited social and spiritual paralysis upon the nation, and that the people of Kars would be delivered at last from the religious prejudices that had too long excluded them from modern life and prevented women from enjoying equality with men. Once again, Life and Art were to merge in a bewitching historical tale of unparalleled beauty. But this time the people of Kars had no reason to fear for their safety, because the central police station and the Martial Law Command had taken every conceivable precaution. Admission was free. Then Kasım Bey, the assistant police chief, appeared on the screen; it was immediately clear that his part had been taped earlier. His hair, so disheveled on the night of the revolution, was now combed, his shirt was ironed, and his tie knotted neatly in place. After assuring the people of Kars to have no qualms about attending that evening's great artistic event, he announced that a large number of religious high school students had already reported to the central police station to promise decorous attendance and warm applause in all the appropriate places, just as one did in Europe and other parts of the civilized world. Furthermore, he admonished, this time no rowdiness would be tolerated; no one would get away with shouting or hissing or making coarse comments of any sort, which should only be too clear to the people of Kars, who issued from a civilization that had been prospering for a thousand years, after all, and so knew exactly how to behave at the theater—and with that he vanished.

The announcer returned to the screen to discuss that evening's fare, explaining how the lead actor, Sunay Zaim, had been waiting many years to do this piece. There followed a montage of wrinkled posters from the Jacobin plays in which, so many years ago, Sunay had played Napoleon, Robespierre, and Lenin; several black-and-white head shots of the cast (how thin Funda Eser had been in those days!); and a variety of theatrical mementos that Ka imagined to be just the sort of detritus a traveling theatrical couple might be carting around with them in a suitcase (old tickets and programs, clippings from the days Sunay aspired to play Atatürk, tragic scenes staged in sundry Anatolian coffeehouses). Annoying though this promotional montage was, it was reassuring to see Sunay on screen every other moment, and in one shot, apparently very recent, he had an air of such ravaged determination as to appear every inch the dictator, whether from Africa, the Middle East, or the Soviet bloc. Having by now watched a full day of this footage, the people of Kars were coming to believe that Sunay had indeed brought peace to their city; he was one of them now, a bona fide citizen, and they were secretly beginning to nurture hopes for their future. Eighty years earlier, when the Ottoman and Russian armies had abandoned the city, leaving the Turks and the Armenians to massacre each other, the Turks had somehow devised a brand-new flag to announce the birth of a nation: Seeing this same standard now, now stained and moth-eaten but defiantly displayed on the screen, Turgut Bey decided that something terrible was about to happen.

"This man is crazy. He's heading for disaster, and he wants to take us too. On no account should Kadife go onstage."

"You're right, she shouldn't," said İpek. "But if we tell her you're the one who's forbidding it—well, you know what Kadife's like, Father. She'll run straight out there and uncover her head just to be obstinate."

"What can we do, then?"

"Why not let Ka go straight to the theater and talk her out of it?" said İpek, turning around to look at him with her eyebrows raised expectantly.

Ka, who had been gazing for the longest while not at the TV but at her, could not fathom what had led to this abrupt change of heart about their scheme, and his puzzlement made him very nervous.

"If she wants to bare her head, it's better for her to do it at home, after all this is over," said Turgut Bey to Ka. "It's clear that Sunay has planned another unspeakable outrage for this evening's performance. I feel like a fool, having fallen for Funda's assurances and let my girl go off with those lunatics."

"Ka can talk her out of it, Father."

"Yes," Turgut said to Ka, "right now you are the only person who could reason with her, and Sunay trusts you. What happened to your nose, my lamb?"

"I fell on the ice," Ka said guiltily.

"You fell on your forehead too, I see?"

"Ka's been walking around the city all day," said İpek.

"Take Kadife aside when Sunay isn't watching," said Turgut Bey. "Don't let on that it was our idea, and make sure she says nothing to Sunay suggesting it was yours. She shouldn't even discuss it with him— better to offer some perfectly plausible excuse, like 'I'm feeling rather ill,' and maybe add, 'I'll bare my head tomorrow at home.' Yes, she should promise to do that. And please, tell Kadife how much we all love her. My child!" Tears welled in Turgut Bey's eyes.

"Father, may I speak to Ka alone for a moment?" said İpek. She took Ka over to the dining table and sat him down. Zahide had set the places but not yet served the food.

"Tell Kadife that Blue is in a quandary. Say he's in trouble or he wouldn't have her do something like this."

"First tell me why you changed your mind," said Ka.

"Oh, my darling, there's nothing to be jealous about, please believe me. It's just that I realized my father is right, that's all. Right now the most important thing is to keep Kadife from this catastrophe."

"No," said Ka, choosing his words carefully. "Something's happened to make you change your mind."

"Not true. If Kadife must bare her head, she can do it later, at home."

"If Kadife doesn't bare her head this evening," said Ka cautiously, "she'll never do it in front of her father. You know this as well as I do. What are you hiding from me?"

"Darling, there's nothing. I love you very much. If you want me, I'll go back to Frankfurt with you. And once we've been there awhile and you see how surely I am bound to you, how much I love you, you'll put these few days behind you and you'll love and trust me, too."

She put her hand, which was warm and moist, on Ka's. In the mirror over the sideboard was İpek's beautiful reflection; he was speechless at the beauty of her back under the straps of the black velvet dress; he could hardly believe how close he was to those enormous eyes.

"I'm almost certain something terrible's about to happen."

"Why?"

"Because I'm so happy. I can't say how or where they came from, but since coming to Kars I've written eighteen poems. One more and I'll have written an entire volume, or perhaps I should say it will have written itself. I believe what you say about wanting to go back to Frankfurt with me, and I can see an even greater happiness stretching out before us. It just seems dangerous to be this happy. That's how I know something terrible is going to happen."

"Something like what?"

"Like this: I go off to talk to Kadife, and you go off to meet Blue."

"Oh, that's ridiculous," said İpek. "I don't even know where he is."

"It's because I wouldn't tell them where he is that they beat me like this."

"And you'd better not tell anyone else, either! I'm serious!" İpek cried, knitting her brows. "Soon enough you'll see that you have nothing to fear."

"So what's going on? I thought you were going off to talk to Kadife," said Turgut Bey. "The play starts in an hour and fifteen minutes. They've just announced on television that the roads are about to reopen."

"I don't want to go; I don't want to leave the hotel," whispered Ka sheepishly.

"Please understand that we can't leave the city if Kadife's in distress," said İpek, "because if we did, we wouldn't be happy either. The least you can do is go over there; it will make us all feel better."

"An hour and a half ago, when Fazıl brought me the message from Blue," said Ka, "you were telling me not to leave the hotel at all."

"All right. Just tell me what proof you'll accept that I haven't left the hotel while you're at the theater—but quickly; we're running out of time," said İpek.

Ka smiled. "Come upstairs to my room. I'll lock you in, and while I'm gone for a half hour I'll keep the key with me."

"Fine," said İpek cheerfully. She stood up. "Father dear, I'm going up to my room for half an hour. You're not to worry, because Ka is going straight to the theater to talk to Kadife. Please don't get up; we have something to take care of upstairs first and we're in a hurry."

"I'm very grateful," said Turgut Bey to Ka, but he still looked uneasy.

İpek took Ka by the hand, and by that hand she led him through the lobby and pulled him up the stairs.

"Cavit saw us," said Ka. "What do you think he thought?"

"Who cares?" said İpek blithely. In his room, there was a faint lingering scent of their lovemaking from the night before. "I'll wait for you here. Be careful. Don't get drawn into an argument with Sunay."

"So when I ask Kadife not to go onstage, should I say it's because you and her father and I don't want her to, or because Blue doesn't want her to?"

"Because Blue doesn't want her to."

"Why?" asked Ka.

"Because Kadife's in love with Blue, that's why. The reason you're going there is to protect my sister from danger. You have to forget you're jealous of Blue."

"As if I could."

"When we get to Germany, we're going to be very happy," said İpek, her arms around Ka's neck. "Tell me about the cinema you'll take me to."

"There's a cinema in the Film Museum that shows undubbed American art films late on Saturday nights," said Ka. "That's where we'll go. We'll stop along the way at one of those restaurants around the station and have *döner* and sweet pickles. After we come home, we can relax in front of the television set. Then we'll make love. We can live on my political exile allowance and the money I'll make doing readings from this new poetry book of mine—and neither of us has to do anything more than that: just make love."

İpek asked him what the title of his book was, and Ka told her.

"That's beautiful," she said. "But now you've got to go, darling. If you don't, Father will get so worried he'll decide to go himself."

"I'm not afraid anymore," he told her. This was a lie. "But whatever happens, if there's some sort of mix-up, I'll be waiting for you on the first train that leaves the city."

"If I can get out of this room, that is," İpek said, with a smile.

"Would you wait at this window and watch me until I've disappeared around the corner?"

"Of course."

"I'm so afraid I won't see you again," said Ka.

He closed the door, locked it, and dropped the key into his coat pocket. He wanted to make sure he'd be able to turn around and take one last leisurely look at İpek in the window, so when he reached the street he kept several paces ahead of his two army bodyguards. Sure enough, when he turned around there she was, like a statue, in the window of Room 203 of the Snow Palace Hotel, still wearing the black velvet evening gown, her honeyed shoulders now covered with goose bumps from the cold. Standing there bathed in the orange light of the bedside night-light, she was his image of happiness, an image Ka would hold close to him throughout the last four years of his life.

He never saw her again.

CHAPTER FORTY

It Must Be Hard Being a Double Agent

THE FIRST HALF OF THE CHAPTER

The streets Ka took to the National Theater were mostly empty—here and there he could see a restaurant open for business, but all the other shopowners in town had rolled down their shutters. The last stragglers were leaving the teahouses, exhausted by their long day of drinking tea and smoking cigarettes, but even on the way out, their eyes remained glued to the television. As he approached the National Theater, Ka saw three army vehicles. They all had their lights on, and when Ka looked down the lane he saw the shadow of a tank nestling among the oleanders. The thaw had begun in earnest that evening, and the icicles that had formed on the eaves of houses were dripping water onto the pavements below. Walking under the live transmission cable that stretched across Atatürk Avenue, he entered the theater, and, taking the key from his pocket, pressed it into the palm of his hand.

The theater was empty except for the soldiers and policemen lined up along the aisles, listening to the echoes of the actors rehearsing. Ka settled down into one of the empty seats to enjoy Sunay's deep rich voice and perfect diction, Kadife's weak and wavering answers, and Funda Eser's hectoring direction ("Say it with feeling, darling Kadife!") as she rushed about the stage moving the props, a tree and a vanity table.

While Funda Eser was rehearsing a scene with Kadife, Sunay noticed the ember of Ka's cigarette and came to sit next to him. "These are the happiest moments of my life," he said. He stank of raki but didn't seem at all drunk. "No matter how much we rehearse, everything depends on how we feel when we walk onstage. But it's clear already that Kadife has a talent for improvisation."

"I've brought her a message from her father and also an eye of Fatima for protection," said Ka. "Do you think I could have a word with her in private?"

"We know you've given your bodyguards the slip. I hear the snow is melting and the trains are about to run again. But before any of this happens, we're determined to put on our play," Sunay said. "Has Blue hidden himself well for once?" he added, with a smile.

"I don't know."

Sunay stood up and called Kadife over; then he returned to the rehearsal. The spotlight came on, and as he looked at the three figures framed onstage, Ka could sense their deep affinity for one other. Looking at Kadife, at the scarf still draped around her head, he was alarmed at the ease with which she now negotiated the intimate world of the stage. And if she was to bare her head, Ka thought, what a shame that she would still be wearing one of those ugly raincoats favored by all covered women; how much closer to her he would have felt if like her sister she'd been wearing a skirt and showing off those long legs of hers. But when she left the stage to sit with him, there was a moment when he understood why Blue had left İpek and fallen in love with Kadife instead.

"Kadife, I've seen Blue. They released him and he's found himself a hiding place. But he doesn't want you to go onstage and bare your head tonight. He sent you a letter."

Lest Sunay should see him, he passed her the letter under his arm, as one might pass the answers to a friend during an exam, but Kadife made no effort at concealment; she read the letter openly and smiled, so it was some time before Ka saw the tears in her angry eyes.

"Your father thinks the same thing, Kadife. You might be right in deciding to bare your head, but it would be insane to do it this evening, in front of all those angry religious high school boys. There's no need for you to stay. You can tell them you're ill."

"I don't need an excuse. Sunay's already told me I'm free to go home if I wish."

It was clear to Ka that he was not dealing with some young girl upset at failing in her last-minute bid for permission to appear in the school play; the anger and heartbreak he read in her face were far too deep.

"So are you planning to stay here, Kadife?"

"Yes. I'm staying here and I'm doing the play."

"Do you know how much this will upset your father?"

"Give me the evil eye he sent me."

"I just mentioned an evil eye so they'd let me speak to you privately."

"It must be hard being a double agent."

He could tell Kadife was heartbroken, and it was with some pain that he realized the girl's mind was far away. He wanted to take her by the shoulders and embrace her, but he did nothing of the sort.

"İpek has told me about her old relationship with Blue," Ka said.

Kadife took out a pack of cigarettes, slowly raised a cigarette to her lips, and lit it.

"I gave him the cigarettes and the lighter you sent with me," Ka said clumsily. For a few moments, neither spoke. "Are you doing this because you're so in love with Blue? What is it about him that makes you love him so much, Kadife? Tell me, please."

When Ka saw that he was digging himself into a hole, he fell silent.

Funda Eser called from the stage to announce that they'd come to Kadife's next scene.

She gave Ka a tearful look and stood up. At the last moment, they embraced each other. Still feeling her presence, still smelling her scent, Ka lingered for a while to watch the play, but his mind was elsewhere; he did not understand a thing. He could no longer trust his instincts; he was missing something. Jealousy and remorse were defeating his every effort to think logically. He could barely manage to identify what was causing him such pain; what he couldn't fathom was why this pain was so destructive, so violent.

Looking ahead to those years he hoped to spend with İpek in Frankfurt—assuming he succeeded in getting her to go with him—he could now see that this crushing, soul-destroying pain would eat away at their happiness. And as he thought this he lit a cigarette, his mind stubbornly refusing to make order of things. He went off to the toilet where he'd met with Necip two days earlier and walked into the same stall. Opening the window high on the wall, he looked out at the black night and stood there, puffing helplessly.

At his first intimation that another poem was on the way, he could hardly believe it. Holding his breath, he pulled out his notebook to jot it down. He hoped the poem had been sent to console him, to give him hope. But when it was done, he still felt crushing pain throughout his body, so he left the National Theater in distress.

When he reached the snowy pavement, he decided the cold air would do him good. His two army bodyguards were still with him, and his mind was in total disarray. At this point, to enhance the enjoyment of my story and make it easier to understand, I must cut short this chapter and start a new one. It doesn't mean that Ka did nothing more worth narrating but, rather, that I must first locate "The Place Where the World Ends," the poem Ka jotted down with so little effort, which would be the last in the book he would entitle *Snow*.

CHAPTER FORTY-ONE

Everyone Has His Own Snowflake

THE MISSING GREEN NOTEBOOK

"The Place Where the World Ends," the nineteenth poem Ka wrote in Kars, was also his last. As we already know, he recorded eighteen of his poems in the green notebook he carried everywhere he went; he wrote them down just as he first "heard" them, even if a few words here and there were missing. The only poem he did not write down was the one he read onstage the night of the revolution. Ka alluded to it in two of his letters from Frankfurt, written but never sent to İpek. In both instances he called it "The Place Where God Does Not Exist" and as he'd been unable to get it out of his mind, he said there was no finishing his new collection until he'd found it; he would be grateful if İpek could search the Border City Television archives on his behalf. When I first read this letter in my hotel room in Frankfurt, I sensed a certain disquiet between the lines. It was almost as if Ka was worried that İpek would think he was using the problem of the poem as an excuse to write her love letters.

In the twenty-ninth chapter, I described how, on returning to my hotel room in Frankfurt one evening, feeling pleasantly tipsy and still holding the Melinda tapes in my hand, I happened on Ka's diagram of a snowflake in a notebook picked at random. While I can't possibly know Ka's exact intent, I can say that I spent a few days reading through all the notebooks, and I believed I was beginning to grasp Ka's purpose in giving each of his nineteen Kars poems a position on this snowflake.

After leaving Kars, Ka apparently read a number of books about snow, and one of his discoveries was this: Once a six-pronged snowflake crystallizes, it takes between eight and ten minutes for it to fall through the sky, lose its original shape, and vanish; when, with further inquiry, he discovered that the form of each snowflake is determined by the temperature, the direction and strength of the wind, the altitude of the cloud, and any number of other mysterious forces, Ka decided that snowflakes have much in common with people. It was a snowflake that inspired "I, Ka," the poem he wrote sitting in the Kars public library, and later, when he was to arrange all nineteen titles for his new collection, *Snow,* he would assign "I, Ka" to the center point of that same snowflake.

Applying the same logic to "Heaven," "Chess," and "The Chocolate Box" he was able to see that each of these poems, too, had its natural and unique position on the imaginary snowflake. Soon he was certain that every poem in his new collection—and, indeed, everything that made him the man he was—could be indicated on the same set of crystalline axes. It was, in short, a snowflake that mapped out the spiritual course of every person who had ever lived. The three axes onto which he mapped his poems—Memory, Imagination, and Reason—were, he said, inspired by the classifications in Bacon's tree of knowledge, but he wrote extensively about his own efforts to elucidate the meaning of the six-pronged snowflake's nineteen points.

Ka's three notebooks recording his thoughts about the poems he wrote in Kars are, for the most part, attempts to discover the significance of that geometry, but it should be clear by now that he was also trying to puzzle out the meaning of his own life, and we should take care to see these objectives in the same light. For example, to read his musings on where to place the poem "To Be Shot and Killed" is to be struck by the priority he gives to the fear that inspired the poem. He explains why it is that a poem inspired by fear belongs near the axis labeled Imagination, at the top of the axis labeled Memory, and near enough the poem entitled "The Place Where the World Ends" to be under its influence. Lurking throughout these commentaries is the belief that his poetic materials were shaped by mysterious external forces. And by the time he was recording these thoughts in the notebooks, Ka was convinced that everyone has his own snowflake; individual existences might look identical from afar, but to understand one's own eternally mysterious uniqueness one had only to plot the mysteries of his or her own snowflake.

Ka's exegesis of his new poetry collection and of his personal snowflake was vast (Why was it that "The Chocolate Box" was located on the axis labeled Imagination? How had the poem called "All Humanity and the Stars" shaped Ka's own snowflake?), but we shall not dwell on these notes any longer than our novel requires. As a young poet, Ka had many unkind things to say about older peers who took themselves too seriously, especially those poets who spent their later years convinced that every bit of nonsense they produced would one day inform serious literary debate and who carved their own statues, oblivious of the fact that no one wanted to look at them.

In the harsh light of many years spent criticizing poets of obscure verse, in thrall to the myths of modernism, there are but one or two excuses for Ka's extensive self-commentary. A careful reading reveals that Ka did not believe himself to be the true author of any of the poems that came to him in Kars. Rather, he believed himself to be but the medium, the amanuensis, in a manner well exampled by predecessors of his modernist bêtes noires. But as he wrote in several places, having produced the poems, he was now determined to throw off his passivity, and it was by coming to understand them—by revealing their hidden symmetry—that he hoped to achieve this purpose. But there was a more practical urgency as well: Without understanding what his Kars poems meant, he could have no hope of filling in the blanks, of completing the half-finished lines—or of recovering his lost poem, "The Place Where God Does Not Exist"—and thus no hope of completing the book. For after Ka returned to Frankfurt, no poem ever came to him again.

It's clear from his notes and letters that by the end of his fourth year back in Frankfurt, Ka had managed to divine the hidden logic of his poems and bring the book to its final form. This is why, when I returned to my Frankfurt hotel room with the papers and notebooks and other belongings rescued from his apartment, I sat there until dawn, drinking raki and sifting through the remains: I kept telling myself that his poems had to be among his things. I stayed up all night, poring over his notebooks and inspecting his old pajamas, his Melinda tapes, his ties, his books, his lighters (I realized that one of these was the lighter that Kadife had asked him to pass on to Blue), until finally I drifted off to sleep on a sea of nightmares and yearnings, dreams and visions. (Ka came to me in one frightening dream to say, "You are old.")

It was noon when I awoke to spend the rest of the day roaming the wet and snowy streets of Frankfurt, and although I no longer had Tarkut Ölçün at my side, I did my best to gather as much information on Ka as I could. The two women with whom he had had relations during the eight years before his visit to Kars were happy to speak to me; I told them I was writing my friend's biography. His first lover, Nalan, didn't even know he was a poet, so it was hardly surprising that she knew nothing of his new collection. She was married now and with her husband ran two *döner* shops and a travel agency. After telling me baldly that Ka had been a contentious, peevish man, always quick to take offense, she cried a little. (The thing that grieved her most was having sacrificed her youth to her ideals.)

His second lover, Hildegard, was still single, and I guessed at once that she would know nothing of the contents of his last poems, or indeed of his having completed a collection entitled *Snow*. I may have overstated Ka's fame as a poet in Turkey, and certainly she played upon my sheepishness at having been caught out; in a rather flirtatious manner she told me that after her involvement with Ka she had stopped taking her summer holidays in Turkey. Ka, she said, was a dutiful, clever, lonesome child whose life was dominated by a restless hunger for mothering—he knew he'd never find it, but also that if he did he'd run the other way—so while he was an easy man to love, he was an impossible one to live with. Ka had never spoken to her about me. (I've no idea why I asked her that question or, indeed, why I mention it here again.) After an interview that lasted an hour and a quarter, Hildegard showed me something I had failed to notice: The top segment of the index finger on her beautiful slender-wristed right hand was missing. She added with a smile that once, in a moment of anger, Ka had mocked her for this defect.

Ka had finished writing out his book in longhand and, as usual, refrained from having it typed or copied; instead, just as he had done with his previous books, with manuscript in hand he went on a reading tour, visiting Kassel, Braunschweig, Hannover, Osnabrück, Bremen, and Hamburg. At the invitation of the various city councils, and with the assistance of Tarkut Ölçün, I embarked on my own lightning tour of literary evenings in those same cities. Like Ka, ever the great admirer of Germany's efficient and immaculate trains, I traveled from city to city enjoying the very Protestant comforts Ka had described in one of his poems; as he must have done, I sat by the window peacefully watching the reflections of the grassy plains, the villages with the sweet little churches nestled in the mountain foothills, and the little stations full of children with their bright raincoats and backpacks; the two Turks sent by the association to greet me would listen impassively, with cigarettes hanging from their mouths, as I explained my wish to do exactly as Ka had done on his own tour seven weeks earlier; and so in every city I checked into a cheap little hotel like Ka's and went off with my hosts to a Turkish restaurant where over spinach *börek* and *döner* we discussed politics and agreed what a shame it was that Turks had so little interest in culture; after the meal I would wander through the cold empty city and pretend I was Ka walking the same streets to escape the painful memories of İpek. In the evening, before a gathering of fifteen or twenty people interested in politics, literature, and things Turkish, I would read halfheartedly a page or two of my most recent novel, and then, switching to the subject of poetry, I would announce that I was a close friend of the great poet Ka, who had recently been shot dead on a street in Frankfurt; did anyone remember anything about his last poems, "which he read here only a short time ago?"

Most of those on hand at these literary evenings had skipped Ka's poetry reading, and it was clear that those who had attended had done so for political reasons or simply by chance, judging by the little they could tell me about his poems as compared with the copious notice they had taken of the charcoal-colored coat he had never taken off, his pale complexion, his unkempt hair, and his nervous mannerisms. But even those uninterested in Ka's life and poetry were quick to take interest in his death. I heard quite a few conspiracy theories: He'd been assassinated by Islamists, the Turkish secret service, Armenians, German skinheads, Kurds, and Turkish nationalists. But it also turned out that at every event there had been a few sensitive souls who had paid Ka careful attention. Those keenly interested in literature confirmed that he had indeed just finished a new collection, that he had read several poems from it— "Dream Streets," "Dog," "Chocolate Box," and "Love"—but they were unable to recall anything useful about the individual pieces, apart from their being very difficult. At several events, Ka had mentioned that he'd written the poems in Kars, sometimes implying he meant them as elegies, particularly for those longing for the towns and villages they'd left behind. At the end of one event, a dark-haired woman in her thirties came forward and, after explaining that she was widowed with a child, she told me of having approached Ka in a similar manner after his reading and that they had discussed a poem called "The Place Where God Does Not Exist"; she believed he had read only four lines of this long poem because he didn't want to offend anyone. No matter how hard I tried to draw her out, this careful poetry lover couldn't remember any of the poem's words, only that it described "a terrifying landscape." But having sat in the front row during Ka's Hamburg appearance, she could at least confirm he'd been reading from a green notebook.

That evening I took the same train that Ka had taken from Hamburg to Frankfurt. When I left the station, I took the same route also—walking down the Kaiserstrasse and stopping now and then to wander through a sex shop. (Although it had been only a week since my arrival in Germany, there was already a new Melinda video.) When I arrived at the place where my friend had been shot, I stopped, and this time I acknowledged what I had already accepted unconsciously: that when Ka fell to the ground, his assassin must have made off with the green notebook. Now I could hold but one consoling hope following this futile weeklong hunt across Germany and all the evening hours poring over Ka's notes: Perhaps I might retrieve one poem from the video archives of a television station in Kars.

Back in Istanbul, I found myself tuning in to the state channel's end-of-day news broadcasts, to hear the Kars weather reports and to judge in what sort of climate I might be received. Like Ka, I arrived in Kars in the early evening, after a bus journey lasting a day and a half; bag in hand, I timidly negotiated a room for myself at the Snow Palace Hotel (where there was no sign of the father or his two mysterious daughters). I then went out to explore the city, taking those same snow-covered pavements Ka told of having walked four years before, and while I wouldn't say the compass of my walk equaled his, I did go far enough to discover that the establishment he had known as the Green Pastures Café was now a wretched beer hall. In any event, I shouldn't want my readers to imagine that I was trying to become his posthumous shadow. As Ka had so often suggested to me, I simply did not understand poetry well enough, nor the great sadness from which it issues, and so there had been a wall between us, a wall that now divided me not just from the melancholy city described in his notes but from the impoverished place I was now seeing with my own eyes. There was, of course, one person who nevertheless observed a resemblance between us; it is that person who now binds us together. But let's not talk about that yet.

Whenever I remember the astonishment of first seeing İpek that evening at the dinner the mayor held in my honor, I only wish I could ascribe my addlement to too much raki, that I could say the drink made me lose myself and emboldened me to believe I had a chance, and that there was no other basis for the jealousy I began to feel for my dead friend. Later, at the Snow Palace Hotel, as I stood at my window watching a far less poetic snowfall—a wet snow that melted on contact with the city's muddy pavements—than the one Ka had described, I could not stop wondering how, having read my friend's notebooks so closely for so long,

I had failed to grasp the extent of İpek's beauty. Without quite knowing why, I took out a notebook—just like Ka, you might say, and, indeed, this was an expression I found myself using more and more—and I wrote down those thoughts that could be called the germ of the book you are reading. I remember trying to describe Ka's story, and his love for İpek, as he might have described it himself. In a smoky corner of my mind I was reminded of a truth drawn from bitter experience: Immersing oneself in the problems of a book is a good way to keep from thinking of love.

Contrary to popular opinion, a man can shut love out if he wants to. But to do so, he must free himself not only from the woman who has bewitched him but also from the third person in the story, the ghost who has put temptation in his way. I, however, already had an appointment with İpek the following afternoon at the New Life Pastry Shop, and the express purpose was to discuss Ka.

Or perhaps it was my desire to talk about Ka that allowed me to open up to her. We were the only customers in the shop; on that same black-and-white television in the corner, two lovers were to be seen embracing near the Bosphorus Bridge. İpek confessed at the outset that she could talk about Ka only with the greatest difficulty. She could describe her pain and disillusionment only to someone who would listen patiently, so it was a comfort to her to know I was a close friend who cared enough about Ka's poetry to have come all the way to Kars. And if she could convince me that she had not treated him unfairly, she could find release at least for a time from her sorrow. But she also warned that it would cause her great pain if I failed to accept or understand her story. She wore the same long brown skirt in which she'd served Ka breakfast on the "morning of the revolution," and there, around her waist, was the same wide outdated belt (both virtually recognizable to one who'd read Ka's notes). There were flashes of anger in her eyes, but her expression was sorrowful; it reminded me of Melinda.

She talked for a long time; I hung on her every word.

CHAPTER FORTY-TWO

I'm Going to Pack My Suitcase

FROM İPEK'S POINT OF VIEW

When, on his way to the National Theater with his two army bodyguards in tow, Ka stopped and turned for one last glimpse of her, İpek was still hopeful, still convinced she'd learn to love him dearly. The knowledge that she could learn to love a man had always meant more to her than loving him effortlessly, more even than falling in love, and that was why now she felt herself to be on the threshold of a new life, a happiness bound to endure for a very long time.

So she was not particularly disturbed to find herself locked in a room by a jealous lover during the first twenty minutes following Ka's departure. Conveniently, her mind was on her suitcase: if she could concentrate now on those things she wanted to keep with her throughout her life, she would, she thought, have an easier time parting from her father and her sister, and if she could finish planning what to take during this unavoidable captivity, they'd have a better chance of leaving Kars in one piece at the earliest opportunity.

After a half hour had passed with no sign of Ka, İpek lit a cigarette. By now she was wondering whether she hadn't been a fool to think everything was going according to plan; her confinement to this room only fed her agitation, and she grew as angry at herself as at Ka. Seeing Cavit the receptionist dashing across the courtyard, she was tempted to open the window and shout to him, but before she could resolve to do so, the teenager had scampered out of range. She was still unsure, but she still expected Ka to return at any minute.

Forty-five minutes after Ka's departure, İpek managed to force open the icy window; she called to a youth who was passing in the street below—a bewildered religious high school student who had somehow managed not to be carted off to the National Theater—and asked the boy to go into the hotel to tell reception that she was locked in Room 203. The youth seemed very suspicious, but he did go inside. Moments later, the phone in the room rang.

"What on earth are you doing in Ka's room?" said Turgut Bey. "If you were locked in, why didn't you just pick up the phone?"

A minute later, her father had opened the door with a skeleton key. İpek told Turgut Bey that she'd wanted to accompany Ka to the National Theater, but Ka had locked her in the room to keep her from danger, and with the phone lines down throughout the city, she'd assumed the hotel phones weren't working either.

"But the phones *are* working again, not just here but everywhere in the city," said Turgut Bey.

"Ka's been gone a long time, I'm beginning to worry," said İpek. "Let's go to the theater and find out what's happened."

Despite his panic, Turgut Bey dawdled in getting ready. First he couldn't find his gloves, then he said he was sure Sunay would take offense if he didn't put on a tie. He insisted on walking very slowly, partly because he didn't have the strength but also because he had much advice to give İpek and wanted her to listen carefully.

"Whatever you do, don't cross swords with Sunay," said İpek. "Don't forget that he's a Jacobin hero who's just been endowed with special powers."

Seeing the curious onlookers milling about at the entrance to the National Theater, and the religious high school boys who'd been herded in on buses, and the hawkers and soldiers and policemen who'd been longing endlessly for this sort of crowd, Turgut Bey remembered his own excitement as a youth over attending political meetings. He clutched İpek's arm tighter as he looked around, hopeful yet afraid, looking for the conversation that might make him feel a part of this event, for the initiative to which he might lend his support. When he saw that most of the crowd were strangers, he shoved aside one of the youths standing in the entrance, but then he immediately felt ashamed.

The hall wasn't yet full, but already there was a family atmosphere in the large theater; it reminded İpek of those dreams in which you see everyone you've ever met assembled before you in a crowd. But there was no sign of Ka or Kadife, and this worried her. A sergeant moved them into the aisle.

"I'm the father of the leading lady, Kadife Yıldız," complained Turgut Bey. "I must see her at once."

Turgut Bey sounded every bit like a father who'd come at the last minute to bar his daughter from playing the lead in some objectionable school play, and the panic-stricken sergeant acted rather like a teacher putting aside his job to help that father—whose concern he knew in his heart to be justified. After they'd waited a short time in a room lined with pictures of Atatürk and Sunay, Kadife appeared alone at the door. Seeing her, İpek knew at once that whatever they said, her sister would still be taking to the stage that evening.

İpek asked about Ka, and Kadife said that they'd spoken briefly but that Ka had headed back to the hotel. İpek wondered why they had not run into him on the way over, but soon she dropped the subject: Turgut Bey, now in tears, was imploring his daughter not to go onstage.

"At this late hour, after all they've done to advertise this play, it would be more dangerous not to go onstage, Father dear," said Kadife.

"When you bare your head, Kadife, do you have any idea how much you'll enrage the religious high school boys, not to mention everyone else?"

"Frankly, Father, after all these years isn't it ironic that you're now telling me to cover my head?"

"There's nothing funny about it, little Kadife," said Turgut Bey. "Tell them you're feeling ill."

"I'm not ill."

Turgut Bey cried a little. İpek felt that her father staged his tears, as he always did when he saw the opportunity to focus on the sentimental aspect of a problem. There was about the old man's anguish something so ready and superficial as to make İpek always suspect that in his heart of hearts he was in fact grieving for the opposite of what he tearfully professed. In the past she and her sister had thought this trait of their father's endearing, but now, faced with a subject they urgently needed to address, they found his behavior embarrassingly trivial.

"What time was it when Ka left?" İpek whispered.

"He should have been back in the hotel quite some time ago," said Kadife, with equal alarm.

They could see the fear in each other's eyes.

When I met with her in the New Life Pastry Shop four years later, İpek told me that at that moment they were worried not about Ka but about Blue, and as they communicated this to each other silently with their eyes, they were paying little mind to their father. By now I could not help seeing İpek's frankness as a token of feeling close to me, and imagined I would be unable to see the end of this story from any other point of view than hers.

For a while, neither sister spoke.

"He told you that Blue doesn't want you going onstage, didn't he?" said İpek.

Kadife shot her sister a look of warning that their father could hear her. Both girls glanced at him and saw that, even through the tears still streaming from his eyes, he was paying close attention.

"You won't mind, will you, Father dear, if we leave you for a moment to have a word alone as sisters?"

"When you two put your heads together, you always know so much more than I do," said Turgut Bey. He left the room without closing the door behind him.

"Have you thought this through, Kadife?" said İpek.

"I have thought it through."

"I'm sure you have," said İpek. "But do you realize you may never see him again?"

"Maybe not," said Kadife carefully. "But I'm very angry at him, too."

Kadife's affair with Blue had been full of ups and downs, arguments that gave way to peace offerings that led to jealous fits, and İpek thought back to the couple's long secret history with some despair. How many years had it been? She wasn't quite sure, particularly as she was trying not to think about how long Blue had been seeing both of them. She thought lovingly of Ka. Thanks to him she'd be able to forget Blue.

"Ka is very jealous of Blue," Kadife said. "And he's madly in love with you."

"I've found it hard to believe he could be head over heels after such a short time," said İpek, "but now I believe it."

"Go with him to Germany."

"As soon as we get home, I'm going to pack my suitcase," said İpek. "Do you really think Ka and I can be happy in Germany?"

"Yes, I do," said Kadife. "But stop telling Ka about your past. He already knows too much, and he can guess a great deal more."

İpek hated it when her younger sister spoke so condescendingly, like some seasoned woman of the world. So she said, "You're talking as if you have no intention of coming home after this play is over."

"Of course I'm coming home," said Kadife, "but I thought you were leaving right away."

"Do you have any idea where Ka might have gone?"

As they looked into each other's eyes, İpek sensed that they both feared the same thing.

"Let's go," said Kadife. "It's time for me to put on my makeup."

"The thing that makes me happier than seeing you take off that scarf is seeing the last of that purple raincoat," said İpek.

The raincoat in question reached all the way to the ground, and now Kadife did a defiant little two-step that sent its hem flying upward. When they saw that Turgut Bey, who'd been watching from the door, was now finally smiling, the two sisters threw their arms around each other and exchanged kisses.

He must have resigned himself to Kadife's going onstage, for this time he neither cried nor offered advice. His performance was done. He embraced his younger daughter with a kiss on both cheeks and started with İpek through the packed auditorium.

On their way out the bustling entrance and back to the hotel, İpek kept her eyes peeled for Ka; seeing no sign of him, she began to search for someone who might know his whereabouts, but there was no one to be found on the city's pavements who could help her. As she would tell me, "Just as Ka could find any reason for pessimism, I spent the next forty-five minutes coming up with idiotic reasons for optimism."

Once home, Turgut Bey made straight for the television, and as he sat hypnotized by the endless announcements about the live broadcast, İpek prepared her suitcase. Whenever she began to wonder where Ka was, she'd try to focus instead on the happiness awaiting them in Germany and on picking out the clothes and other things she wanted to take with her. Then she started to pack another suitcase with the things she'd already excluded on the theory that there were "probably things of far higher quality in Germany," and as she rummaged through her stockings and underwear, wondering whether she might find to her dismay nothing quite like them for sale there, something told her to take a look outside. Entering the courtyard was the army truck that had been ferrying Ka around the city.

She went downstairs and saw her father was at the door. A clean-shaven, hook-nosed official she'd never seen before said, "Turgut Yıldız," and pressed a sealed envelope into his hands.

With an ashen face and trembling hands, Turgut Bey opened the envelope to find a door key. Seeing that the letter also enclosed was addressed to his daughter, he handed it to İpek.

As a matter of self-defense, but also to ensure that whatever I was to write about Ka would reflect all available facts, İpek decided to let me see the letter when we met four years later.

Thursday, 8:00 P.M.
Turgut Bey:
If I might ask you to use this key to let İpek out of my room and then to pass this letter on to her, it would be best for all of us, sir. I offer my apologies.

Respectfully yours,
Ka

My darling, I was unable to change Kadife's mind. The soldiers have brought me to headquarters for my own protection. The track to Erzurum has reopened, and they are forcing me to take the first train, which leaves at half past nine. You'll need to pack my bag as well as yours and come at once. The army truck will pick you up at a quarter past nine. On no account should you go out on the streets. Come to me! I love you very much. We are going to be very happy.

The hook-nosed man said they'd be back after nine and left.

"Are you going?" Turgut Bey asked.

"I'm still worried about what's happened to him," said İpek.

"The soldiers are protecting him; nothing can happen to him. Are you going to leave us and go?"

"I think I can be happy with him," said İpek. "Even Kadife said so."

In her hand was a document certifying her future happiness, and now, as she read it again, she began to cry, but she wasn't quite sure why.

"Perhaps it was because I dreaded leaving my father and my sister," she would tell me four years later. At the time I believed my intense interest in every detail of İpek's feelings stemmed from my need to hear her story. Then she said, "And perhaps I was worried about the other thing in my mind."

When İpek had managed to stop crying, she and her father went to her room to make a final check of the things she would take with her, and then to Ka's room to put all his belongings into his large cherry-colored valise. Father and daughter were both hopeful now; they were telling each other that, fingers crossed, Kadife would soon complete her course, and then she and Turgut Bey would come to visit İpek in Frankfurt.

When the bags were packed, they went downstairs and huddled in front of the television to watch Kadife.

"I hope it's a short play so you can know this business is over and done with before you get on the train!" said Turgut Bey.

They stopped talking and nestled against each other just as they did when they watched *Marianna,* but İpek could not concentrate on what she was seeing. Years later, all she could remember of the first twenty-five minutes was Kadife coming onstage in a head scarf and a long bright-red dress, and her line, "Whatever you want, Father dear." Sensing my sincere curiosity as to her thoughts at that moment, she added, "Of course my mind was elsewhere." Over and over, I asked her where particularly that might have been, but she would allow only that her thoughts were on the journey she was about to make with Ka.

Later her mind would be gripped by fears but she could never admit to herself what those fears were, much less manage to articulate them for me. With the windows of her mind blown open, everything but the television set looked very far away; she felt like a traveler who returns from a long journey to find that during her absence her house has changed in mysterious ways—every room much smaller than she remembered, and every stick of furniture much more worn. As she looked around her, everything—the cushions, the table, even folds in the curtains—surprised her. Faced with the chance to go to an utterly foreign place, she could now see her own home through the eyes of a stranger; that, she told me, is how she felt. And this careful account of hers given to me at the New Life Pastry Shop was, in her view, clear proof that she was still planning to set out for Frankfurt with Ka that evening.

When the bell rang, İpek ran to the hotel entrance. The army truck that was to take her to the station had come early. Swallowing her fear, she told the official at the door that she'd be ready in a moment. She ran straight back to her father, sat down beside him, and embraced him with all her strength.

"Is the truck here already?" asked Turgut Bey. "If your bag is packed, we still have some time."

İpek spent the next few minutes staring blankly at Sunay on the screen. Unable to keep still, she ran off to her room, and after packing the slippers and her little sewing kit with the mirror that she'd inadvertently left by the window, she sat for a few minutes on the edge of the bed, crying.

According to her recollection, by the time she went downstairs she was in no doubt as to her decision to leave Kars with Ka. Now rid of the lingering hesitations that had been poisoning her mind, she was at peace again, determined to spend her last minutes at home watching television with her father.

When Cavit the receptionist told her that there was someone at the door, İpek was not unduly concerned. Turgut Bey asked her to get him a Coke from the refrigerator, and she brought it with two glasses so they could share it.

İpek said she would never forget Fazıl's face as he stood there waiting at the kitchen door. It was clear from his expression that something terrible had happened, and so it was that İpek felt for the first time that Fazıl was a member of their family, someone very close to her.

"They've killed Blue and Hande!" said Fazıl. Breathless, he gulped down half the glass of water that Zahide had given him. "Only Blue could have dissuaded her."

İpek watched motionless as Fazıl cried a bit. In a dazed voice that seemed to come from deep inside him, he explained that Blue had gone into hiding with Hande, and a group of soldiers had raided the premises and killed them. He was sure someone had tipped them off: If not, they'd never have sent so many troops. And, no, there was no chance Fazıl had been followed: By the time he got there, everything was over and done with, and Fazıl watched with a number of children from the surrounding houses as the army searchlight shone on Blue's body.

"May I stay here?" Fazıl asked. "I don't want to go anywhere else."

İpek took out another glass so he, too, could share the Coke. In her distraction, she couldn't find the bottle opener; she kept looking in the wrong drawers and searching cupboards where she ought to have known it couldn't be. She suddenly thought of the flowery blouse she'd been wearing the day she met Blue and then remembered having packed it in her suitcase. She took Fazıl inside and sat him down on the chair by the kitchen where Ka, after getting so drunk on Wednesday night, had sat down to write his poem. Then, like an invalid suddenly relieved of the pain shooting through her body, she relaxed; leaving the boy to watch Kadife and sip his Coke, she went to the other end of the room and gave the second glass to her father.

She went up to her room and stood there for a minute in the dark. She stopped by Ka's room to pick up his cherry-colored valise, and then she went out into the street. She walked in the cold over to the official standing by the army truck and told him she had decided not to leave the city.

"We can still make the train," said the official, trying to be helpful.

"I've changed my mind. I'm not going, but thank you. Please give this bag to Ka Bey."

She went back inside, and as she sat down next to her father they heard the army truck revving its engine.

"I sent them off," İpek told her father. "I'm not going."

Turgut Bey put his arms around her. For a while, they watched the play on television, but without taking in a single thing. The first act was just coming to an end when İpek said, "Let's go see Kadife! I've got something to tell her."

CHAPTER FORTY-THREE

The Main Reason Women Commit Suicide Is to Save Their Pride

THE FINAL ACT

I t was very late in the day when Sunay decided to change the title of the drama originally inspired by Thomas Kyd's *The Spanish Tragedy* but which in its final form showed many other influences; in fact, it was only during the last half hour of the relentless promotional campaign that the television announcers began referring to *The Tragedy in Kars*. The revision came too late for those already in the theater. Many had been brought in by military bus; others had seen the play advertised and came to show their faith in a strong army; a fair number didn't care how catastrophic the result, as long as they had the chance to see it with their own eyes (there were already rumors that the "live broadcast" was really a tape shipped in from America); there were the city officials as well, whose presence had been ordered (this time they'd decided not to bring their families). Hardly any of these people were aware of the new title, but even those who were could little fathom the content and, like the rest of the city, had a hard time following the action.

Four years after its first and last performance, I found a videotape of *The Tragedy in Kars* in the Kars Border Television archives. The first half is almost impossible to summarize. I could make out a blood feud in some "backward, impoverished, and benighted" town, but when its inhabitants started killing one another, I had no notion of what it was that they'd been unable to share, nor could the murderers or their victims offer a clue as to the reason for so much bloodshed. Only Sunay raged against the backwardness of blood feuds and of people who allowed themselves to be drawn into them; he debated the matter with his wife and a younger woman who seemed to understand him better (this was Kadife). Though he was a rich and enlightened member of the ruling elite, Sunay's character enjoyed dancing and joking with the poorest villagers and, indeed, engaged them in erudite discussions of the meaning of life, as well as regaling them with scenes from Shakespeare, Victor Hugo, and Brecht, if only to furnish the promised "play within the play." He also offered an assortment of short soliloquies on such matters as city traffic, table manners, the special traits Turks and Muslims will never give up, the glories of the French Revolution, the virtues of cooking, condoms, and raki, and the way fancy prostitutes belly dance. These discussions, no more than his subsequent exposés of adulterated brands of shampoo and cosmetics, shed little light on the bloody scenes they interrupted, and as one outburst followed another, it grew harder to imagine that they conformed to any logic at all.

But the wild series of improvisations was somehow still worth watching, if only for the passion of Sunay's performance. Whenever the action began to drag, whenever he sensed the people of Kars losing interest, Sunay could always find something to bring them back under his spell; he would fly into a fury and, borrowing a fine theatrical pose from one of the most illustrious roles of his career, he would rail against those who had brought the people low; with tragic abandon he would then pace the stage recounting youthful memories and quoting Montaigne on friendship as he mused on the quintessential loneliness of Atatürk. His face was wet with perspiration. During my visit to Kars, I was able to meet with Nuriye Hanım, the teacher who loved literature and history and had been so enthralled by Sunay's performance on the night of the revolution; she told me that everyone in the front row for the second performance could smell the raki fumes. Still, she insisted Sunay wasn't drunk; she preferred *enthusiastic*. But others in her row more than confirmed this so-called enthusiasm. It was a disparate group: Many were middle-aged officials who'd risked their lives to get as close to this great man as decorum allowed. Some were widows, others perhaps best described as young admirers of Atatürk—and they had already seen these images hundreds of times. There were also a few hungry for adventure, so to speak, or at least interested in power. But they all spoke of the light shining in Sunay's eyes, radiating in all directions; it was dangerous, they said, to stare into those eyes for more than a few seconds.

I would one day have corroborating testimony from one of the religious high school boys who'd been piled into a military transport and frog-marched to the National Theater. His name was Mesut (he'd been the one opposed to burying atheists and believers in the same cemetery). He confirmed how Sunay held them all spellbound. We can only assume he had no ax to grind because, after four years with a small Islamist group based in Erzurum, he had lost faith in armed struggle and returned to Kars to work in a teahouse. He told me it was very difficult for the other religious high school boys to speak openly about their attraction to Sunay. Perhaps it had to do with Sunay's absolute power, the thing to which they also aspired. It may be that they were relieved by the many restrictions he'd imposed on their movements, which made it impossible to take stupid risks like inciting a riot. "Whenever the army steps in, most people are secretly thankful," he told me, and then confessed that his classmates had been most impressed by Sunay's courage. There he was, the most powerful man in the city, unafraid to stride onto the stage and bare his soul to the teeming multitudes.

Watching the Kars Border Television archive videotape of the evening's performance, I was struck by the silence in the hall; it was as if the audience had left behind the struggles that defined them—the tussle of fathers and sons, the skirmishes between the guilty and the powerful—to sink into a collective terror; and I was not immune to the power of that shimmering fiction that any citizen of an oppressive and aggressively nationalistic country will understand only too well: the magical unity conjured by the word *we*. In Sunay's eyes, it was as if there were not a single outsider in the hall: all were inextricably bound by the same hopeless story.

But Kadife threatened to break this trance, and this may explain why the people of Kars couldn't quite bring themselves to accept her presence onstage. The cameraman taping the live broadcast seems to have been aware of this ambivalence: In the happy scenes, he zoomed in on Sunay, not showing Kadife at all, so the only time the broadcast audience got a glimpse of her was when she was serving the great and the good, just like one of those maids in a boulevard comedy. Still, everyone had heard the announcements that had been running on TV since lunchtime, and they were now very curious to see whether she would bare her head. There'd been the usual spate of conflicting rumors—some holding that Kadife was merely following army orders to remove her scarf, while others had it that she was planning not to go onstage after all—but after half a day of saturation publicity, even those only vaguely acquainted with the head-scarf affair now knew all about Kadife. This is why there was such broad disappointment at her low visibility in the early scenes—and her long red dress was hardly any consolation for the scarf, whose fate remained unclear.

Twenty minutes into the play, an exchange between Kadife and Sunay gave the audience the first hint of what was to come. They were alone onstage, and Sunay asked if she had made up her mind, adding that he "could not condone killing oneself just out of anger."

Kadife gave the following reply: "In a city where men are killing each other like animals just to make it a happier place, who has the right to stop me from killing myself?" Then, seeing Funda Eser striding toward her, she made a quick exit—leaving it unclear whether this was part of the play or a hastily improvised escape.

When I'd spoken to everyone who would speak to me, I tried to reconstruct from their testimony a minute-by-minute time line synchronizing the performance with the action offstage; and this is how I was able to establish that Blue's last glimpse of Kadife came when she delivered this line. For according to neighbors who witnessed the raid, and also various police officers still working in Kars at the time of my visit, Blue and Hande had been watching television when the bell rang. According to the official report, Blue took one look at the soldiers and the police officers assembled outside and rushed to get his weapon; he did not hesitate to open fire, though several neighbors and the young Islamists who would turn him into a legend almost overnight remember that after getting off a few rounds he'd cried, "Don't shoot!" Perhaps he was hoping to save Hande, but in vain; Z Demirkol's special operations team had already taken up positions around the perimeter, and in less than a minute not just Blue and Hande but every wall of their safe house was riddled with bullets. It was a fierce noise, but hardly anyone but a handful of curious neighborhood children paid much attention. It was not only that the people of Kars were accustomed to such nocturnal raids; they simply wouldn't be distracted from the live broadcast from the National Theater. All the sidewalks in town were empty, all the shutters closed, and apart from the odd teahouse with a television no one was open for business.

Sunay was well aware that all eyes in the city were on him, and this made him feel not just secure but extraordinarily powerful. Knowing her very presence onstage was subject to Sunay's sufferance, Kadife courted his approval more than she might have done otherwise; she had to make the most of the opportunities Sunay had given her if she was to have any hope of accomplishing her own ends. (Unlike İpek, she would refuse to give me her own version of events, so I cannot know what else she was thinking.) Over the next forty minutes, as the audience began to grasp that Kadife was faced with two important decisions—one about baring her head, the other about committing suicide—their admiration for her grew and grew. And as her stature increased, the play evolved into a drama more serious than that implied by Sunay and Funda's half didactic, half vaudevillian fury. Although they could not completely forget Kadife the head-scarf girl, many still grieving for her years later told me that her new persona had won the hearts of the people of Kars. By the middle of the play, the audience was falling into a deep silence whenever Kadife walked onstage; whenever she spoke, those watching in houses full of noisy children would frantically ask one another, "What did she say? What did she say?"

It was with the National Theater caught in just such a moment of silence that one could hear the whistle of the first train to leave Kars in four days. Ka was riding in the compartment in which the army had forcibly planted him. When my dear friend had seen the army transport return not with İpek but only his valise, he desperately implored his guards to let him see her or at least talk to her; when they refused, he persuaded them to send the army transport back to the hotel; when the transport returned empty a second time, he begged the officers to hold the train for five more minutes. When the whistle blew, there was still no sign of İpek, and even as the train began to move, Ka's wet eyes were still scanning the crowds on the platform; training them on the station entrance, the door that looked out at the statue of Kâzım Karabekir, he continued trying to conjure up a tall woman walking straight toward him, bag in hand.

As the train gathered speed, it blew its whistle once again. İpek and Turgut Bey were on their way from the Snow Palace Hotel to the National Theater when they heard it.

"The train's on its way," said Turgut Bey.

"Yes," said İpek, "and any minute now the roads will be reopened. The governor and the military chief of staff will be back in the city soon." They talked for a while about how this ridiculous coup would now draw to a close and everything would soon return to normal, but İpek would later allow that she had no particular interest in these subjects; she wanted to speak lest her father deduce from her silence that she was thinking about Ka. Was her mind really on Ka, though? How much was she thinking about Blue's death? Even four years later, she herself wasn't sure, and finding my questions and my suspicions irksome, she tried to deflect them. But she did say that far stronger than any regret at missing her chance for happiness was her anger at Ka. After that night, she knew, there was no hope of ever loving him again. When she heard Ka's train pull out of the station, the only thing she felt was heartbreak, and perhaps that came with a bit of surprise. In any case, all she wanted was to share her grief with Kadife.

"It's so desolate, you'd think everyone's fled the city," Turgut Bey said.

"It's a ghost city," said İpek, just to say something.

A convoy of three army transports turned the corner to pass in front of them. Turgut Bey took this as proof that the roads had reopened. They watched the trucks roll off into the night until only their lights were visible. According to my later inquiries, but at the time unbeknownst to them, the middle jeep was carrying the bodies of Blue and Hande.

A moment earlier, the lights of the last jeep had shone on the offices of the *Border City Gazette* just long enough for Turgut to see that tomorrow's edition was hanging in the window. He stopped to read the headlines: DEATH ONSTAGE; ILLUSTRIOUS ACTOR SUNAY ZAIM SHOT AND KILLED DURING YESTERDAY'S PERFORMANCE.

They read it twice and then walked as fast as they could to the National Theater. The same police cars were standing outside the entrance, and down the road, far, far away, the same tank nestled in the shadows.

As they were searched at the entrance, Turgut Bey announced that he was the leading lady's father. The second act had begun, but they found two empty seats in the very last row and sat down.

This act also contained a number of the stock gags that Sunay had been falling back on for so many years, including a modified belly-dance parody by Funda Eser. But the atmosphere had grown heavier, and the silence in the hall deeper, from the cumulative effect of Kadife and Sunay's long scenes alone onstage.

"May I again insist that you explain to me why you wish to kill yourself?" said Sunay.

"It's not a question anyone can really answer," said Kadife.

"What do you mean?"

"If a person knew exactly why she was committing suicide and could state her reasons openly, she wouldn't have to kill herself," said Kadife.

"No! It's not like that at all," said Sunay. "Some people kill themselves for love; others kill because they can't bear their husbands' beatings any longer or because poverty is piercing them to the bone, like a knife."

"You have a very simple way of looking at life," said Kadife. "A woman who wants to kill herself for love still knows that if she waits a little her love will fade. Poverty's not a real reason for suicide either. And a woman doesn't have to commit suicide to escape her husband; all she has to do is steal some of his money and leave him."

"Very well, then, what is the real reason?"

"The main reason women commit suicide is to save their pride. At least that's what most women kill themselves for."

"You mean they've been humiliated by love?"

"You don't understand a thing!" said Kadife. "A woman doesn't commit suicide because she's lost her pride, she does it to *show* her pride."

"Is that why your friends committed suicide?"

"I can't speak for them. Everyone has her own reasons. But every time I have ideas of killing myself, I can't help thinking they were thinking the same way I am. The moment of suicide is the time when they understand best how lonely it is to be a woman and what being a woman really means."

"Did you use these arguments to push your friends toward suicide?"

"They came to their own decisions. The choice to commit suicide was theirs."

"But everyone knows that here in Kars there's no such thing as free choice; all people want is to escape from the next beating, to take refuge in the nearest community. Admit it, Kadife, you met secretly with these women and pushed them toward suicide."

"But how could that be?" said Kadife. "All they achieved by killing themselves was an even greater loneliness. Many were disowned by their families, who in some cases refused even to arrange the funeral prayers."

"So are you trying to tell me that you plan to kill yourself just to prove that they are not alone, just to show that you're all in this together? You're suddenly very quiet, Kadife. But if you kill yourself before explaining your reasons, don't you run the risk of letting your message be misinterpreted?"

"I'm not killing myself to send any message," said Kadife.

"But still, there are so many people watching you, and they're all curious. The least you can do is say the first thing that comes into your mind."

"Women kill themselves because they hope to gain something," said Kadife. "Men kill themselves because they've lost hope of gaining anything."

"That's true," said Sunay, and he took his Kırıkkale gun out of his pocket. Everyone in the hall could see it flashing. "When you're sure that I'm utterly defeated, will you please use this to shoot me?"

"I don't want to end up in jail."

"Why worry about that when you're planning to kill yourself too?" said Sunay. "After all, if you commit suicide you'll go to hell, so it makes no sense to worry about the punishment you might receive for any other crime—in this world or the next."

"But this is exactly why women commit suicide," said Kadife. "To escape all forms of punishment."

"When I arrive at the moment of my defeat, I want my death to be at the hands of just such a woman!" cried Sunay, now spreading his arms theatrically and facing the audience. He paused for effect. Then he launched into some tale of Atatürk's amorous indiscretions, cutting it short when he sensed interest flagging.

When the second act ended, Turgut Bey and İpek rushed backstage to find Kadife. Her dressing room—once used by acrobats from St. Petersburg and Moscow, Armenians playing Molière, and dancers and musicians who'd toured Russia—was ice cold.

"I thought you were leaving," said Kadife to İpek.

"I'm so proud of you, darling; you were wonderful!" said Turgut Bey, embracing Kadife. "But if he'd handed you that gun and said, 'Shoot me,' I'm afraid I would have jumped up and interrupted the play, shouting, 'Kadife, whatever you do, don't shoot!' "

"Why would you do that?"

"Because the gun could be loaded!" said Turgut Bey. He told her about the story he'd read in tomorrow's edition of the *Border City Gazette*. "I know that Serdar Bey is always hoping he can make things happen by writing about them first, but most of his stories turn out to be false alarms. I wouldn't especially care about this one's coming true anyway," he said. "But I know that Serdar would never dream of proclaiming an assassination like this unless Sunay had talked him into it—and I find that very ominous. It may just be more self-promotion, but who knows; he could be planning to have you kill him onstage. My darling girl, please don't pull that trigger unless you're sure the gun isn't loaded! And don't bare your head just because this man wants you to. İpek isn't leaving.

We're going to be living in this city for some time to come, so please don't anger the Islamists over nothing."

"Why did İpek decide not to go?"

"Because she loves her father and you and her family more," said Turgut Bey, taking Kadife's hand.

"Father dear, would you mind if we spoke alone again?" said İpek, instantly seeing her sister's face go cold with alarm. Turgut Bey crossed to the other end of the dusty high-ceilinged room, joining Sunay and Funda Eser, and İpek hugged Kadife tightly and sat her on her lap. Seeing the gesture had only made her sister more fearful, İpek took her by the hand toward a corner separated from the rest of the room by a curtain. Just then, Funda Eser emerged with a tray of glasses and a bottle of Kanyak.

"You were excellent, Kadife," she said. "You two make yourselves at home."

As Kadife's anxieties mounted with every second that passed, İpek looked into her eyes in a manner that said, unambiguously, I have some very bad news. Then she spoke. "Hande and Blue were killed during a raid."

Kadife shrank into herself. "Were they at the same house? Who told you?" she asked. But seeing the sternness in İpek's face, she fell silent.

"It was Fazıl, that religious high school boy, who told us, and I believed him because he saw it with his own eyes." She paused for a moment, to give Kadife a chance to take it in. Kadife grew only paler, but İpek pressed on. "Ka knew where he was hiding, and after his last visit to see you here, he never returned to the hotel. I think Ka betrayed them to the special operations team. That's why I didn't go back to Germany with him."

"How can you be so sure?" said Kadife. "Maybe it wasn't him; maybe someone else told them."

"It's possible. I've considered that myself. But I'm so sure in my heart that it was Ka, it almost doesn't matter: I know I'd never be able to convince my rational self that he didn't do it. And so I didn't go to Germany because I knew I could never love him."

Kadife was spent, trying to absorb the news. Only on seeing Kadife's strength failing could İpek tell that her sister had begun to accept that Blue was really dead.

Kadife buried her face in her hands and began to sob. İpek folded her arms around Kadife's and they cried together, though İpek knew they were crying for different reasons. They had cried this way before, once or twice during those shameful days when neither of them could give up Blue and they dueled mercilessly for his affections. Now İpek realized that this terrible vendetta was over, once and for all; she wasn't going to leave Kars. She felt herself age suddenly. To reconcile and grow old in peace, and have the wit to want nothing from the world—this was her wish now.

She could see that her sister's pain was deeper and more destructive than her own. For a moment she was thankful not to be in Kadife's place—was it the sweetness of revenge?—and guilt swept over her. In the background they were playing the familiar taped medley that the National Theater's management always played during intermissions to encourage sales of soda and dried chickpeas: The song right then was one she remembered from the earliest years of their youth in Istanbul: "Baby, come closer, closer to me." In those days, both of them had wanted to learn to speak good English; neither succeeded. It seemed to İpek that her sister only cried harder on hearing this song. Peeking through the curtains, she could see her father and Sunay in animated conversation at the other end of the room, as Funda filled their glasses with more Kanyak.

"Kadife Hanım, I'm Colonel Osman Nuri Çolak." A middle-aged soldier had yanked open the curtain. With a gesture evidently acquired from a film, he bowed so low he almost wiped the floor with his pate. "With all due respect, miss, how can I ease your pain? If you do not wish to go onstage, I have some good news for you: The roads have reopened and the armed forces will be entering the city at any moment."

Later on, at his court-martial, Osman Nuri Çolak would offer these words as evidence that he'd been doing all he could to save the city from the ludicrous officers who'd staged the coup.

"I'm absolutely fine, but thank you, sir, for your concern," said Kadife.

İpek saw that Kadife had already assumed a number of Funda's affectations. At the same time, she had to admire her sister's determination to pull herself together. Kadife forced herself to stand: She drank a glass of water and then began to pace quietly up and down the long backstage room like a theater ghost.

İpek was hoping to get away before her father could talk to Kadife, but Turgut Bey crept up to join them just as the third act had begun. "Don't be afraid," said Sunay, nodding to his friends. "These people are modern."

The third act began with Funda Eser singing a folk song about a woman who'd been raped, an engaging number to make up for earlier parts of the drama that the audience had found too intellectual or otherwise obscure. It was Funda's usual routine: One moment she was crying and cursing the men in the audience, and the next moment she was showering them with whatever compliments came into her head. Following two songs and a little commercial parody only the children thought funny (she tried to suggest that Aygaz filled their canisters not with propane gas but with farts), the stage grew dark, and—in an ominous reprise of the finale two days earlier—two armed soldiers marched onstage. The audience watched in tense silence as they erected a gallows center stage. Sunay limped confidently across the stage with Kadife to stand right beneath the noose.

"I never expected things to happen so quickly," he said.

"Is this your way of admitting you've failed at this thing you've set out to accomplish, or is it simply that you're old and tired now and looking for a way to go out in style?" said Kadife.

İpek saw Kadife was drawing on unsuspected reserves of strength.

"You're very intelligent, Kadife," said Sunay.

"Does this frighten you?" said Kadife, her voice taut and angry.

"Yes," said Sunay in a lecherous languor.

"It's not my intelligence that frightens you, you fear me because I'm my own person," said Kadife. "Because here in our city, men don't fear their women's intelligence, they fear their independence."

"To the contrary," said Sunay. "I staged this revolution precisely so you women could be as independent as women in Europe. That's why I'm asking you to remove that scarf."

"I am going to bare my head now," said Kadife, "and then, to prove that I'm motivated neither by your coercion nor by any wish to be a European, I'm going to hang myself."

"You do realize, don't you, Kadife, that when you act like an individual and commit suicide, the Europeans will applaud you? Don't think you haven't already turned some heads with your animated performance in the so-called secret meeting at the Hotel Asia. There are even rumors that you organized the suicide girls, just as you did the head-scarf girls."

"There was only one suicide who was involved in the head-scarf protest, and that was Teslime."

"And now you mean to be the second."

"No, because before I kill myself, I'm going to bare my head."

"Have you thought this through?"

"Yes," said Kadife. "I have."

"Then you must have thought about this, too: Suicides go to hell. And since I'm going to hell anyway, you can kill me first with a clear conscience."

"No," said Kadife. "Because I don't believe I'm going to hell after I kill myself. I'm going to kill you to rid our country of a microbe, an enemy of our nation, our religion, and our women!"

"You're a courageous woman, Kadife, and you speak with great frankness. But our religion prohibits suicide."

"Yes, it's certainly true the Nisa verse of the glorious Koran proclaims that we shouldn't kill ourselves. But this does not prevent God in his greatness from finding it in his heart to pardon the suicide girls and spare them from going to hell after all."

"In other words, you've found a way to twist the Koran to suit your purposes."

"In fact, the contrary is true," said Kadife. "It happens that a few young women in Kars killed themselves because they were forbidden to cover their heads as they wished. As surely as the world is God's creation, he can see their suffering. So long as I feel the love of God in my heart, there's no place for me in Kars, so I'm going to do as they did and end my life."

"You're going to anger all those religious leaders who've come to Kars through snow and ice to deliver their sermons hoping the helpless women of Kars might be delivered from their suicidal wishes—you do know that, Kadife, don't you? And while we're on the subject, the Koran—"

"I am not prepared to discuss my religion with atheists or, for that matter, with those who profess belief in God out of fear."

"Of course you're right. Mind you, I don't bring it up to interfere with your spiritual life; it's only that I thought the fear of hell might keep you from shooting me with a clear conscience."

"You have nothing to worry about. I am going to kill you with a clear conscience."

"That's wonderful," said Sunay, looking a little offended at the alacrity of the reply. "Now let me tell you the most important thing I've learned in my twenty-five years of professional theater: When any dialogue goes on longer than this, our audiences can't follow it without getting bored. So with your permission we will stop our conversation here and turn our words to deeds."

"Fine."

Sunay produced the Kırıkkale gun he had brandished in the last act and showed it both to Kadife and to the audience. "Now you are going to bare your head. Then I shall place my gun in your hands and you will shoot me. And as this is the first time anything like this has happened on live television, let me take this last opportunity to explain to our audience how they are to understand—"

"Let's get on with it," said Kadife. "I'm sick of hearing men talking about why suicide girls commit suicide."

"Right you are," said Sunay, playing with the gun in his hand. "But there are still one or two things I wish to say. Just so our viewers in Kars won't be unduly alarmed—after all, some may have actually believed the rumors in the papers—please look at this gun's magazine clip." He removed the clip, showing it to Kadife and for effect to the audience as well before putting it back again. "Did you see that it was empty?" he asked, with the assurance of a master illusionist.

"Yes."

"Let's be absolutely certain about this!" said Sunay. He took the clip out again, and like a magician about to saw a woman in half he showed it to the audience again before snapping it back. "Now, finally, let me say a few words on my own behalf. A moment ago, you promised you would shoot me with a clear conscience. You probably detest me for having staged this coup and opening fire on the audience, just because they weren't living like Westerners. But I want you to know I did it all for the fatherland."

"Fine," said Kadife. "Now I'm going to bare my head. And please, I want everyone to watch."

Her face flashed with pain and then, with a single clean stroke, she lifted her hand and pulled her scarf off.

There was not a sound in the hall. For a moment Sunay stared stupidly at Kadife, as if she had just done the utterly unexpected. Both then turned to the audience and gaped like acting students who'd forgotten their lines.

All of Kars gazed in awe at Kadife's long, beautiful brown hair, which the cameraman finally screwed up his courage to show in tight focus. When he had found the nerve to zoom in on her face, it became clear that Kadife was deeply embarrassed, like a woman whose dress had come undone in a crowded public place. Her every movement bespoke a terrible pain.

"Hand me the gun, please!" she said impatiently.

"Here you are," said Sunay. He was holding it by the barrel, and when she had taken it in hand, he smiled. "This is where you pull the trigger."

Everyone in Kars expected the dialogue to continue. And perhaps Sunay did too, because he said, "Your hair is so beautiful, Kadife. Even I would certainly want to guard you jealously, to keep other men from seeing—"

Kadife pulled the trigger.

A gunshot sounded in the hall. All of Kars watched in wonder as Sunay shuddered violently—as if he'd really been shot—and then fell to the floor.

"How stupid all this is!" said Sunay. "They know nothing about modern art, they'll never be modern!"

The audience expected Sunay now to launch into a long death monologue; instead, Kadife rushed forward with the gun and fired again and again: four times in smart succession. With each shot, Sunay's body shuddered and lurched upward; every time it fell back to the floor, it seemed heavier.

There were still many who thought Sunay was only acting; they were ready for him to sit up at any moment and deliver a long instructive tirade on death; but at the uncommonly realistic sight of his bloodied face, they lost hope. Nuriye Hanım, whose admiration for theatrical effects surpassed even her reverence for the script itself, rose to her feet; she was just about to applaud Sunay when she too saw his bloody face and sank fearfully back into her seat.

"I guess I killed him!" said Kadife, turning to the audience.

"You did well!" shouted a religious high school student from the back of the hall.

The security forces were so preoccupied by the murder they'd just witnessed onstage they failed to identify the student agitator who'd broken the silence. And when Nuriye Hanım, who'd spent the last two days watching the awesome Sunay on television and who'd determined, before the announcement of free admission, to sit in the front row regardless of the cost so long as she had her chance to see him up close—when Nuriye Hanım broke down in tears, everyone else in the hall, and everyone else in Kars, was forced to accept the reality of what they had just seen.

Two soldiers, running toward each other with clownish steps, pulled the curtains shut.

CHAPTER FORTY-FOUR

No One Here Likes Ka These Days

FOUR YEARS LATER, IN KARS

As soon as the curtain was closed, Z Demirkol and his friends arrested Kadife "for her own safety"; removing her through the stage door into Little Kâzımbey Avenue, they pushed her into an army jeep and headed straight for the central garrison, where they deposited her in the old fallout shelter where Blue had been kept his last day on earth. A few hours later, all the roads to Kars had reopened; several military units rolled in to suppress the city's "little coup" and met with no resistance. The governor, the military chief of staff, and a number of other officials were dismissed for dereliction of duty; the small band of conspirators who had staged the coup were arrested, along with a number of soldiers and MİT agents, who protested that they'd done it all for the people and the state. It would be three days before Turgut Bey and İpek were able to visit Kadife.

Turgut Bey had no doubt that Sunay had died onstage, and he was hopeful that nothing would happen to Kadife; all he wanted was to find a way to take his daughter home, but when midnight had come and gone he gave in and walked home through the empty streets, arm in arm with his older daughter. İpek went straight to her room; as she unpacked her suitcase, putting everything back in the drawers, her father sat on the edge of the bed and cried.

Most Kars residents who'd watched the events unfold onstage would discover that Sunay had in fact died after his theatrical death throes only when they read the *Border City Gazette* the next morning. After the curtain closed, the audience at the National Theater quietly filed out, and the television station never again mentioned the events of the past three days.

But as Kars was well accustomed to military rule and to the sight of police and special operations teams chasing "terrorists" through the streets, it wasn't long anyway before those three days ceased to seem exceptional. And when the general staff office launched a full inquiry the following morning, prompting the office of the prime minister's inspectorate to spring into action as well, everyone in Kars could see the wisdom of regarding the stage coup more as a strange theatrical event than a political one. Their fascination lingered over questions such as this: If Sunay had just shown the clip to be empty in full view of a live audience, how could Kadife have shot and killed him with the same gun?

As I have referred several times to the inspecting colonel sent by Ankara after things had returned to normal, my readers will have already deduced my indebtedness to this man and his detailed report on the stage coup; his own analysis of the gun scene confirms it was less a case of sleight of hand than actual magic. Since Kadife refused to speak to her father or her sister or even her lawyer, much less the prosecutor, about what happened that night, the inspecting colonel was obliged to undertake the same sort of detective work I would do four years later; interviewing as many people as he could (although it would be more accurate to say that he took their depositions), he finally satisfied himself there was not a rumor or theory that had escaped his attention.

There were, of course, many stories suggesting that Kadife did knowingly and willfully kill Sunay Zaim, and without his real permission; to refute these allegations, the inspecting colonel showed it would have been impossible for the young woman to have switched guns or to have replaced the empty clip with a loaded one so quickly. And so, despite the amazement Sunay's face registered with every shot, the fact remains that searches carried out by the armed forces, the inventory of Kadife's personal effects at the time of her arrest, and even the video recording of the performance all confirm that she was in possession of only one gun and one clip. Another popular local theory had it that Sunay Zaim was shot by a different gunman firing from a different angle, but that one was put to rest when the ballistics report and autopsy results came back from Ankara to confirm that all the bullets in the actor's body had come from the Kırıkkale gun in Kadife's hand.

Kadife's last words ("I guess I killed him!") turned her into something of an urban legend; the inspecting colonel saw them as proof that this was not a case of premeditated murder. Perhaps out of consideration for the prosecutor who would open the trial, the colonel's report digressed to give a full discussion of premeditation, wrongdoing with intent, and other related legal and philosophical concepts; still, he wound up alleging that the true mastermind—the one who had helped Kadife memorize her lines and taught her the various maneuvers she would deftly perform—was none other than the deceased himself. In twice showing the audience that the clip was empty, Sunay Zaim had duped Kadife and indeed the entire city of Kars. Here, perhaps, I should quote the colonel himself, who took early retirement not long after the publication of his report. When I met him at his home in Ankara and pointed to the rows of Agatha Christie books on his shelves, he told me that what he liked most about them were their titles. When we moved to the case of the actor's gun, he said simply, "The clip was full!" A man of the theater would have hardly needed to know magic to trick an audience into taking a full clip for an empty one: Indeed, after three days of merciless violence visited upon them by Sunay and his cohorts in the name of republicanism and westernization (the final death toll, including Sunay, was twenty-nine), the people of Kars were so terrorized they would have been prepared to look at an empty glass and see a full one.

If we follow this line of reasoning, it becomes clear that Kadife was not Sunay's only accomplice; Sunay, after all, had gone so far as to advertise his death in advance, and if the people of Kars were so eager to see him kill himself onstage, if they were still prepared to enjoy the drama, telling themselves it was just a play, they too were complicit. Another rumor, that Kadife had killed Sunay to avenge Blue's death, was refuted on the grounds that anyone handed a loaded gun with the express notification that it was empty could not be accused of using it with intent to kill. There were those among Kadife's Islamist admirers and her secularist accusers who still maintained that this was precisely what was so crafty about the way Kadife killed Sunay but then refused to kill herself, but the inspecting colonel, whose own patience with the fanciful was limited, held that this was to confuse art with reality.

The military prosecutor stationed in Kars gave the inspecting colonel's meticulous report great weight, as did the judges, who ruled that Kadife had not killed for political reasons; instead, they found her guilty of negligent homicide and lack of forethought and sentenced her to three years and one month. She would be released after serving twenty months in jail. Under Articles 313 and 463 of the Turkish Penal Code, Colonel Osman Nuri Çolak was charged with establishing a vigilante group implicated in murders by unknown assailants; for this he received a very long sentence, but six months later the government declared a general amnesty and set him free. Although he had been amply admonished under the conditions of his release that he was not to discuss the coup with anyone, it was not unheard of for him to go to the officer's club of an evening to see his old army friends, and after enough to drink he'd allow that whatever else had happened he had at least found it in himself to live the dream of every Atatürk-loving soldier; without undue rudeness, he would accuse his friends of bowing to the religious fanatics for want of courage.

A number of other soldiers and officials involved in the coup tried to portray themselves as well-meaning patriots and helpless links in the chain of command, but the military court was unmoved; they too were convicted of conspiratorial collusion, murder, and use of state property without permission and held for a time before the same general amnesty. One of them, a young but high-minded low-ranking officer who turned to Islam after his release, published his story *(I Was a Jacobin Too)* in the Islamist newspaper *Covenant,* but the memoirs were censored for insulting the army. By then it was common knowledge that Goalkeeper Vural had started working for the local branch of MİT the moment the revolution began. The court found that the other actors in Sunay's troupe were but simple artists.

Funda Eser had gone on a rampage the night her husband died, leveling wild accusations against every person who crossed her path, threatening to denounce them all; when it was established that she had suffered a mental breakdown, she was sent to the psychiatric wing of the military hospital in Ankara, where she spent four months under observation. Years after her discharge, she was to become famous throughout the country as the voice of the witch in a popular children's television cartoon; she told me she remained grief-stricken over the slanders that had prevented her husband (whose death she now termed "a work-related incident") from taking on the role of Atatürk; her sole consolation was to see how many of the newest statues of the great man showed him striking poses created by her husband. Because the inspecting colonel's report had also implicated Ka in the coup, the military court summoned him as a witness; after his failure to appear at two hearings, they charged him with obstruction and issued a warrant for his arrest.

Every Saturday, Turgut Bey and İpek visited Kadife, who served her sentence in Kars. During spring and summer, when the weather was fine, the kindly warden gave them permission to spread a white tablecloth beneath the mulberry tree in the prison's spacious courtyard, and they would while away the afternoon eating Zahide's stuffed peppers with olive oil, offering her rice meatballs to the other inmates, cracking and peeling hard-boiled eggs, and listening to Chopin preludes on the Philips cassette player that Turgut Bey had managed to repair. To keep his daughter from seeing her sentence as a cause for shame, Turgut Bey insisted on treating the prison like a boarding school, a place through which all proper folk had to pass sometime; occasionally he would invite friends along, like the journalist Serdar Bey.

One day Fazıl joined them on a visit, and Kadife said she'd like to see him again; two months after her release, this young man four years her junior became her husband. For the first six months, they lived in a room in the Snow Palace Hotel, where Fazıl now worked as a receptionist, but by the time I visited Kars they had moved to a separate apartment. At six o'clock every morning, Kadife would take their six-month-old, Ömercan, to the Snow Palace Hotel; Zahide and İpek would feed the baby and then Turgut Bey would play with his grandson while Kadife busied herself with hotel business; by now Fazıl had decided it was better not to be too dependent on his father-in-law so he was working two other jobs. The first was at the Palace of Light Photo Studio and the other was at Kars Border Television: he told me with a smile that his job title was production assistant but really he was nothing more than a glorified errand boy.

As I've reported, on the day of my arrival the mayor gave a dinner in my honor; I met with Fazıl at noon the next day at their new home on Hulusi Aytekin Avenue. As I was gazing out at the enormous snowflakes bouncing softly against the walls of the castle before sinking into the dark waters of the river, Fazıl innocently asked why I'd come to Kars. Thinking he might say something about the way İpek had turned my head at the mayor's dinner, I panicked and launched into a long, somewhat exaggerated account of my interest in the poems Ka had written while in Kars and my tentative plans to write a book about them.

"If the poems are missing, how can you write a book about them?" he asked, in a friendly well-meaning voice.

"That's as much a mystery to me as it is to you," I said. "But there must be one poem in the television archives."

"We can find it this evening. But you spent the whole morning walking around every street in Kars. So maybe you're thinking of writing a novel about us too."

"All I was doing was visiting the places Ka mentioned in his poems," I said uneasily.

"But I can tell from your face that you want to tell the people who read your novels how poor we are and how different we are from them. I don't want you to put me into a novel like that."

"Why not?"

"Because you don't even know me, that's why! Even if you got to know me and described me as I am, your Western readers would be so caught up in pitying me for being poor that they wouldn't have a chance to see my life. For example, if you said I was writing an Islamist science-fiction novel, they'd just laugh. I don't want to be described as someone people smile at out of pity and compassion."

"Fine."

"I know I've upset you," said Fazıl. "Please don't take offense, I can tell you're a good person. But your friend was a good person too; maybe he even wanted to love us, but in the end he committed the greatest evil of all."

I found it difficult to hear Fazıl imputing evil to Ka's alleged betrayal of Blue, and I could not help thinking that it was only on account of Blue's death that Fazıl had been able to marry Kadife. But I held my tongue.

"How can you be so sure this allegation is true?" I asked finally.

"Everyone in Kars knows this," he said. He spoke with warmth, even compassion, and took care not to blame Ka or me.

In his eyes, I saw Necip. I told him I was happy to look at the science-fiction novel he had wanted to show me, but he explained that he wanted to be with me when I read it. So we sat down at the table where he and Kadife ate their evening meal in front of the television set and read the first fifty pages of the science-fiction novel Necip had first imagined four years earlier, and which Fazıl was now writing in his name.

"So what do you think, is it good?" Fazıl asked, but only once, and apologetically. "If you're bored, just leave it."

"No, it's good," I said, and I read on with curiosity.

Later, when we were walking down Kâzım Karabekir Avenue, I told him truthfully how much I liked the novel.

"Maybe you're just saying that to cheer me up," Fazıl said brightly, "but you've still done me a big favor. I'd like to reciprocate. So if you decide to write about Ka, it's fine to mention me. But only if you let me speak directly to your readers."

"What do you want to say to them?"

"I don't know. If I can think of what to say while you're still in Kars, I'll tell you."

We parted company, having agreed to meet at Kars Border Television in the early evening. I watched Fazıl race down the street to the Palace of Light Photo Studio. How much of Necip do I see in him? Could he still feel Necip inside him in the way he had described to Ka? How much can a man hear another's voice inside him?

That morning, as I walked the streets of Kars, talking to the same people Ka had talked to, sitting in the same teahouses, there had been many moments when I almost felt I *was* Ka. Early in my wanderings, while I was sitting in the Lucky Brothers Teahouse, where Ka had written "All Humanity and the Stars," I too dreamed about my place in the universe, just as my beloved friend had done. Back at the Snow Palace Hotel, as I went to pick up my key, Cavit the receptionist told me I was rushing "just like Ka." As I was walking down a side street, a grocer came outside to ask, "Are you the writer from Istanbul?" He invited me inside to ask whether I could write that all the newspaper reports four years earlier about the death of his daughter Teslime were false; he talked to me in just the way he must have talked to Ka and offered me a Coke, just as he had offered one to him. How much of this was coincidence; how much was just my imagining? At one point, realizing I was on Baytarhane Street, I stopped to look up at the windows of Sheikh Saadettin's lodge, and then, to understand how Ka felt when he visited the lodge, I went up the steep stairs that Muhtar had described in his poem.

I'd found Muhtar's poems in Ka's Frankfurt papers and took this to mean that he'd never sent them to Fahir. But it must have been five minutes after we were introduced that Muhtar, proclaiming Ka to have been "a true gentleman," described how Ka had been so taken with Muhtar's poems that he had volunteered to send them to a conceited Istanbul publisher with a cover letter praising them to the skies. Muhtar was happy with the way his life was going. Although the Prosperity Party had been shut down, he was sure to be the candidate of the new Islamist party the next time there was an election and was confident of a time to come when he would be mayor. Thanks to Muhtar's warm, ingratiating manner we were able to visit police headquarters (though they didn't let us see the basement) and the Social Services Hospital where Ka had kissed Necip's lifeless head. When Muhtar took me to see what was left of the National Theater and the rooms he had converted into an appliance depot, he conceded that he was partly to blame for the destruction of this hundred-year-old building, and then by way of consolation he added, "At least it was an Armenian building and not a Turkish one." He showed me all the places Ka had remembered whenever he found himself longing to return. My thoughts remained with Ka as we walked through the snow and through the fruit market; as we walked down Kâzım Karabekir Avenue, Muhtar pointed out the hardware stores one by one. Then he led me into the Halıl Paşa Arcade, where he took his leave, after introducing me to his political rival, the lawyer Muzaffer Bey. The former mayor reminisced at length about the city's glory days during the early years of the Republic, just as he had done with Ka, and as we proceeded through the gloomy corridors of the arcade a rich dairy owner standing in front of the Association of Animal Enthusiasts cried, "Orhan Bey!" He invited me in and flaunted his remarkable memory by describing how Ka had visited the association around the time of the assassination of the director of the Institute of Education, and how he had gone off in a corner and lost himself in thought.

It was difficult to listen to his description of the moment Ka had realized he was in love with İpek, just as I was about to meet İpek at the New Life Pastry Shop. It was, I think, to calm my nerves, to ease my fear of being swamped by love, that I stepped into the Green Pastures Café to down a raki. But the moment I sat down across from İpek at the New Life Pastry Shop, I realized that my precaution had left me only more vulnerable. I'd drunk the raki on an empty stomach, so instead of calming me it had set my head swimming. She had enormous eyes, and just the kind of long face I like. As I struggled to make sense of her beauty—although I had been thinking about it incessantly since first seeing her the night before, I had yet to fathom its depths—I inflamed my own confusion and despair by reflecting that I knew every detail of her time with Ka and the love they'd known. It was as if I'd discovered yet another weakness in myself; it was a painful reminder that while Ka had lived his life in the way that came naturally to him, as a true poet, I was a lesser being, a simple-hearted novelist who like a clerk sat down to work at the same time every day. Perhaps this is why I now gave İpek such a colorful and sympathetic account of Ka's daily routines in Frankfurt, how he'd got up every morning at the same hour and walked the same streets to the same library, to sit and work at the same desk.

"I really had decided to go to Frankfurt with him," said İpek, mentioning several facts to prove it, including the suitcase she'd packed. "But now it's hard to remember why I found Ka so charming. That said, out of respect for your friendship I would like to help you with your book."

"You've already helped enormously. Ka wrote brilliantly about his time here, and this was all thanks to you," I said, hoping to provoke her. "He filled several notebooks with a minute-by-minute account of his three-day visit. The only gap is the last few hours before he left the city."

She proceeded to fill that gap with astonishing frankness, concealing nothing, it seemed, though it must have been hard to be so open in public. I could not help but admire her honesty as she offered her own minute-by-minute account of Ka's last hours in town: what she had seen with her own eyes, and what she had guessed about the rest.

"You had no solid proof, but you still decided not to go to Frankfurt?" I said, again by way of provocation.

"Sometimes, you sense something in your heart and simply know it's true."

"You're the first one to mention hearts," I said, and as if to make up for this I told her what I had gathered from the letters Ka had written to her from Frankfurt but never sent. I told her Ka had never been able to forget her. He'd been utterly distraught, needing two sleeping pills every night for a year after his return to Germany; he would regularly drink himself into a stupor; walking the streets of Frankfurt, he couldn't go fifteen minutes without seeing some woman in the distance whom he mistook for her. Until the end of his life Ka had spent hours every day musing on the happy moments they'd spent together—the same film playing in slow motion over and over in his head—he'd been overjoyed every time he managed to go even fifteen minutes without thinking of her; he'd never again had relations with any other woman, and after losing her he saw himself as not a real person at all, but a ghost. When I saw her face succumbing to her compassion even as it cried wordlessly, Please, that's enough!, when her eyebrows rose up as if taking in a puzzling question, I realized with horror that I wasn't pleading my friend's case but my own.

"Your friend may have loved me a great deal," she said, "but not enough to come back to Kars to see me."

"There was a warrant out for his arrest."

"That needn't have stopped him. He could have appeared in court as ordered, and that would have been the end of the matter. Please don't take this the wrong way—he was right not to come—but the fact remains that Blue managed to make many secret visits to Kars to see me even though there'd been orders to kill him on sight for years and years."

It pierced me to the core to see that when she mentioned Blue, her hazel eyes lit up and her face filled with a melancholy I could tell was entirely genuine.

"But it wasn't the courts your friend was most afraid of," she said, as if to console me. "He knew very well what his real crime was, and this crime is the reason I didn't come to the station."

"You've never offered a shred of proof he was actually guilty," I said.

"All I have to do is look at your face; you're carrying his guilt for him." Satisfied with her clever response, she put her lighter and her cigarettes back into her bag to let me know our interview was over. Clever, indeed: I held up a mirror forcing me to see what she could see, that I was jealous not of Ka but of Blue. Once I had also admitted this to myself, I knew I was defeated. Later on I would decide that I'd overread her—all she'd intended was a simple warning not to let guilt get the better of me. She rose to put on her coat. How tall she was, with everything else!

I was confused. "We'll see each other again tonight, won't we?" I said. There was no call for me to say this.

"Of course. My father is expecting you," she said, and moved away with that sweet walk of hers.

I tried to feel sorry that in her heart she believed Ka was guilty, but I knew I was fooling myself. As I sat there invoking "my dear departed friend," I had really intended only to speak of him wistfully and then, little by little, to expose his weaknesses, his obsessions, and then his "crime," finally to blot out his noble memory as I boarded the same ship with her to embark on our first journey together. The dreams I'd entertained during my first night in Kars—of taking İpek back with me to Istanbul—now seemed very far away: Faced with the shameful truth, all I wanted now was to prove my friend's innocence. Can we assume then that, as for dead men, it was Blue who had provoked my jealousy and not Ka?

Walking through the snowy streets of Kars after nightfall only darkened my mood. Kars Border Television had moved to a new building on Karadağ Avenue, just across from the gas station. It was a three-story concrete affair heralded on its opening as a sign that Kars was moving up in the world, but two years later, its corridors were as muddy, dark, and dingy as any others in the city.

Fazıl was waiting for me in the second-floor studio; after introducing me to the eight others who worked at the station, he smiled affably and said, "My colleagues want to know if you'd mind saying a word or two for the evening broadcast." My first thought was that this might help the cause of my research. During my five-minute interview, their youth programs presenter, Hakan Özge, said unexpectedly (though perhaps at Fazıl's direction), "I hear you're writing a novel set in Kars!" The question threw me but I managed to mutter noncommittally. There was no mention of Ka.

We then went into the director's office to examine the shelves lined with videocassettes; the law required that they be dated, so it wasn't long before we were able to locate the tapes of the first two live broadcasts from the National Theater. We took them into a small airless room and sat in front of the old TV set with our glasses of tea. The first thing I watched was Kadife's performance in *The Tragedy in Kars*. I must say I was impressed by Sunay Zaim and Funda Eser's "critical vignettes," not to mention their parodies of various commercials popular at the time. At the scene in which Kadife bared her head to reveal her beautiful hair before killing Sunay, I paused, rewound, and repeated, trying to see exactly what had happened. Sunay's death really did look like so much theater. I guessed that only the front row would have had any chance of detecting whether the clip was full or empty.

When I put in the tape of *My Fatherland or My Head Scarf*, I quickly realized that many elements in the play—the impersonations, the confessions of Goalkeeper Vural, Funda Eser's belly dances—were no more than little sideshows that the troupe inserted into every play they did. The roaring and shouting and sloganeering in the hall, to say nothing of the age of the tape, made it almost impossible to work out what anyone said. But I rewound several times in my attempt to hear Ka recite the poem that had come to him on the spot and would later become "The Place Where God Does Not Exist." Miraculously, I was able to transcribe most of it. When Fazıl asked me what could have possibly made Necip jump to his feet while Ka was reciting the poem, and what could Necip have been trying to say, I handed him the sheet on which I had jotted down as much of the poem as I'd been able to hear.

When we got to the part where the soldiers fired into the audience, we watched it twice.

"You've been all over Kars now," said Fazıl. "But there's another place I'd like to show you." With slight embarrassment, but a certain air of mystery too, he told me that the place he had in mind was the religious high school. The school itself was closed, but since I was probably going to put Necip in my book too, it was important that I see the dormitory where he had spent his last years.

As we were walking through the snow down Ahmet Muhtar the Conqueror Avenue, I happened to see a charcoal-colored dog with a round white spot in the middle of his forehead, and when I realized he must be the dog Ka had written the poem about, I went into a grocery store to buy a boiled egg and some bread: the animal wagged its curly tail happily as I quickly peeled the egg for him.

When Fazıl saw that the dog was following us, he said, "This is the station dog. I didn't tell you everything back there, maybe because I thought you might not come. The old dormitory is empty now. After the coup, they closed it; they called it a nest of terrorists and reactionary militancy. Since then no one's lived there, which is why I've borrowed this flashlight from the station," and he shined the light into the anxious eyes of the black dog, still wagging its tail. The dormitory, an old Armenian mansion, had been the Russian consulate, where the consul had lived alone with his dog. The door to its garden was locked. Fazıl took me by the hand and helped me over the low wall. "This is how we used to get out in the evenings," he said. He pointed to a large high window; slipping through the paneless frame with accustomed ease, he turned around to light my way with the flashlight. "Don't be afraid," he said. "There's nothing in here but birds." Inside it was pitch-dark. Many of the windows were boarded up, and the glazing in others was so caked with ice and dirt that no light came through them, but Fazıl made his way to the stairs without difficulty. He climbed fearlessly but kept turning around like an usher in a cinema to show me the way. Everything stank of dust and mold. We went through doors that had been kicked in on the night of the raid, and past walls riddled with bullet holes; overhead, pigeons flew in a panic from the nests they had built in the elbows of the hot-water pipes and in the corners of the high ceilings.

On the top floor, we walked among empty, rusting bunk beds. "This one was mine, and that was Necip's," said Fazıl. "On some nights, to make sure we didn't wake anyone with our whispering, we'd sleep in the same bed and watch the stars and talk."

Through a gap in one of the top windows, we could see snowflakes sailing slowly through the halo of the streetlamp. I stood there paying them my full attention, my deepest respects.

"Necip used to watch them from his bed," said Fazıl. He pointed down to a narrow gap between two buildings: On the left—just beyond the garden—was the blind wall of the Agricultural Bank; to the right another blind wall, the back of a tall apartment building; the two-meter gap between them was too narrow for a street and so is best described as a passageway. A fluorescent tube on the first floor cast a purple light on the muddy ground below. To keep people from mistaking the passageway for a street, a NO ENTRY sign had been posted somewhere in the middle of the wall. At the end of this passage, which Fazıl said had inspired Necip's vision of the "end of the world," there was a dark and leafless tree, and just as we were looking at it, it suddenly turned red as if it were on fire.

"The red light in the sign of the Palace of Light Photo Studio has been broken for seven years now," whispered Fazıl. "It keeps going on and off, and every time we saw it blink from Necip's bed, the oleander over there looked like it was on fire. Necip would frequently dream of this vision all night long. He called the vision 'that world,' and on mornings after sleepless nights, he'd sometimes say, 'I watched that world all night!' He had told the poet Ka about it, and your friend put it into his poem. I figured this out while we were watching the tape, and that's why I brought you here. But your friend dishonored Necip by calling the poem 'The Place Where God Does Not Exist.' "

"It was your friend who described this landscape to Ka as 'the place where God does not exist,' " I said. "I am sure of it."

"I do not believe that Necip died an atheist," said Fazıl carefully. "Except, it's true, he had doubts about himself."

"Don't you hear Necip's voice inside you anymore?" I asked. "Doesn't all this make you afraid of turning into an atheist so gradually you don't even notice, like the man in the story?"

Fazıl was not pleased to learn that I knew of the doubts he'd expressed to Ka four years earlier. "I'm a married man now; I have a child," he said. "I'm no longer interested in such matters." It must have occurred to him that he'd been treating me like someone who'd flown in from the West to lure him toward atheism, because he immediately relented. "Let's talk about that later," he said, in a gentle voice. "We're expected at my father-in-law's for dinner, and it wouldn't be right to keep them waiting, would it?"

But before we went downstairs he took me to a grand room that had been the main office of the Russian consulate. Pointing at the table, the chairs, and the broken raki bottles in a corner, he said, "After the roads opened, Z Demirkol and his special operations team stayed here for a few days so they could kill a few more Islamists and Kurdish nationalists."

Up until that moment, I'd managed to keep this part of the story out of my mind, but now it came back to me with a vengeance. I had not wanted to think about Ka's last hours in Kars at all.

The charcoal-colored dog had been waiting for us at the garden gate and followed us back to the hotel.

"You look very upset," said Fazıl. "What's wrong?"

"Before we go in to eat, would you come up to my room for a moment? There's something I'd like to give you."

As I took my key from Cavit, I looked through the open door of Turgut Bey's office and saw the bright room beyond, I saw the food spread on the table, I heard the dinner guests talking and felt İpek's presence. In my suitcase I had the photocopies Ka had made of the love letters Necip had written to Kadife four years earlier, and when we got to my room, I gave them to Fazıl. Only much later would it occur to me that I wanted him to be as much haunted by the ghost of his friend as I was by Ka's.

Fazıl sat on the edge of the bed to read the letters, while I went back to my suitcase to take out one of Ka's notebooks. Opening it up to the snowflake I had first seen in Frankfurt, I saw something that a part of me must have recognized a long time ago. Ka had located "The Place Where God Does Not Exist" at the very top of the Memory axis. This suggested to me that he had been to the deserted dormitory Z Demirkol and his friends had used as their base at the tail end of the coup, had looked through Necip's window, and so discovered, just before leaving Kars, the true origins of Necip's landscape. All the other poems on the Memory axis referred to his childhood or his own memories of Kars. So now I too was sure of the story all of Kars had always believed to be true: After Ka had failed to persuade Kadife to give up the play, and while İpek was sitting locked up in his room, he'd gone to pay a visit to Z Demirkol, who was waiting in his new headquarters for Ka to tell him where to find Blue.

I am sure I looked just as dazed as Fazıl at that moment. The voices of the dinner guests floated faintly up the stairs; the sighs of the sad city of Kars rose from the street. Each lost in memory, Fazıl and I bowed to the unassailable presence of our more complex, passionate, and authentic originals.

Looking out the window at the falling snow, I told Fazıl that time was passing; we really should be getting downstairs. Fazıl left first, loping off with a hangdog look as if he'd just committed a crime. I lay down on the bed and imagined Ka's thoughts as he walked from the National Theater to the dormitory; how he must have struggled to look Z Demirkol in the eye; how, unable to furnish the exact street address, he must have ended up getting in the car with those who'd been sent for Blue, to show them the way. What sorrow I felt to imagine my friend pointing out the building in the distance. Or was it something worse? Could it be that the writer clerk was secretly delighted at the fall of the sublime poet? The thought induced such self-loathing I forced myself to think about something else.

When I went downstairs to join Turgut Bey and his other guests, I was undone anew by İpek's beauty. Recai Bey, the cultivated book-loving director of the electricity board, did his best to lift my spirits, as did Serdar Bey and Turgut Bey. But let me pass quickly over this long evening, during which everyone treated me with the most beautiful solicitude and I had far too much to drink. Every time I looked at İpek sitting across the table, I felt something come loose inside me. I watched myself being interviewed on television; to see my nervous hand gestures was excruciating. I took out the little tape recorder I'd been carrying around Kars to record my hosts and their guests giving me their views on the city's history, the fate of journalism here, and the night of the revolution, but I did all this in the dutiful languor of one who no longer believes in his work. As I sipped Zahide's lentil soup, I began to imagine myself as a character in a provincial novel from the 1940s. I decided that prison had been good for Kadife; she was more mature now, more assured. No one mentioned Ka—not even his death—and this broke my heart. At one point İpek and Kadife went into the room next door where little Ömercan was sleeping. I wanted to follow them, but by then your author had "drunk a great deal, as artists always will." I was, in fact, too drunk to stand.

But I still have one very clear memory of that evening. At a very late hour, I told İpek that I wanted to see Ka's room, Room 203. Everyone at the table fell silent and turned to look at us.

"Fine," said İpek. "Let's go."

She took the key from reception, and I followed her upstairs. The room. The window, the curtains, the snow. The smell of sleep, the perfume of soap, the faint whiff of dust. The cold. As İpek watched, still keen to give me the benefit of the doubt but not entirely trustful, I sat on the edge of the bed where my friend had passed the happiest hours of his life making love to this same woman. What if I died here, what if I declared my love to İpek, what if I just stayed here to look out the window? They were all waiting for us, yes, they were all waiting for us at the table. I babbled a bit of nonsense that amused İpek enough to make her smile. I remember her giving me an especially sweet smile when I uttered the mortifying words that I told her I had prepared in advance.

"Nothingmakesyouhappyinloveexceptlove . . . neitherthebooksyou-writenorthecitiesyousee . . . Iamverylonely . . . ifIsaythatIwanttobehere-inthiscityclosetoyoutilltheendofmylifewouldyoubelieveme?"

"Orhan Bey," said İpek, "I tried hard to love Muhtar, but it didn't work out. I loved Blue with all my heart, but it didn't work out. I believed I would learn to love Ka, but that didn't work out either. I longed for a child but the child never came. I don't think I'll ever love anyone again, I just don't have the heart for it. All I want to do now is look after my little nephew, Ömercan. But I'd like to thank you anyway, even though I can't take you seriously."

For the first time in my presence, she hadn't said "your friend"; she used Ka's name, and for this I thanked her effusively. Could we meet again, at noon the next day, at the New Life Pastry Shop, just to talk about Ka a little longer?

She was sorry to say she'd be busy. But, still determined to be a good host, she promised that she and the rest of the family would come to see me off at the station the following evening.

I thanked her and then confessed I hadn't the strength to return to the dinner table (I was also afraid I might start crying), whereupon I threw myself on the bed and passed out.

The next morning I managed to leave the hotel unnoticed and spent the day walking around the city, first with Muhtar and later on with Serdar Bey and Fazıl. As I'd hoped, my appearance on the evening news had put the people of Kars at ease about talking to me, so I was able to gather up many essential details that clarified the end of my story. Muhtar introduced me to the owner of the *Lance*, the first political Islamist newspaper in Kars (circulation seventy-five); I also met the retired pharmacist who was the paper's managing editor, though he arrived for our meeting quite late. The two men went on to tell me that the antidemocratic measures launched against it had sent the Kars Islamic movement into retreat, and even the popular demand for a religious high school was waning. Only after they had finished speaking did I remember how Fazıl and Necip had once plotted to kill this aging pharmacist after he had twice kissed Necip in an odd manner.

The owner of the Hotel Asia was now writing for the *Lance*, and when we turned to the discussion of recent events, he remembered how thankful he was that the man who had assassinated the Institute of Education director four years earlier had not been from Kars, a detail I'd somehow managed to forget. The assassin, he said, had turned out to be a teahouse operator from Tokat; it was later proved that he had committed another murder around the same time using the same weapon; when the ballistic reports came back from Ankara, the man from Tokat was charged with the murder, and he confessed that it was Blue who'd invited him to Kars. A brief submitted at trial claimed he had suffered a nervous breakdown, so the judge sent him to the Bakirköy Mental Hospital, and when they released him three years later, he decided to make his home in Istanbul, where he now ran the Merry Tokat Teahouse and wrote columns on the civil rights of head-scarf girls for the newspaper *Covenant*.

The cause of the head-scarf girls in Kars had been greatly weakened four years earlier, when Kadife bared her head, and although it now showed signs of resurgence, so many girls involved in the court cases had been expelled, and so many others had transferred to universities in other cities, that the Kars movement had yet to show the dynamism of those in Istanbul; Hande's family refused to see me.

The fireman with the strong baritone who'd been yanked into the television station the morning after the revolution to sing Turkish folk songs had gained such a following that he was now the star of his own weekly program on Kars Border Television, *Songs of the Turkish Borderlands*. They taped it on Tuesday and aired it on Friday evening; the music-loving janitor from Kars General Hospital (a close personal friend and one of His Excellency Sheikh Saadettin's most devoted followers) accompanied him on a rhythmic *saz*.

Serdar Bey also introduced me to "Glasses," the young boy who'd appeared onstage on the night of the revolution. Forbidden by his father ever to appear onstage again, even for a school play, Glasses was now a grown man, and he still worked as a newspaper distributor. He brought me up-to-date on the Kars socialists who depended on the Istanbul papers for their news. Still stouthearted admirers of the Islamists and the Kurdish nationalists who were prepared to lay down their lives to oppose the state, they occasionally issued indecisive statements that no one bothered to read. These days their activities amounted to little more than sitting around bragging about the heroes they'd been and the sacrifices they'd made as younger men.

It seemed that almost everyone I met on my walks around Kars was waiting for just such a hero, some great man ready to make the large sacrifices that would deliver them all from poverty, unemployment, confusion, and murder; perhaps because I was a novelist of some repute, the whole city, it seems, had been hoping that I might be that great man they'd been waiting for. Alas, I was to disappoint them with my bad Istanbul habits, my absentmindedness and lack of organization, my self-regard, my obsession with my project, and my haste; what's more, they let me know it.

There was Maruf the tailor, who, having told me his life story in the Unity Teahouse, said I should have agreed to come home with him to meet his nephews and drink with them; I should also have planned to stay two more days to attend the Conference of Atatürk Youth on Thursday evening; I should have smoked every cigarette and drunk every glass of tea offered me in a spirit of friendship (I almost did).

Fazıl's father had an army friend from Varto who told me that in the past four years most Kurdish militants had either been killed or thrown into prison; no one was joining the guerillas anymore. As for the young Kurds who'd attended the meeting at the Hotel Asia, they'd all abandoned the city, though at the Sunday-evening cockfight I saw Zahide's grandson the gambler, who greeted me warmly and shared some of his raki, which we sipped surreptitiously out of tea glasses.

By now it was getting late, so I made my way back to the hotel, plodding slowly through the snow like a traveler without a friend in the world although laden with all its sorrows. I still had plenty of time before my departure, but I was hoping to leave without being seen and went straight up to my room to pack.

As I was leaving through the kitchen door, I met Saffet the detective. He was retired now, but he still came every night for Zahide's soup. He recognized me straightaway from my television interview and said he had things he wanted to tell me. At the Unity Teahouse, he told me that while he was officially retired he still worked for the state on a casual basis; there was, after all, no such thing as retirement for a detective in Kars. He'd been dispatched because the city's intelligence services were keen to know what I was trying to dig up here (was it to do with the "Armenian thing," the Kurdish rebels, the religious associations, the political parties?). Smiling graciously, he added that if I could tell him my true business, I'd be helping him make a little money.

Choosing my words carefully, I told him about Ka; I reminded him that he had followed my friend step by step around the city during his visit four years earlier. What did he remember about him? I asked.

"He was a man who cared about people, and he loved dogs too—a good man," he said. "But his mind was still in Germany, and he was very introverted. No one here likes Ka these days."

For a long time we remained silent. Hoping he might know something, but still apprehensive, I finally asked about Blue, and I discovered that a year ago, just as I was now here asking about Ka, several young Islamists had come from Istanbul to ask about Blue, this enemy of the state. They left without finding his grave, probably because the corpse had been dumped into the sea from an airplane, to keep his burial site from becoming a place of pilgrimage.

When Fazıl came to join us at the table, he said he'd heard similar stories; he'd also heard that those same young Islamists were following the same path Blue had taken on his own pilgrimage. They'd escaped to Germany, where they founded a fast-growing radical Islamist group in Berlin; according to Fazıl's old classmates from the religious high school, they'd written a statement—published on the first page of a German-based journal called *Pilgrimage*—in which they'd vowed revenge against those responsible for Blue's death. It was this group, we guessed, that had killed Ka. Perhaps the only existing manuscript of his book was now in Berlin, in the hands of Blue's Pilgrims—or so I imagined for a moment as I gazed out at the snow.

At that point another policeman joined us at the table to tell me that all the gossip about him was untrue. "I don't have gray eyes!" he said. He had no idea what it meant to have gray eyes. He'd loved the late Teslime with all his heart, and if she hadn't committed suicide they would certainly have married. It was then I remembered from Ka's notebooks how, four years ago, Saffet had confiscated Fazıl's student identity card at the public library. It occurred to me that both Saffet and Fazıl had long forgotten the transaction.

When Fazıl and I returned to the snowy streets, the two policemen came out with us—whether in a spirit of friendship or professional curiosity, I couldn't tell—and as we walked, they spoke unbidden about their lives, the emptiness of life in general, the pain of love and growing old. Neither had a hat, and when the snowflakes landed on each man's thinning white hair, they didn't melt. When I asked whether the city was now even poorer and emptier than four years earlier, Fazıl said everyone had been watching a lot more television in recent years, and that, rather than spend their days sitting in a teahouse, the unemployed now preferred to sit at home watching free films beamed from all over the world by satellite. Everyone in the city had scrimped and saved up to buy these white dishes about the size of stewpot lids now hitched to the edge of every window; this, he said, was the only new development in the city.

We stopped off at the New Life Pastry Shop, where we each bought one of the delicious nut-filled crescent rolls that had cost the director of the Institute of Education his life: It would be our evening meal. When the police had ascertained that we were heading for the station, they said their farewells, and as Fazıl and I walked on past shuttered shops, empty teahouses, abandoned Armenian mansions, and brightly glistening shop windows, I looked up from time to time at the snow-laden branches of the chestnut and poplar trees above streets unevenly illuminated by the odd neon light. We took the side streets since the police weren't following us. The snow, which had given signs of abating, now began to fall more thickly. It may have been the emptiness of the streets, or it may have been my pain at the prospect of leaving Kars, but I began to feel guilty, as if I were somehow abandoning Fazıl to solitary life in this empty city. I could see that the icicles hanging from the bare branches of two oleander trees had intertwined to form a tulle curtain; in a nest of ice I saw a sparrow fluttering; it took off into swirls of giant snowflakes and flew away over our heads. The blanket of fresh white snow had buried the empty streets in a silence so deep that, apart from our footsteps, all we could hear was our own breathing. The longer we walked, the more labored and thunderous our breathing became, the shops and houses remaining silent as a dream.

I stopped for a moment in the middle of a street to watch a single snowflake fall through the night to its ultimate resting place. At that same moment, Fazıl pointed above the entrance of the Divine Light Teahouse: There, high up on the wall, was a faintly lettered poster, now four years old:

HUMAN BEINGS ARE GOD'S MASTERPIECES
AND
SUICIDE IS BLASPHEMY

"This teahouse is popular with the police, so no one dared touch that poster," said Fazıl.

"Do you feel as if you're God's masterpiece?" I asked.

"No. Only Necip was God's masterpiece. Ever since God took his life, I've let go my anxieties about atheism and my desire to love God more. May God forgive me."

The snowflakes falling so slowly now seemed suspended in the sky, and we did not speak again until we'd reached the train station. The beautiful stone station house, the early republican structure I'd mentioned in *The Black Book*, was gone now; they'd replaced it with the typical concrete monstrosity. We found Muhtar and the charcoal-colored dog waiting for us.

Ten minutes before the train's scheduled departure, Serdar Bey arrived with some back issues of the *Border City Gazette* that mentioned Ka. Giving them to me, he asked me if I could take care not to say anything bad about Kars or its troubles, the city or its people, when I wrote my book. When he saw Serdar Bey bringing out a present, a nervous, almost guilty-looking Muhtar handed me a plastic shopping bag; inside was a bottle of cologne, a little wheel of the famous Kars cheese, and a signed copy of his first poetry collection, printed in Erzurum at his own expense.

I bought my ticket and a sandwich for the little dog my friend had mentioned in his poem. The dog wagged his curly tail happily as he approached me, and I was still feeding him the sandwich when I saw Turgut Bey and Kadife rushing into the station. They'd only just heard from Zahide that I'd gone. We exchanged a few pleasantries about the ticket agent, the journey, the snow. Turgut Bey reached shamefacedly into his pocket and pulled out a new edition of *First Love*, the Turgenev novel he'd translated from the French while he was in prison. Ömercan was sitting on Kadife's lap, and I stroked his head. His mother's head was wrapped in one of her elegant Istanbul scarves, and the snow it had collected was falling from the edges. Afraid to look too long into his wife's beautiful eyes, I turned back to Fazıl and asked him whether he knew now what he might want to say to my readers if ever I was to write a book set in Kars.

"Nothing." His voice was determined.

When he saw my face fall, he relented. "I did think of something, but you may not like it," he said. "If you write a book set in Kars and put me in it, I'd like to tell your readers not to believe anything you say about me, anything you say about any of us. No one could understand us from so far away."

"But no one believes in that way what he reads in a novel," I said.

"Oh, yes, they do," he cried. "If only to see themselves as wise and superior and humanistic, they need to think of us as sweet and funny, and convince themselves that they sympathize with the way we are and even love us. But if you would put in what I've just said, at least your readers will keep a little room for doubt in their minds."

I promised I would put what he'd said into my novel.

When Kadife saw me eyeing the station entrance, she came toward me. "I hear you have a beautiful little daughter called Rüya," she said. "My sister isn't coming, but she asked me to send warm wishes to you and your daughter. And I brought you this memento of my short theatrical career." She gave me a photograph of herself with Sunay Zaim on the stage of the National Theater.

The stationmaster blew the whistle. I think I was the only one boarding the train. One by one, I embraced them. At the last moment, Fazıl passed me a plastic bag; inside were the copies he'd made of the videos and a ballpoint pen that had once belonged to Necip.

By now the train was moving, and it took some effort to jump into the car with my hands so full of presents. They were all standing on the platform waving, and I leaned out the window to wave back. It was only at the last moment that I saw the charcoal-colored dog, its pink tongue hanging from its mouth. It ran happily alongside me, right to the end of the platform. They all disappeared into the thick-falling snow.

I sat down and as I looked out the window through the snow at the orange lights of the outermost houses of the outlying neighborhoods, the shabby rooms full of people watching television, and the last snow-covered rooftops, the thin and elegantly quivering ribbons of smoke rising from the broken chimneys at last seemed a smudge through my tears.

April 1999–December 2001

THE ORDER IN WHICH
KA WROTE HIS POEMS